T0274504

COUNTDOWN

ROBERT DORSEY SMITH

ISBN 979-8-35092-682-8 (paperback)
ISBN 979-8-35092-683-5 (digital)

Printed in the United States of America

CONTENTS

Acknowledgments 1

Prologue 3

Chapter 1 – Friday, September 12 (Ten Months Later) 11

Chapter 2 – Saturday, September 13 19

Chapter 3 – Sunday, September 14 33

Chapter 4 – Monday, September 15, Morning 50

Chapter 5 – Monday, September 15, Afternoon 72

Chapter 6 – Monday, September 15, Evening 101

Chapter 7 – Tuesday, September 16, Morning 126

Chapter 8 – Tuesday, September 16, Afternoon 176

Chapter 9 – Tuesday, September 16, Evening 226

Chapter 10 – Wednesday, September 17, Morning 269

Chapter 11 – Wednesday, September 17, Afternoon and Evening 304

Chapter 12 – Wednesday, September 17, Night, and Thursday, September 18 329

Epilogue – Friday, September 19 339

About the Author 353

ACKNOWLEDGMENTS

I have learned through my years of military service and business how important it is to obtain unbiased opinions about what you write. In my consulting work, my partner and I review each other's emails before we send them out. This practice has saved us from embarrassment or worse on many occasions.

How much more important it is to have your creative writing evaluated before the digital equivalent of putting your pencil down. I do this with all of my song albums and have done it again with this book. Therefore, I thank Shirley Smith, Erik Nelson, Brad Elliott, Nic Torelli, and John Prim, all of whom have read and commented on the content of this work prior to its publication.

I also thank the members of the United States armed services, government civil servants, and federal and local law enforcement officials who work tirelessly to keep our country safe from horrific acts of terrorism similar to the one described in this book, as well as so many others.

Finally, I thank God for the ability he has given me to write words, lyrics, and music. With no formal training in either creative fiction or songwriting, there has to be a divine source for this talent. For this gift, I am most grateful.

PROLOGUE

The man's mood was as dark as the November day that surrounded him, although the feeling was nothing new. In fact, if he gave the subject any thought, he would conclude that there was scarcely a day during the past several years when he had not experienced some aspect of the darkness. His unique attitude was born of a frustrated career filled with unrealized goals and was intensified by the notable achievements of professional rivals. It was manifested as a blend of anger, resentment, envy, and a host of other destructive emotions, depending upon the day and the hour.

For years, the man had tried to internalize his feelings, but of late the task had become much more difficult. He felt the emotions building up inside of him, like the pressure of a volcano on the verge of erupting. Small destructive actions, the steamy precursors of eruption, periodically relieved the pressure, but the relief was temporary and the actions were directed at those not deserving of his malice. He knew that unless he acted soon, he would disintegrate, either physically or emotionally.

Now, as the cloudy autumn darkness loomed over the Maryland countryside, signaling an impending storm, the man's own personal darkness consumed his entire being, signaling the beginning of his treachery.

* * * * * * *

By 4:00 p.m. on Thanksgiving Eve, the Fort Detrick Army Installation north of Frederick, Maryland resembled a ghost town. Most of the military personnel, civil servants, and contractors who worked on the base had left for the long weekend. A collection of custodians quickly completed their cleanup tasks so they too could join their family or friends for the holiday.

In the building on the base where remnants of the defunct United States offensive biological warfare program were stored and safeguarded, a lone janitor hastily swept the corridors while contemplating a Thursday of watching football and consuming massive amounts of turkey, dressing, potatoes, and pumpkin pie. As he made his way down the second floor hallway, he observed a light left on in one of the offices and made a mental note to turn it off as he passed. As he walked past the doorway of the illuminated office, he reached in with one hand for the light switch while continuing to push his broom forward with the other.

"Don't touch that!" the man ordered, causing the preoccupied custodian to simultaneously jump, shriek, and drop his broom.

"Sorry, sir," he responded, shaken by the scare. "I had no idea anyone was still working; the holiday, you know."

The man did not acknowledge the apology. His eyes returned to the paperwork in the center of the drab gray metal and Formica desk of the type that populated the offices of most low-to-mid-level civil servants.

"No holiday plans, sir? Seems a shame to be working so late the day before Thanksgiving. I'm gonna finish sweeping up just as soon as I can and get home to the wife and kids. You got a family, sir?"

The janitor wanted to chat. The man did not. He continued to ignore the custodian, who was now in the center of the doorway, one hand resting on the jamb while the other played with the broom handle.

"None, huh? Too bad. My family means everything to me." The janitor sensed that the conversation was destined to be one-sided, so he wrapped it up. "Sir, wherever you're going, you better head out soon. Those clouds look threatening. I think a big storm's about to hit us. I can see you're still working, so I'll say so long. Have a good holiday." He retreated from the doorway and continued pushing his broom across the ugly industrial vinyl squares toward the end of the hallway.

In truth, the man was not working at all, but waiting—waiting until he was the sole occupant of the building. As the sound of the footsteps faded, he felt a twinge of guilt, knowing he had vented his anger, albeit passively, at yet another undeserving victim. However, the feeling disappeared nearly as quickly as the footsteps. He rose from his desk and glanced around the corner of the doorway in time to see the custodian entering the stairwell at the end of the corridor. The man paced back and forth in his office for the next ten minutes, looking out the window every thirty seconds. Finally, he saw the custodian walk from the building into the parking lot, his jacket on, and head toward the next-to-last car in the lot. When the car was finally gone from the lot and out of view, the man felt safe.

* * * * * * *

Many military and government service jobs require access to highly sensitive materials, such as nuclear weapon components and the cryptographic keys used to decode highly classified messages transmitted over the airwaves. Men and women entrusted with the handling and protection of such material are carefully screened to ensure the highest standards of reliability and competence. Still, the screening process is imperfect and people can change. Therefore, as an extra measure of security, the government requires two-person accountability during those times when these sensitive materials are not under lock and key.

For the past several years, the samples of biological warfare agents in the laboratory four doors down from the man's office had been designated as substances requiring two-person control, and the weekly inventory of the toxin samples was one of the times such control was implemented. As one of the two people responsible for the sample inventory, the man was well versed in the access procedure for both the laboratory and the refrigerated storage locker containing the toxin samples. He also knew the exact shape and color of the bottles holding the deadly liquid slush and the precise temperature at which the locker was kept.

Preparation for the swap had been time consuming, though not overly complex. First, the man needed to find two bottles identical to those in the cabinet. The task was trivial, as the bottles were a stock item from a variety of laboratory supply vendors. He then needed to track down the same typewriter used to create the labels on the actual toxin bottles. The typewriter he sought consistently mis-typed the "i," omitting the upper horizontal and the dot. He finally found the machine after testing twenty others and felt fortunate that Fort Detrick hadn't gone completely high-tech and replaced all of the old IBMs with word processors and printers. Next, he needed to create an innocuous liquid substitute for the toxin samples. He experimented with different combinations of water, alcohol, and food coloring until his concoction, when cooled to the temperature of the locker in the lab, matched both the color and consistency of the genuine toxin slurry.

By far, the most difficult of the preparations was duplicating the magnetic signature coded onto his inventory partner's picture badge. Finding an unused badge and learning how to imprint a code onto the magnetic strip was relatively easy. Separating the partner from his badge long enough to read and store the badge's code for later use had been the more difficult task. However, the opportunity presented itself one afternoon when the partner, who was also his office-mate, returned from lunch. Instead of taking the badge from his jacket pocket and clipping it to his shirt, as was his normal habit, he threw the badge onto his desk and headed for the bathroom. When he picked up a news magazine, the man knew it would be an extended visit.

The well-rehearsed action was accomplished punctually, but not without an uncomfortable level of tension. The man grabbed the partner's badge and walked to the security office on the first floor using the largest strides possible without appearing conspicuous. The closed door to the office indicated that the security manager had not yet returned from lunch. He punched in the loosely guarded three-number code that opened the door's cipher lock and entered the room unnoticed. Less than a minute later, he exited the office and pulled the door shut behind him. He'd taken only three steps down the hallway before he noticed the security manager coming in the front door of the building. After wiping a bead of perspiration from his brow, he hustled back to his own office to find the partner rifling through the clutter on his desk, saying, "I know I left it here somewhere." Thinking quickly, the man suggested checking the jacket pocket. In the five seconds it took to confirm the badge was not in the jacket, the man slipped the badge under some papers on the partner's desk. The next search of the desk uncovered the missing badge, and both men breathed a sigh of relief.

* * * * * * *

As an extra measure of security, the man waited a full five minutes after the custodian's car departed the parking lot before putting the next part of his plan into action. He took the small security box from the bottom drawer of his desk, unlocked it, and removed two labeled bottles, the counterfeit badge, an alligator clip, three telescoping pointers, and a roll of duct tape. The contents of the two bottles were liquids at room temperature, but he knew that the refrigerated locker would readily turn the liquids into frozen slushes.

The man extended the three pointers to their full lengths and joined them with tape to create a six-foot arm. He attached the alligator clip at a ninety-degree angle to one end of the arm and slipped the badge into the clip's jaws. With this apparatus, he would be able to span the six-foot separation necessary to insert two badges—his and the phony—into the code reader slots simultaneously, a procedure required for access to both the laboratory and the toxin locker. He grabbed the bottles and proceeded to the lab.

The device worked like a charm. Within two minutes, the man was staring at the rows of refrigerated bottles, as he had done hundreds of times before, although never alone. He marveled at the destructive power of what he was facing. He used to believe that the Biological Weapons Convention of 1972 was a sensible step toward eliminating the threat of toxin weapons. Then he realized how flawed and unverifiable the treaty really was and how much offensive weapon research and development continued around the world despite the treaty. He sensed that the United States was falling behind everyone, including the third world, and he observed new efforts beginning in synthetic toxin development and genetic research that would put the country even further behind. His reaction was to embark upon a personal crusade to correct what he perceived to be a serious national policy error.

For several years, he encouraged his superiors to sanction a clandestine biotoxin R&D program with himself as the senior researcher. He tried to convince them through endless memos and briefings that the world desperately needed a biological warfare equivalent to nuclear detente and that to refrain from such technology development would seriously jeopardize national security. His single-minded persistence so infuriated his bosses that they transferred him to another department and relegated him to tasks well below his potential.

On many occasions since, he had contemplated standing where he was now, beginning his own secret research effort. He would of course offer his product to the government and accept the kudos when the country finally woke up to the woeful inadequacy of its biological warfare policy.

The man blinked away the daydream and returned to the reality of the present. His destiny was finally at hand. However, the circumstances were very different now that the darkness had taken over. His motivation had shifted from patriotism to vengeance. His objective was no longer constructive, but destructive. Only the means to the end remained unchanged.

There was no guilt in the man as he replaced two bottles from the locker, one labeled anthracis and the other botulinum, with his two bottles of harmless fluid. After the swap, he quickly closed the locker, then left the lab, disassembled his apparatus, and departed Fort Detrick with the toxin samples. With the first critical step now complete, there was no turning back.

CHAPTER 1 -

FRIDAY, SEPTEMBER 12

(TEN MONTHS LATER)

Commander Glen Hargrove, United States Navy Medical Corps, didn't like being called Commander or Doctor, though he deserved both titles. In fact, he would have rather pursued his life's work, the training of one's own immune system to seek out and destroy all toxic invaders, outside the boundaries of any formal structure. However, the Navy had provided for his education, his research facility, and an annual budget sufficient to fund him and half a dozen associate researchers. So Glen Hargrove played by the Navy's rules, though sometimes reluctantly.

Within his Biological Defense Research Directorate at the Navy Medical Research Center (NMRC) in Silver Spring, Maryland, just outside the boundaries of Washington, D.C., he bent the rules only slightly to foster a close working relationship among his researchers. He invented the one-up rule for first names. First names could be used to address anyone up to one rank above one's own rank. Anyone two or more ranks higher was addressed more formally.

"Good night, Glen. Have a great vacation." Lieutenant Commander Cheryl Forrester was Glen's right-hand person for his immunotoxicology project at NMRC.

"See you later, Cheryl. I place the entire project in your capable hands. I'm doing nothing for one glorious week."

"Give me a break," Cheryl said with a touch of sarcasm. "The phrase 'do nothing' is not in the workaholic's vocabulary. And you, Glen, are a certified workaholic."

"Perhaps. But I'm going to do my best to put you and this laboratory in the farthest reaches of my mind on this trip."

"Good. You need the break. Same place as last year?" she asked.

"You bet. The New Hampshire condo. I plan on doing a lot of hiking, swimming, fishing . . ."

"And worrying about all the carcinogens in the air and water," Cheryl finished his sentence.

"No way; it's God's country up there, the purest environment I've ever seen." The concerns of his job started to fade from his face and voice as he pictured his time-share home on Squam Lake, miles from the nearest civilization.

"Have a great time, Commander," added Lieutenant Jim Thunderhill, one of Glen's bright young and upcoming researchers.

"Thanks. By the way, I'm counting on you two to make some significant progress in the next week." The comment was directed mostly at Cheryl. She was the senior and more experienced of the two associates.

Cheryl knew they would make some progress, but without Glen's direction, it would be minimal. She admired his talent and trusted his insight. "We'll be done by the time you get back," she said straight-faced, but knowing Glen would catch her true message.

"I'm out of here. Don't let them zero our funding," were Glen's parting words, a final stab at the bureaucracy that he felt often impeded, rather than encouraged, his work.

* * * * * * *

At the same time that Glen Hargrove was bidding farewell to his colleagues at NMRC and emerging into the glorious afternoon sunshine of metropolitan Washington, D.C., most residents on the West Coast of the United States and Canada were finishing their Friday lunches. Shift change had just occurred at the Lynden border crossing between Washington State and British Columbia, and the usual collection of workers and tourists was making its way back to the United States after work or play in the most southwestern of the Canadian provinces.

Derek Morgan loved his job as a border guard. It was much less stressful than his former job as an office supply manager for a Seattle tax consulting corporation, and it allowed him to meet all kinds of people. In addition, it was much more in tune with his personality. Office work, he concluded after only a year in the business, was for wimps.

In the four years of his current employment, he had developed what he called a sixth sense about suspicious entry attempts. He felt that all illegals would give themselves away at some point in the entry interview, partially because of his clever set of interview questions and partially because people couldn't maintain a consistent lie throughout the questioning. "They just don't do their homework," he was fond of saying to his friends and fellow guards. Morgan was supremely confident in his ability to sniff out the perpetrators of evil in the world, his post-Cold War replacement phrase for the word "commies." In truth, if you looked up either egotist or bigot in the dictionary, you might find a picture of Derek Morgan.

When the blue Chevy Malibu pulled up to his station, there was no reason to suspect a problem, but Morgan put his interview plan in motion anyway. The first thing he noticed was the Avis license plate holder.

"US citizens?" he asked.

The driver replied with a simple yes as both he and his passenger produced California driver's licenses. Morgan noted the license information, compared the pictures to the faces, the nationality of which he couldn't quite place, and returned the cards.

"Anything to declare?"

"No."

"A little sightseeing?"

"Yes, a lot of sightseeing," came the response in flawless English. "We spent a few days in Victoria, then took the ferry to Vancouver and spent two days there."

"A bit cooler than . . . where was that you're from?" Morgan continued with his surefire plan.

"San Francisco. Actually no, about the same weather."

IDs check out okay, Morgan concluded. *And they know the climate.* "What did you like the most on your trip?"

"Butchart Gardens near Victoria. We both garden."

Definitely tourists with an interesting hobby for men, Morgan thought. "No wives on this trip, guys?"

"No, just us guys. The ladies had their own plans for the week."

"Mind if I look at your rental papers?" The final check.

"Please do." The driver handed Morgan the rental agreement.

Morgan quickly reviewed the paperwork. The car was picked up at Sea-Tac airport five days ago—in line with the time spent in Canada. Everything checks out.

Morgan returned the papers. "You can be on your way, guys. Have a nice day." As the Malibu pulled away from his station and the next car pulled up, he said quietly to himself, "I am good at my job."

* * * * * * *

"Do you really think he wants us to have a nice day?" the Chevy passenger chuckled.

The driver shook his head. "Americans, they are so gullible. They are full of words that mean nothing, and they are blind to the reality of the world. They have had it too easy for too long. The American worker believes the world owes him a living. He has become soft and nonproductive. His complacency will be the downfall of this country."

"You're not referring to that guard back at the crossing, are you?" the passenger responded sarcastically.

"He and everyone like him. He thought his thoroughness would reveal something sinister, but I read him like a book. What Mister Border Guard doesn't realize is that his smug, overconfident attitude has contributed to the ultimate success of our mission, much to the detriment of his beloved country."

The passenger agreed with a nod, and the next thirty miles were spent in silence.

The first thing that Derek Morgan didn't realize was that the Malibu's occupants were not two men on vacation from San Francisco, but two highly trained and experienced terrorists. The driver, Ahmad Ad-Faddil, and his accomplice, Shakir Hassan, were highly potent weapons for nefarious activity, partly because of their heritage. Although the mixed marriages of their grandparents and parents had diluted their Middle Eastern blood and lightened their skin color, they nevertheless maintained a fierce animosity toward the United States. What made these men even more dangerous was that they had no allegiance to any particular country or religion. They were mercenaries, pure and simple—terrorists for hire. Money was their god.

Though prior Middle Eastern sponsors could not comprehend the financial aspect of their motivation, they forgave them this vice because of their excellence at clandestine terrorist activities. In truth, the money motivation helped to sharpen their skills and sensitize their instinct for survival.

The current mission of Ad-Faddil and Hassan was so motivated. They knew that several Middle Eastern nations would be pleased at the embarrassment and humbling of the mighty United States in such an innovative way. But they were also being paid handsomely for the transport, placement, and if necessary, release of their precious hidden cargo, which was the second thing of which Derek Morgan was unaware. Carefully concealed within the interior of the right rear passenger-side door were three explosive metal canisters and one small Lucite-encased vial, each containing one of the most deadly biological toxins ever developed. Their mission was an inconceivable act of environmental terrorism; their hostage: the city of Seattle.

The next several days would be very busy, but only one task remained on this particular day—preparation of a package for overnight shipment to an address on the other side of the country in the state of Virginia.

* * * * * * *

As Glen Hargrove drove his Toyota Camry southward on the Washington Beltway en route to his Fairfax home, the car stereo volume was on minimum and he was deep in thought. His team was so close to a breakthrough. They had worked hard on a generic immunogen, a drug that when ingested into the human body, would permanently enhance the immune system's capability to seek out and destroy a variety of invading toxins, regardless of their type and source. They had even created a prototype in the lab. The problem was that the immunogen stimulated the production of antibodies that were not as selective as those produced by the body to fight specific diseases. They tended to destroy some of the cells that should have been recognized as self and miss some of the pathogenic cells. Until the missing link to selective destruction was found, the project was at a standstill.

As he crossed the state line between Maryland and Virginia, Glen wondered whether the timing of this vacation was a mistake. They were so close, yet he knew that he owed himself and his wife a break. After all, of the thirty days of annual leave he received from the Navy, he rarely used more than ten. He eased up the volume on the stereo. One of his favorite oldies from the '60s, "We Gotta Get Out of This Place" by The Animals, was playing on the classic rock station to which his radio was semi-permanently tuned. He decided to agree with Eric Burdon. From that moment on, he fixed his mind on Squam Lake and fishing. Eric reminded him that his lovely wife was going on the trip too. "Girl, there's a better life for me and you."

CHAPTER 2 -
SATURDAY, SEPTEMBER 13

Glen and Jennifer Hargrove had a solid twelve-year marriage based on complete honesty, mutual respect and trust, and a strong Christian faith. Other than an occasional argument about money or conflicting schedules, they were rarely at odds with each other.

The lack of children in their lives was not a conscious decision. A serious pregnancy problem early in their marriage had forced a hard but sensible decision about trying again to have a baby, while adoption had never been considered a serious alternative. In time, they had both come to cherish the freedom that being childless offered and were able to pursue their respective professions with a dedication that would otherwise have been impossible. Moreover, they had enjoyed many exciting and wonderful times together without the encumbrance of kids. It's not that they were selfish about their time. If things had turned out differently, Glen and Jen would have been excellent parents.

After all the years of marriage, Glen still adored his wife. Time had been kind to Jennifer Hargrove. A consistent exercise regimen had kept her five-foot-five-inch body well distributed, and not a fleck of gray inhabited her shoulder-length blond hair. In her red shorts and white halter-top, Jen was now loading vacation supplies into her trusted Volvo SUV.

Glen brought the last of the baggage out of the house into the bright Saturday morning sunshine. "Nice shorts," he said, making sure the intended meaning was obvious.

"Why do I think it's not the shorts you're interested in?"

"How well you know me, dear." He crammed the last few small bags into what little space remained in the SUV and slammed the rear door. "That's it."

"Great. It's nice that the bags ran out at the same time as the room to put them."

"I'll check the house one more time and lock up, and we'll be on our way." Glen headed back inside just as the Federal Express van pulled up to the curb outside the house. When he emerged two minutes later, the FedEx courier, a pleasant-looking twenty-something man, was standing next to Jennifer with a package for Glen.

"Were you expecting a package?" Jen asked.

"I don't believe so," Glen replied, a quizzical expression on his face.

"I can see you folks are busy," the courier said, holding out the package and a ballpoint pen. "Just sign here. I'll be on my way and let you two go wherever you're going."

"No return address?" Glen asked the courier as he signed the document.

"I noticed that too," the courier replied. "It is strange. We usually require a return address before we accept a package. That's a problem at the other end, though. I'm just the delivery guy for this one."

Glen signed the receipt and handed the multiple copies together with the pen back to the courier, who ripped out the recipient's copy and gave it to Glen. "See you later, folks," the courier said, as he hopped back into his van and drove off.

Glen had no idea what was in the package. "I have to open this before we leave, Jen. I'll just be a couple minutes." He unlocked the front door, while Jennifer made herself comfortable in the passenger seat of the Volvo.

Inside the house, Glen slit the tape with his penknife and opened the FedEx box. He removed several wads of empty packing paper before he found a wad containing something cube-shaped and hard. He unwrapped the paper to find a small transparent plastic box in two segments, sealed with epoxy glue. Inside the box was a small vial containing a thick liquid, also transparent. As he studied the object from all sides, his eyes caught a glimpse of the note attached to one of the removed wads of paper. As he read the note, the color in his face drained, his mouth became dry, and a lump developed in his throat. The brief message carried an ominous threat and placed a weight of responsibility on his shoulders that he could only begin to comprehend.

> *Your analysis of this small sample will prove that we are not joking. Hundreds of thousands of lives will be lost if this biotoxin is released into the reservoirs of Seattle. Keep quiet and don't leave town. If you say anything or leave, the deed will be done. Further instructions and our demands will follow soon.*

Anonymity was something Glen Hargrove had cherished, even though he was one of the best scientists in his field. Now his private world had been violated, and a thousand questions were racing through his mind. Who were these people? Whom did they work for? What did they want? How did they know him? What kind of toxic agent did the vial contain? Was there an antidote? On the other hand, was it all a cruel joke? Whatever the case, his vacation was on hold . . . Jennifer!

It had been several minutes since he brought the unopened package into the house. As he walked to the front door, he tried in vain to push the fear and anxiety behind his face.

Jennifer asked, "What's wrong?" as he approached the front passenger side window.

"Look, Jen, I can't go with you today. Go without me. I'll be there as soon as I can, probably tomorrow," he lied, uncharacteristically.

"What was in the package, Glen? Why is it so important?"

"I can't say."

"You're scaring me."

"Trust me. I wouldn't keep anything from you unless it was very important. Now go have fun."

"Glen, I can't have a good time in New Hampshire knowing you're back here facing some sort of crisis alone."

"Believe me, there is nothing at all that you can do." Glen tried to change the mood of the conversation. "Besides, I know you can have a great time all by yourself with just a good book and a little bit of sunshine."

"True, but . . ."

"No more buts." He was actually smiling a little now. "On your way. I'll fly up as soon as I can."

"All right, you win. But I'll be worried sick the whole trip."

"I'll be fine."

They kissed through the window, she moved to the driver's side, and they waved to each other as she pulled out of the driveway, both uncertain of where the events of the next several days would lead.

* * * * * * *

Glen went over every word of the note time and time again until he was sure he understood its every meaning, explicit or implied. He decided on a course of action that would first determine how serious the threat actually was. Then, he would confide in the only man in the world he knew he could trust. He grabbed the plastic box, the note, and two apples for lunch, then headed out the door to his Camry.

It was now 1:20 on Saturday afternoon. If Cheryl and Jim had worked today, they would be gone by now, and he would have the lab to himself. He tried to convince himself that the whole thing was a bluff and pictured himself arriving by air at the condo before Jen arrived there by car. He would know the truth within an hour. A few simple tests would determine the toxicity of the fluid and possibly the identity.

* * * * * * *

As the winter snow in the North Cascade Mountains of Washington State melts, millions of miniature rivulets trickle down the western mountain slopes. These rivulets feed thousands of small streams, which in turn feed larger and larger streams until the waters pour into the north and south forks of the Cedar River, the primary sources of water for the Chester Morse Lake/Masonry Pool Reservoir Complex. Similarly, mountain streams feed the South Fork Tolt Reservoir, which together with the Morse provides ninety-four percent of the fresh water for metropolitan Seattle. These bodies of water were logical targets for the terrorist act of Ad-Faddil and Hassan.

The plan was inherently simple. They would install one of the canisters to a secure structure in each of the two water sources, the Morse today and the Tolt tomorrow. The third canister was a backup in case one of the others failed. They would deliver their ultimatum to Hargrove on Sunday at 6:00 p.m. Eastern Time. If, in ninety-six hours, their demands were not met or both of them were killed or placed out of action, the release mechanism on the canisters would actuate automatically. If there was any indication that the media had been informed or any other unanticipated incident occurred, they would trigger the release early. Even if widespread death could be avoided initially through prompt alerting of the public, some would not get the word. And since the bacteria contained in the canisters thrived in fresh water, the US Government would have an environmental disaster of colossal proportions on its hands for years to come. The best part of all was that no matter which scenario played out, barring an untimely end to their lives, they would be paid and they would receive the notoriety they had sought for so long.

* * * * * * *

Rear Admiral Herman "Bud" Kershaw looked like a cross between Popeye the Sailor and a pit bull. With a five-foot-ten-inch frame and 220 pounds of solid muscle, a completely bald head, and a tattoo with the name of a long forgotten love on his forearm, he was not your stereotypical Navy admiral. His physical features reflected the tough and aggressive side of his personality. One of the last products of the now defunct US diesel submarine Navy, he had remained in the Washington, D.C. arena since his command tour, bouncing between various defense acquisition jobs while pursuing a PhD in biophysics. He had become known as a smart and savvy debater when it came to defense spending programs, and like the late Admiral Hyman Rickover, he had a talent for quickly raising the blood pressure of many a congressional representative, senator, and senior officer. Kershaw himself was not immune to fits of rage. One need only call him Herman to determine his threshold of self-control. He had achieved flag rank and his current position as Chief of Naval Research despite his hard-nosed and often defiant approach. He had learned over his long career that those in power respected someone who stood up for what they believed in, as long as that someone was right. Bud Kershaw was right most of the time, and those who questioned his judgment usually learned a lesson in futility.

The other side of Bud Kershaw was very supportive and protective of subordinates who had helped him throughout his career. Six years ago, on short notice, Lieutenant Glen Hargrove had put together a comprehensive point paper on potential long-term effects of exposure to a variety of chemical warfare agents. Kershaw's presentation of this paper was enthusiastically received and sparked a multimillion-dollar research effort into chemical and biological antigens. The initial work grew into Hargrove's current program. Kershaw never forgot Glen's help and told him that if there was ever anything he could do for him, just let him know. Somehow, from the moment Glen said hello at 3:50 this Saturday afternoon, Bud Kershaw knew he was going to be called on his promise.

"Good afternoon, Admiral. Glen Hargrove here."

"It's Bud, Glen. Remember, we're out of uniform," Kershaw replied, trying to loosen the obvious tension in Hargrove's voice.

"Of course, sir. I'd like to see you this afternoon, if possible."

"I take it this isn't a social call."

"No, it isn't. I can't really say any more over the phone. Please, can we meet?" Glen pleaded.

"Sure, how about in a half hour at the Pentagon City Mall?"

"I'm not sure that will be private enough, Admiral, uh, Bud."

Kershaw's interest was piqued now. "Okay, the Doubletree Hotel lounge in Crystal City. I know we can find a quiet table there this time on a Saturday."

"Fine. I'll be there at 4:30. I really appreciate this, sir," Glen said, ending the conversation on a more formal note.

As Kershaw hung up the phone, he knew something serious was up. Glen had called him many times for some career advice or his professional opinion on a technical matter. This time, it was different. He grabbed the keys to his car and told his wife that he'd be back in two hours.

* * * * * * *

As the business of the US Government had grown over the years, the borders of Washington, D.C. proper could no longer contain the burgeoning bureaucracy that kept the country "moving forward." Like ivy on a Georgetown brick home, government organizations had spilled outward and upward over the surrounding Maryland and Virginia countryside. From the city of Washington to Interstate 495—the Washington Beltway—and beyond, entire communities of high-rise buildings had sprouted to contain these government organizations and their supporting contractors.

Crystal City, a two-mile by half-mile section of Arlington, Virginia along the bank of the Potomac River, was one such community. Aptly named, Crystal City was a square mile of glass, metal, and cement extending from fifty feet below to three hundred feet above street level. Strategically located within minutes of the Pentagon, Crystal City was home to much of the Defense Department's supporting structure. Its high rises and underground contained office spaces, homes, hotels, shopping malls, cinemas, restaurants, transportation, and just about everything else, barring nature, to support the day-to-day life of a worker for the US Government.

Bud Kershaw arrived first at the Doubletree on Army Navy Drive in Crystal City and found a quiet table in a corner. When the server came, Bud looked briefly at his watch, then ordered a Tanqueray and tonic. "Four twenty-five," he mumbled to himself. "Close enough." Glen walked in five minutes later and headed for the table.

Kershaw stood and offered his hand. "Good seeing you, Glen. How's that wife of yours?"

"Jen's fine, Bud. And Eileen?"

"Good. As always, the perfect Navy wife. You sounded so serious on the phone. What's up?"

"To be honest, I'm scared to death." Glen handed him the note that was in the FedEx package. "I know you're not in my chain of command, but I need the advice of someone I can trust. This note came by FedEx late this morning with a small vial of toxic liquid."

Kershaw spent over a minute reading the note, absorbing its every inference. He had years of experience in digesting documents of various types, storing the data like a computer memory, then formulating the questions that would extract every bit of information necessary to move the decision process forward. Despite his earlier suggestion of informality, he now went into his Navy admiral mode of operation.

"Okay, Glen, what's the background?" he started.

Glen told him about the arrival of the Federal Express package without a return address, the package contents, his sending off of Jennifer on vacation alone, and his initial analysis of the vial contents in the lab this afternoon prior to his phone call.

Kershaw listened attentively, allowing him to complete the entire story without interruption.

"Tell me more about your findings in the lab." Kershaw was giving orders now, not asking questions.

"I won't know the degree of toxicity until I observe the effects on the specimen I infected. From the few tests I ran, though, I can tell you it's some nasty stuff. Like botulin in some ways, unlike it in others."

"Are you saying you don't know exactly what it is?" Kershaw asked.

"Not until I do some more tests. Some theoretical research has been done on genetically altering known bacterial toxins to increase lethality and resistance to therapy. I haven't seen any practical application, though."

"All right, the stuff's a mystery for now. They mention the reservoirs. Can it live in water?"

"Unfortunately, yes. The organism producing the toxin will probably reproduce in almost any environment. We're talking some serious widespread and long-term contamination if it gets into the water system."

"Where's the sample now?"

"Locked in one of the liquid nitrogen freezers in the lab."

Kershaw had heard enough for the time being. "Okay, Glen, here's what you do. First, go to the hardware store and pick up a new lock for the freezer. Go back to the lab, replace the lock on the freezer, and keep both keys on you. Then go shopping for food, enough for a few days. Do you have a way of recording entire phone calls?"

"Yes, I have an app on my phone."

"Good," Kershaw continued. "After you pick up your groceries, head home and stay there. Call your wife and let her know that you won't be joining her. Don't get very far from your phone, and keep the app ready to record. We don't know when they'll make their next move. They may test you on the note's content to confirm you haven't given it to anybody, so keep the note handy. After they call, get in touch with me ASAP, day or night. You have my numbers. In all your free time before the call, start thinking about anybody you may have stepped on, slighted, or had friction with during your career. Somebody who knows you is behind this. You're good at what you do, Glen, but you're not a household word. And these people didn't get your name from a Google search for 'Rat and Mouse Death, Dispensers of.' Any questions?"

Glen managed a smile. This was the take-charge attitude he hoped his admiral friend would have. "No, sir. Acknowledge all of the above."

"One more thing. Try to stay detached; don't dwell on what could happen if this stuff is released."

Glen's mood suddenly turned somber. "That'll be tough. Jen's parents, brothers, sisters, and their families all live in the Seattle area."

Kershaw lowered and shook his head. "I didn't know. Do your best to keep them out of your thoughts. You need to keep a clear head through all this."

"Okay, I'll try. And thanks for everything."

"My pleasure. By the way, my lips are sealed. The ball's in their court."

Kershaw and Hargrove rose and shook hands. Glen left the lounge, while Bud ordered the second of his four drinks.

* * * * * * *

Glen headed south out of Crystal City on I-395 and picked up the Beltway west toward the Maryland state line. As he drove, he started to recall people, places, and events from his past that could provide a clue as to who was behind the incident and why.

He wished he could look down on the tapestry of his life from far above and home in on the irregular pattern, the point where something he did or said planted a seed of contempt in a friend or associate. Unfortunately, from the perspective of the present, he could only go back and pull on the threads one at a time, hoping some of the fabric unraveled.

He arrived home about 8:00 p.m. after following Kershaw's instructions to the letter. He was, for some unknown reason, relieved to find no messages on his home phone answering machine. He smiled to himself as he played back an imaginary message. "Hi, Glen, it's your mother. Just kidding. It's really us terrorists. Sorry we didn't catch you in; we'll call later. By the way, you weren't out snitching on us, were you? That would make us very unhappy, and we'd have to poison a million or so Pacific Northwesterners."

He couldn't believe how his life had been turned upside down in just the past ten hours. It seemed like days. He was physically and emotionally drained and decided to call it a night after calling Jennifer.

As he reached for his cell phone, it rang. Caller ID was "restricted." Second ring. He felt his heart speed up. He grabbed a pencil and paper and turned on the call record app. Third ring. *Calm down, Glen.* He answered and said, "Hello." Click. "Hello." Nothing. *Great,* he thought. Was it them? Wrong number? Crank caller? He was too nervous to call Jen now. He would call first thing in the morning. Give them both a good night's sleep before breaking the bad news.

After fixing himself a turkey and cheese sandwich and a glass of orange juice, Glen watched the news for half an hour, and then headed to bed.

His head hit the pillow at 9:30, but sleep would not come. Thousands of fragmented thoughts raced through his brain, inhibiting the rest he so desperately needed. Every half hour, he would get up, walk around the bedroom, and verbally will his body to sleep, but to no avail. Finally, at half past two in the morning, his mind could no longer outrace his fatigued body, and he drifted into a welcomed but fitful sleep.

CHAPTER 3 - SUNDAY, SEPTEMBER 14

After rising at 7:30, showering, and shaving, Glen sat down to a breakfast of cheesy scrambled eggs and toast, washed down with orange juice and French Roast coffee. He felt surprisingly refreshed, despite his few hours of sleep. As he ate, he started walking through his life in reverse chronological order, trying to recall any acquaintances that could fit the mold of a terrorist activity supporter. With each name, he tried to attach a motive. After an hour of thinking, he came up with a short list of four names, none of whom he believed would really do such a despicable thing. However, it was a start, and at this point, he couldn't afford to leave any stone unturned. He jotted notes on each of the four potentials:

Name: Jack Broussard

Occupation: Immunotoxicologist; specialty: warfare agents

Last Contact: Seventh Review Conference of the Biological Weapons Convention, Geneva

Current Location: Probably somewhere in the Washington, D.C. area

Motive: Professional jealousy

Analysis: Day late and a dollar short on several key technological developments. May feel I am personally responsible for career defeats. May also harbor malice toward the Government because it wouldn't fund one of his proposals for biotoxin technology development. Been known to steal technology developed by others, repackage it, call it his own, and resell it. Always out for his own interests.

Name: Captain Martin Corrigan

Occupation: Retired Navy medical officer

Last Contact: Reporting senior at NMRC before being relieved of duties for cause

Current Location: Probably home in front of the TV, drinking

Motive: Latent resentment for a career gone awry

Analysis: Confused my open and verbal concern for the welfare of the research team and advancement of the project with insubordination. Often demonstrated unpredictable behavior and publicly humiliated his fellow officers, including me. Extremely paranoid. Tendencies recognized by his superiors. Fired after one of his temper tantrums. Loose cannon, capable of almost anything if the right button is pushed. Probably considers me responsible for his downfall. My attitude toward the establishment is because of him.

Name: Lieutenant David Levy

Occupation: Research associate

Last Contact: Eight months ago, when informed that he was being transferred at my request

Current Location: Unknown

Motive: Retaliation

Analysis: Brilliant, but reckless lab procedures needlessly endangered equipment, personnel, and laboratory animals. So sure that one bacterium was innocuous, he exposed himself and every specimen in the lab to it. Killed two dozen mice and made himself sick for two weeks. When transferred, claimed anti-Semitism and told me to watch my back. If terrorists happen to be Middle Eastern, this candidate probably doesn't fit.

Name: Troy Halpin

Occupation: Likely unemployed

Last Contact: Amateur beach volleyball tournament, Virginia Beach, over ten years ago

Current Location: Probably some beach, hastening the onset of skin cancer

Motive: Vengeance for marrying his girlfriend

Analysis: Jen dated Troy for a while, then decided she would rather spend her life with someone more cerebral. Never got over it; still sends love letters on occasion. During last encounter, asked how the divorce was coming along. Hates me more than anyone, but too stupid to pull off anything this sophisticated.

When he was finished, Glen tucked the notes into a file folder he, in a lighter moment, had labeled Excedrin Headache Number 101, cleaned up his dishes, and decided it was time to call Jen.

* * * * * * *

In her dream, Jennifer Hargrove was giving a corporate presentation on the impact of North Korea's nuclear weapons capability on the stability of the Pacific Rim nations. Ingram International, Incorporated, the company for which she worked, was a forward-looking research firm or think tank that specialized in analyzing the world power balance heading into the next decade.

The ring of the phone annoyed her more than anything. She had told the receptionists that she did not want to be interrupted during her briefing. They would answer for their incompetence. It wouldn't stop. She answered on the fifth ring.

"I-cubed. Jennifer Hargrove. May I help you?"

"I woke you up. Sorry."

"Huh?" she replied groggily.

"It's Glen, honey. Sorry I woke you. Dreaming about work again?"

"What?" She was starting to realize where she really was.

"You answered the phone 'I-cubed.' You must have been dreaming about work."

"I guess you're right." Jen was now wide awake. "Good thing for those receptionists. I was about to have their jobs."

"What are you talking about?" It was Glen's turn to be confused.

"Never mind. How are you? More importantly, where are you?"

"Home," Glen responded, his voice a shade darker. "I'm afraid I've got some news you don't want to hear."

"You're not coming at all. I knew it," she said, with a touch of anger mixed in with her disappointment.

Glen's defensive nature took over. "It absolutely can't be avoided. I'm really sorry, but this thing I'm involved in is very important."

"Can you talk about it yet?"

"No, not yet."

"Glen, I don't want to spend this vacation alone."

"And I don't particularly want to spend my vacation here. But it can't be helped. Look, you know some of the neighbors up there with the same time-share week. How about Alice . . . what's her name? She likes to golf, doesn't she? You can spend some time with her."

"Alice DuPriest. I guess I'll have to do something like that. I have no other choice if you're not coming."

"I'll make it up to you, Jen. I promise." Glen's feeble attempt at consoling her fell on deaf ears.

"Right," Jen replied, with about as much sincerity as your average "Have a nice day" comment.

"Call me tomorrow, or I'll call you. Okay?"

"Sure, Glen. I just want you to know how frustrated I am. It's not the first vacation I've spent alone, and it probably won't be the last."

"I understand your frustration. We don't feel all that different. If there was any way I could change these circumstances, I . . ."

"I know you would," she completed his thought. "Look, take care with whatever it is you're doing. It would be nice to have a husband up here, but first and foremost, I want to keep having a husband."

Glen shuddered at her unknowing perception of the situation's gravity. "I'll be careful. Let's talk tomorrow."

"All right, Glen, so long. Love you."

"Love you too. Bye." As he hung up the phone, Glen was once again asking the "why me" question. He would have been totally blown away if he knew the answer.

* * * * * * *

Nineteen-year-old Joey Caviletti loved to fish. The first generation son of Italian immigrants, he spent a lot of time fishing on his own since his father died two years ago. Bruno Caviletti had been a commercial fisherman out of the Port of Seattle and had worked hard to support Joey, his mother, and his little sister until a freak storm in the Strait of Juan de Fuca washed him over the side of his trawler. Never much of a swimmer, Bruno quickly drowned in the choppy waters of the strait.

Joey preferred fresh water fishing, partly because of his father's death at sea. During the summer, he would go fishing almost every day, and his mother could count on him bringing home enough fish for the family supper. Joey was a good fisherman because of the simple lesson he learned from his dad. He could remember his father's accented voice so clearly. "You gotta hava good technique; ana you gotta hava da spot. You only hava one a da two, you no catcha da fish. I teacha you technique, but you gotta finda your own spot, you unnerstan?"

Joey had found the perfect spot, on a small cove in the Tolt Reservoir not far from where the river water entered. The spot was perfect because a lot of big steelhead trout called the cove home. He wasn't sure why the fish liked it. Maybe it was the way the water swirled into and out of the main reservoir. Maybe it was the natural rock pier that attracted them. Whatever the reason, the fish liked it, and that's all that mattered to Joey.

Most of all, the spot was perfect because it was secret. For as long as Joey had been coming here, he had never seen another soul fishing. Once last year, a man and woman he guessed were in their early twenties had found the spot, but all they wanted to do was hold hands and neck. He figured other fishermen couldn't find the spot because there was no obvious way to get to it. There was no established footpath from the nearest road, which was no more than a ten-foot-wide dirt clearing a couple hundred yards away. Joey did his best to preserve the spot's isolation. He would park his Chevy Blazer in the trees a quarter mile down from the nearest part of the road, then walk through the woods to the water, using a slightly different route each day to avoid making a noticeable pathway.

He was proud of his secret fishing spot, which is why he was surprised and dismayed to hear the sound of approaching footsteps and voices on this cloudy Sunday morning in September. He quickly reeled in his line and ducked behind some tall grass as two men emerged from the woods. He breathed a small sigh of relief when he realized they were not there to fish. Their street clothes and leather shoes were definitely not fishing attire.

One of the men carried a shiny metal bottle that resembled a miniature fire extinguisher. The men looked around in all directions, pointed a lot, and talked in a language Joey couldn't understand. They walked over to the rock pier and then nodded as if they had reached some sort of agreement. They spent about three minutes stooping or kneeling near the rocks. Joey couldn't see exactly what they were doing because their backs were turned toward him. When they stood up and walked back toward the woods, neither of them had the bottle in his hands.

Curious and bold beyond his years, Joey decided to follow, staying behind about twenty-five yards. His dad would have done the same thing, but now Joey was the man of the family. A good fisherman has to be observant, he told himself, so he took note of everything: their heights, weights, clothes, and facial characteristics.

A loud snap interrupted his observations. Joey knew he had stepped on and broken a dry twig and instinctively jumped behind the nearest tree. The two men also heard the sound and quickly turned around. One of them pulled a pistol out of a shoulder holster as he spun to look back the way they came.

From behind the tree, Joey heard one of them say, "See what it is," in English. Then he heard the sound of footsteps getting closer. He felt his heart pounding so hard in his chest that he thought the sound of it could surely be heard by the nearer man. He figured the man was no more than ten feet away when he said, "Probably just a rabbit or squirrel." Then thankfully, the sound of the footsteps diminished as the man turned and walked away.

As the two joined up and moved on, Joey allowed another fifteen yards of distance to separate them from himself. As he continued trailing them, he often looked down to see where he was walking. When the men emerged from the woods, they walked to either side of a mid-size car and got in. With the additional sound barrier of car doors working for him, Joey now stooped and moved faster toward the edge of the woods. The engine started, and the car started to pull out. It was about thirty feet away when Joey reached the road. He noted four things as the car rounded the bend and disappeared from view: the car's blue color, the word Malibu on the trunk door, an Avis license plate holder, and the plate number: Washington State 742-JKB.

Joey returned to his fishing spot and walked over to the rock pier where the men were working. He looked into the clear waters of the cove and saw the metal bottle attached to a narrow rock with electrical ties. Then he saw something that scared the pants off him. At the narrow end of the bottle, there was a small rectangular display with red numbers on it. The arrangement of the numbers indicated a time. The numbers on the timer read 102:14:36. The numbers were counting down.

* * * * * * *

When Ad-Faddil and Hassan returned to the mobile home in the Shady Retreat Trailer Park near Issaquah that had been leased to them for two weeks, they were confident that all was proceeding according to plan. No one would ever find the canisters; they were both in isolated locations of the respective reservoirs. They had personally been careful to cover their tracks at every move and felt that they were virtually untouchable. The only weak link in the chain was their employer. It seemed from their few conversations with him that the whole business was too personal. And when the game got too personal, carelessness slipped in, and with carelessness came mistakes.

That was why it was important to plan for contingencies. They had been careful to place insulating layers between themselves and the man they knew only as Mr. Fox. They knew each other's voices but not the faces. The IDs were delivered without photos, which they added themselves. The car was driven into Canada by a third party and left with the keys at a predetermined location. Likewise, the cargo was well hidden, but not accompanied, at a specified drop-off point. Their only required contact was a phone call to Fox at certain times during the execution of the plan. With the planting of the canisters now complete, this was one of those times.

Ad-Faddil dialed their sponsor's number from the landline phone in the kitchen, and Hassan picked up the extension in the living room.

"Yes?" came the response after three rings.

"Brown and Roberts here," the ID names by which Fox knew Ad-Faddil and Hassan.

"Are both canisters in place?" Fox asked.

"Right on schedule," Ad-Faddil replied.

"The third?"

"Still hidden in the door panel. I doubt we will need it. The installation was conducted without incident." Ad-Faddil's supreme confidence in himself was obvious in his voice.

"Good. And Hargrove?"

Ad-Faddil continued to do all the talking. "The package was delivered yesterday. He has had considerable time to sweat. We will call him later this afternoon."

"I trust you have come up with demands of your own in addition to my payment."

"We will seek an additional ten million dollars; after this mission, we are considering retirement. And of course, we have a few political objectives."

"That's up to you. I'm only concerned about my objective."

"You go to great extremes for revenge, Mr. Fox." Hassan spoke for the first time.

"It's more than revenge. It's power . . . control. You gentlemen should understand power's intoxicating effect."

"Certainly, Mr. Fox," Ad-Faddil responded, now anxious to end the conversation.

"Keep up the good work, gentlemen. And keep me informed of your progress at the prescribed times."

"We will."

Both parties hung up without goodbyes.

When Hassan returned to the kitchen, he said, "That man scares me."

"He's harmless," Ad-Faddil replied; the tone of his voice was that of the dominant partner. "And he's a man with money, which is all I care about."

* * * * * * *

The phone call came at precisely 6:00 p.m., and Glen was well prepared. He answered after two rings. "Hargrove here," were the last words he said for the entire conversation.

Ad-Faddil was the communicator. He spoke in slow, precise, and unaccented English. "Hargrove, listen closely. You are probably recording. That is fine. If not, take good notes. Do not waste your time tracing this call. It will not be sufficiently long, and it is being made from an untraceable landline. Our demands are clear and simple. One: the release of prisoners responsible for the Willis Tower and Baltimore Harbor Tunnel bombing plots. Two: ten million dollars, bills no larger than fifties with random serial numbers. Three: complete media silence. Any information given to the press will result in the toxin being released. You can involve your president, his senior advisors, and the head of the Environmental Protection Agency. No CIA or FBI. Remember, the more people involved, the greater the probability of leaks. So keep silent. Your government has ninety-six hours to comply. Be near your phone between six and seven o'clock each evening for further instructions. Warn your president, Hargrove. Any tricks and many people will die. We know where to find you also. That's all for now. Get to work."

From Ad-Faddil's perspective, only demands two and three were significant. Prisoner release was a distraction only, its purpose to keep the bureaucrats from focusing their attention on any plan disruption.

Glen stared at his phone for nearly a minute after the terrorists hung up. He was amazed at the composure and confidence of the spokesman. "He talks of mass murder as calmly as he would order dinner in a restaurant." Glen was talking to himself, trying to believe that calm killers did not exist in the world. After listening to the call playback twice, he called Bud Kershaw.

* * * * * * *

"Hello," came the familiar voice of Eileen Kershaw.

"Hi, Eileen. Glen Hargrove here. Is Bud there?"

"Certainly, Glen. Wait one." After years of being married to an admiral, Eileen had unconsciously adopted some of the more common Navy colloquialisms.

Less than ten seconds later, Bud Kershaw was on the line. "Glen, what's up?"

"They called at six."

"And . . .?"

"It's all recorded. I've confirmed it. Basically, they want ten million bucks . . ."

"No problem with that." Kershaw had limited experience with terrorist activities but he knew that coming up with ten million dollars was a piece of cake. *The government could do a lot worse with some of its defense contractors,* he thought to himself.

". . . and they want some of their buddies who have been having fun with bombs released."

"That will be much harder. Like the last several administrations, this one is not inclined to deal in hostage swapping."

"But we're talking about a whole city held hostage," Glen protested.

"They don't care if it's an entire state. It's a matter of principle," Kershaw replied.

"They are also insisting on complete media silence," Glen concluded his summary of the demands.

"Maybe the toughest one of all," Kershaw said pensively. "There are leaks in the White House, but nobody can seem to plug them. Remember the Supreme Court Justice nomination fiasco?"

"How could anyone forget! I think the *Washington Post* knew the president's short list before half of his staff members."

"How much time?"

"Four days."

"Anything else?"

"They want me close to my phone between six and seven each evening. And speaking of short lists, they've specified exactly who can be involved in the discussions."

"Oh, who's on the list?" Bud asked, knowing for a fact he was not.

"The president, his senior staff, and the head of the EPA. The CIA and FBI were specifically not invited."

"No surprise. Okay, Glen. Let's meet for breakfast. Do you know the Rosslyn Station Brasserie on Moore Street?"

"Uh huh."

"Good. Bring the recording, the note from Saturday, and any info you have on possible suspects. I'll call the National Security Advisor tonight and try to set up a meeting with the president for tomorrow morning, if possible. Considering the short fuse, he should be agreeable to meeting soon."

"Sounds good, Bud. What time do you want to meet?"

"Seven okay?"

"Fine. See you then."

* * * * * * *

Bud Kershaw knew the National Security Advisor personally. Although they were by no means friends, their relationship was characterized by mutual respect. Fortunately, Kershaw had managed to avoid alienating Lou Bernstein as he had so many others in politics. Their conversations of late had been frank, but cordial. This one was no different. Kershaw was brief and to the point. Bernstein understood the gravity of the situation without the need for embellishment. He told Kershaw he would call the president immediately and get back to him as soon as possible. Within fifteen minutes of the first conversation, Bernstein called back and told Kershaw that he was on the president's agenda at 9:30 the following morning.

* * * * * * *

Glen Hargrove's phone rang at 9:15 p.m. Though he had conversed with the terrorists only a little over three hours ago, he instinctively got his materials ready and turned on the recording app. He answered, "Hargrove here."

"Aren't we being a bit formal?" The chipper voice of his wife was on the other end of the line.

"Hi, Jen. Sorry, I was expecting it to be someone else. You sound like you're in a better mood than this morning."

"I am."

"Decided that you could have a good time without me?"

"Not exactly."

"Okay. You and Alice played golf, and you made par for the course."

"Not really." She was playing telephone tease, a game they often played.

"You found a new lover, and this is a Dear John call."

"Sounds interesting, but not true."

At this point, Glen was tired of playing. "Okay, I give up. Tell me why you're so disgustingly cheerful."

"Well, do you remember I told you I didn't want to spend my vacation alone?"

"Yes."

"And I had all those frequent flyer miles from last year's business travel."

"Right."

"So I decided to come visit my parents for the week. Caught a morning flight from Boston."

The news hit him like a Mack truck. Inside, Glen lost his composure completely, but he couldn't let it show in his voice. She was in Seattle. Of all the places to be right now, Jennifer was in Seattle.

The prolonged silence baffled Jen. "Glen, are you all right?"

"Yeah. Just a little surprised, that's all. How are your folks?" He tried to conceal his anxiety with idle talk.

"Fine. Are you sure . . ."

"Yes, I told you I was fine," he interrupted with a raised voice, the only way of disguising his fear. He wanted desperately to tell her to pack up and leave now and take her parents with her. But he knew it was not an option. Too many lives depended upon his silence. It would be selfish and dangerous to even suggest that she leave. He would have to let her stay and hope the situation could be resolved. "Look, I'm just stressed out to the max, and this was an unexpected twist to my day. I'm not upset, really."

"If you say so. I have to go now and help Mom with dinner. I'll talk to you in a day or two. Will you be okay?"

"I'll be fine. Take care. Bye, Jen."

"Get some rest, Glen. Good night."

Glen's legs went wobbly after he hung up. It had been years since tears had visited his eyes. He had always been the strong one emotionally. But now, the realization of the danger Jen faced and the awful thought that he might never see her again flooded his eyes and brought him to his knees. "Dear God, protect her," he cried out loud. "And help me do whatever I can to prevent a tragedy."

After several additional minutes on his knees, he stood and fell into bed with his clothes on. Exhausted but unable to sleep, he stared at the ceiling. The night before, sleep was fitful when it came. Tonight, it would elude him altogether.

CHAPTER 4 - MONDAY, SEPTEMBER 15, MORNING

When Glen Hargrove walked into the Rosslyn Station Brasserie at 7:05 Monday morning, Kershaw noticed the exhaustion and apparent distress. He rose to greet Glen as he approached the table, which was already set with two large glasses of orange juice, two mugs of coffee, and two of the largest cinnamon buns ever created by humans.

"What's wrong? You look terrible," Kershaw commented.

"I didn't sleep at all. Jen called last night after I talked to you. She decided that since I couldn't join her on vacation, she was going to visit her parents for the week."

"In Seattle? Did you stop her?"

"She called from Seattle. She flew out yesterday."

"Oh no. This whole thing couldn't get any more personal for you," Kershaw said in his most sympathetic tone. "Did you let anything slip over the phone?"

"No, she sensed something was wrong, but I just told her I was stressed out."

"That was not a lie."

"I know. I'm trying to cope, but it licked me last night. Every time I closed my eyes, I could see her face."

"How are you doing now?"

"Despite the way I look, my head's on straight today. I'm ready to go to work."

"Good, keep thinking positively, Glen. It'll help you pull through the tough times ahead."

"Where do we stand on the meeting?" Glen asked, shifting the talk to business as he took a bite of the warm and tasty bun.

"Lou Bernstein set me up to meet with the president at 9:30 this morning. Do you have the materials?"

Glen handed Kershaw an envelope containing a mini digital audio recorder to which he had transferred the recording of the call, the note from the FedEx delivery, and his own notes on possible suspects.

"Good," Kershaw said as he accepted the package. "I won't need you there today, but if the conversation goes as planned, you can expect to join me at our next Oval Office meeting. It's critical that you find out as much as you can about the poison we're up against as soon as possible: short-and long-term symptoms, incubation period, and mortality rate. Get your whole team on the analysis today. Tell them it's important, but don't give them any details of the situation. Work the problem hard for eight hours, then go home and wait for today's phone call, if it comes. After the call, get out of the house. Go see a movie or something. Make it a comedy. Anything to get your mind off Jennifer for a while. Then go home, have a couple of shots of strong liquor, and crash. I'll give you a wakeup call at 6:30 tomorrow morning."

Again, Bud Kershaw amazed Glen with his thoroughness. He assumed Bud also had an agenda for his meeting with the president and a follow-up plan that left no stone unturned. Glen was convinced he had confided in the right man. Now it was up to him to do his part: find out what kind of toxin they were dealing with. "I appreciate your involvement in this, Bud," he said with the utmost respect and sincerity.

"It's a pleasure, Glen. I'm happy to share your burden on this one."

They spent the rest of the time until 7:30 finishing breakfast, mostly in silence. They engaged in a few moments of small talk about the Baltimore Orioles' hot streak and the changing Washington weather. Kershaw made sure the conversation stayed clear of toxins, terrorists, and Jennifer. Glen appreciated the short respite.

* * * * * * *

"What on earth are you doing here?" Cheryl Forrester nearly dropped a petri dish when Glen walked through the door to the lab.

"The best laid plans . . ." Glen replied, avoiding discussing the crisis for the moment.

"What about Jennifer?"

"She went on vacation without me."

"C'mon, Glen. Nothing around here was so important that you couldn't enjoy a week off," Cheryl protested mildly, clearly pleased to have him around. She had always been attracted to Glen, but she knew he was a happily married man, and so never pushed their relationship beyond the close friends stage.

"Look, Cheryl," Glen said, getting down to business, "something big has come up. There is a new biotoxin on the street. It's potent, it's resilient, and we don't know much about it yet. I need the whole crew to focus on analyzing it today. I have enough of the stuff for twenty ten-milliliter samples and plenty of specimen doses, with some left over for backup."

"Where did it come from?" Cheryl asked with a puzzled expression, not used to radical changes in her daily schedule.

"That's not important. But time is. Have the crew assemble in fifteen minutes over by the specimen cages. I'm going to do a quick thaw on the stuff." Glen noticed that Cheryl's expression hadn't changed. He added, "Please trust me on this. You'll have to be content with few details."

"Whatever you say, Glen."

* * * * * * *

Certain naval officers whom Glen Hargrove had known over the years exercised a dictatorial form of leadership, sometimes achieving near-term results, but at the high cost of the respect, dedication, and morale of the junior members of their commands. These officers often abused their positions, using the power associated with rank as a substitute for a more creative and inspirational managerial approach.

Glen Hargrove, on the other hand, was a Bud Kershaw clone when it came to leadership technique. Bud had taught him that you must earn, not demand, the followership of subordinates by combining a strong command presence with the equally essential qualities of fairness, compassion, and understanding. Glen learned from his own experience over the years that the key ingredients to long-term productivity were a sense of individual self-worth and a feeling of accomplishment. He applied these principles in leading his research directorate at NMRC. He never thought of himself as the boss, but as the senior member of a committed and focused team of researchers with a common purpose. As an ironic consequence of his nonconventional approach, his team would have followed him to the ends of the earth if he asked.

When the lab crew, consisting of Cheryl, Jim Thunderhill, recent Academy grad Paula Uhrig, two summer interns from the University of Richmond, and a post-doc from Johns Hopkins University, assembled at 8:45, Glen was prepared with his analysis plan, and his team was ready and willing to implement the plan.

"We have a critical short-fused task that will temporarily displace our normal work," he started. "We have a sample of a potent biotoxin requiring thorough analysis over the next couple of days. I have an approach, but as usual, I solicit your inputs. Before we get into the details, I need to ask each one of you to maintain strict silence concerning all aspects of the project. This includes not telling your spouses or close friends. I can't tell you why we need to do this project or why it needs to be done so quickly, so please don't ask."

Glen gave the team a short breather to absorb his initial comments before continuing. "Now, we have a limited quantity of the substance. I've divided it up to allow each test to be performed.

Paula, your job is critical. I'd like you to take charge of investigating reproduction and recapturing samples. We need to know how quickly the bacterium spores in a freshwater environment. After you've gathered enough data to determine the population-doubling rate, centrifuge the water to create additional samples. We can never use up the last of the toxin. It's up to you to make sure we don't."

Paula appreciated being assigned such an important part of the project.

"Cheryl, you'll head up the investigative analysis team, which will include everyone else but Jim. Find out everything you can about the substance. My initial tests indicate that it's different from anything we've encountered, possibly a genetically altered variety of the botulinum toxin. We're striving for both a vaccine and an antidote, so first we need to understand how it responds to current treatments. You've done this work before and have my full trust and confidence."

Glen noticed that the mood was too serious. The situation was critical, but the best results would be achieved if everyone remained loose and calm. He decided to lighten their collective load.

"Jim, pathology and mortality rates will be your area. All doses should be given orally. The objective is to determine the dose rates for fifty and one hundred percent mortality and the average time for each dosage group. I have a hunch these numbers won't be far apart." He winked at Cheryl, and she knew something was up. "By the way, Jim, you can get started on your first autopsy. I infected a specimen on Saturday, but I'm afraid Alfie didn't make it."

The comment achieved the desired effect. Jim Thunderhill's mouth dropped open, his eyes widened, and his look of horror was priceless. Alfie was his pet mouse. Originally designated as a specimen, Jim saved the rodent's life just prior to administering a lethal oral dose of anthrax. He claimed that the mouse looked up at him with saddened eyes and that a tear actually formed in one of them. Even more unbelievable was his assertion that the mouse uttered a sound reminiscent of the human words "not me." So Jim placed his new friend, which he named Alfie, in a cage in an out-of-the-way corner of the lab. To the outside of the cage, he attached a three-by-five card that read: "My name is Alfie, and I do not wish to die." Jim's steadfast devotion to his small buddy was both admired and joked about, depending upon the day of the week.

Glen couldn't hold the serious look for more than five seconds before he burst out laughing. Cheryl followed in kind, then everyone else in one uproarious howl.

Finally, Jim himself managed a smile and said, "I knew you were kidding."

"NOT!" added one of the Richmond students, completing one of the more familiar movie-inspired phrases of the 1990s.

After the howls died down and everyone wiped the tears of laughter from their eyes, Glen brought everyone back to reality, but not without the desired mood shift.

"One more thing for everyone," he concluded. "Please be careful with this stuff. Until we know more about it, protect yourselves with anti-contamination clothing. Are there any questions?"

Glen gave everyone a few seconds to respond. When no one did, he clasped his hands together and said, "Okay, let's get to work. We'll meet again at 1700."

* * * * * * *

Jackson Tyler had entered politics from the equally visible world of professional sports. A mediocre third baseman over the course of his seven-year career with the St. Louis Cardinals, he had managed to sandwich one spectacular year between three rather unimpressive years on either side. But that one year, in which he won the batting title, RBI title, and fell only three home runs short of the Triple Crown, cemented his place in baseball history and his position as a Missouri hero. It was a fairly easy transition from baseball to state politics.

Tyler's opportunity to graduate to national politics came in the form of a hotly contested race for a US Senate seat vacated when the senior senator from Missouri was fired for sexual misconduct. It seems the not-so-honorable Rufus Carlisle was making the rounds with at least six of the Senate Office Building administrative assistants after hours, in their offices, and without his wife's knowledge—a truly remarkable feat for the eighty-four-year-old senator. The affairs may have continued unchecked, had he not stumbled one evening half-naked into a late meeting between the junior senator from Michigan and some of his constituents. Carlisle was simply one floor off from his other appointment. In his case, the mind actually was the first thing to go.

Front-runners quickly emerged in each party after Carlisle's dismissal. The ensuing campaigns were so negative and bitter that the candidates completely discredited each other. Enter Jackson Tyler with his relatively low profile, noncontroversial voting record, and baseball superstar credentials. As the Republican and Democratic candidates self-destructed, Tyler was swept into the Senate as an independent by a landslide.

After two Senate terms, during which he served on all the right committees, Tyler declared his alignment with the Democratic Party and his candidacy for the office of president. The focus of his campaign was the restoration of technological superiority and economic preeminence in the United States through such measures as sweeping educational reform and broad foreign trade restrictions. However, it was his buddy-of-the-people demeanor as much as the substance of his campaign that got him elected. His imposing six-foot-four-inch frame and the fact that both his names belonged to former presidents probably didn't hurt.

Now, in the last year of a presidency that was as lackluster as most of his baseball career and a dozen points behind the Republican frontrunner in the polls, Jackson Tyler was once again seeking that Hall of Fame season before time ran out.

When Admiral Herman Kershaw was escorted into the Oval Office by Lou Bernstein and introduced, Tyler swiveled his chair away from the window out of which he was staring, rose, extended his hand, and made his first social blunder of the day. "Admiral Kershaw, glad to meet you; may I call you Herman?"

Kershaw bit his tongue, then in deference to the President of the United States, said politely, "I would prefer to be called Bud, sir."

"Very well, Bud it is. Now, Bud, please sit and brief me on the situation as you see it."

"Perhaps, Mr. President, it would be best to let the terrorists speak for themselves," Kershaw started. "I've made a copy of a note received by Commander Hargrove . . ."

"Hargrove?" Tyler interrupted.

"Yes, sir. Navy Medical Corps, stationed at the Navy Medical Research Center."

"Okay, continue please." Tyler had to at least create the impression of being in control of the conversation.

"As I was saying, the note was received by Federal Express delivery on Saturday morning together with a small vial containing a potent biotoxin. As you can see, they intend to plant, or have already planted, toxin containers in the Seattle water supply."

Tyler scanned the note handed to him by Kershaw. "How do we know it's not a bluff?"

"Of course there is no way to be absolutely sure," Kershaw said, "but I think it's a fair assumption that since the vial's contents are genuine, sufficient quantities to back up their claim could be in their possession."

"Tell me more about this toxin, Bud."

"Commander Hargrove's initial analysis indicates that it's highly toxic and in some ways unlike anything he's dealt with before."

"You mean to say we don't even know what we're dealing with?" The concern was beginning to show on Tyler's face.

"It has some recognizable characteristics, but Hargrove believes a common bacterium may have been genetically altered so that drugs we currently use as treatments won't work."

Until now, Jack Tyler had thought he knew the solution. Just neutralize the stuff in the water supply or give everyone in Washington State a vaccine. Put half a dozen PhDs on the problem and make it go away like we made smallpox go away. He now spoke very slowly. "Are you saying that if this toxin gets in the water supply, there's nothing we can do about it?"

"Not before some serious damage is done. I'm sure Mr. Wilkes can estimate the impact better than me." George Wilkes was the EPA chief, who had specifically been invited to participate by the terrorists.

"Ultimately," Kershaw continued, "a toxoid can be developed, but . . ."

"Toxoid?" Tyler interrupted again.

"Sorry, sir, this isn't exactly my area of expertise either." Kershaw's apology for getting too technical was genuine. "From what I understand, you create a toxoid by heating or chemically treating a toxin. This eliminates the toxic qualities while retaining the antigenic properties."

"Makes sense. Thank you for the biology lesson."

"As I was saying," Kershaw continued, "developing a toxoid takes time, and then you have the problem of producing it in quantities sufficient to treat an entire city. I don't think we can reasonably count on this solution."

"All right. This means we need to prevent release." Tyler stated the conclusion that everyone in the room had now reached. "What do we know about the people behind the threat?"

Kershaw suggested that he play the recording of the phone call made to Hargrove, and the president concurred. About thirty seconds of silent head shaking followed the playback, after which Tyler made the first comment.

"They sound like they're from around the corner."

Kershaw responded, "I assure you they are not. Did you note the phrasing: your government and your president? What you just heard is the ultimatum of one or more professional terrorists who are not from the United States and who are very skilled at what they do."

"Do we know what country might be behind this, Bud?" Tyler asked.

"That's just it, Mr. President; I don't think a country is behind this. If it were a country, the demands would have been delivered to a fairly well-known person in your administration or the military. Glen Hargrove is not well known outside of his research community. All of this has something to do with him, either personally or professionally."

Tyler was incredulous, and his voice reflected a combination of frustration and anger. "Somebody is holding an entire city hostage to get back at some medical researcher?"

"It's the only motivation I can think of right now," Kershaw replied. "However, I suggest that we focus not on the why, but on how to stop these people from doing the unthinkable."

"And I take it you're prepared with a plan of attack."

"Absolutely, I was a Boy Scout before I joined the Navy."

"Okay. Shoot. But I'll advise you now, no part of the plan will involve releasing terrorists being held in prison. I'll pay money to save lives, but I will not trade convicted prisoners for hostages."

Kershaw understood that limitation before he entered the Oval Office. He began presenting his approach. "We follow three parallel paths. First, we try to find the toxin containers and/or the guys doing the dirty work. It's a bit like a needle in a haystack, but clues are always left behind. The terrorists said no CIA or FBI. Fine. I have some Defense Security Service buddies who would love to get involved, and they know how to keep a low profile. They can fly to Seattle and check out things like hotel records, short-term lease agreements, and rental car contracts. They're good at turning over all the stones while staying invisible. If our poison-toting friends have slipped up, these guys will find them."

Kershaw paused, partially for effect and partially to let the first prong of his three-pronged attack sink in. "Understood so far?" he asked after ten seconds.

The collective nod was his signal to continue.

"Second, we try to find the perpetrator. I believe we're looking for someone who is now or has in the past been involved in government. Maybe he or she is disgruntled, out for revenge, or just plain crazy. Whatever the case, two things are true: this person is no patriot and somehow there is a connection with Glen Hargrove. Glen has prepared a list of four men he's had run-ins with in the past. It's as good a place as any to start."

The White House Chief of Staff Clive Donner spoke for the first time. "And who, Admiral, do you suggest we get to perform this investigation?"

"Someone outside of the government. I know a reputable PI who uncovered a fraud, waste, and abuse scam that government auditors couldn't trace a couple of years back. He's perfect for this work."

"Isn't it dangerous going outside of the government, in light of the demands for silence?" Donner asked.

"He won't know the whys and the wherefores. I'll just tell him to find out what these guys have been up to and report back to me."

"What about payment?" Donner continued the line of questioning. "I assume your PI friend won't work for God and country alone."

"Not a problem," Kershaw replied, as if he knew the question was going to be asked. "I control some discretionary funds that I can spend pretty much as I please. With your approval, Mr. President, I'd like to use some of it for this purpose."

Tyler nodded once.

Kershaw continued with the third prong. "Finally, gentlemen, although it's a long shot, we need to pursue a treatment for the toxin itself or the bacteria that produces the toxin. Glen Hargrove has his entire team on the analysis today. Hopefully by tomorrow this time, we'll know more about what we're up against."

"Speaking of Commander Hargrove," Tyler interjected, "how is he doing? This whole affair must be taking its toll."

"More than you realize," Kershaw replied to the entire group. "Glen's wife and her whole family are in the Seattle area. He's pretty frazzled, but he's still capable of work."

"Sounds like it's in his mind's best interest to keep working," Tyler said. "One more question, Bud. Is there any way we can monitor the water supply to see if any of the toxin has been released? That would signal us to issue a public warning."

Kershaw suddenly got very enthusiastic. "I'm glad you asked that. I know a scientist at the Naval Research Laboratory who is in the test and evaluation stage of a new toxin sensor. This sensor can detect minute amounts of toxin in just about any liquid. I'm sure she would be thrilled with a field test of her equipment."

"I assume you can make that happen also?" Tyler asked, by now recognizing the extent of Kershaw's contacts and influence.

"That one's easy, Mr. President. NRL is part of my command. I'll be on it within the hour."

"Is there anything, Admiral Kershaw, that you haven't thought of?" The tone of Donner's rhetorical question reflected the group's appreciation of Kershaw's thorough preparations.

"Certainly," came the confident, albeit unsolicited, reply. "But sooner or later, I will cover all the bases."

"We're glad to have you on the team, Bud," Tyler commented. "Lou, you've been pretty quiet. What do you think about the admiral's plan?" Bernstein had been sitting without comment for the entire meeting.

"I agree on all points," Bernstein answered unemotionally.

"I bet you wish you could get Helen to say that once in a while." Tyler's crude humor at Bernstein's expense was his second social blunder of the morning and made the room very uncomfortable. Eyes turned away from both men. Everyone except Kershaw was well aware that the twenty-year marriage of Lou and Helen Bernstein was souring and that Lou was taking it hard. Now the man to whom he had devoted a large part of his adult life, both as campaign manager and staff member, was again trivializing his torment. He didn't need the additional anguish.

The awkward silence prompted Jack Tyler's closing remarks. "Well, it sounds like we have a plan. Gentlemen, you all heard the call. Nothing we said leaves this room. Of course, Bud, you'll need to brief the DSS operatives going to Seattle, but that's the furthest this information goes. Clive, cancel my trip to Savannah to inspect the hurricane damage. This is more important. George, put an EPA team on a project to determine the potential environmental impact of a 'hypothetical' poison spill in the reservoirs surrounding Seattle. Bud, you know better than me what you need to do. Please call me directly if any more phone calls are received. We're still lacking some specifics on these demands. Otherwise, everyone provide reports on the status of your action items every six hours to me through Mr. Donner. We'll meet again here at nine tomorrow morning. Time is of the essence, gentlemen; we have only a few days. Any questions?"

Silence across the room provided the answer.

"One more thing, Bud. I think it's important that Commander Hargrove plan to attend our next meeting. His personal insight may be helpful. What do you think?"

"I agree, sir," Kershaw replied. "I'll bring him with me tomorrow."

"Thank you for your time." Everyone recognized President Tyler's standard dismissal line and started filing out of the office.

As the last of the visitors left, Jackson Tyler once again swiveled his chair toward the window and stared out, much more worried than before the meeting. As he surveyed the White House grounds, he said quietly to himself, "Getting out of this one unscathed would be equivalent to a .400 batting average for the season. There's still hope, slugger, there's still hope."

* * * * * * *

The Chief of Naval Research (CNR) presides over a community unlike any other in the Navy. While most of the Navy functions under the direction of the Chief of Naval Operations (CNO), the

CNR works not for the CNO but for the Secretary of the Navy. In addition to commanding a traditional naval hierarchical structure, the CNR also manages a multi-billion dollar budget and a 15,000-person organization composed of some of the best military and civilian research scientists in the world.

The jewel of the CNR's command is the Naval Research Laboratory (NRL), which in itself is a bit of a misnomer. Because there is no identical Army or Air Force equivalent, NRL satisfies a broad spectrum of multi-service technology needs, extending from the bottom of the ocean to the farthest reaches of space.

In 1915, Thomas Edison said in an interview for the *New York Times Magazine*, "I believe the Government should maintain a great research laboratory, jointly under military and naval and civilian control." From Edison's vision came the organization that today stretches from Washington, D.C. to Monterey, California, providing scientific advancements in everything from superconductivity to charged particle beam weaponry, and from advanced submarine sonar systems to spaceborne sensing and imaging devices.

Although NRL is the principal organization under the CNR, the D.C. NRL facility does not contain his primary office spaces, which are located ten miles away in Ballston, Virginia. Therefore, when the black sedan bearing the blue flag with two white stars pulled into the NRL complex unexpectedly at 11:00 a.m. on Monday morning and headed straight to the biochemistry building, a bit of a commotion ensued.

"Carry on," were Rear Admiral Kershaw's frequently repeated words as he made his way from the car to the building entrance and then down the main corridor, quickly dismissing those who cast special attention in his direction.

When he arrived at the outer office of Dr. Lisa Kennelly, head of the biosensor technology project, the office assistant spilled her coffee and dumped her paper clip tray as she vainly tried to conceal her emery board and copy of *Ms. Magazine*. "Admiral Kershaw, sir, may I help you?" she said, embarrassed even further as she rose barefoot from her chair. She was very familiar with the visitor's face because, like most Navy facilities, NRL had pictures of its chain of command up to and including the President of the United States hanging in every lobby of every building.

"I'm here to see Dr. Kennelly," came the curt reply.

"She's giving a briefing in the conference room. Shall I interrupt her, sir?"

"I think that would be wise, Ms. . . .?"

"Pratt. Darcy Pratt, sir."

"Ms. Pratt, please interrupt Dr. Kennelly."

"Yes, sir. Just a moment, sir. Please make yourself comfortable, sir. Coffee, sir?"

"No, thank you." Kershaw thought that if he heard Ms. Pratt say "sir" one more time in her heavy Bronx accent, his smile would far exceed that which was normally worn for common courtesy.

Unaccustomed to having an admiral in her office, Darcy Pratt was well beyond the point of being flustered. She grabbed her shoes and hopped out of the office on one foot while simultaneously placing a shoe on the other.

* * * * * * *

Dr. Lisa Kennelly could have been a model, or a singer, or an artist, or just about anything else she wanted to be. She was one of those rare people who never knew the taste of failure at any of life's pursuits. But it was the challenges of higher education and scientific research that finally lured her from the more visible and financially rewarding professions she could have chosen.

When she was twenty-six, Lisa received her first PhD, a chemistry degree from Georgetown. She was then invited to Yale on a full scholarship to pursue a second doctorate in molecular biology. After graduation at the age of twenty-nine, she sought a position that would allow her to put both degrees to work. NRL offered her an assignment she couldn't resist.

She was given total technical and budgetary authority over a project to pioneer the development of an ultrasensitive sensor for liquid-borne chemical and biological toxins. Biomolecular sensor research, or the "biosensor project" as it came to be known, had been an all-consuming passion for Lisa Kennelly over the past two years.

The breakthrough came only seven months ago, while talking with an associate in the optical sciences division. It struck her that fiber optic technology had enormous potential for her project as well as the more traditional applications, such as acoustic arrays and stress measurement devices.

After the light bulb went on, the progress came quickly. The basic sensor was constructed by stripping the coating from a strand of fiber optic cable and coating the core with an antibody. The treated fiber was then suspended in a solution containing the same antibody chemically attached to a phosphor, like that on a TV screen. Adding a second fluid containing the toxin specific to the antibody would result in toxin molecules being compressed between the two antibodies. A laser beam focused down the fiber would activate the phosphor, now also attached to the fiber, and be reflected back down the fiber, indicating the toxin's presence. With her prototype ready for testing, Lisa Kennelly was currently averaging a briefing a day to muster interest in field evaluation and full-scale production of the biosensor.

When Darcy Pratt knocked on the door of the conference room and entered, she was immediately met with the "I thought I told you I didn't want to be disturbed" look. Expecting this greeting, she said, "Excuse me, Doctor, but Admiral Kershaw is here to see you."

"Admiral Kershaw!?" half exclamation and half question was Lisa's response.

Darcy nodded once and left.

Lisa, realizing that the admiral's visit was likely to be neither social nor short, excused herself from the briefing, asking if they could reconvene at another time. She quickly packed up her laptop and hurried out of the room with the full understanding of the attendees.

As she walked into her office, Kershaw rose and extended his hand, which she accepted. "Admiral Kershaw, what an unexpected surprise," she said, as they shook hands.

"Lisa, it's good to see you again." Kershaw's smile was now genuine, unlike that worn in Darcy Pratt's presence.

"Good to see you too, Admiral," she said, as they parted hands and sat down.

Bud Kershaw had first met Lisa Kennelly at her project status briefing for senior staff members in March. He remembered being floored by her beauty as she stood up for her presentation, but he was even more overwhelmed when she began to speak. It had been hard for him to believe that God had combined so much elegance and intellect within a single body. Since the March briefing, they had seen each other twice, first in a chance encounter at a Georgetown restaurant, and a month later at the annual Navy ball. In both situations, only a blind person could have mistaken his attraction to her. Eileen Kershaw was certainly not blind, but she was forgiving of an old admiral's occasional wayward stare. She knew that looking and pursuing were two very different things. Now in Lisa's presence again, the feelings came for an instant but were quickly suppressed by the urgent nature of his visit.

"I'll get right to the point, Lisa. How many prototype biosensors have you built?" Kershaw asked.

"About a dozen remote sensors and two processing units. Each processor can receive inputs from six sensors. Why the interest, if I might ask?"

Kershaw began answering her question with another question. "Are they completely ready for on-site evaluation?"

"Yes, they are. I've been trying to find the right opportunity to check out the entire system."

"Good," Kershaw said, getting ready to deliver the punch line. "Can you and your team be ready to fly to Seattle tomorrow morning for a full-fledged field evaluation?"

Lisa was both stunned and elated. "Absolutely!"

"Then it's set. Get everything packed and ready as soon as possible. Make your reservations for an early flight tomorrow, then drop by my office at 3:00 p.m. for a more detailed briefing."

"I'll be there, Admiral."

"Now that business is out of the way, tell me how you've been and what you've been doing." Kershaw decided to stay and chat for a few minutes—the privilege of rank.

Fifteen minutes later, they rose together and shook hands again. Kershaw held on perhaps a moment longer than a normal handshake. "See you at three," he said, as he reached for his cap and turned to leave. He walked into the outer office, where Darcy Pratt was busy at her computer, putting the finishing touches on a piece of fabricated work designed to impress a man who was not easily impressed.

CHAPTER 5 - MONDAY, SEPTEMBER 15, AFTERNOON

Bud Kershaw arrived at his Ballston office after a quick stop at McDonald's. He always enjoyed noticing the expressions on the faces of the employees at the drive-through window as the shiny black, chauffeured Navy sedan pulled up to collect his favorite Monday lunch: a Big Mac, fries, and a coke.

His agenda for the afternoon prior to Lisa's arrival included a phone call to a friend who had helped him out many times over the years and one to a PI with whom he shared an occasional round of either golf or drinks. Being a bit old school and never fully committing to the technological capabilities of cell phones, he flipped through the B section of the Rolodex on his massive mahogany desk and dialed the local office of the Defense Security Service (DSS).

The overly cordial voice of a nonperson spoke at the other end of the line. "Thank you for calling the offices of . . ."

Kershaw quickly punched in the three-digit extension of Harry Boland, a thirty-year veteran of the DSS and a colleague for almost as long.

"DSS, Boland." By the enthusiasm in the voice, one might believe it was 5:00 p.m. Friday rather than 1:00 p.m. Monday.

"Harry. Bud Kershaw here. Been drinking your lunch again?"

"Bud, my friend. No, I'm just buried in paperwork with no signs of relief. There are too many contractors needing background investigations, and my office is in the midst of a hiring freeze. I just can't get the work done."

One of the primary responsibilities of the DSS is to ensure that all military personnel, civil servants, and contractors who work on classified projects for the government are cleared to the appropriate security level—confidential, secret, top secret, or higher. Ninety-nine percent of those investigated have squeaky-clean backgrounds. However, finding the one percent that could pose a risk to national security was one of the DSS investigator's main areas of work. The Walker, Ames, and Snowden scandals made the work all the more important. Though Harry Boland often lamented that his job was a thankless one, he knew it was critical to his country's security interests, and so he did it well without complaining openly. That's what Harry felt being a patriot was all about.

"Well," Kershaw said, "I'm not about to make life any easier for you."

"If this is another special assignment, I'm ready to go. Anything to get out of the office for a while." Boland had a sudden excitement in his voice.

"But your workload," Kershaw said with mocked sympathy.

"It can wait. What's up?"

"I can't say on the phone, Harry. Can you be at my office in an hour?"

"Sure can, Bud."

"By the way, does Wolczyk still work with you?"

"Yeah, Darrell's still around."

"If the office can spare him for a few days, bring him along."

"Will do. Be at your office at two."

"See you then, Harry."

* * * * * * *

Bud Kershaw had first met Harry Boland and Darrell Wolczyk decades ago when he was Commanding Officer of the *Blueback*. The last of the US Navy's operational diesel submarines, *Blueback* was a fixture in the Pacific fleet before being decommissioned in 1990. *Blueback* spent plenty of time in the Western Pacific, often visiting Asian ports that offered some special liberty for the crew.

Most of the crewmembers sampled one aspect or another of the nightlife. Some came back to the ship with one or more outrageous tattoos. Some drank a little and some drank too much. No one was driving though, so a little overindulgence in alcohol was tolerated. Many of the crew also partook in the offerings of the local women of the night. But rarely did anyone pursue more than a one-night stand.

Then came the Wheeler incident. During one Hong Kong port visit, Radioman First Class Charles Wheeler fell in love with a lovely young lady named Kwan Ch'iang. Despite repeated lectures about the dangers of falling for a prostitute, Wheeler insisted that the love was both real and reciprocal. When the boat returned to Subic Bay in the Philippines, he flew Kwan over and they were married by the Navy Base Chaplain.

Kershaw had suspected something from the start. Kwan was a strikingly beautiful young woman, while Wheeler's visage was remarkably similar to that of a camel. Kershaw also surmised that Kwan was very intelligent and that much more was going on behind her impassive eyes than she let on. On the other hand, Wheeler often gave the impression that he was in the back of the line when brains were handed out. In short, despite Wheeler's claims of true love, there was a physical and intellectual mismatch between the two.

The suspicions grew one day when the chief yeoman reported finding a classified communications document left face down on the photocopier in the ship's office. When the radiomen were confronted with the evidence, each in turn claimed ignorance, but Kershaw noticed that Wheeler appeared to sweat a bit more than the others. Unable to prove anything, Kershaw drafted a letter documenting his concern about a possible breach of security and sent it up the chain of command. Within a week, two rookie agents named Harry Boland and Darrell Wolczyk were sent to the Philippines to investigate. From the start, Kershaw was impressed with their efficiency and enthusiasm. Within three days, the two agents had obtained phone conversations and photographs implicating Kwan in the theft of classified material from the Navy. Within another two days, they had identified her contact in the Philippines and had a complete history of her operations on behalf of the Chinese Communist Party. On day six, they arrested her, her contact, and Wheeler.

Kershaw wasn't one to forget those who demonstrated rare competence. So several times over the course of his Washington tours of duty, he had called upon Boland and Wolczyk to help him do a little special investigating. He appreciated the prompt and professional results, and they appreciated the break from the more mundane aspects of their job. The next few days, however, could prove to be their toughest test.

* * * * * * *

The next item on Kershaw's agenda would be somewhat easier. His fingers were once again flipping through the Rolodex, this time the M section, stopping at the name and number of Rudolf J. Moss, Private Investigator. He dialed, and after three rings, heard Moss's voice.

"Hello . . ."

"Hi, Rudy, this is . . ."

"Hello . . ."

"Yeah, Rudy, Bud Kersh . . ."

"Hello . . . wait! I know why I can't hear you. I'm just a dumb answering machine. Please leave a message and I'll get right back to you."

Rudy Moss, always the joker. "Rudy, Bud Kershaw here. Very entertaining message. How many potential clients never call back, though? Give me a ring when you return from your extended lunch break. Bye."

With forty-five minutes left until the arrival of Boland and Wolczyk, Kershaw decided to do some paperwork. He looked first at his in-box and the four inches of paper that had accumulated just this morning, then at the empty out-box below it. He wished he still had the gag routing boxes that had been given to him as a parting gift from the staff at his previous Pentagon command. In place of the solid bottom of a normal routing box, the in-box on top had a hinged trap door. With a quick flip of the lever on the side of the box, all of the in-box's contents were deposited into the out-box. End of paperwork problem.

Realizing the futility of his wish, he started plodding through the documents. As he scanned, read, and signed, his mind drifted to his first encounter with Rudy Moss, which also involved the wife of a young enlisted man in his command. The sailor was convinced his wife was cheating on him. He cited her numerous quiet disappearances in the evenings, his many visits home during the daytime to find no one there, and multiple hushed and secretive phone calls. In no way convinced that the claims were valid, Kershaw nonetheless recommended a so-called reputable private investigator that the kid could hire at his own expense. Bud actually found the PI by a totally random selection process.

Rudy Moss got on the case. It took him all of four hours to uncover the underhanded plot of a cruel and wicked wife: the planning of her husband's surprise twenty-fifth birthday party. The kid had to be told. He paid good money for the information. The wife was livid and didn't speak to him for a month. Bud and Rudy had a terrific laugh over the matter and continued a friendship over the years. Every now and then, Bud threw a little work Rudy's way that didn't exactly fit within the context of an official investigation.

His daydreaming was interrupted by the voice of his Flag Lieutenant through the intercom. "Admiral, Mr. Moss is on the phone for you."

"Thanks. Please put him through."

"I got your message, Bud. And I say if they can't take a joke, I don't want them as clients."

"Good for you. Say, Rudy, do you have some time for a little work?" Kershaw asked, already knowing what the answer would be. One thing about working for Uncle Sam, he always pays his bills, and he usually pays them on time. Rudy was well aware of this fact and had gotten stiffed by enough nonpaying clients to know that you never say no to a sure thing.

"Absolutely. Always willing to serve my government . . . at the standard rate, that is."

"Let's see, that was five hundred a day plus expenses if my memory serves me correctly."

"It's six now, Bud. Inflation, you know. And of course there's the divorce, in which I'm being taken to the cleaners."

"I thought you and Cindy were going to split everything fifty-fifty," Kershaw commented.

Moss laughed. "We were, until she found a lawyer who redefined the term. Now she's convinced that fifty-fifty means she gets the house and I get the payments."

"Sorry to hear that, Rudy. Okay, it's a deal. Six hundred a day, but you pick up greens fees our next time out."

"No problem, Bud. Now tell me what I can do for you."

"I'm going to fax you a list with the names of four guys and their probable locations. I'd like you to track them down and find out what they've been up to for the past three months. Be on the lookout for any inconsistencies or irregularities in their schedules. Check out their recent travel, who they've visited, who they've phoned the most, unusual purchases . . . you know the kind of stuff that indicates whether or not somebody's been up to no good."

"What kind of no good are we talking about here?" Rudy asked the question that Bud knew he couldn't answer with specifics.

"Can't say, Rudy. And whatever you find out is just between me and you, got it?" Kershaw was as serious as he ever got with Rudy Moss.

"Sure. Whatever you say. One more thing. Do you want me to check these guys out in any particular order?"

"I'd like a cursory investigation on all of them within the next twenty-four hours, then you can do a detailed look at each, starting at the top of the list."

"I'll get on it right away."

"Good. The list will be coming in three minutes. Talk to you tomorrow."

"Later, Bud."

As they hung up, Kershaw stood and walked to his outer office, feeling confident that if any of the guys on Glen Hargrove's short list was responsible for the Seattle situation, Rudy Moss would find something to implicate him. He handed the list to the Flag Lieutenant together with Moss's fax number and returned to his paperwork.

* * * * * * *

Joey Caviletti thought long and hard about whether to tell the police what he had seen out at the Tolt Reservoir on Sunday morning. After all, it was just a little bomb. Probably would scare a few fish and move a few rocks around, that's all. After the dust and water settled, his fishing spot wouldn't be all that different, and it would still be his secret. On the other hand, if he went to the police, they would probably send ten police cars, complete with a bomb squad. They would all chuckle as they removed the tiny little bottle from the rock and turned off the clock. Then the next day, two dozen cops and explosives experts would show up with their rods and tackle boxes and that would be the end of Joey's secret fishing spot.

Every time Joey decided that he would not go to the police, however, the voice of his departed father would start speaking to him again: "Joey, ma boy. America, sheeza beena good to dissa family. Firs ana foremos, you gotta be a good citizen. You helpa dissa country, she taka cara you." Joey knew his father was right. Those guys yesterday were not Americans. They were speaking a language he'd never heard before, and at least one of them was carrying a gun. And maybe the bottle was not just an ordinary bomb. Why would anyone want to blow up a few trout anyway? So Joey finally decided to tell the police what he saw and accept whatever consequence it would bring.

Now he was enjoying himself immensely, riding for the first time ever in a police cruiser on the way to the South Fork Tolt Reservoir. Officer Bernard Cushman had said to call him Bernie. He liked being on a first-name basis with adults. The two of them were going over the details of Sunday's events one more time.

"Okay, Joey, tell me again what happened after they put the bottle in the water." Cushman was checking for inconsistencies between the first and second accounts of the events.

"They started back into the woods," Joey recalled. "Then I followed them. But I stepped on a branch, and it made a loud noise. One of the guys turned and . . ."

"Which guy?"

"The shorter one."

"The one with the moustache?"

"They both had moustaches, but the shorter guy's moustache was bushier."

"Okay, go on."

"Right. So when he turned, he pulled out a gun, and I ducked behind a tree. He walked back toward where I was hiding. But I guess before he got to me, he figured it was just an animal that made the noise."

"Then you followed them again, but from further back, right?"

"Right. They got in the blue car . . ."

"The Chevy Malibu?" As they conversed, police headquarters was tracing a Blue Malibu with the Washington license plate 742-JKB.

"Yeah, that's it. Then the car was around the bend, and that's the last I saw of them. I went back to see what they had put in the reservoir. That's when I found the bottle with the red numbers."

"Counting down?"

"Yeah, with around 102 hours left," Joey concluded his story.

"Why didn't you come to us yesterday?" Cushman asked.

Joey's expression showed slight signs of guilt from having delayed reporting the incident for almost a day. "I didn't want anyone else to know about my secret fishing spot."

A novice fisherman himself, Cushman could relate to Joey's indecision. "Well, Joey, we won't tell anyone who doesn't need to know about your fishing spot, all right?"

"Sounds good to me," Joey said, with renewed optimism. He now felt that he had done the right thing, and he could see in his mind's eye his father smiling down on him.

The rest of the trip to the Tolt was relatively quiet. At one point, when Joey figured they were a good distance from civilization, he asked Bernie if he would turn on the siren and lights for a few seconds. Cushman was happy to oblige. Being the father of three girls whom he dearly loved, he nonetheless enjoyed having a boy with him for a change and was anxious to make this day a little special for Joey.

When the two of them reached the reservoir, they parked near the place where Joey normally parked and took his indirect path to the water's edge. Until this point, Cushman wasn't sure whether the so-called bomb was real or the product of a teenager's active imagination. But there in the shallow water tied to the rock, just as Joey had described, was the shiny metal bottle with the red number display, which now read 76:27:39 and was still counting down.

This discovery changed the complexion of the visit to the reservoir. Not being an explosives expert, Cushman was reluctant to do anything other than make some observations, take some notes, and report his findings. First, the object appeared exactly as Joey had described it. He had to give credit to the kid's attention to detail. This would lend further credence to his descriptions of the men and their car.

As Cushman observed the canister through the clear, still water, it occurred to him that the device did not have the appearance of a typical bomb. In fact, it looked as if it might dispense something rather than disintegrate when detonated. The neck of the bottle was longer and narrower than a typical bottle of its size and was surrounded by an inch-in-diameter casing connected to the timer with two small wires. The ruggedness of the canister indicated that the contents could be under pressure.

Cushman decided that he would not attempt to touch or remove the device on the chance that there was an anti-tamper circuit in the detonator. Judging by the numbers on the timer and the rate of countdown, there were still over three days remaining until time zero. That would give him the opportunity to report his findings to the appropriate authorities, who would then put the real experts on the case.

As he walked back to the car with Joey, additional thoughts flooded his mind. Why would someone set a bomb to detonate several days in the future unless he or she was trying to negotiate for something in the meantime? He was not aware of any ultimatums given to his office. Could this be a US Government problem? Should his office inform the Feds? His list of action items grew with each step he took on his way back to the car.

The ride back was mostly a silent one. Cushman reassured Joey on a couple of occasions that he had done the right thing by reporting what he saw. He knew, however, that Joey's fishing spot would be getting a lot of attention over the next couple of days. He also had the sickening suspicion that if the device in the Tolt released its contents, no one would be fishing there for a very long time.

* * * * * * *

Harry Boland and Darrell Wolczyk were the Mutt and Jeff of their DSS office. At six feet three inches and 175 pounds, Boland could eat a horse a day and not gain an ounce. The five-foot-nine-inch

Wolczyk, however, need only inhale the aroma from a bowl of pierogies for his waistline to grow an inch.

Boland was the human equivalent of a mongrel, his bloodline traceable to at least a dozen countries, but he considered himself one hundred percent American. Although he was born and raised in Michigan, somewhere along the way he picked up the speaking mannerisms of a southerner. Those who didn't know him often mistook him for a redneck. However, the only intolerance Harry Boland had was for individuals or groups that were a threat to America. Wolczyk, on the other hand, was pure Polish. With his full moustache, close-cropped hair, and blue-collar worker style of dress, he could have passed for a member of Lech Walesa's Solidarity Union of the past. They had only one trait in common—their finely honed investigative skills—and that is why at 2:00 p.m. this Monday afternoon, they were being escorted into the office of the Chief of Naval Research.

"Gentlemen," Kershaw started, "it's good to see you again."

Both DSS agents returned the greeting.

"Before I brief you, I have to ask for your complete silence on the details of this project. No discussions with superiors, no follow-up reports. Any problems?"

Boland was the unofficial spokesman of the pair. "Not a problem, Bud. We're finally senior enough that no one questions our comings and goings."

"Good," Kershaw continued. "A couple more preliminary questions. How's your travel budget and how suspicious will a trip to the Seattle area for a few days look?"

"We're pretty flush on travel funds," Boland replied, "and there's always good reason to head out to the Puget Sound area. There's a lot of defense work going on at Boeing and at the shipyard in Bremerton. DSS has a local office, but they often get overloaded and cry to headquarters for help."

"Also good." Kershaw invited the agents to make themselves comfortable, offered coffee, then spent the next ten minutes explaining the chronology of events since Saturday morning. He left out only the details of the biological agent, which to date were sketchy at best. He then gave them a few recommendations on things to check out, but left the details to them.

"Now, a few things I consider the most important," he concluded. "First, it's absolutely essential that you keep as low a profile as possible. They've threatened to release the toxin if any word gets leaked to the press. If the local authorities suspect something is going down, they may not like being left out, but you'll have to keep them in the dark. We don't know who we can trust. Second, it's critical to keep at least one of these terrorists alive. I don't know how many we're dealing with, but if they should all be killed and the toxin dispensers are on some kind of timer, we've lost the battle. Third, if these guys are willing to murder who knows how many people in metropolitan Seattle, they won't think twice about blowing away a couple of snooping federal agents. Even though it's out of the ordinary for you to carry weapons, I think you should be prepared to defend yourselves." Kershaw breathed a heavy sigh, indicating that he was finally done speaking for the moment.

Darrell Wolczyk spoke for the first time. "I don't know, Harry, sounds like just too much fun to me. Think we can handle it?"

Boland put on his widest grin. He was a Navy Seal before he joined the DSS and still had a craving for real action. "Just point me in the right direction. I'm ready to roll."

"I knew I could count on you two," Kershaw said, as he rose and came around the huge desk to escort them to the door. "I think there's a nonstop United flight out of Dulles at about 5:00 p.m. It gets you into Sea-Tac about 8:00 p.m. Pacific Time. You can get settled tonight and on the case first thing tomorrow."

"We'll be on it," Boland said, still grinning with delight at the opportunity they were being offered.

"Call me at work or home whenever anything breaks," Kershaw said, "but at least twice a day with an update."

"We'll be in touch often," Boland said, as they all shook hands and parted company.

Kershaw returned to his desk, convinced that the best possible people were on the job.

* * * * * * *

By the time Lisa Kennelly arrived, the in-box on the mahogany desk had been empty for a half hour, and Bud Kershaw had spent some time trying to find holes in his own plan. He was concerned about White House leaks, but he had no idea who the source was and whether the leaks were intentional or caused by carelessness. He concluded that since he had no control over that matter, it was not worth the worry.

Glen Hargrove's continued mental health was critical to the operation. Kershaw wasn't worried about the time Glen spent at work, because he knew he would be busy and around his co-workers.

It was the time Glen spent at home alone about which he was concerned. He decided to minimize the amount of time Glen was alone in order to keep his mind off Jennifer and her family. He had already suggested plans for tonight, so he decided he would invite Glen to dinner at his home tomorrow night.

By far, the largest of Kershaw's concerns was the sheer magnitude of the hunt. He had a gut feeling that Rudy Moss would discover no connection whatsoever between the four men on Glen's list and the events in Seattle. Even if one of them was involved, the bad guys in Washington State could very well be operating autonomously at this point, ready to carry out the plan with or without further instruction.

He concluded that the huge burden of preventing an incident from happening rested squarely on the shoulders of Harry Boland and Darrell Wolczyk. As competent as they were, their success was going to depend on a fair measure of good fortune as well.

As the Flag Lieutenant escorted Lisa Kennelly into the inner office, Bud rose and walked around the desk to greet her. "Have a seat, Lisa," he said cordially.

"Thank you," she said as she sat down, opened a thin valise, and removed a notepad and pen.

Kershaw sat in one of the visitor chairs rather than returning to his own chair on the other side of the huge desk. He often did this when he wanted to maintain an air of informality, or in this case, friendship, during a conversation.

"How are your preparations going?" he asked.

"Fine. I have two associates preparing the systems as we speak. Four of us have flights out of Reagan National Airport at 9:00 a.m., scheduled to arrive in Seattle around noon Pacific Time. I just need a few more details on what we're actually doing."

Kershaw spent a few moments giving the same lecture about confidentiality that he gave Boland and Wolczyk, but for some reason with Lisa, it sounded more like a request than an order. Then he presented a somewhat truncated discussion of the situation in Washington State. Lisa needed to know that there was a possibility of contamination in the city's water supply by a new and potent biotoxin and that it could originate from one or more reservoirs providing water to the system. She also needed to know as much information as possible about the toxin itself. She didn't need to know that the source of the potential threat was the intentional introduction of the toxin by terrorists, so Kershaw spared her these details.

"Sounds serious. If this is a new type of toxin, though, how am I going to know which antibody to use to coat the sensor fibers?"

"Good question. Glen Hargrove—I don't think you know him—is a medical researcher at NMRC and is performing the investigation. He says that the toxin is similar to the botulinum toxin and that a botulin antibody on your fibers should detect it."

"Fine, I'll treat the fibers this evening. What about monitoring sites? I'll need to know where to get my samples and how often."

"Another good question, and this time, I don't have a good answer. I suggest that as soon as you arrive, you contact the local public utilities organization. They probably have a department that controls their water management. I will call them after you leave, introduce you in advance, and urge their cooperation. If they seem reluctant, I have a few lines in my bag of tricks that should get their attention. You want these folks to help you pick sample sites that cover multiple feeds into the system. This should increase your probability of successful detection if contamination occurs. It's important, though, that they don't know what you're really doing, so our stories need to match. I'll tell them you'll be doing some routine water analyses over the next few days. You can elaborate when you get there. I trust your imagination."

"Not a problem. Now, what if one of the biosensor readings comes up positive?"

"Call me right away at my office, home, or cell. You can get the numbers from my aide on your way out. When you arrive out there, buy burner phones for all of your associates. This mission is a sensitive one, and I don't want any of your team's personal information compromised."

"Absolutely, Admiral. Does that about cover it?"

"I think so. You know, Lisa, as much as I want you to have a successful field test, if any of your readings turn out positive, it means the rest of our efforts have failed. So don't feel bad if you get nothing but nice clean water for the next several days."

"I won't, sir. Believe me, just packing, moving, and deploying the sensors in the field is all I could have hoped for this early in the project. I want to thank you for the opportunity."

"Don't mention it. Maybe you can tell me how it went over lunch some day after you get back."

"I'd be delighted," Lisa responded, as she rose and headed for the door with Kershaw right behind.

"Best of luck out there, Lisa. Be careful and keep in touch."

"Will do, Admiral. Goodbye," she said, stopping to collect the promised phone numbers on her way out.

Kershaw returned to his desk after asking the Flag Lieutenant to track down the main number of the Seattle Public Utilities (SPU) offices. When the number was brought in, he placed the call and was referred to Water Management by the SPU operator. He called the number he was given and asked for the senior field supervisor. He figured he would get much further with someone who got his hands a little dirty than with some starched-shirt pencil pusher sitting in an office. He was right. Mr. Craig Evans, who took the call, happened to be a former first-class machinist mate in the amphibious Navy. He knew exactly what an admiral was and how much clout one carried. He assured Admiral Kershaw that Dr. Kennelly would have the total cooperation of the department and that he would personally attend to her specific needs. Kershaw was pleased that he didn't have to reach into his bag of admiral tricks. He made note of the address given to him to pass on to Lisa when they next talked.

* * * * * * *

At exactly 5:07 p.m., United flight 406 took off from the Dulles International Airport serving greater Washington, D.C., bound for Washington State's Seattle-Tacoma International Airport, better known as Sea-Tac. Seats 11A and 11C were occupied by Harry Boland and Darrell Wolczyk. Their carry-on bags were, as the flight attendant had directed, securely tucked underneath the seats in front of them. However, each man checked one bag because a portion of its contents would have never made it through the security checkpoint. Normally when Boland and Wolczyk traveled together on airplanes, they talked a lot of shop. On this trip, however, silence was the order of the day. They decided to enjoy the flight. They had a drink apiece and a nice snack by airplane standards. Then they watched a movie and caught an hour or so of sleep. Before they knew it, the Airbus A319's wheels were touching down on Runway 34 Right at Sea-Tac.

* * * * * * *

At around the same time Boland and Wolczyk took off, Glen Hargrove was assembling his research staff to determine the results of the day's work. A combination of exhilaration and exhaustion dominated the mood, as each researcher had made significant progress, but only by working at breakneck pace throughout the day. Glen asked for reports—first Paula, then Jim, and finally Cheryl.

Ensign Paula Uhrig was well prepared and organized. The valedictorian in her Naval Academy class, she graduated with a 4.0 grade point average and immediately pursued a master's degree in infectious diseases, which she obtained in twelve months with another perfect GPA. Her extended time in academia prepared her well for a research job at NMRC. Though she still lacked experience, she more than made up for it with intelligence and enthusiasm.

"Well, Commander," she started her report with her thick Alabama drawl, "I've worked with a lot of toxin-producing organisms, but I have to admit, I've never seen anything like this one in terms of reproduction rate."

"What kind of rate are we talking about?" Glen asked.

"It's a variable, sir. I know this is going to sound strange, but the multiplication rate seems to depend upon the water volume into which the organism is introduced."

"Wait a minute. Are you saying that the greater space this organism has to grow, the higher the resultant concentration?"

"Not more, Commander, faster. In all of the volumes I tested, the toxin levels reached a consistent final value, somewhere around 125 parts per thousand. But as the test volume was increased, the levels reached that plateau faster."

"That's incredible. Let me get this straight. You put this organism into water, and it replicates like there's no tomorrow. Then before it runs out of room to spread out its little bacterial arms and legs, it starts practicing birth control."

"That's an interesting way of putting it, but essentially, that's what's happening." Paula always enjoyed her boss's analogies and the way he could keep a serious situation from getting too serious. "I hate to admit it, but we humans could learn something from these organisms," she added.

"You're right there, but I doubt if we'll ever learn. Okay, Paula, when does the reproduction rate start to level off?"

"For the samples I tested, which went from ten milliliters to four liters, it didn't."

"What are you saying?" Glen asked incredulously. "It has to taper off at some point."

"All I'm saying, sir, is that for the sample volumes I used in my tests, the rate of acceleration of the division process was totally linear."

"I'll accept that for now, but tomorrow, please check out larger volumes, much larger volumes. We have to find the reproduction rate limits."

"Care to volunteer your swimming pool, sir?"

Glen chuckled and everyone else with him. "I don't think so, Paula. I trust your capability to find suitable containers with sufficient volume. So, what's your bottom line?"

"Well, sir, we have a very active organism on our hands. Someone has gone to great lengths to maximize its reproduction rate in order to attain a self-sustaining population in the fastest possible time, no matter the volume of water. More detailed conclusions will of course require further evaluation."

"Thank you, Paula, very thorough report. All right, Jim. What have you got to tell us?"

Jim Thunderhill had spent the first part of the day performing a postmortem on the specimen Glen had infected on Saturday and thanking the stars that it wasn't Alfie. He spent the major portion of the day administering carefully measured toxin doses to thirty-two specimens: four groups according to dosage level with eight mice per group. All of the toxin was administered orally in a sugar water solution as per Glen's instructions. The specimens were returned to their individual cages, and the plastic cards on the cages were labeled, using a grease pencil, with the dosage and the time of administration. Although personally, Jim felt some sympathy for the animals being used as specimens, his professional side knew that saving human lives was the objective of this type of research and that animal experimentation was a critical part of the process. At 5:00 p.m., when the first results of the group's research were being reported, all of the specimens infected earlier in the day were still living, so Jim's report was brief.

"The cause of death in the specimen you infected, Commander, was asphyxiation caused by complete paralysis of the respiratory muscles. There were, however, some interesting non-related indications, including localized swellings on different parts of the body and bloody discharges from the ears, mouth, and rectum. Realizing the trauma associated with this specimen's mortality, I limited my dosages on the test group to levels below the one you used. I think we'll get a better indicator of the course of disease. All of the specimens infected today are still alive, but most are starting to react in some way. They're showing a variety of inconsistent symptoms. Some specimens alternate between states of extreme excitement and depression, while others are trembling or experiencing spasms. Some are vomiting and some are showing early signs of muscle weakness. A few keep stretching their necks as if there's a constriction in their throats. I should know more by tomorrow as the symptoms converge. Meanwhile, I have a digital camera rolling, striped with time code, so the animals' progress will be monitored throughout the night. That's about it, Commander."

"Good work, Jim." Glen was clearly pleased with the work his associates had accomplished during the past eight hours. "Cheryl, in addition to your own report, how about giving us your insights into what Paula and Jim have learned."

Cheryl Forrester had handed out assignments to her own mini-team shortly after Glen's morning task briefing. Likewise, she had assembled her group and collected reports a half hour prior to 5:00 p.m. She now presented the collective results.

"Although you haven't given us any background, Glen, I have to assume that this biotoxin was created for destructive, as opposed to constructive, purposes. Paula says the bacteria reproduce at a phenomenal rate. Jim's analysis indicates a high degree of toxicity. My report won't make things any brighter. I have to start out by saying that if the person who created this organism didn't have a destructive personality, he or she would be the kind of scientist we should think about hiring. There's a genius mind at work here.

"Okay, specifics. The organism is basically bacterial in origin, which we all assumed in advance. I've examined both botulinum and anthracis toxins under the microscope in the past. This stuff has characteristics of both. At the cellular level, the nucleus is unusually large compared with the overall cell size. This may hold the key to the speed of reproduction."

Cheryl, like Glen, was sensitive to the collective mood and saw this one turning a bit too dark. She had an absurd thought and decided she would share it. "Or maybe it multiplies so quickly because the inventor spliced in some blue whale DNA."

"What!" Glen was visibly surprised by the unexpected comment. Everyone else saw it coming from Cheryl's expression.

"The blue whale: fastest growing organism in the plant and animal kingdom. Don't you ever play trivia games, Glen?"

"Yes, but I don't remember that question."

"It's a fairly common one."

"All right, so I'm not much of a game person. You can continue now," Glen said, ending the short respite from the bad news.

"Anyway, we performed several toxoid reaction tests: anthrax, botulin, ricin, and about half a dozen other treatments. The cells danced around in the stuff like they were having the time of their lives. They acted as though they were weaned on the very substances that could kill them, and now that I think about it, that could very well be the case. That might explain the rather dense cell wall structure. Over the course of its development, the organism may have been conditioned to ward off any threat to its existence by building its own little suit of armor at the cellular level. Interesting concept." Cheryl paused to let her conclusions sink in.

"We've got a lot more to examine, but let me summarize what I think. All biotoxins pose a threat to humans, but in my opinion, an extremely dangerous toxin has to satisfy three criteria. It must be very virulent and its parent organism must be both prolific and hard to kill. By these measures, we could be dealing with one of the most potent biotoxins in the world. God help us if this stuff gets into the hands of an enemy."

Cheryl wanted to ask the logical follow-on question: "Or is that why we're here analyzing it?" But when she glanced at Glen and noticed him shaking his head slightly, she knew the answer to her question, and she also knew that he knew she knew.

Glen spoke quickly to prevent Cheryl from saying any more. "Well, you've all done an exceptional job today. It's just a shame that for all the successful analysis, there's nothing truly optimistic to report. Does anybody have any good news?" he asked, hoping there might be a ray of sunshine somewhere.

Paula raised her hand shyly and said, "Sort of, sir."

"Let's have it."

"The good news is . . . well, uh . . . we're never going to run out of toxin for our experiments."

"Thanks a lot, Paula."

* * * * * * *

As Glen Hargrove was concluding his meeting and sending his people home for a well-deserved evening of rest, Bernie Cushman and Joey Caviletti were arriving back at the police headquarters.

Cushman was still uncertain as to how he should handle Joey's discovery. He knew he had to tell someone; the question was whom. His immediate superior was incompetent, his opinion reinforced by the fact that the request for a trace on the blue Malibu was still sitting on his desk, no action taken. The department chief, although a skilled administrator, was indecisive when it came to field matters. The more he thought about it, the more convinced he became that the situation warranted bringing in federal investigators. He decided that he would make the call himself. If later questioned why he hadn't reported the incident through the internal chain of command, he could claim that he couldn't locate either of his bosses and felt at the time that prompt action was required. In truth, his immediate boss was on the golf course, as he usually was by this time most afternoons.

"What are you going to do, Bernie?" Joey asked.

"I'm going to call the FBI," Cushman replied. "I think it's the best course of action."

Joey was impressed. He had seen TV shows and read books with FBI agents, but had never actually met one. Maybe he would have the opportunity soon.

Cushman lifted the phone from the receiver and started dialing the number for the local FBI office. Suddenly and from out of nowhere came the most irritating voice in three counties, and unfortunately a voice all too familiar to Cushman. "Hey Bernie, got a scoop for old Scoop?"

Cushman placed the handset back in the cradle, turned slowly, and eyed his not-so-welcomed visitor.

Herbert Whitaker Scanlon felt it necessary to adopt a nickname that represented his profession. He selected the name "Scoop" more than ten years ago when he first became a newspaperman. To call him a journalist would be stretching the term beyond reason. In retrospect, it was probably a good thing that he went by the name Scoop, because there was little other evidence of his life's work. Certainly, his portfolio of articles didn't qualify.

When it came to reporting, Scanlon was more into sensation than sensibility. He accepted the idle comments and speculation of his sources without question and, as a result, his articles were usually more fabrication than fact. Scanlon had his critics and had been slapped with more than one lawsuit in the past. But in each case, he successfully hid behind his article's carefully worded sentences such as "Unofficial sources report . . ." or "An unidentified bystander said that . . ." To sum up Scoop Scanlon, he would have made an excellent reporter for a tabloid like the *Star* or *National Enquirer*. Unfortunately, he worked for the *Seattle Times*.

Cushman's lack of verbal response prompted Scanlon to ask his trademark question again. "C'mon, Bernie, got a scoop for old Scoop? There's got to be something going on around here."

"No, Scanlon. Nothing's going on right now. And even if there was, what makes you think I'd tell a weasel like you?" Cushman chuckled at the accuracy of his own comment. In addition to being sneaky like a weasel, Scanlon's face strongly resembled that of a weasel, thin and gaunt with a nose that pointed to his shoes and spaghetti-thin lips pressed into a perpetual crooked grin. Cushman figured that if a weasel could talk, it would have a voice quite similar to Scanlon's. Joey followed Cushman's lead and joined in the mild laughter.

Scanlon was not amused. "C'mon, Cushman, what's the kid doing here? Why were you gone for three hours? You're never out of headquarters that long. And why is there mud on your tires? You've been outside your normal beat. Let's have it."

With the humor in the situation now passed, Scanlon was quickly becoming an annoyance. Cushman silently cursed the day that the past regime, all now either retired or relocated, gave Scanlon an open invitation to the station because of his superb coverage of a policeman's ball that was now ancient history. "I know I can't kick you out of the building, Scanlon, but I can ask you to leave me alone and let me get back to work. And that's exactly what I'm doing. Now, if you'll excuse me . . ."

"I'll find out what you've been up to, Cushman," Scanlon interrupted. "You can't hold back information forever. I'll be around and when you slip up, I'll find it. The public has a right to know."

Cushman wanted to assault the weasel, either verbally or physically, but thought twice and regained control of his emotions. Just before he turned his back on Scanlon for the last time, he calmly said, "Scanlon, go dig up your dirt somewhere else. I've got better things to do than talking to you."

Scanlon hung around for another minute; then when he was certain he'd lost Cushman's attention for good, the little weasel slithered away defeated, but only for the time being.

Cushman looked at his watch and sighed; five till three, almost time for shift change. Scanlon had moved beyond visual range, but there was no guarantee he was beyond hearing distance. The clock on the device at the Tolt would now be reading just over seventy-two hours. He was frazzled by the Scanlon encounter and a bit tired. All things considered, Cushman decided to postpone his call to the FBI until morning. “How ’bout we call it a day, Joey?” he suggested to his young companion.

“Sure,” Joey answered. “You want me here tomorrow, don’t you?”

“Of course. Until we get to the bottom of this, I’m going to need your help.”

“Okay, see you tomorrow morning around . . .”

“Eight will be fine.”

“Eight it is. Bye.”

“Bye. And thanks.”

“Anytime,” Joey said as he swung around on his chair, got up, and headed for the door.

Just as Joey was about to reach for the handle of the station’s huge wood and glass front door, Scanlon appeared from out of nowhere and placed himself between Joey and the door. “Hey kid, you want to fill me in on what’s going down?”

Somewhat startled, it took a moment for Joey to regain his composure. After he recovered, he thought for a moment longer before answering. His father had taught him to respect his elders, but he figured the guidance applied to elders worth respecting. Judging by Bernie’s reaction to Scanlon, the man didn’t fall into that category. Joey’s response was blunt and only mildly disrespectful. “I don’t know what you’re talking about, but if I did, I can think of a lot of people I’d tell before you. Now if you’ll please move, I have to get home.”

Scanlon reluctantly complied. As he backed away from the door, he swore under his breath. Two put-downs within ten minutes, one by a teenage punk, was not his idea of a good afternoon.

CHAPTER 6 - MONDAY, SEPTEMBER 15, EVENING

With the phone call preparations almost being second nature now, Glen was ready after the first ring. Though clearly not pleased to be wrapped up in this whole affair, his voice nonetheless reflected a growing experience in dealing with dangerous men and circumstances. "Hargrove here."

"You seem to follow instructions well, Hargrove. Keep it up and everyone will come out of this situation unharmed. We shall begin with the money. The ten million dollars will be delivered on Thursday at 9:00 a.m. Pacific Time. The location will be specified tomorrow. However, you can begin arranging for a courier and a flight to ensure that she arrives in Seattle on time. You heard correctly, a female courier. Now, concerning our imprisoned comrades, are appropriate preparations for their release being made?"

During both conversations with the terrorists, Glen had, until this moment, not said a word other than his brief greeting. Realizing that he might have to answer questions during today's call, he had talked with Bud Kershaw just before 6:00 p.m. to solicit advice on how to respond. Kershaw urged him to simply agree with anything they said and to reassure them that all of their demands would be met on time and in accordance with their instructions. Glen's answer reflected Kershaw's advice. "The preparations for release of the prisoners are being made as we speak. I see no problems with meeting all of your requests."

"They are demands, Commander Hargrove, not requests." Ad-Faddil, again the spokesman, raised his voice for the first time, but only slightly. "Please remember who is in control of these events. However, let us not dwell on semantics. You will continue to be the link between ourselves and your government. It is important that we communicate with each other clearly and concisely. Remember, if so much as a hint of a problem in this region of your country appears in any of the news media, the weight of countless deaths will rest upon you and your government. Keep in mind that American lives are as meaningless to us as a swarm of menacing insects. Take great care with the information with which you have been entrusted. Continue to follow instructions, and catastrophe can be avoided. We will call again tomorrow. Goodbye, Hargrove."

As he hung up, Glen was even more numbed by the ruthlessness of his antagonists. The senseless destruction of human life was a tragedy ingrained in history. Wars between and within nations had helped shape the world's chronology. However, there was normally a certain regret and sadness associated with the cost of war in terms of human pain and suffering. Likewise, natural disasters, such as earthquakes or weather events, often claimed countless lives, but attitudes of compassion and concern inherent in the human spirit brought individuals and nations to the aid of those in dire need. Even in people who were normally selfish with their time and resources, tragedy usually evoked a rare demonstration of empathy and support.

From all indications, however, the people with whom Glen was now dealing would not show a shred of remorse if half a million people were killed by their actions. He spent a few moments pondering whether such an impenitent attitude was caused mostly by upbringing, environment, or heredity. With the answer far beyond his grasp, he shook off the notion and called Bud Kershaw.

"Hello, Glen," Kershaw said, recognizing the familiar caller ID. "What's new with our friends out west?"

"Friends . . . I wish," Glen said, with obvious revulsion in his tone of voice. "At least they let me speak for a change. As you suggested, I assured them that all of their demands would be met on time. They used the opportunity to lecture me on who was in charge and just how merciless they would be if we don't play by their rules."

"A standard terrorist line. Don't let it get to you. Anything substantive?"

"A couple of things. They want the money delivered at nine in the morning their time on Thursday. We can choose whom we want to deliver the money, with one constraint. The courier must be a woman."

"A woman!" That was a new one on Kershaw. "Maybe they think a woman will be less threatening."

“Obviously they never met any of the fine young ladies in my class at the Academy,” Glen retorted. “I wouldn’t want to meet some of them in a boxing ring or in an alley on a dark night.”

“I hear you, Glen. Nevertheless, I can’t think of any other reason for them wanting a female courier. Anything else?”

“They reemphasized the consequence of leaking information to the press. That was when I realized just how callous these people are. Why do you think avoiding media leaks is so important to them?”

Kershaw pondered a moment before answering. “My guess is that they’re not opposed to media coverage per se. In fact, American press coverage would probably bring them even greater notoriety when they return to their own country. I think they just want to hold off the story hounds until their mission is completed. Any TV or newspaper visibility before that time will focus attention on them and increase the probability of failure. If they happen to be successful, God forbid, I believe they’ll welcome the coverage. Who knows, they may offer phone interviews to whoever will talk to them.”

“We have to stop these guys, Bud. My mind can’t comprehend their self-righteous faces gloating all the way to the bank.”

“We’re doing all we can. You just keep working on that toxin. Speaking of which, we need to talk about what you found out today and the meeting tomorrow with the president.”

“I take it I was invited.”

“Of course. Tyler thought your insight would be helpful, and I agree with him.” Kershaw was trying to boost Glen’s morale after an obviously disheartening phone call with the terrorists. “Now, what about the toxin?”

"No good news, I'm afraid," Glen started. "As I guessed on Saturday, it's different from anything we've encountered before. The biotoxic organism was created at the genetic level using one of several possible processes."

"There's more than one?" Kershaw asked.

"Yes," Glen answered. "Most people have heard of recombinant DNA, you know . . . gene splicing. That's where you splice and recombine different DNA fragments to give a particular DNA strand a new genetic identity. This manufactured strand is called the donor DNA. Then you produce as many copies of the donor DNA that you want by a cloning process."

"Cloning? Has the process really come that far?" Kershaw asked.

"At the cellular level and for a variety of animal species," Glen continued. "It's a tricky process, but molecular biologists are becoming quite good at it. Cloning for a biotoxic organism would be done by first joining the donor DNA strand to the DNA strand from a host species, something that reproduces quickly like the E. coli bacteria you find in the intestines. The new double-stranded DNA is then absorbed by the bacteria. You can speed up this process by putting the bacteria in a saline solution, which makes the membranes more permeable. Once the new DNA is inside the bacteria, it duplicates right along with the cells. After you've cultured the amount of bacteria desired, you centrifuge out the DNA and heat it up. The heat causes the strands to separate. Then when the DNA cools off, the like strands reattach, isolating the DNA of interest from the bacteria DNA. Voila. A new species is born."

"But for this toxin, isn't the bacteria the final product?"

"That's right. My guess is that the person who engineered this stuff used something like botulinum as his host, and then skipped the strand separation step. The host DNA was probably created from an equally potent bacterium like ricin or anthrax. I wouldn't be surprised if the inventor attached a gene or two to the donor DNA fragment that gave it some unique survival properties that the constituent organisms don't have."

"Like what?" Kershaw asked.

"Like the ability to live in the presence of oxygen. The botulinum bacteria can't survive in the presence of oxygen. This species seems to have no problem with it."

"Sounds like this whole business is too much like playing God." Kershaw was outside his technical area of expertise, so he threw in a philosophical comment.

"I don't agree completely," Glen countered. "Genetic engineering offers a lot of potential for understanding and controlling diseases involving cell mutations, like cancer, and helping to increase the body's ability to combat these illnesses. When it gets to restructuring human embryos though, I agree with you. There are serious ethical questions that need to be addressed."

"You mentioned other genetic engineering processes."

"Uh huh. There are other methods of gene manipulation. The entire nucleus of one cell can be transferred to the cell of a different organism from which the nucleus has been removed. Also, new genes can be inserted into a foreign DNA using a process called microinjection. However, neither of these processes is as popular as gene splicing."

Kershaw was amazed at the rate of technology development in the area of genetics. Although he had a strong technical background, the focus of his recent jobs on management and politics had precluded his keeping up with many of the latest scientific advances. "This bacteria creation . . . I don't know whether to call it genius or madness," he said.

"It's a bit of both," Glen retorted. "The development process didn't end with creation, though. After the basic organism was produced, the inventor nurtured it, like a mother nurtures a newborn, feeding it, strengthening it, and training it to reproduce rapidly and to ward off threats to its destruction, thereby maximizing its toxic potential."

"Training? Are you kidding?"

"Not at all," Glen continued. "Remember that the organism isn't the poison. The toxin it produces is what kills, and the toxin is secreted only by a healthy organism as it multiplies. For the organism to be a continuing long-term danger, it must first survive all threats to its existence and second, replicate in sufficient numbers to avoid a diminishing population. This organism is an expert at survival and produces offspring faster than oversexed rabbits."

"So how was this training accomplished?"

"The incredibly fast reproduction rate is a mystery we're continuing to investigate. The resistance to toxoids was probably accomplished in a manner similar to vaccinations or flu shots in people. Exposing the organism to minute doses of the same substance that can injure or kill it results in a tolerance build-up. Increasing the dosage over time increases the tolerance until the end result of total immunity is achieved."

"So nothing we know can kill the organism?"

"Not yet. Something will, and we'll find it. It's just a question of time."

"Unfortunately, time is not an abundant commodity right now." Kershaw stated the obvious. "So how dangerous is the toxin produced by this organism?"

"That's the worst news of all. Let me put it into perspective. The most potent biotoxin we know of is botulinum type H, a hybrid of types A and F. Theoretically, one ounce of the substance is enough to kill every man, woman, and child on earth. By initial indications, the toxin we're dealing with is deadlier than botulinum H."

Silence was Kershaw's response for a full fifteen seconds as the gravity of the situation sank in. He then spoke slowly and with a combination of anger and disbelief. "What kind of monster would create such a thing and use it as a weapon against innocent human beings?"

"If we knew, Bud, we would have him committed for life."

"Not painful enough. I'd make him drink his own poison and watch him suffer." Kershaw was not known for his tolerance of inhuman behavior.

They both shook their heads on opposite ends of the call. Finally, Glen interrupted the extended silence. "With that discussion out of the way, tell me how I should act in the presence of the president tomorrow."

It was difficult for Kershaw's mind to shift subjects. He answered Glen's question without giving it much thought. "Just be yourself. I mean, be respectful, but not overly polite. Answer his questions as directly and honestly as you can. I won't let you get in over your head."

"How technical should I get?" Glen asked.

"I think you'll be safe if you steer clear of Latin terms. Believe me, he'll stop you if he doesn't understand something."

"Cut me off if you think I'm headed down a wrong path, okay?"

"Don't worry, I will." Kershaw looked at his watch. "Glen, do you realize we've been talking for over half an hour? It's time for you to get out of the house and catch that movie we talked about this morning. And plan on joining Eileen and me for dinner tomorrow. Any problem with that?"

"None at all. You're right. It's important that my mind stays off Jennifer," Glen admitted.

"I'm not giving up on her situation either," Kershaw said.

Glen was confused. "What are you . . ."

"Never mind, I have to think about it some more. We'll talk tomorrow. Remember, your wake-up call is at 0600. Good night, Glen."

"Night, Bud." Glen hung up, wondering what other sly and devious plans his friend Bud Kershaw had up his gold-braided sleeve.

* * * * * * *

Suite 500 of 1100 13th Street NW houses the Washington, D.C. offices of the Associated Press (AP), the oldest and largest of the cooperative news agencies. Like its competitor services, UPI and Reuters to name a couple, the AP makes its money via subscriptions from client news services and broadcast or online media that do not have the staff or time to be everywhere the news is happening. The competition for subscribers is intense, and the service that consistently comes through with the hot stories first wins the lion's share of subscribers. Inside information from reliable sources can give one service a leg up on the competition, so informants are aggressively sought, closely guarded, and well paid. A reporter never knew when a news tip might come in, so many worked well into the evenings, cell phones at hand and close to their computers. One reporter in particular spent three or four nights a week until 9:00 p.m. by his desk: reading, writing, and waiting.

Ever since childhood, Nathan Crowe had wanted to become a journalist. His hunger for the news began soon after he started reading. While his siblings and friends spent their time focused on sports and entertainment, Nathan devoured the news. World news, local news, good news, bad news, fact, opinion, he loved it all. He wrote his first editorial at the age of twelve and was a regular contributor to the op-ed page of his hometown paper until he went off to college to obtain a degree in journalism. After graduation, he worked a couple of years for a respectable small town paper, where he established a reputation for solid and aggressive reporting. While on assignment to cover some racial turmoil in Washington, D.C., he met a lovely young woman who worked for the Associated Press. Attracted to her physical as well as journalistic attributes, he decided to pursue a relationship. The attraction turned out to be a mutual one. Both of them realized that a long distance love affair wouldn't work, so she introduced him to some people with influence at the AP. Crowe's credentials served him well, and he was offered a job in the Washington office. Now three years later, his lady friend was a distant memory, but Nathan Crowe still worked for the AP in D.C.; his assignment was the White House.

In Crowe's opinion, which was the same as many of his young contemporaries who attended the more liberal colleges and universities, the public's right to know the complete truth and his freedom to pursue and report the truth were unconditionally guaranteed by the First Amendment. On his journalistic rights scale, there were no shades of gray, only black and white. Black was represented by the politicians, whom he believed were committed to keeping people in the dark. At best, they selectively filtered the information they dispensed under the guise of protecting the public. He cringed every time these politicians referred to themselves as public servants. Crowe believed he represented the white end of the scale, and it was his solemn conviction to extract every shred of information possible out of the Washington establishment. One day several years in the future, when the rough edges of his youthful idealism were smoothed over by experience, Nathan Crowe would learn to meet the politicians somewhere in the middle. However, on this evening of September 15, as he sat at his desk in the AP offices consuming his daily ration of news, Crowe was as determined as ever to ensure the American public's right to the whole truth.

The ring of his office phone interrupted his perusal of the front page of the *New York Times*. He put down his paper, punched the blinking button, and answered with his last name.

"This is Jeremiah," said the muffled and purposely altered voice on the other end of the line.

Crowe immediately grabbed a pad and pen. "Jeremiah, we haven't spoken for a while. I was beginning to think you'd forgotten about me."

Crowe had himself given the informant his code name. When the first call came in a few months before, the snitch was naturally nervous and uncomfortable with what he was about to do. Crowe made him feel at ease. He told him he didn't want to know who he was or why he was doing what he was doing. That was no lie. Blowing the whistle on an informant wouldn't benefit anyone, and Crowe wasn't the blackmailing type. He also told him that the source of information for any particular article to which he provided input would never be shared with anyone. Finally, he suggested the concept of financial incentives for the provision of reliable information. When the subject of choosing a code name for future calls came up, the informant asked for suggestions. Crowe pulled the name Jeremiah out of thin air. Having never known anyone named Jeremiah in his life, he suggested that the caller would be immediately recognized by the name. No objections forthcoming, the name was adopted. Although he suspected that Jeremiah was an office assistant or janitor who had found a way to access privileged information during off hours, Crowe didn't waste a lot of time conjecturing. All that mattered was that Jeremiah's intelligence on activities in the Oval Office was accurate, and it always was. That's why a phone call from Jeremiah was a special event in the daily routine of Nathan Crowe.

"I haven't forgotten you, Mr. Crowe. There has just been no reason to talk to you recently."

"I take it there's something going on in the White House that's not receiving the coverage it deserves."

"I believe I have a few facts that might be of interest to you, assuming my fee will be forthcoming," Jeremiah said.

"Don't worry. If the info is good, you'll get your grand. Okay, let's have it." Crowe had his pen poised, ready to take notes.

"The president was scheduled to fly to Savannah, Georgia tomorrow morning to personally inspect the damage caused by hurricane Carly. He is a little outraged at the amount of federal assistance being requested by the Georgia governor and wants to show that he will not simply rubber-stamp these requests."

"Right," Crowe said, irritated at being read back the news from today's papers and broadcasts. "Everybody knows this already. Tell me something I don't know."

"Don't be impatient, Mr. Crowe," Jeremiah responded, "I'm merely establishing the background for what I'm about to tell you. This trip has been postponed indefinitely so that the president can focus his attention on a much more urgent domestic crisis. The current situation in . . ."

Suddenly the line went dead. Crowe said hello four or five times before he gave up and put down the receiver. He sat in silence for five minutes, and then, certain that Jeremiah was not going to call back soon, he analyzed what he had been told. It was practically nothing. The Savannah trip was canceled. The reason was a more urgent domestic crisis. Okay, so it wasn't a foreign policy issue. The crisis couldn't be another act of God or it would be common knowledge by now. Was it a fiscal crisis? A labor crisis? An energy crisis? He went through every Cabinet post in his mind and concluded that there were no hints in what Jeremiah said. He had ended with the phrase, "The current situation in . . ." That could imply something outside of the Washington, D.C. area, a regional crisis of some sort.

Crowe had little to go on, but he turned to his word processor and started typing anyway. The brief report would say exactly what he knew. "The president has canceled his trip to Savannah to inspect hurricane damage in order to focus on a more urgent domestic crisis. No details of the crisis were available at this time." Crowe read the text over once and hit the send key. The story went into the transmission queue and, within two minutes, was headed for a satellite that would relay it to all of the AP's subscribers. Maybe his little article would encourage the administration to come forth with a few more details.

* * * * * * *

In the study of a suburban D.C. colonial home, Jeremiah sat in deep contemplation. Since the argument with his wife, he'd been having second thoughts about the call to Nathan Crowe. Originally, her intrusion into his privacy infuriated him. He had told her on several occasions that he did not want to be disturbed when the study door was shut. This was one of his many standing requests that she did not care to respect. When she came bursting into the study demanding ten minutes of his time to address an issue of vital importance to her, he quickly ended his phone call in mid-sentence. The ensuing discussion was typical of nearly every discussion lasting more than a minute during their previous three months together. Specifics quickly turned to generalities, and the conversation degenerated into a bitter shouting match. The seed of the argument long forgotten, she ended the discussion by storming out of the room, arms waving in the air, exclaiming at the top of her lungs, "A man like you just can't be reasoned with." Such was the rocky relationship of Lou and Helen Bernstein.

Again deprived of the opportunity to have the last word, Lou "Jeremiah" Bernstein silently boiled for five minutes before falling into his current mental state, a combination of depression and indecision. When Jackson Tyler had first started to demean him openly at staff meetings, it was done in a joking fashion. Even Bernstein himself got an occasional chuckle out of Tyler's comments. With time, however, the comments became more coarse and insensitive, especially when it came to his worsening relationship with his wife. He felt he had to strike back, but direct confrontation was never considered an alternative. Its impact would be temporary, and he would end up losing his job. One day, it occurred to Bernstein that his knowledge of privileged information was the key to inflicting frequent and long-lasting injury. He could administer his blows silently and covertly, while having the pleasure of witnessing the effect of the counterattack.

After observing many representatives of the media in action, he selected Nathan Crowe as his voice to the world. Crowe's youth, aggressiveness, and reputation as a maverick would serve his purposes well. The first call was accompanied by the usual discomfort. However, subsequent calls were easier. The call leaking the prime candidates for the Supreme Court Justice nomination was great fun. It was pure enjoyment seeing the expression on his boss's face when confronted with the article in the *Washington Post.* His allegiance to Tyler presumed to be unwavering, Bernstein was never seriously considered as the source of the leaks. Until tonight, Bernstein's agenda for retaliation was skillfully executed. He was seeing the results personally and in Tyler's plummeting approval rating. Finally, the extra money would come in handy in the event of a nasty divorce trial.

Tonight's phone call to Crowe, however, was taking on a different complexion. His outrage at Tyler's comment during the morning meeting with Kershaw and the others had clouded his judgment. He was beginning to realize the extent of damage that could result from the information he was leaking. He finally decided the phone call was a mistake and that he'd said too much already. Crowe would not be called back regarding the Washington State toxin crisis. Ironically, his wife brought him to his senses with her unwelcome visit to the study. His mind turned to thoughts of a possible reconciliation, but the thoughts were fleeting. For all intents and purposes, he and Helen were already divorced.

* * * * * * *

Having only infrequently visited the Seattle area in the past, Harry Boland and Darrell Wolczyk were content to stay at the first decent hotel they could find. After renting a mid-size Nissan at National Car Rental, they drove around the airport perimeter looking for a place with a bit of class. The Sea-Tac Red Lion Hotel filled the bill. They were given adjacent rooms on the top floor of the hotel and agreed to meet for a quick meal at a nearby chain restaurant. On the way to dinner, Boland stopped by the hotel convenience store and picked up a tourist guide to Seattle and vicinity. The map in the guide was detailed and extended sufficiently far to the east to cover the primary sources to the city's water supply.

The first table they were shown didn't provide the privacy they desired. They were then led to a small booth in a corner, which was ideal. Boland ordered a turkey club sandwich, while Wolczyk selected the chef salad with ranch dressing. Both ordered a Tropic Haze IPA from the Silver City Brewery after being advised that it was one of the better local beers. They both started to focus on the enormous task ahead.

"Where do you suggest we begin?" Boland asked his partner. He had formulated an outline for a plan on the plane, but always liked to keep Wolczyk's mental juices flowing.

"Before we begin looking for these characters, I think we should at least make a courtesy call to the local police," Wolczyk started. "I know Kershaw told us to keep them in the dark, but we could arouse a lot of suspicion by showing up unannounced on their turf and conducting our own little investigation."

"The thought crossed my mind too," Boland agreed. "And who knows, they may provide us with some useful leads." He did a quick Google search for phone numbers of the various federal, state, and local organizations in the metropolitan Seattle area, thinking to himself how convenient it was to rarely have to say "I wonder" anymore. A few words spoken or typed into a cell phone, and the answers were right in front of you.

Boland studied the search results for a few minutes and discovered that the city was served by multiple independent law enforcement agencies—the Seattle Police Department, several surrounding city police departments, and the King County Police Department, which was also called the Sheriff's Office. After comparing the street addresses to locations on the map in his tourist guide, he concluded that the Seattle Police Department was more centralized in the downtown area and probably more concerned with city affairs. On the other hand, a couple of law enforcement entities on the outskirts of the city appeared to cover the region to the east of Lake Washington, where the water sources to the city converged. He concluded it would be beneficial to interact with two specific entities—the third precinct of the King County Police Department in Maple Valley and the Bothell Police Department. Boland suggested that they first visit the King County third precinct, which was closer to their hotel, and then drive north to Bothell. After briefing the respective police chiefs, they could start their search for the terrorists.

Wolczyk agreed with Boland's suggestion. "What about our cover story?" he asked.

"We'll tell them we're here to investigate a potential security violation at one of the local defense contractors. Boeing is a good candidate. The company is huge and dispersed throughout the region. If we're friendly and appear to be honest, we shouldn't have any problems."

Their meals and beers arrived, so they suspended the discussion briefly until their server moved on to another table. While consuming their food and washing it down with the beers, they lamented about the magnitude of the task.

"Touching base with the local authorities is the easy part," Wolczyk said. "Talk about your needle in a haystack. How on earth are we going to track down these terrorists in the middle of a metropolitan population of four million people?"

"Logically," Boland countered, "these people are professionals. They're not going to leave an obvious trail. We have to look for the more obscure clues, the tracks they leave behind during the course of their daily routine. I also believe we should focus on the present time and not some event several days ago. Even if we did find out how, when, and where they got into the country, that doesn't help us figure out where they are now. Remember Bud saying that their first message specified the Seattle reservoirs as the target? Well, I've been trying to put myself in their shoes. If I were going to set up an operation to pollute several reservoirs at once, I'd establish a home base about equal distance from all of them. Then I'd have an easy commute to different reservoirs on different days."

Boland pushed aside his half-empty plate and placed the regional map on the table facing Wolczyk. "Look here, Darrell," he said, pointing to the western foothills of the Cascade mountain range. "The reservoirs run north and south in this area." His finger bisected the line connecting the bodies of water, then moved west until it hit civilization near the city of Bellevue. "Here's where I'd set up my base of operations."

"Makes sense," Wolczyk commented. He realized Boland was on a mental roll now and let him continue without interruption. If past experience was any indication, a mild alcohol buzz would help inspire Boland's pearls of wisdom. He waved to catch the server's attention, pointed to an empty beer can, then held up two fingers. The international hand sign for "bring us two more brews" was understood and acknowledged.

Boland continued, "Okay, Darrell, think about who we're dealing with. These people want money, but they also want some of their friends released from prison. The guys that plotted to take out the Willis Tower and the Baltimore Harbor Tunnel were definitely Middle Eastern. I distinctly remember seeing their defiant faces on the front page of every newspaper. I believe there's a fair chance that the people we're trying to find are from the same neck of the woods. Now think about where we are. This is the Pacific Northwest. I'm no regional expert, but I'm pretty sure Middle Easterners are still a significant minority here. If we can be thankful for one thing, it's that we're not looking for Scandinavians. There are plenty of them around here. So, what do we have? A couple or three Middle Eastern looking people, one or more of them male, hanging around the eastern suburbs of Seattle, walking on the streets, eating out, asking directions, buying groceries and other essentials, generally living life in a place where they don't quite belong. I think they'll stand out in a crowd."

The beers came, and Boland paused only long enough to take three long swallows. "Also, Darrell, they're driving a car. They can't get out to these reservoirs using public transportation, and they're certainly not walking or hitchhiking. Finally, they're living somewhere. I don't know whether it's a house, a condo, a trailer, or a hotel room, but there's bound to be something that'll lead us to the place." Boland took a few more swallows, and no more words followed for the moment.

"So, Harry, how does all of this knowledge translate into a plan?" Wolczyk asked.

"We've got to rely on a process of elimination," Boland answered. "There's no way of knowing how they came into the country. Plane? Car? Ship? Who knows, but who cares? That information doesn't lead us to their current location. We're almost certain they're driving a car now, and there's a high probability that it's a rental. We also know they're in town for a specific short-term mission. They probably came into the United States less than a week ago, and they'll probably leave as quickly as possible when they're done. Judging by their ultimatum, they expect to be gone by the end of the week. While they're here, they have to sleep and eat, so they're living somewhere and shopping somewhere nearby. If they are from some country in the Middle East, their looks and mannerisms might cause suspicion among the locals. I suggest we focus on who they are, where they're staying, and what they're driving. I think we should concentrate our search on this geographic area." Boland's index finger created an imaginary five-mile-radius semicircle on the east side of Lake Washington with its center in downtown Bellevue.

"Details, you ask," Boland continued, anticipating Wolczyk's next question. "One of us should cover the car rental agencies and the other should check out hotels, motels, and real estate rentals. The length of the stay is key. We limit the search to those visiting the area for six to ten days."

"That should shorten the list to ten or twenty thousand," Wolczyk retorted with mild sarcasm.

"Maybe that many, but maybe a lot fewer," Boland continued undaunted. "After that, we continue the process of elimination to further shorten the list. There are plenty of folks who just don't fit the mold: those who are too old or too young, those with homes of record in the United States, those in the military, a lot of groups. The car agencies require renters to provide a local address. That can be another clue. After we shorten the list to something manageable, we start making the rounds and asking a lot of questions until we find them. So there's my plan. What do you think?"

Wolczyk pondered all that Boland had said for a moment, then spoke. "Okay, Harry, suppose these people are sympathizers and not really aligned with some Middle Eastern country. Kershaw said they sounded like they were Americans, so they may not cause any suspicion at all. And suppose they're from out of the area, but all of their arrangements are being handled by a local resident, maybe someone who's lending them a car and letting them stay at his place, which is probably not a hotel. And suppose this friend is bringing them in all of the food and other supplies they need for their week-long stay in Seattle. And suppose . . ."

"Enough, Darrell," Boland cut him off sharply, then sighed deeply. "Of course you're right. I've thought of all these possibilities too. I guess I just choose to believe that there's a trail somewhere. Do you have any better ideas?"

Wolczyk had played the devil's advocate well, but didn't have any suggestions for improving upon Boland's plan. "Not really, Harry. We have to start somewhere. There are holes in your plan, but at least it's a plan."

They engaged in a minute of contemplation, during which the server came with the check. Boland grabbed the bill and offered to pay for this meal if Wolczyk picked up the next tab, then threw a fifty on the table. As they both rose to leave the restaurant, Boland philosophized. "It's not fair that we should be at such a disadvantage, Darrell. These criminals are out to kill Americans and destroy our environment. We have less than three days to prevent a major catastrophe and no solid leads to go on. It's probably the toughest challenge we've had since we first started working together. Something has got to happen to either make the needle a lot bigger or the haystack a lot smaller."

"All we can do is our best," Wolczyk responded half-heartedly, not really knowing whether a response was solicited.

They reached the doors of their respective hotel rooms. "Our best may not save Seattle," Boland said quietly to prevent being overheard. He paused for a few moments, during which time his face seemed to take on a new look of determination. Then with a renewed assertiveness, he proclaimed, "We're going to get these guys, Darrell. I feel it in my bones. They're going to slip up, and when they do, we'll be all over them. Let's get some sleep now. Tomorrow, bright and early, the chase begins. We need to be at our best."

They unlocked their doors simultaneously and silently slipped into their rooms. Sleep came easily. As far as their bodies were concerned, it was close to midnight, even though their watches said it was before 9:00 p.m. The six o'clock wake up calls they requested wouldn't be necessary. Their bodies would wake up suddenly and completely at 3:00 a.m., and the thoughts would start to creep into their collective consciousness—the plans, the uncertainties, the odds against success, the dangers. Though they remained in bed, their busy minds would keep them awake and alert until the rising sun took over the job three hours later.

* * * * * * *

Most residents of the Emerald City of Seattle were still awake when Boland and Wolczyk fell asleep. Among them was Scoop Scanlon, who often paid an after-hours visit to the *Times* Building on Denny Way. He made his usual rounds, first checking the reception desk for messages from visitors and then his answering machine for phone calls. Finally, he sat down at his computer and accessed the Associated Press stories received since late afternoon, when he had stopped by the office after his disastrous encounter with Cushman and the kid.

He skimmed the first half-dozen new articles one by one, pressing the DEL key after each to delete it from his personal queue. The seventh and last article, which concerned the cancellation of a planned trip by the president so that he could focus on a more urgent domestic crisis, piqued Scanlon's interest but was devoid of details. Besides, he needed to focus his attention on the local crisis he knew Cushman and the kid were hiding. His finger went back and forth between the SAVE and DEL keys several times before he finally tapped DEL. He then turned off his computer and headed home to his one-bedroom apartment for the night.

* * * * * * *

Glen Hargrove was still laughing to himself as he pulled into his garage after driving home from the movie theater. The film was a hilarious spoof that brought lawyers, cowboys, cops, soap opera stars, and comic book superheroes together, all on the same screen.

The laughter quickly subsided as he opened the front door and immediately saw the red number “2” on his answering machine, indicating the receipt of two phone messages while he was out. He took a breath and hit the *Play* button. The first one contained a busy-like signal, indicating that the caller hung up without leaving a message. The second one was from Jennifer.

“Hi, honey, it’s me. I hope you’re out enjoying yourself right now instead of being at work. I just called to say hello and to let you know we’re all doing fine out here in Seattle. Mom and Dad say hi also. They’re concerned about you, and I am too. Please take care of yourself. I miss you and wish you were here. Bye, hon.”

The sound of her voice should have brought comfort, but once again, uncertainty about the situation in Seattle and her safety brought on a fearful chill. As he prepared for bed, her image filled his thoughts. He longed to reach out three thousand miles and pull her body to him, to hold her close, to kiss her lips, and to lie close to her. As he fell into bed, he clutched his pillow, imagining the softness of the linen to be that of his wife. The illusion lasted only a moment, and then was supplanted by an anger unlike any he’d ever known before. He was furious at the dispassionate actions of the men who were threatening the lives of his wife and a million other unsuspecting people. He tried to push aside the anger with revived thoughts of Jennifer, but it would not be displaced. Though exhausted from a hard day at work and two nights of sleep deprivation, Glen’s attempts to rest were again frustrated, this time by his lingering outrage at an unseen enemy.

Well after midnight, he drifted into an unusual body state consisting partly of sleep and partly of a semi-conscious thought process. Kershaw's comment earlier in the day about not giving up on Jennifer's situation came back to him while in his pseudo-slumber. In his own mind, he began to formulate a strategy for extracting Jennifer from Seattle and its associated peril. He knew his privileged knowledge of the situation gave him an unfair advantage over the thousands of others having relatives in the region, but in his mentally and physically exhausted condition, he yielded to the selfish motivation. The strategy far from being solidified, the sleep portion of Glen's state finally took control at 2:00 a.m. His last conscious sensation was a revived optimism that Jennifer would be safe in his arms in the very near future.

CHAPTER 7 - TUESDAY, SEPTEMBER 16, MORNING

"Hello," Glen answered groggily.

"Rise and shine, Glen," Kershaw said on the other end of the connection. "We've got a big day ahead."

"How can you be so alive?" Glen asked.

"Are you kidding?" Kershaw answered. "I've been up for an hour and a half. I did fifty push-ups, thirty leg raises, a hundred sit-ups, and an assortment of other calisthenics, ran two miles, showered, shaved, dressed, put out the trash, and fed the dog before calling you."

"You don't have a dog, Bud."

"Okay, so I listened to the news for five minutes, brushed my teeth, and ran a comb through my hair."

"You don't have any hair, Bud."

"So you caught me. I just woke up, got vertical, and called you. Nevertheless, it's wake-up time."

"I need about three more hours of sleep," Glen protested mildly, realizing that any more shut-eye was out of the question.

"Another bad night?" Kershaw asked.

"Yeah. When I got back from the movie, there was a message on the answering machine. It was Jen. I couldn't stop thinking about her again." Glen suddenly recalled his last waking thoughts and Kershaw's comment about Jennifer during the previous evening's conversation. "Did you imply last night that you were working on a plan to get her out?" Glen asked, still not quite lucid.

"I've been thinking about it more, but let's wait until breakfast to talk about it. We both need to get ready for our meeting."

"Summer whites?" Glen assumed that the normal uniform worn in Washington between May and October would be appropriate for the meeting with the president.

"Whites are fine," Kershaw answered. "The meeting is at 0900, so we should plan to be at the White House ten minutes early. I suggest we meet at my office an hour before that. You can park in my Flag Lieutenant's space; he'll be over at NRL all morning. Then we can catch the Metro to downtown and grab a bite within walking distance of 1600 Pennsylvania Avenue."

Glen smiled, now almost fully awake. Bud Kershaw was never without a plan. "Sounds good to me," he said. "See you then."

"Ciao, Glen."

* * * * * * *

Anxious to see how his specimens fared over the course of the night, Jim Thunderhill was the first to arrive at the NMRC immunotoxicology laboratory on Tuesday morning. Only Glen Hargrove and Cheryl Forrester had personal keys to the lab, but there was a spare key hung on a hook by the door in case anyone planned to arrive early the next day or work on the weekend. Jim had grabbed the key on his way out the night before and now used it to open the passage lock.

It was an improbable series of events that had brought Jim Thunderhill to the current place and time. A full-blooded Navajo Native American, Jim was born and raised on the Ramah Reservation in West Central New Mexico. Realizing that there was a world beyond the reservation that they would never fully experience, Jim's parents tried to integrate him into the "whole of society" at an early age by enrolling him in the public school system. They were reluctant, however, to sacrifice his identity by allowing him to adopt society's standards of dress and appearance.

With his long and flowing hair, tanned leather clothes, and moccasins, Jim was ostracized by his contemporaries from the start. The mockery he endured during his elementary school years turned physical as he entered junior high school, where his emotional anguish was frequently accompanied by bodily pain. On many a day, Jim came home limping or with a black eye because of a fight that he neither started nor desired. His parents visited the school authorities on several occasions, but none of their efforts could stem the derisive assault against their son.

The conflict reached crisis proportions during the second week of Jim's ninth grade, when a group of boys under the leadership of a recent Los Angeles import named Hank Masterson cornered Jim in the bathroom. Four of the boys held him down while Hank and another boy took scissors to his head, leaving him with a poor facsimile of a Mohawk haircut. Two dozen bruises and a fat lip later, Jim was released by the boys. The incident was the last straw for his very tolerant family. Jim was removed from public school and returned to the reservation.

His mother, however, didn't give up on her dream of seeing her son become successful in the outside world. She took on the task of home-schooling Jim, a task that was made even more difficult by her own limited education. Despite the obvious hurdles, she bought the required textbooks, studied them herself, and then passed on her newfound knowledge to Jim. She kept him on a rigorous learning schedule for four years, then, because of the family's limited finances, encouraged him to apply to a service academy. Jim wrote to all of New Mexico's legislators about appointments to all three academies. Harold Miller, the representative from the congressional district bordering the Ramah Reservation, was willing to give Jim an interview.

West Point and the Air Force Academy would not even consider an applicant without a high school transcript. However, with the growing emphasis in the military on equal opportunity for minorities, the Naval Academy was willing to accept Jim's application, provided that a grade equivalency could be established through testing and that there would be no partiality shown in evaluating competitors for the billet.

The day that the congressional appointee to the Naval Academy was to be announced was an anxious one for the Thunderhill family. The announcement was to be made in the auditorium of the high school Jim had left over three years ago and not set foot in since.

Silence greeted the family as they entered the large room and walked toward their assigned seats in the front. Then the chatter and offensive sounds started, and all of the painful memories of years ago flooded Jim's mind. He saw many of the faces of the boys who had taunted him. The faces were older but wore the same patronizing expressions. Only one boy spoke to him directly. As he headed for his seat with the other Naval Academy candidates, Hank Masterson purposefully walked right up to Jim and said, loudly enough so that everyone in a ten-foot radius could hear, "Hey, Geronimo, come back to school for another trim?" The outburst of laughter was so distressing that Jim's mother started to get up to leave. However, Jim took hold of her hand and looked her straight in the eye, smiling and nodding, until she settled back into her seat. Only the principal's introduction of the speaker for the assembly, the Honorable Harold Miller, quieted the group.

Miller had gotten into the US Congress by being in touch with his constituents. Though in certain public events, he often gave one the impression that he had lost consciousness, he was always mindful of his surroundings. For the previous five minutes, he had been sitting in his seat on the stage, arms folded and eyes closed, absorbing the course of the conversation in the first row. He squinted an eye open just in time to see Jim Thunderhill's reaction to the arrogant comment from the other candidate. He was immediately gratified that the result of his staff's candidate evaluation had turned out the way it did and quickly altered his upcoming remarks.

"Ladies, gentlemen, and students," Miller started, "it is my privilege and pleasure to be here today to announce the name of the individual whom I am nominating for an appointment to the United States Naval Academy this year. Before I do, however, I would like to say a few words about the kind of person I believe is deserving of this honor and this opportunity to serve our great nation. While academic excellence and athletic ability are certainly prerequisites for the difficult four-year curriculum at Annapolis, I believe another more important human quality defines the truly exceptional naval officer, an attribute that is nurtured in the home and put into practice every day until it becomes a natural extension of one's being. I might add that it is a rare quality in this day and age. I'm talking about the attribute of integrity. Men and women with integrity have helped make America great. Those without it have strived to tear this country down. Integrity has many meanings. It means being honest even when dishonesty is the path of least resistance. It means having high standards of morality and ethics. It means being a person of principle and of your word."

Miller shifted his gaze to Hank Masterson before continuing with his next few sentences. "Integrity means being a fair and decent person, a person who does not consider himself better than others or treat those who are of different heritage with contempt and prejudice, a person who understands the words of our forefathers when they stated in the Declaration of Independence that all men are created equal."

The sweat began to appear on Masterson's brow as he realized that Congressman Miller's comments were being directed at him personally.

"One therefore might assume," Miller concluded, "that if not quite synonymous, the terms integrity and American certainly go hand in hand. I now announce with great pride that this year, my appointment to the Naval Academy goes to a young man of great integrity, to one of the finest young Americans I have had the privilege of meeting . . . Jim Thunderhill."

At first, there were quiet gasps and sarcastic whispers in the auditorium. An Indian going to Annapolis! Unbelievable. Then after about twenty seconds of collective discomfort, a single set of hands somewhere in the middle of the room was brought together at even one-second intervals. The murmurs quickly died down, and then one by one, additional hands joined in the unison clapping until the entire assembly was participating in a near deafening round of applause.

Jim and his family were overwhelmed by the spontaneous outburst of long overdue approval. Even Masterson made a begrudging offer of congratulations. The demands for a speech forced Jim to the podium, but the only words he could muster in the midst of the emotional moment were, "Thank you to my family, and I thank you all very much."

No other event in Jim's life had been quite so climactic as Congressman Miller's message nominating him to Annapolis and the resultant outpouring of approval. However, the years since had brought many successes and many realized dreams. Jim graduated with a 3.4 GPA and was a member of the varsity cross-country team. He was selected for the immediate graduate education program (IGEP) in biomolecular research and was transferred to the Medical Services Corps after receiving his master's degree. He'd been working and learning at NMRC for more than three years now and was thrilled with his current assignment.

As Jim opened the door to the laboratory on the morning of September 16, the first thing that struck him was the unusual silence. Even when you were the only human being in the lab, you were never alone. The clicking of claws, nibbling of food, and general motion of the specimens in their cages reminded you of the abundance of life around you. This morning was different, though. At first, Jim surmised that the whole group hadn't yet woken up. Then he remembered why he came in early.

He flipped on the lights and rushed over to the specimen cages, where his fears were realized. All of the specimens he infected the day before were dead. Not only were they dead, it was obvious that they died under very unpleasant circumstances. Mouths were agape as if gasping for a breath but unable to succeed. Normally expressionless eyes were open, giving the small faces a look of shock and disbelief. Blood-laced urine, feces, and vomit littered the cages, and signs of a struggle were evident in every cage. One mouse was hanging by two of its extremities halfway up the side of its cage. One had slammed so hard into the cage wall that its neck was broken. Its relatively peaceful visage indicated that it was spared the more painful death of the others. One specimen had actually pushed its head through the cage's wire frame, the spacing of which was originally half the size of the head. Only Alfie, in his haven in the corner of the room, was alive and well, and even he seemed to know that something terrible had happened during the night.

As Jim went from cage to cage inspecting the results, he tried to remain detached and scientific, but even for a seasoned veteran of animal research like himself, the scene was overwhelming. As he completed his inspection, he walked over to the DVR and hit the << button. He wasn't looking forward to watching the specimens' deaths in progress, but it would help him in his further analysis of the toxin's specific effects on the body. When the video was reset to the beginning, he pushed *Play*, took a seat in the nearest chair, propped his feet up on the DVR cart, and prepared for the worst.

* * * * * * *

Glen Hargrove scanned the names, ranks, and positions painted on the wall of the parking garage until he saw the words "Reserved for Flag Lieutenant," then pulled his Camry into the space. From his window on the ninth floor of 800 North Quincy Street in Arlington, Bud Kershaw had seen Glen's car pulling into the garage and decided to save him a trip. By the time Glen reached the elevator at the second sub-level of the building, Kershaw was exiting the stairwell.

"Forget it, Glen, I'm right here," Kershaw said, slightly out of breath from the multi-story descent. "Let's head straight to the Metro."

The pair climbed the two flights of stairs back to ground level, further taxing Kershaw's wind capacity. "I'm not in the shape I used to be in," Kershaw commented, a short breath thrown in between every couple words.

"Desk jobs will do that to you," Glen said, himself being a victim of diminishing stamina and a slight midsection bulge.

They headed along Quincy Street and Fairfax Drive toward the Ballston Metro Station, engaging in some small talk until they arrived at the station. Each man deposited the required amount in the fare card machine and then headed through the turnstile and down the escalator, just in time to catch the eastbound Orange Line train. They would transfer to the Blue Line toward downtown D.C. in Rosslyn and finally surface again at the Federal Triangle Station, completing their half-hour ride on one of the nation's finest and most well-maintained subway systems.

During the ride, the conversation remained casual. Talking loudly enough to be heard over the train noise meant being heard by the ears of the city. In Washington, where information was literally worth its weight in gold, it was unbelievable how far and fast presumably privileged information traveled. Entire publishing empires had been built upon the reporting of hearsay and idle chatter. One might be inclined to believe that even the walls of buildings and train cars had ears. In many cases, it was probably true.

The two naval officers could afford to be a little more relaxed about talking shop when they finally exited the subway into the morning D.C. sunlight. Realizing that their breakfast conversation should remain confidential, Kershaw suggested a pastry and cup of coffee at a local street vendor, which was fine with Glen.

They purchased their food and drink, then found an isolated bench on the Ellipse near the White House. Kershaw brought up the subject of Jennifer without a prompt from Glen. "We can't get her whole family out, you know," he began. "There's too great a risk of the word getting out on the street. Who else lives with her mother and father?"

"Nobody," Glen replied. "It's just the three of them out there right now."

"Good," Kershaw said, "then that's who we'll extract. Here's what I'm thinking. She wanted to spend this week with you in New Hampshire. Your situation caused her to choose the best alternative—visiting her parents. Now we give her both. Suppose a messenger shows up at their front door tonight with two e-tickets for her parents to fly to Boston tomorrow morning and an itinerary change for Jen to return on the same flight. Of course the tickets are from you, even though the government picks up the tab."

Glen continued the thought process. "I'm sending her the tickets because my crisis is over and I want to salvage the rest of the vacation week up at Squam Lake."

"Exactly," Kershaw continued. "The three of them arrive in Boston and drive in Jennifer's car back to the condo . . ."

". . . and I keep making excuses as to why I can't join them for another two or three days until this mess is over." Glen finished Kershaw's sentence, describing the least palatable part of the plan.

"Right," Kershaw agreed. "Have you been reading my mind?"

"You know," Glen answered, "it's uncanny, but as I fell asleep last night, my mind concocted an almost identical plan."

"That's not unusual. After all, you are a Kershaw-trained man," Bud joked. "How did your plan differ?"

"Well, in my plan, I bought the tickets. That's why I like your plan better."

They both laughed. "It's the least Uncle Sam can do for you, considering what you're going through this week," Kershaw said. "Now, first and foremost, do you think she'll go for it?"

"If the tickets show up at her parents' front door, I don't see that she has a choice. Jennifer is too frugal to waste a couple thousand dollars in airplane fares. Her parents are seasoned travelers and love to fly, so there won't be a problem there. One question, though. Who's going to be the messenger?" Glen asked.

"There are a couple of DSS agents in Seattle as we speak, trying to track down the bad guys. They're going to be busy, but maybe

I can persuade Harry Boland to take half an hour off tonight and make the delivery. What airline does she normally fly?"

"American," Glen answered.

"Okay, we'll reserve three adjacent seats on an American flight, then get Boland to print out the e-ticket specifics and make the delivery."

Kershaw concluded, looking at his watch and rising to search for a trash can. "Fine, it's a done deal."

Glen also rose and said, "Let's just hope it works."

After doing their part to keep Washington litter-free, the two men, who in their summer uniforms could have been mistaken for Good Humor ice cream vendors, began their short walk to the White House. As they walked, their voices were silent, while their minds were totally focused on the important roles they would play in the meeting to follow.

* * * * * * *

As Kershaw and Hargrove made their way on foot to 1600 Pennsylvania Avenue, the final boarding call for Alaska Air Flight 942 to Seattle was announced at the Ronald Reagan Washington National Airport. Lisa Kennelly and her group of three associates made their way through the jetway to the plane, each loaded down with the more sensitive of the biosensor components. At the ticketing counter, the group had annoyed and frustrated more than a few travelers with their wooden crates full of gear, each of which had to be separately weighed and inspected for adequate packaging.

After delicately placing their parcels in the overhead compartments, the group took their seats, and Lisa placed a call to Admiral

Kershaw's office before phones were required to be placed in airplane mode. She was greeted by his voicemail message, indicating both he and his Flag Lieutenant were out of the office. She hung up without leaving a message and decided to call back in flight using the plane's Wi-Fi.

Fortunately, the 737 wasn't crowded, so Lisa and her assistants, the four of them seated on opposite sides of the aisle in row 12, had open middle seats between them. Kurt Wagner, seated at the window next to Lisa, was the senior of the three. With a master's degree in physics, a concentration in the optical sciences, and nearly two years' experience on the project, his knowledge of the sensing end of the system was unsurpassed. Across the aisle from Lisa was Robin Stoddard, who was four years out of MIT with a bachelor's degree in electrical engineering. She knew the biosensor's signal processing circuitry inside and out. Finally, seated in the window seat next to Robin was Sanjay Bhuttar, the prodigy of the group. Having graduated from high school in New Delhi at the age of fourteen, he spent the next eight years collecting more degrees than any random group of ten people obtain in a lifetime, most of them related to the computer sciences. His latest acquisition was a master's degree in satellite telecommunications, which was being applied to the transmission of the remote biosensor data to the master processing units, affectionately called the "mothers."

Somewhere over northern West Virginia, Lisa started discussing her plans for setting up and monitoring the biosensor network. She mentioned that the precise locations of the sensor stations wouldn't be known until she had a chance to talk with their point of contact in the Seattle Public Works Department. Admiral Kershaw would hopefully be providing the name of the contact when they talked. She did, however, have a general plan of action, which, as the plane reached its final cruising altitude of 33,000 feet, she started to explain.

"The network will consist of two sets of six sensors, each set sending data to its mother via cellular telecommunications links. I anticipate that we'll be able to group the sensor sites into two geographic groups. After the network is assembled and checked out, which I hope will be completed by mid-afternoon, the three of you will go into a shift work rotation. Two of you will be on duty at any given time, one assigned to each set of six sites, while the third can rest. I think six-hour shifts are reasonable, although I'm flexible on this matter. Your job while on duty will be to continuously travel between the sites, take water samples at each, analyze the samples, and initiate the transmission of the data back to the respective mother. I'll be on full-time duty with the mothers, comparing the results, recording the data, and keeping the admiral informed. Any questions?"

Her three team members shook their heads, and Lisa nodded and said, "Great, let's enjoy the flight."

They all leaned back and reclined their seats. Kurt and Robin put on their headsets and listened to music, while Lisa and Sanjay read. None of them noticed the man in seat 11C who, after Lisa finished talking, had pulled a three-by-five card out of his shirt and jotted down some notes. They were not trained to realize that airplanes could also have ears.

* * * * * * *

The cut was a small one, but when dealing with such a potent substance, there is no margin for error. At first, Jim Thunderhill didn't realize he had been cut at all, but when he did, the full impact of the accident hit him hard.

An hour before, he had turned on the DVR and settled into the unpleasant task of watching thirty-two of his lab specimens meet their demise. He had observed, with both curiosity and revulsion, as the toxin poisoning was manifested as a multitude of debilitating symptoms. The symptoms observed the day before had intensified in less than three hours after his afternoon brief to the analysis team. All of the specimens suffered frenzied motor activity, coupled with uncontrollable convulsions. The activity grew panicky as other advanced symptoms were exhibited: breathing difficulty, loss of continence, and uncontrollable vomiting. Near the end, which occurred for all of the animals within an hour of 9:00 p.m., the activity became even more frantic, as little legs and feet swiftly and erratically carried spasmodic bodies between the corners of the cages, apparently without the aid of any of the senses. After all of the motion on the TV screen had ceased, Jim stopped the playback and reset the video to its start.

Prior to the last few moments of the video, Cheryl Forrester and Paula Uhrig had arrived at the lab. When they started to walk toward Jim with the video in progress, he had suggested that they protect their half-digested breakfasts and head to the cafeteria for an extra cup of coffee, a request with which they gladly complied.

Alone for another half hour, Jim had then returned to the cages and selected a specimen for a necropsy, the pathobiologist's term for animal autopsy. It really didn't matter which one; they had all suffered a similar misery. After taking all of the appropriate precautions for protecting his skin from contamination, Jim had performed the gross necropsy, inspecting the various body cavities and organs for abnormal conditions. He had then proceeded with the microscopic necropsy, which required carving very thin layers of various organs and inspecting the slices under the electron microscope. He had just finished dissecting the liver when he made his only procedural mistake. Instead of returning the scalpel to its proper holder, he had set it down horizontally on the worktable. He had then taken the microthin slice of liver, placed it on a glass slide, and slipped it under the microscope lens. His observations had indicated an unusually high concentration of the toxin-producing organism in the liver, still replicating and still very active.

It was during this period of intense concentration on the image under the microscope that one of the University of Richmond interns had silently moved up next to Jim. The louder than necessary "whatcha looking at" comment had so utterly startled Jim that he jerked his head up from the scope and backed up two steps before regaining his senses. It was the second step that had proved disastrous. If alone on the worktable, the scalpel would have been pushed out of the way by Jim's hip. Unfortunately, the handle was positioned against a dissection tray, which leaned against a book, which in turn was flush against the wall of the room.

Annoyed as much as startled by the interruption, Jim's first reaction had been to have a few harsh words with the intern. At some point during the admonishment, however, he had started to feel something warm and sticky on his hip. By the time he had looked around to inspect the area, the red stain was already starting to blossom on his white lab coat. This was when Jim Thunderhill's legs had gone weak and nearly buckled under him.

Cheryl and Paula arrived back from the cafeteria in time to see Jim nearly collapse on the floor. They immediately came to his aid, while the intern claimed ignorance of what had happened during the last thirty seconds. As the women helped Jim to the nearest chair and the intern continued to make excuses, Jim kept repeating the words "I'm infected" and "I'm contaminated" over and over again. He had every right to be terrified. If all of the reactions to the toxin he'd observed in the specimens translated directly to humans, his future hours would be both painfully unpleasant and numbered.

It took Cheryl a few minutes to calm Jim down so he could tell her what had happened. When it finally became obvious to her that a scalpel just used to dissect a toxin-rich liver had penetrated his skin, she also became distraught and started to bark orders. She threw her keys at Paula and told her to bring her car to the front of the building. Then she told the intern to call the Walter Reed National Military Medical Center emergency room and have them prepare for an acute case of intravenous poisoning. When she was certain Jim could be left on his own for thirty seconds, she bolted to the sink and returned with some cold compresses.

Cheryl sat in the chair next to Jim, who was now shivering with fear, and pulled his head and upper body toward her. With his head cradled in one arm, she applied a compress to his forehead and rocked him gently, as a mother comforts a crying baby. But as their eyes met, they both knew that, unlike the problems of a whimpering infant, Jim's problem would not go away with a simple feeding or a little affection.

* * * * * * *

"Commander Hargrove, it's a pleasure to meet you. May I call you Glen?" Jackson Tyler asked, always the gracious, as well as predictable, host.

"Certainly, Mr. President. An honor to meet you, sir," Glen replied, doing his best to appear relaxed.

After the brief introduction, Tyler quickly got down to business. "I'd like you to start this morning, Bud. How are things progressing from your perspective?"

"As good as can be expected this early in the crisis, Mr. President. The DSS agents are already in Seattle. They caught a late flight yesterday and will start their search for the terrorists as soon as they wake up out there, which should be soon. I have a lot of confidence in these guys, but I have to admit they have a monumental task and not much time to complete it."

"We all understand that, Admiral," Lou Bernstein threw in. "All we can ask is that they do their best."

"Well, thanks, Lou; how insightful," Tyler said sarcastically, throwing his first jab of the day at his NSA.

After clearing his throat to disperse the tension in the air, Kershaw continued. "I've talked with the PI that I mentioned yesterday. He has Glen's list of possible nemeses and will get back to me with his broad brush analysis by early afternoon."

"Glen, any more names come to mind over the past twenty-four hours?" the president asked.

Glen thought briefly, then replied, "Not a one, sir. But I've been preoccupied and haven't devoted any real time to thinking of more people who might have it out for me."

"That's understandable," Tyler said, "with your wife and her family being in Seattle and all."

The eyes of Glen Hargrove and Bud Kershaw met briefly. In that instant, they both realized that it would have been better to not have disclosed Jennifer's whereabouts to this group. Kershaw grimaced in self-reproach as he remembered his comment of yesterday revealing her location. If there truly was a White House leak, the source could very well be part of the present company, and the plans to extract Jennifer could be in jeopardy.

Rather than dwelling on the mistake, Kershaw picked up where he left off. "Moving on, gentlemen, Dr. Lisa Kennelly, head of the biotoxin sensor research project at NRL, is flying to Seattle as we speak to set up toxin monitoring stations at a dozen sites where source water enters the water distribution system. A Seattle area point of contact has been arranged to assist her in selecting appropriate locations. Her knowledge concerning details of the situation is limited, so I can't imagine any breach of information security through her."

"What if the local authorities get suspicious and start asking questions she can't answer?" Clive Donner asked.

"I never send anybody on a mission like this without a cover story. Her story revolves around some routine water analyses and the field testing of her sensors. Also, the point of contact is a former white hat . . ."

"White hat?" Tyler displayed his ignorance of Navy jargon.

"Sorry, sir. A sailor . . . a Navy enlisted man," Kershaw explained.

"White hat. Got it," Tyler repeated, as he added the expression to his mental dictionary.

"Anyway," Kershaw continued, "because he and I were once part of the same organization, I could communicate with this former enlisted man using terminology he could comprehend. I explained the importance of Dr. Kennelly's mission and the critical contribution he would make by cooperating fully with her requests."

George Wilkes, the EPA chief and a former officer in the Naval Oceanography Corps, instantly picked up on the doublespeak. "So you gave him a few orders, and he said, 'Aye aye, sir.'"

"Exactly," Kershaw said, giving the group their first opportunity to chuckle during the meeting.

After the laughter subsided, Tyler asked, "Did the terrorists call last evening as promised?"

"Right on time," Kershaw replied, "and perhaps now is an appropriate time to play the recording."

When no one objected, Kershaw started the playback.

The response from those listening was as expected—a collection of shaking heads, a few clenched fists, and several expletives spoken under the breath.

Clive Donner was the first to break the silence after the recording was turned off. "Animals," he said. "Only animals kill without conscience."

"I think we've just seen that some humans have not risen very high above their animal instincts," Bernstein added.

"Very few animals kill for pleasure, Lou," Tyler retorted. "Most kill for food or survival. What we're really seeing here is a form of humanity that has not risen *up* to the level of the animals."

From anyone else, the comment would have seemed a logical rebuttal to the comments of both staff members, but from Bernstein's perspective, it was just another personal putdown from Jack Tyler. "Of course, you're correct," he added, both quietly and cynically.

"Okay, let's talk specifics here," Tyler said, moving on quickly to avoid further discussion on the idiosyncrasies of the animal kingdom. "First, the money. How's it going, Clive?"

"I talked with Treasury after our meeting yesterday. Ten million is a piece of cake. Less than a couple pennies per taxpayer."

"Somehow I don't think the American public would see it that way," Tyler commented.

"Nevertheless," Donner continued, "I think everyone here knows that the money is not the demand that should be concerning us."

"Which brings us to the prisoners," Tyler said. "Glen, you told the terrorists that preparations were being made for their friends' release."

"That was my doing, sir," Kershaw interjected before Glen could respond. "I think we all agree that no matter what our true intentions are, we have to convince these people that we plan on meeting all of their demands."

"Fine," Tyler said, "as long as we all understand that I do not intend to put convicted prisoners back on the streets so they can wreak more havoc."

"But, sir," Bernstein protested, knowing in advance that no matter how valid his point, it would be readily dismissed by Tyler, "if releasing a few dangerous men saves half a million lives in the short term, isn't it worth the risk?"

"Your assumptions are flawed, Lou," Tyler answered. "First, there are no guarantees that these guys aren't going to release the toxin even if we do let their buddies out of prison. Second, if we let these guys go free, we set an extremely dangerous precedent. Terrorists are going to think they can pull any stunt they want to in this country. And you know what, they're going to be right, because if they go to jail, it's no big deal. The next group of terrorists just makes the previous ones' release a condition for not blowing up some railroad or something, and so on and so forth. Anytime terrorists are in prison, there's going to be a strong incentive for getting the next job on track so the prisoners get out sooner. Terrorist activities against the United States will become more frequent and more grandiose. If we give in now, the world is going to know that common criminals can hold up the most powerful nation in the world and get away with it. I don't plan on letting that happen."

Tyler paused a moment before making his third point. "Finally, we haven't yet heard from Mr. Wilkes or Commander Hargrove. I'm not at all convinced we have an insurmountable problem if the toxin does get into the reservoirs. All right," the president concluded, "is there anyone here who doesn't understand my position on this matter?"

No one said a word.

Kershaw was somewhat impressed with Tyler's comments on the impact of releasing convicted terrorists, although he didn't quite buy the concept of a perpetual string of terrorist acts, each in part designed to liberate the perpetrators of the preceding act. As to the president's doubts concerning the hazards of releasing the toxin, Kershaw believed a lesson in biological warfare agents was about to be presented and learned.

"I'd like to hear what you have to say first, George," Tyler said, swiveling his chair to face the EPA chief.

"Well, Mr. President," Wilkes began, "we had to make some basic assumptions about the variables, such as the toxicity of the poison, the number of reservoirs in which it would be introduced, and the volumetric flow rates of the rivers that are the sources of city water. Not knowing much about the specific toxin posing the threat, we assumed a toxicity equivalent to strychnine, which is a fairly potent poison."

As Wilkes stated his first assumption, Hargrove and Kershaw glanced at each other. They both rolled their eyes at the absurdity of equating the potency of the biotoxin with which they were dealing to strychnine. However, they withheld comment for the time being.

"There are roughly half a dozen rivers that are fed by Seattle area reservoirs," Wilkes continued. "We assumed that three reservoirs would each be polluted with ten kilograms of the toxin, and that all of the toxin would be transferred to the rivers. This was a conservative estimate, as we believe much of the toxin would likely be deposited at the bottom and banks of the reservoir. Finally, we assumed a combined mean discharge rate of .0005 cubic meters per second per square kilometer. The Mississippi River has a rate of about .005, so we believe that crediting these small rivers with one-tenth the discharge rate of the largest river in the country was again conservative. After entering these figures into our model for determining waterborne contaminant concentrations and running the model, we arrived at a final concentration at the river effluent of less than .05 parts per million. Quite honestly, Mr. President, there is a higher concentration of naturally occurring strychnine in most sources of drinking water than would result from this incident."

Tyler seemed to be quite pleased with the EPA chief's report, primarily because it was exactly what he wanted to hear. "Thank you, George. Good report. Anyone care to comment?"

Kershaw was compelled to speak frankly. "My only comment is that Mr. Wilkes's forecasts are grossly inaccurate. Even the best models give poor results when the assumptions are flawed or the input data are in error. In this case, both are true."

"Would you care to explain your reasoning, Admiral?" Tyler asked, suddenly getting very formal.

"I'm sure Commander Hargrove can do a much better job than me, Mr. President," Kershaw replied, maintaining the air of formality.

"Very well," Tyler said. "Glen, you have the floor."

Glen cleared his throat and launched into the response he'd been preparing in his mind ever since Wilkes first mentioned strychnine. "I find no argument with Mr. Wilkes's assumptions about the number of polluted reservoirs or the volumetric flow rates of the rivers. And I don't doubt the validity of his model, given appropriate input parameters. I'm sure that for a poison like strychnine, you could dump a thousand kilograms into the reservoirs and still have an insignificant concentration at the spigot. The problem is that we're not dealing with strychnine. Strychnine is an alkaloid, an organic compound that comes from a plant, similar to morphine or nicotine. The only thing it has in common with a biotoxic organism is a few of the same elements. Strychnine doesn't eat, grow, or reproduce. The concentration in water is always going to be the amount you start with divided by the amount of water; the more water, the lower the concentration.

"On the other hand, biotoxins are produced by living microorganisms, usually bacterial in nature. My guess is that the terrorists have in their possession billions of spores, which are probably dormant and stored in containers under pressure. If the contents are discharged into the reservoirs, the spores will release the bacteria, which will in turn secrete the toxin as they multiply. Our initial tests show that these multiplication rates are phenomenally large and directly proportional to the volume of water given to replicate. So unlike strychnine, with a biotoxin, there is no relationship between the amount you start with and the final concentration."

Glen paused for a brief moment to let everyone's brains catch up with their ears. "Now, if we can move over to the subject of toxicity, it's time for a dose of reality. There's no doubt that strychnine can be lethal. I wouldn't want to drink a soda pop laced with the stuff. But compared to most biotoxins, strychnine is practically innocuous. You might have heard of ricin, which comes from castor beans. Ricin is one of the least potent of the common biotoxins, yet it is twenty-five-thousand times as lethal as strychnine.

"If you came prepared for the worst, you're about to hear it. Botulinum toxin type H, which to date is the most lethal of the biotoxins, is two hundred and fifty times as lethal as ricin, and the toxin being used to hold Seattle hostage is very similar to botulinum H, only deadlier. So you see, gentlemen, we're dealing with a poison that's about ten million times more potent than strychnine. I just don't believe it's realistic to compare the two. It's sort of like comparing the damage from a .22 caliber bullet to that of a nuclear detonation."

Clive Donner, who had a course or two in biology, tried to dispute some of Glen's conclusions. "Now wait just a minute.

Botulin—that's the stuff you find in canned food that hasn't been sterilized properly and in Botox injections. I know for a fact that those bacteria can't survive in oxygen. So how is your toxin going to live and reproduce in the reservoirs and rivers?"

"You're right about botulin, Mr. Donner. Alone it is anaerobic, and with regard to Botox, those injections use only a very small amount of a purified form of the toxin. However, the toxin we're dealing with has been genetically altered. I'm sure one of the intended byproducts of the DNA engineering was the capability for the organism to survive in a number of oxygen-rich environments. In fact, my technicians haven't confirmed it yet, but we speculate that even after its introduction into the human body, the bacterium continues to thrive and reproduce. Theoretically, a single microbe could enter the body via something as routine as brushing your teeth or washing off a cut. Once inside, the bacteria would multiply and continue to secrete toxin until the host's death occurred. Even then, it would continue to prosper until the oxygen was gone."

Everyone in the room was numbed by Glen's discussion. The full significance of the threat to the Seattle area environment and population was beginning to sink in.

George Wilkes was the first to speak following the prolonged silence. "If Commander Hargrove is correct, and I have no reason to doubt that he is, my projections are in fact erroneous. At this point, I don't see the need to revise my numbers. It appears as though the release of any quantity of this toxin into the environment would result in an environmental disaster of immeasurable consequence. Not only for Washington State, I might add, but for California, which buys some of its water from Washington. It must be concluded that release of this toxin into a single reservoir is an unacceptable alternative."

Throughout the Oval Office, heads nodded in agreement.

"Does that bring us back to the subject of possibly releasing convicted terrorists from prison?" Lou Bernstein asked, this time with the support of most present in the room.

"I think we have to readdress the issue, sir." Donner directed his response to Bernstein's question at Jack Tyler.

"At this point," Tyler said, "I will only state that I will give the matter further consideration. I still feel very strongly about the negative effect of acquiescing to this demand, and I want to exhaust all other alternatives prior to releasing these prisoners."

The assembly was relieved that the president at least agreed to give the matter some more thought.

"I believe it's time for action items," Tyler said, looking at his watch and realizing that the meeting, originally scheduled for twenty minutes, was now pushing an hour.

Donner grabbed a pad off a nearby table and a pen from his pocket to take notes.

"First, the money," Tyler began. "It sounds like putting a package of bills together on time is no problem. Now we need to find a courier. Does anyone know a woman who might want to volunteer for a job like this?"

"How about Birnbauer over at the Justice Department?" Donner suggested. "She has experience in these matters."

"Good suggestion," Tyler said. "She was the one involved in that touchy hostage exchange at the Chase Manhattan Bank, wasn't she?"

"Right," Donner continued. "Plus, if the terrorists are requesting a woman courier in order to deal with someone they can intimidate, they'll be in for a rude awakening when they meet Birnbauer. She could have been a linebacker for the Ravens."

With a nod, Tyler approved the selection. "Clive, talk to the Attorney General and see if Birnbauer can take the job. Also, insist that she wears a dress when the transfer is made so they don't have to look twice to confirm that . . ." Tyler cut himself off. "Never mind, that was uncalled for."

Despite the retraction, everyone in the room got the point. Suggesting that Birnbauer was femininity-challenged would have been political suicide if said in public, but in this company, the statement merely turned down the tension a notch.

"It's a good thing the cameras aren't rolling, Jack, or tomorrow, you'd be history," Donner said, half-jokingly. He periodically had to keep his boss from making politically incorrect statements.

Bernstein briefly flirted with the notion of making a phone call to Crowe about an insensitive sexist comment made by the nation's leader, but decided that it was both too trivial and too risky.

Tyler continued with the action items. "Bud, yours is the longest list, I guess. I take it you'll be getting periodic updates from your people on the West Coast and your PI friend."

"They'll be calling a couple of times a day with routine reports and whenever anything noteworthy occurs," Kershaw said. "I'll keep your Chief of Staff informed when I have anything to report."

"That's fine for the routine stuff, but call me directly with any major twists." Tyler turned to Donner and said, "Clive, make sure the White House operator knows the admiral's name and patches him through directly upon his request."

"Yes, sir."

Tyler turned back to the two naval officers, who were seated in adjacent seats. "Glen, keep working on your analysis of the toxin and report through Admiral Kershaw. Do you think there's any possibility you'll be able to come up with a vaccine or an antidote within a couple of days?"

"It's possible, but unlikely," Glen replied. "There's still so much to learn about the toxin, and its creator went to great lengths to hone the bacterium's survival instincts. We'll work hard at it, sir, but I don't think you can count on neutralizing the threat with some miracle drug. It's an impractical solution to our problem."

The president was not thrilled with Glen's response but accepted it without further question. "By the way, Glen, excellent job so far. I appreciate the effort you're putting into this. Keep up the good work; I know you'll do your best." Tyler could see that Glen needed some encouragement with all he'd been going through.

"Thank you, sir. I appreciate your confidence."

"All right, any further items?" Tyler's question was directed at the entire group, which responded in the negative.

With the primary business of the meeting concluded, Tyler brought up the subject he'd been saving for last. "Finally, gentlemen, I would like to briefly address a small article in today's *Washington Post*." He snatched the paper from his desk and read the short Associated Press article about his canceled trip to Savannah. "Now, many people could have access to the knowledge that I postponed this trip. However, no one outside this room knew why the trip was canceled. That reason is spelled out right here on page 1. Our friends at the wire service have either been working overtime on their clairvoyance skills, or there's a little bird who's been talking. I don't know if the chatter is intentional or just plain carelessness. I certainly hope it's the latter, but for the moment, I don't care. My only request—not a request, insistence—is that it stops. There are a million or more lives at risk here, and I will not allow these lives to be jeopardized by idle conversation outside of this office. I should not have to remind those present that the media in this city is not our ally. If any of you has any insight into where or how this information leak occurred, please remain after the meeting. I'd be very interested in hearing what you have to say. For now, I trust nothing we've discussed today goes past that door. Unless there are any further questions, that's all I have. There's a lot to do, gentlemen. Let's get on it. Thank you for your time."

One by one, all of the meeting participants filed out of the Oval Office. As Lou Bernstein left, he was thanking God he'd hung up with Nathan Crowe when he did. As Bud Kershaw left, he was reflecting on how calmly and skillfully Jackson Tyler had just handled the loose lips situation. The man was starting to grow on him.

* * * * * * *

As the meeting in the Oval Office concluded, Harry Boland and Darrell Wolczyk were finishing their breakfasts at the hotel. They had compared notes on the negative effects of flying three time zones to the west and going to bed early, then solidified their agenda for the morning.

The dreary and drizzly overcast skies that typify half of the September days in Seattle greeted them as they emerged from the

Red Lion and walked to their car. Boland drove while Wolczyk handled the navigation chores and gave directions. They headed northeast on Interstate 405 out of Sea-Tac to Renton, then southeast on the Renton-Maple Valley Road. Boland and Wolczyk would discover, as most King County visitors do, that navigating in a car around the region is as simple as knowing where you are and where you're headed, as most of the roads are named after those two places. They found the headquarters of the third precinct of the King County Police Department, parked, and went into the building.

After showing their credentials to the receptionist at the front desk, they were escorted to the office of the precinct chief. Boland explained to the attentive but wary lieutenant that their office in D.C. had received information citing potential security violations at Boeing aircraft and that they would be conducting an investigation within his jurisdiction as well as several others in the metropolitan area. When pressed for details, Boland referred to the potential illegal sale of military aircraft components to an unnamed Middle Eastern nation and told the lieutenant that any further amplification would be impossible due to the classified nature of the investigation. He then requested the opportunity to question the precinct's officers about any suspicious activities of which they might be aware.

Though somewhat skeptical of their story's accuracy, the precinct chief gave Boland and Wolczyk five minutes in conference with all of the on-duty officers at the same time. During the meeting, Boland presented the same briefing he had given the chief and then asked about questionable activities in the area by people who could be of Middle Eastern descent. The response from the group was negative, so Boland wrote the Red Lion phone number and both his and Wolczyk's cell numbers on the white board in the briefing room and suggested that a phone call be placed if anything came up. With their five minutes up, the DSS agents excused themselves, thanked the chief, and left the third precinct headquarters.

* * * * * * *

After the Oval Office meeting, Bud Kershaw and Glen Hargrove made their way back to Ballston on the Metro, the differences from the earlier trip being the direction, the cheaper non-rush-hour fare, and the near-empty subway car. During the trip, Kershaw had provided his insights on the meeting and assured Glen that he had done a superb job. They parted company at Glen's car in the garage, and then Kershaw headed for the elevator.

Not knowing how many times the phone had already rung, Kershaw bolted for his office and lifted the receiver just in time to beat the voicemail message. This was fortunate for Lisa Kennelly, who was growing tired of listening to the recording.

"Yes," Kershaw said, needing to catch his breath before attempting a second syllable.

"Admiral, it's Lisa. I've been trying to reach you."

"I've been meeting with the president, Lisa."

"Of course," she said, "I should have guessed. I wanted to let you know that our plane took off on time, and we're about halfway to the West Coast."

"Good. Do you have a pen and paper handy? I have your point of contact out in Seattle."

"Yes, I'm ready to write," she said, lowering her tray table to provide a writing surface.

Kershaw looked at the note from the day before on his desk blotter and started reading slowly to allow the information to be written down at the other end. "His name is Craig Evans, and he works for the Water Management Branch of Seattle Public Utilities. You can meet him at his office, which is on the 49th floor of the Seattle Municipal Tower, located at 700 5th Avenue in downtown Seattle."

Lisa scrawled the data on the back of one of her business cards, repeating back the name, department, and address as they were read to her. "Got it," she said as she finished writing. Not being fond of cold introductions, she then asked, "He's expecting me, right?"

"He knows you, he's expecting you, and he's promised to help you in any way he can," Kershaw explained.

"Great. Thank you for making the arrangements, Admiral."

"No problem, Lisa. Call me again when you're all set up, okay?"

"Will do. Talk to you later."

"Good luck."

"Thanks." Lisa put away her phone and returned the pen to her purse. As she reclined to relax for the rest of the flight, the passenger in seat 11C returned his pen and three-by-five card to his shirt pocket.

* * * * * * *

When Glen walked through the door of the NMRC lab, the scene was not what he expected. No one seemed to be working on the toxin analyses, and Cheryl Forrester and Jim Thunderhill were nowhere in sight. Paula Uhrig seemed to be comforting a distraught intern, while the rest of the team stood around in a stupor. At the sound of the door closing, Paula turned and walked toward Glen, intercepting him and pulling him aside before he was three steps into the lab.

"There's been an accident, Commander," she said soberly. "Lieutenant Thunderhill has been contaminated with the toxin. Apparently, he was startled by Roger over there while he was looking at something in the microscope, and he backed up into a dissection scalpel."

The Navy had trained Glen to handle bad news without showing emotion. His response was calm and detached. "All right, Paula, where is the lieutenant now?"

"Lieutenant Commander Forrester drove him to Walter Reed Hospital, sir. It's been a couple of hours since they left."

"And our young intern, how is he doing?" Glen asked.

"At first, he was walking around denying any responsibility for what happened, but then he calmed down and realized that he probably did startle Jim badly. For the past half hour, he's been full of self-blame. He was nearly in tears a few minutes before you got here."

"Keep reassuring him that it was an accident, will you, Paula?"

"Sure thing, Commander."

"Meanwhile, I think it's best for everyone to get back to their work. This accident hasn't reduced the importance of the analysis we're doing. In fact, it's all the more important that we continue with the effort. I'm going to head over to the hospital. You're in charge, Paula."

"Yes, sir."

The telephone in the lab rang while Glen was finishing his discussion with Paula, and the other Richmond intern answered it. "Commander Hargrove, it's for you," he said.

"If it's not the hospital, please take a message and I'll call the person back," Glen said.

After a moment on the phone, the intern said, "Sir, he says it will only take a minute."

"Who is it?" Glen asked.

Another moment on the phone. "He says he's your Naval Academy roommate, sir."

Glen stood for a moment in shocked disbelief. "You've got to be kidding me. Okay, I'll take it," he said, as he walked over and took the receiver from the intern's hand. "Chuck, is that you?"

"You bet, roomie. Long time, no see . . . or hear from . . . or anything else for that matter."

"Look, Chuck, I'd like to talk, but you're catching me at a very bad time."

"I understand. We're all busy. I just decided it was time to renew old acquaintances, so I'm having several of our company mates in the D.C. area over for dinner Thursday night at my place. So far, I've gotten Larson, Hopkins, Furneaux, and Zeller to say yes. How about it? We'll have a blast."

Glen was ready to decline, and then remembered what Kershaw had said about staying occupied in the off hours. "Okay, I'll say yes for now, but things may change before then. I'm up to my ears in work, Chuck."

"We all need a break, Glen. Oh, and bring your wife too."

"Wish I could. She's out of town visiting her parents."

"Next time. You know, we all need to do this more often. It's been too long."

"I agree. Gotta run now, Chuck. See you Thursday unless you hear different from me."

"See you then."

As he hung up the phone and headed out of the lab on his way to the hospital, Glen reflected on the lifelong friendships that were the legacy of his Naval Academy years. He and the others in his company had gone through a lot together, both good times and bad, but the comradery had survived it all. He figured the chances of making his roommate's party were about one in ten, but he placed it on his mental agenda just in case. As he got into his car for the short drive across the complex to the hospital, the awesome thought struck him that by Thursday night, according to the ultimatum, the crisis would be over, one way or another.

* * * * * * *

Within fifty minutes of leaving the third precinct of the King County Police Department in Maple Valley, Harry Boland and Darrell Wolczyk were presenting a similar briefing to the captain in charge of the Bothell Police Department, which was a somewhat larger and busier organization than the third precinct. A bit less formal in his management style, the captain gave Boland and Wolczyk the green light to roam the building and talk to the police officers at their discretion.

The first officer they approached knew of no suspicious happenings in the area. The second officer discussed the most exciting event in Bothell in the past week, which was an incident over at the Inglewood Country Club. Apparently, a guy who had a lousy round of golf came back half an hour later and took a rototiller to the practice putting green; it wasn't a pretty sight.

The third officer, a petite and attractive blond who looked like she could have been a ballet dancer as an alternative to being a police sergeant, knew of no suspicious goings-on herself. However, she had noticed that one officer on the force had been rather preoccupied and unapproachable over the past day or so. She also mentioned a teenage boy hanging out with him, which was rather unusual. When Boland asked where they might find him, she pointed to Officer Bernie Cushman's cubicle.

* * * * * * *

Across the metropolitan Seattle area, many were still enjoying their morning coffee and newspaper. Those who limited their reading to the headlines, front page, and sports page would miss the article completely. Others who had time to read more of the *Times* would catch the small story on page two about a canceled presidential trip and a domestic crisis more urgent than the hurricane that hit the East Coast last week. One person in particular who read the article would take its content very seriously. In fact, within one minute of reading the last sentence, Ahmad Ad-Faddil was on the phone with his contact.

"Are you positive it is not related?" Ad-Faddil asked, after Fox assured him that the crisis referenced in the newspaper had nothing to do with their mission in Seattle.

"Absolutely," Fox answered, trying to sound more confident than he was. "Tyler is always canceling trips. He has to keep his schedule flexible. It's the nature of the job."

"Very well, Fox. It is not that I care whether we release the toxin or not. I am merely determining where we stand at this point in time."

"There's no need to get trigger happy, Brown. I'm telling you the media's still in the dark, so for the moment, be cool."

Ad-Faddil detested American idioms, and Fox had just used three within two sentences. "We will retain our self-control for now, Fox. Remember, these are your rules we are following. As long as payment is guaranteed whatever the outcome, we will continue to abide by those rules."

"Don't worry, you'll get your money," Fox said. "By the way, I have one more piece of information you might find useful."

"And that is?"

Fox provided his information, and Ad-Faddil acknowledged.

They both hung up without sharing the courtesy of a goodbye.

* * * * * * *

As he lifted the phone from its cradle and started to dial, Bernie Cushman silently cursed the bureaucratic requirements that represented ninety percent of his job. Since arriving at 7:00 a.m., he had been loaded down with the paperwork and meetings that often prompted him to turn in his resignation letter. Only his love of the remaining ten percent of the job caused him to reconsider whenever the urge hit.

First, he had to complete the vehicle usage report for the day before, which had to be on the chief's desk by 8:30. Then came the daily event synopsis, which had to be carefully worded in light of his decision to turn the Tolt Reservoir matter over to the Feds. Finally, the daily briefing, which usually took ten minutes, lasted well over half an hour, with explicit instructions on maintaining golf course security being provided. On two occasions, Cushman had sent Joey Caviletti to the library next door, once at 7:45 a.m., when he first arrived, and again at 8:15. Five minutes ago at 8:30, when Joey came in for the third time, he had him take a seat.

With the number of the local FBI office half-dialed, Cushman's agenda was again disrupted when two official-looking men in sport coats came around the wall of his partitioned office space. At first, he gave an exasperated sigh at the interruption, then as the US Government IDs were produced, he slowly replaced the handset in its cradle and pointed to the two remaining seats in the cubicle.

"Harry Boland and Darrell Wolczyk, Defense Security Service," Boland said, both agents still standing.

"Bernie Cushman, and this is Joey Caviletti." After a round of hand shaking, Boland and Wolczyk took the offered seats, and Boland continued in his role as spokesman. "I wonder if we might ask a couple of questions."

Cushman nodded and Boland continued. "We're in the area investigating the possible illegal sale of military airplane components to a Middle Eastern nation, and we were wondering if, in the course of your daily routine, you've noticed anyone of Middle Eastern lineage hanging around your area or . . ."

"Middle Eastern, like Omar Sharif," Joey interrupted, demonstrating an uncommon familiarity with classic films. "Yeah, that's who they looked like," he said excitedly.

"Who looked like that?" Wolczyk asked, after exchanging wide-eyed glances with Boland.

Cushman held up a hand to silence Joey, then answered on his behalf. "Look, guys, I don't know a thing about selling airplane parts to foreign countries, but there have been some curious goings-on around here. In fact, as you were walking around the corner, I was in the middle of dialing the local FBI office, because neither I nor anyone else in this department is qualified to handle this type of situation."

"What exactly is this situation?" Boland asked.

"Well, the other day, Joey was out fishing at the South Fork Tolt Reservoir about twenty-five miles east of here. He saw two guys coming through the woods in street clothes with some sort of bottle. They huddled around the edge of the water for a few minutes, then headed back out through the woods without the bottle."

Boland and Wolczyk sat spellbound as Cushman continued. "Joey followed the men out to their car, then went back to the reservoir to get a close look at the bottle. It appeared to be some sort of bomb several inches deep in the water with a timer attached to the neck. He left it alone, then came to see me yesterday. We both took a drive out to the Tolt yesterday afternoon. Everything he told me was true. I saw the bottle myself, red numbers counting down and all. I left it alone too, figuring it was outside my area of expertise. We came back here to the station, and I tried to call the FBI yesterday, but I got interrupted in the process. I was tied up with paperwork today until a few minutes ago, when I was trying to call again. That's when you guys showed up."

"All right," Boland said, not believing his good fortune at stumbling upon Cushman and the boy when he did. "This is definitely related to the reason we're here. First, I need to ask you for your complete silence concerning this bottle you saw. I can't tell you why this is critical, but believe me, it is. Have you talked with anyone else about this? Your superiors in the department, wives, mothers, friends?"

Joey shook his head. Cushman said, "No, but I did ask for a trace on the license plate number of their car."

"You saw the car and got the license plate number?" Wolczyk asked Joey, elated at this additional bit of good news.

"Yep," Joey said with a wide grin, "and I got a real good look at their faces."

"Good, Joey, we'll talk about what they looked like in a minute," Boland said, turning back to Cushman. "Did the trace come up with anything, Officer Cushman?"

"Please call me Bernie. Hold on one minute," Cushman said, as he fished around the papers on his desk, trying to locate the trace results that his boss finally gave him fifteen minutes ago. He found the slip of paper and read it for the first time. "Not much more than Joey has already told me," he said. "It's an Avis car rented somewhere locally. That's too bad. If the car belonged to a resident, we'd already have the person's name and address. I know that doesn't help much, but it's all I've got."

"Don't worry about it," Boland said, amazed that things were falling into place as nicely as they were. "It's a start, and we'll take it from here. By the way, did you tell your boss any of the circumstances surrounding the trace request?"

"Absolutely not, he'd just get in the way," Cushman replied, looking across the room to his superior's glassed-in office to make sure he was in fact not around.

"Good," Boland said. "Now, this timer on the bottle, what did it look like and what was it doing?"

Cushman answered. "It was a typical timing device. It had an LED window with red numbers, two digits each for hours, minutes, and seconds. The time was counting down at the rate of a regular clock. When we saw it yesterday afternoon, the timer read about seventy-six hours."

Boland did a quick calculation in his head, correcting for the time difference between the coasts. He looked at Wolczyk, nodded, and said, "It fits." Then turning to Joey, he said, "Okay Joey, it's your turn. Tell me what they looked like."

Joey spent a couple of minutes describing the appearance of the two men, while both agents took notes.

Then Wolczyk flashed on an idea. "Say, Bernie, do you have one of those computer programs that does facial composites?"

"Not here, but they do downtown at the King County Courthouse."

Wolczyk looked at Boland and commented, "We may want to make use of that program."

"I agree, but later in the day," Boland said. "Right now, I think it's time for a visit to the Tolt Reservoir."

As the foursome rose together, Wolczyk asked for the location of the men's room. When shown, he and Joey headed in together, while Boland and Cushman remained behind in the cubicle.

As Boland tucked his notes into his jacket pocket, Cushman said, "Harry, let me tell you one more thing about this bottle Joey and I saw. It was no ordinary little bottle. It was a large rugged metal canister with a long thin neck. I believe the timer, if it ever ran to zero, would initiate a small detonation that would blow a plug in the neck. And when that plug was gone, whatever was in that canister would be released into the reservoir. Now, you and I both know this has nothing to do with selling airplane technology to enemies. Are you going to be honest and tell me what's really going on?"

Boland shrugged and said, "I can't, Bernie. The order for secrecy comes from the highest level. Maybe later if it's necessary, but for now, you're just going to have to trust me."

Cushman nodded, disappointed but without recourse.

"By the way, do you have a drinking glass I can borrow?" Boland asked, changing the subject before any more probing questions were presented.

"Yeah, I think so," Cushman answered, as he opened one of his desk drawers and looked. "Here," he said, blowing the dust off a glass found in the bottom of the drawer, "but why . . .?"

"Might come in handy," Boland interrupted, taking the glass and putting it in his jacket pocket.

As Wolczyk and Caviletti emerged from the restroom, they were joined by Boland and Cushman. The four of them exited the police headquarters and headed for one of the green and gold striped Ford Crown Victorias that comprised the fleet of police cruisers.

The cruiser exited the parking lot, got onto 101st Avenue NE, then turned onto Route 522, paralleling the Sammamish River. As Cushman glanced in his rearview mirror, he noticed a white Ford Focus turning off 101st behind them and said, "I think we've got trouble."

"What is it?" Boland asked from the passenger-side front seat.

"Scanlon. I recognize his car."

"Who's Scanlon?"

"A pain-in-the-butt reporter from the *Times*," Cushman replied.

"*Seattle Times*?"

"Yeah. Scanlon's always hanging around the office, trying to dig up dirt for his column. He's supposed to report the news, but he peppers his stories with as much sleaze as he can find. He was hanging around the office yesterday trying to figure out what Joey and I were up to. We kept him in the dark, though, didn't we, Joey?"

"That's a fact," Joey replied, proud of his rebuff of Scanlon at the front door of the station the day before.

"In retrospect," Cushman added, "I suppose we should be grateful to the guy. If it weren't for his interruption yesterday, I'd be driving the local FBI agents out to the Tolt instead of you guys."

"Thank God for small favors," Boland said. "He's obviously up to no good now, though. Any plans for losing him?"

"Well, first I'll try to ditch him in town, but that may be tough; this cruiser isn't exactly what you'd call a low-profile vehicle. If that doesn't work, we'll try to outrun him. That's the advantage of being in the cruiser."

Cushman drove the two miles to downtown Bothell, then turned off 522 at the west end of town. For the next five minutes, he deftly maneuvered the cruiser through the streets of the downtown area, finally emerging on the east side. He crossed the Sammamish and jumped on Riverside Drive toward Woodinville, satisfied that the Focus and its persistent driver were at least half a dozen turns behind. Convinced that they had successfully evaded Scanlon, the three passengers congratulated Cushman. The celebration ended suddenly, however, when Scanlon's white car again pulled in behind the cruiser from a street-side parking space at the southeast corner of town.

"I should have known he'd wait here," a dejected Cushman commented, as the traffic on Riverside slowed to a crawl. "He knows we're headed out into the sticks because of the mud he saw on my tires yesterday. Now it looks like plan B may be on hold too. Look at this traffic; it's like a parking lot out here. I could turn on the lights and siren, but there's nowhere for these cars to go to get out of the way."

Then Cushman saw the reason for the hold up. Half a mile ahead, the barrier at the railroad crossing was just completing its downward swing. Cushman instantly put plan C into action, realizing he had exactly eighty-five seconds to pull it off. He flipped on the siren and lights, turned into the nearly non-existent breakdown lane, and yelled, "Hang on!"

As soon as the cruiser was completely in the lane, Cushman put his foot to the floor. He accelerated to a speed of about fifty miles per hour and was passing the cars to his left with less than a foot of clearance. He glanced only once in the rearview mirror and smiled as the Focus sat with its nose halfway into the breakdown lane but unable to clear the car ahead of it.

As the cruiser approached the crossing without slowing, the tension level among the riders increased dramatically, but no one said a word. They didn't want to distract their driver in any way, shape, or form. With twenty yards to go before striking the barrier, Cushman slammed on the brakes and threw the steering wheel to the left, then to the right, then to the left again, executing a perfect S-turn before settling out at a comfortable speed in the right lane on the opposite side of the tracks from where they started.

Boland, Cushman, and Caviletti all looked back at the same time to see the immense, lumbering locomotive that was now in the middle of the crossing.

"Whoa!" Joey said, his heart still beating at an accelerated rate. "Way to go, Bernie."

Words escaped the two DSS agents for the moment.

Finally, Wolczyk spoke, "Wasn't that trick a little risky for a rural cop like yourself? I mean, I've seen the city boys pull stunts like that, but you don't seem to be the type, Bernie."

"It was a calculated risk," Bernie answered calmly, as he eased the Crown Vic's speed up to fifty and turned off the siren and lights. "I've sat at that crossing more times than I care to remember. Sometimes for fifteen minutes or more. The trains are slow when they come through here. The engineers are required to keep them less than twenty miles per hour or else they get cited. After the barrier completes its downward swing, there's a minute and a half, plus or minus five seconds, before the engine arrives at the crossing. The time never varies; I've measured it on many occasions. So I knew if I could get to the barrier quickly enough, we'd make it. I would have stopped if we were too late, but we had just enough time to get through."

"Did anyone notice what happened to Scanlon?" Boland asked.

Cushman chuckled. "I caught a glimpse of him in the mirror. He couldn't make it out of the traffic lane. He should be happy he didn't, or else his Focus would be ready for the scrap heap now with him wrapped up inside."

The four occupants of the cruiser got a good laugh at Scanlon's expense, then relaxed to take in the beautiful rural Washington scenery on the way to the Tolt Reservoir.

* * * * * * *

Glen arrived at the hospital just before noon and was directed to Jim Thunderhill's private room.

Jim had been admitted two hours prior and had since been subjected to a battery of tests, including extensive and frequent blood work. He remained in a state of mild shock and mental anguish, manifested as low blood pressure and cold, clammy skin. He had been given an injection of Demerol mixed with a mild barbiturate to keep him sedated and free of pain.

What remained of Jim's consciousness continued to play back the video scenes of the specimens in their cages: their confused and frightened faces, their frantic and unguided movements, their final struggle for survival. Then the scenes in his tortured mind turned grotesquely surreal, the expressionless faces of mice taking on human features with agonizing expressions, pleading to him personally for help, crying, moaning, screaming . . .

"Jim . . . Jim . . . Jim!"

He came back to reality as the voice of Glen Hargrove interrupted his hideous fantasy.

"Jim, are you all right?" Glen asked.

"Commander, thank you for coming," Jim replied in a weak and faltering voice.

"Of course. Listen, I want you to know that we're doing everything possible for you, both here and back in the lab. Now I want you to tell me as accurately as you can how you're feeling. What symptoms are you experiencing?"

"I'm cold . . . shaking . . . can't get warm. My head hurts. Things are blurry . . . can't seem to focus. Stomach is queasy, like I want to vomit, but can't."

"Anything else?"

"No . . . not yet . . . but soon . . . the mice . . . I'll be like them . . . it was awful . . . suffering . . . can't bear to think . . . horrible pain . . ."

"Jim, try to get your mind off the lab and the specimens. Try to relax. I know it's hard, but you're going to have to try so we can isolate the symptoms of the toxin."

"Okay, I'll try." Thunderhill closed his eyes in an effort to relax and let the Demerol cocktail take over.

Glen turned away and walked toward the door of the room, where the doctor assigned to Jim's case, also a Navy commander and circulatory system specialist, had just joined Cheryl Forrester.

"What have you learned?" Glen directed the question at both of them.

The doctor spoke first. "To date, his symptoms are purely the result of the shock, which is self-imposed I might add. There is no indication of toxic poisoning at this stage."

"However, the blood analysis definitely shows a foreign bacteria present," Cheryl added, "and the concentration levels are on the rise."

"Any migration beyond the blood?" Glen asked.

"So far, there are no bacteria present in any of the other body fluids—urine, saliva, sweat," the doctor answered. "Of course, we don't know about the liver."

"Suggestions?" Glen looked to the doctor first.

"There's really not much we can do. According to Lieutenant Commander Forrester, due to the prolific nature of the organism, any effort to filter or flush his blood supply would be a wasted effort. We can keep him comfortable and out of pain, but as for reversing the course of the toxic poisoning, there's little we can accomplish."

"Cheryl?" Glen's eyes were pleading for a hint of hope that was not forthcoming.

"I'm afraid the commander's right, Glen," she said. "We'll keep up with the periodic blood samples and monitor Jim's progress closely."

"I understand," Glen said, resigned to the experts' prognosis. "Please, somebody stay with him continuously and don't talk to him about this discussion. I'm sure he's already aware of the consequences of the accident, and that's why he's involuntarily placed himself in this state of shock. He doesn't need any confirmation from us."

"What are you going to do?" Cheryl asked Glen.

"I'm going back to the lab and light a fire under everybody. We need to accelerate the search for a treatment. I'm going to send one of our interns back here to relieve you, so you can help with the analysis. We'll work through the night if we have to. We're not giving up on Jim. As long as he's breathing and I'm standing, we're not giving up."

CHAPTER 8 -
TUESDAY, SEPTEMBER 16,
AFTERNOON

Rudy Moss, like many others in the private investigation profession, began his career as a detective in the police force. However, after several years, he was tired of both the paperwork and taking orders from someone he considered incompetent. He started his own business in a tasteful section of Arlington, Virginia, servicing only respectable customers. He had more than once turned down a job because the client appeared to be as sleazy as the person he or she wanted to be investigated. Moss's income was irregular, but fortunately, he had married into a degree of financial stability that allowed him to be selective about the cases he accepted. At least, that's the way it was before the divorce proceedings started.

Regardless of his financial status, Moss had never declined a job from Bud Kershaw and always went out of his way to make sure his friend and his friend's employer, the US Government, got their money's worth. This particular case was straightforward. Each of the individuals on the list Kershaw had faxed him the day before had a first and last name and enough of a background so that tracking him down should be relatively easy. He would have been in big trouble if Kershaw had asked him to find a six-foot guy with dark hair and brown eyes who lived somewhere in North America and every other Thursday went by the name "Bubba."

Moss's methods for obtaining private information on individuals went back to his days on the police force. He had established contacts at a variety of banks, credit card companies, travel agencies, phone companies, and any other businesses with records that could be used to piece together the mosaic of a person's life. Whereas Moss used to obtain the info by showing a badge and an ID with a picture of himself, he now displayed a green piece of paper with a picture of Jackson, Grant, or Franklin, depending upon the value of the information.

Since the fax arrived, Moss had been either on the phone or on the road, trying to obtain information about the four people on Glen Hargrove's list: their identity, where they were living, and a summary of their recent activities. The last three men on the list posed little problem; two of them still lived nearby, and one had moved to California but had retained a credit card with a local bank. The first person on the list, Broussard, was much more difficult. He seemed to take the Privacy Act very seriously.

So far, the information on the men was sketchy, but Kershaw had asked for a cursory investigation within a day, and that was what he was going to get. Moss picked up his phone and dialed the number Kershaw had given him to bypass his Flag Lieutenant. "Bud, Rudy here," he said, when his golfing partner answered his phone.

"How's it going, Rudy?" Kershaw asked.

"Not too bad. I have some basic information on the suspects. I'll start probing deeper into their lives this afternoon."

"Great. Shoot."

"Okay," Moss began. "Let's start with the easy ones—Corrigan, Levy, and Halpin. After Martin Corrigan retired from the Navy last year, he went to work for DuPont up in Wilmington, Delaware, as the manager of all the pharmaceutical testing labs. That job lasted less than six months. He was fired for trying to turn his small part of the company into a military operation, with himself as the commanding officer. Sound familiar?"

"Once a tyrant, always a tyrant," Kershaw commented, alternately writing notes and nervously tapping the same pencil on his desk blotter.

Moss continued, "He moved back to northern Virginia a few months ago, and started his own consulting business out in Vienna. It's called MAC Associates, Inc."

"MAC?" Kershaw questioned.

"His initials; Corrigan's middle name is Alexander. Anyway, as far as I can figure, it's a fledgling consulting business specializing in training its customers on how to obtain grants and find other sources of funding for medical research."

"Has he been up to anything suspicious?"

"I can't say for sure, but I think there's a low probability he's your man. I can tell you from personal experience that the first few months of starting a business are chaotic. I figure this guy's been working at a feverish pace just to get his head above water. I don't know how he'd find the time to focus on anything else."

"All right, Rudy, who's next?" Kershaw asked.

"David Levy," Moss answered. "After Glen Hargrove fired him, he left the Navy and moved to San Diego. He was hired as a hospital administrator and manages patient records for both the nursery and geriatric wards. Looks like if you're either coming into this world or on your way out, Levy gets to process your paperwork."

"And his extracurricular activities?"

"Not much to report there. He's joined a local fitness club, goes to synagogue regularly, and dates a co-worker. No unusual travel, bills, or phone calls. He seems too ordinary to be dangerous."

"You're right," Kershaw said. "Maybe Glen was exaggerating in his notes. Okay, what about Halpin?"

"Let me ask you a question about Halpin. Do you know when Hargrove's wife last received any correspondence from him?"

"No," Kershaw answered. "Why?"

"I think it's probably been a while. Halpin's been married for a year and a half, apparently happily. He and his wife live in an apartment in Norfolk and just had a baby last month. He makes a living teaching physical education at a local junior high. He's not pulling in the big bucks, but he pays his bills on time and stays out of trouble; not even a parking ticket."

"What's your opinion, Rudy?"

"I can't find a motive here. It looks like at some point, he just let the past go and moved on with his life."

"Reasonable assessment," Kershaw agreed. "That leaves us with Broussard."

"Right. Unfortunately, I haven't been able to find much of anything so far. Apparently, he's a very private person, sort of an informational black hole. There are several Broussards locally, but no Johns or Jacks. The two J. Broussards were both women. I'll have to dig further this afternoon."

"Please do that," Kershaw said, "and get back to me when you know anything. Would you agree that the other three aren't worth pursuing further?"

Moss pondered for a moment. "I would say we can forget about Levy and Halpin, but let me do a little more digging on Corrigan; we won't count him out yet. Broussard, however, definitely gets the lion's share of my attention."

"Sounds like a plan," Kershaw said. "Good job so far, Rudy. I'll look forward to hearing more from you later on."

"When I know something, you'll know something. Talk to you soon, Bud."

"Right. Take care."

As the two men hung up, Kershaw reviewed the summaries provided by Moss in his mind. Two of the four men on Glen's list either turned their lives around or were only a threat from Glen's perspective. He wondered if Glen also overstated Broussard's malice toward him. Kershaw was beginning to think that all of the names on Glen's list would lead Moss down dead-end streets, which made the efforts of Boland and Wolczyk in Seattle all the more critical. He hoped they would call with some good news before too long.

* * * * * * *

It would be a while before Kershaw got a call from Boland and Wolczyk, who were at the moment making their way along the winding access road to the Tolt Reservoir. Cushman brought the cruiser to a halt at the same spot he and Joey had stopped the previous afternoon. The foursome exited the vehicle, and Joey led the way to the water's edge.

The canister was visible in the shallow water as expected, the only difference from before being the timer, which now read 53:22:15 and was still counting down the seconds.

"What are you going to do?" Joey asked, anxious to see some real federal agents in action.

Boland crouched down for a closer look. "Well first, Joey, I'm going to figure out what kind of detonator we're dealing with here, and then we'll see if we can disable it to keep all the fish in this cove safe."

He reached into his jacket pocket for the drinking glass he had borrowed from Cushman, then pushed it down into the water to get a view of the detonator wiring not distorted by the shimmering water above it. He silently observed the device for about two minutes, moving the glass around to inspect it from a variety of angles. Finally, he stood up, satisfied that his examination was sufficiently thorough.

"It's a simple mechanism," he said. "I saw hundreds like it while I was in the Navy Seal program. When the countdown reaches zero, the timer sends an electrical signal down the wires to the detonator, which directs a spark into a small squib located in the neck of the bottle. When the squib blows, the neck is either punctured or blown off altogether, and the contents of the bottle, which are undoubtedly pressurized, end up in the water."

Cushman thought, *I figured it was something like that.*

Somewhat disappointed, Joey lamented, "You mean it's not a real bomb?"

"It's like a bomb," Boland answered, "but the damage is not from the explosion itself. The content of the bomb is the real problem. What's in the bottle would hurt the fish and anyone who drinks the water."

"So how do we disable it?" Cushman asked.

"Simple. No wires, no signal, no detonation. I simply disconnect the wires—the order isn't important—and the device will not function."

"How do you know there's no anti-tamper circuitry?" Wolczyk asked.

"I don't know for sure, but it really doesn't make sense that there would be. This is not the typical scenario where you would use a bomb with an anti-tamper mechanism. I mean, they placed this thing in the middle of nowhere. I'm sure they're not expecting anyone to find it, let alone tinker with it."

Boland reached into his pocket and pulled out his Swiss Army knife, then found the screwdriver among the many tools on the gadget. Within thirty seconds, both wires were disconnected. Boland removed them at the detonator end to prevent any stray electrical signal from causing a mishap. After the wires were disconnected, Boland changed tools on his knife, then snipped the plastic ties that secured the canister to the narrow rock. He gently removed the bottle from the water and held it at arm's length to examine it. It looked to be extremely sturdy, which was important in terms of transporting the device.

"Aren't you going to stop the timer?" Joey asked.

"I don't think that would be a good idea." Boland was answering Joey but speaking to the group. "You see, there's a good chance that this timer is being monitored or even controlled remotely. The times on both this clock and the remote clock could be synchronized. Stopping the countdown might let whoever has the remote control, whether it's a cell phone or some standalone device, know that we've tampered with the bottle. I think it's best to let the countdown run. Even if it reaches zero, nothing is going to happen now."

With the device disabled, Boland took the time to notice the scenery. "Nice fishing spot," he said to Joey, who thanked him and told him how it was a secret spot until all of this stuff started happening. As the group began walking back to the car, Wolczyk reassured Joey that after all of this was over, everything would be back to the way it was.

When they arrived at the car, Cushman opened the trunk and produced a large piece of plastic sheeting and an old blanket. Boland wrapped the canister first in the plastic and then in the blanket. He wedged the bulky package into the space normally reserved for the car's jack and other tools. Satisfied that the canister was secure, he shut the trunk door.

The trip back to the Bothell Police Station was far less exciting than the trip out. The agents used the opportunity to question Joey about the two men at the reservoir and the car they were driving. The color, make, and license plate number of the car would be critical to their search effort. If Joey could work with a computer artist to create reasonable facial composites of the terrorists, they would benefit even more.

Tired of the questions, many of which Bernie had already asked him the day before, Joey finally asked a question of his own. "Is anybody going to tell me what's in the bottle and why it's such a big deal?"

Boland looked into the back seat at Wolczyk, who nodded in return, then said, "All right, but both of you must not repeat what I'm about to tell you to anyone. That includes your mother, Joey. It could place the whole city of Seattle in grave danger."

Joey closed an imaginary zipper on his lips, while Cushman said, "Whatever you say stays right here in this car."

Boland started his mini-briefing with a little history. "Ever since the beginning of time, people have been inventing innovative and efficient ways of killing each other. During the past century, the devastation potential of a single device grew with things like nuclear bombs. But in my opinion, human beings reached an all-time moral low when we started building weapons from biological agents. These living poisons don't kill you cleanly like a bullet. They destroy you slowly from the inside out. They're painful and savage weapons in my book."

Boland continued his history lesson. "Back in the early 1970s, the world leaders realized how inhumane these weapons were, so they held a meeting in Geneva called the Biological Weapons Convention. At that meeting, the major powers agreed to ban biological weapons and to stop stockpiling the agents and developing new agents. However, some folks only sign treaties so they can break them later. To make a long story short, development of these agents continues around the world today at an alarming rate, and unfortunately, nobody's doing much of anything to stop it. That bottle in the trunk probably contains enough biological agent to wipe out the entire city. Joey, the men you saw planned to release that agent if they don't get what they want from the government."

"Wow!" was the only comment Joey could muster.

Cushman said, "I had no idea this was so serious."

"Now you see why Darrell and I were so happy to stumble in on you guys this morning," Boland said. "The problem is we don't know how many bottles these terrorists have already placed in other reservoirs. That's why we have to find them before they get a chance to finish the job they came here to do. Joey, you're going to have to give us a hand. After we get back to the station, we'll get you downtown to help a computer artist make pictures of the men you saw. That should help us track them down more easily."

"How on earth are you going to find these guys?" Cushman asked. "There are four million people living in this city and the surrounding region."

"Logically," Wolczyk echoed Boland's strategy from the previous evening. "Fortunately, the needle just got a little bigger and the haystack got a little smaller."

Boland nodded. "Exactly what we were hoping for last night."

* * * * * * *

Cheryl hated leaving Jim at the hospital, but she knew it was in his best interest for her to be at the lab working on an antidote. She had left instructions with the Richmond intern by Jim's bedside to phone her immediately if his condition changed. She knew in time it would, and not for the better.

Cheryl was the sole lab associate with any medical doctor training. After completing her undergraduate education with a pre-med degree from the University of Maryland, she completed Officer Candidate School in Newport, Rhode Island. The Navy sent her to medical school, but after two years, she decided that research, rather than patient care, was her cup of tea. She rearranged her curriculum and graduated with a PhD in immunopharmacology. Now and then, her doctor training still came in handy, and Glen Hargrove had come to rely on it for various aspects of their work. However, she never thought it would be useful in a situation like the current one.

On the short drive back to NMRC, Cheryl went over in her mind what the group had determined thus far about the organism, trying to select a course of action that would prove timely as well as productive.

The bacteria had a unique DNA structure, to which was probably attached one or more genes providing resistance to known antibiotics. If they could undo the resistive qualities at the genetic level and replace them with self-destructive attributes, the basis for an antidote might result. The post-doc from Johns Hopkins had done his thesis on DNA restructuring; his experience could be put to good use. Unfortunately, genetic manipulation was time consuming, and time was not on anyone's side, certainly not Jim's. Also, they did not have the insight of the organism's creator. Their task would be like putting together a jigsaw puzzle with 10,000 pieces, all with similar, but not identical, colors and shapes.

At the cellular level, they had already observed how hardy the organism was. No chemical they administered harmed the bacteria or even slowed down its reproduction rate. They had tested a large enough drug sample that the group felt secure in their conclusion that the organism had a universal immunity.

These thoughts brought Cheryl full circle to the research group's primary purpose for existing. There had to be a way to turn on the human immune system to combat the bacteria.

As she parked her car and headed up the steps to the entrance of the NMRC Building, her focus was on one thing—finding the treatment that would motivate the body's own disease fighters to destroy the organisms that by now were rapidly spreading throughout Jim Thunderhill's body.

By the time Cheryl arrived back in the lab, she had formulated a rough plan of action and immediately sought out Glen for his opinion. She found him in his office, working hard to overcome a lack of sleep and stay focused despite the distractions. She shared with him her plans for segregating a specific immunogen that would stimulate the immune system to attack the biotoxic organism. Glen gave her a few suggestions on her technical approach, followed by full authority over the research effort and an extra measure of encouragement. The two officers worked well together—Cheryl, the brainy scientist, and Glen, the insightful spark that lit the flame of progress. After the brief conversation, Glen left Cheryl and the lab, returning to the hospital to spend more time with his sick associate.

* * * * * * *

Upon arriving at the hospital, Glen first stopped at the office of Jim's doctor. No one was in the office; however, hanging on one of several wall hooks was a clipboard holding a chart marked "Thunderhill." Glen pulled the clipboard off the hook and looked the chart over briefly. Baffled by some of the results, he decided to borrow the chart for the duration of his visit. He left the doctor's office and headed down the corridor.

When he walked into Jim's room, Glen was somewhat surprised to find the patient sitting up in bed conversing with one of the many nurses who had been caring for him since he arrived. The color had started to return to his face, and he appeared alert and animated. Glen glanced into the corner of the room, where the Richmond intern sat in a chair reading a novel.

When Glen caught his attention, the intern shrugged and said, "I don't know what's going on. About half an hour ago, he sort of got a shot of instant energy. He's been like this ever since."

Curious, Glen walked to Jim's bedside, at which point the nurse excused herself. "Jim. I must say, you're looking much better than you did when I was here two hours ago."

"Yes, sir. What you see now reflects how my body actually feels. When I became infected, I allowed fear to take over, and I acted childish and afraid. My body responded to my mind's image of what was ahead for me. I kept seeing those poor animals in their cages suffering so horribly, and I allowed my mind to place me in their circumstances. I was not acting like a naval officer or a Navajo."

"It's understandable. You . . ."

"It's not, Commander," Jim interrupted. "Those animals acted like they did because they didn't comprehend what was happening to them. Their fear of the unknown controlled their actions. Their only realization was of their simple existence. As that realization slipped away, they reacted with confusion and panic. Unlike the animals, we humans have an understanding that transcends life and death. There's honor, dignity, principle, and knowledge of the Creator and a hereafter. Once I allowed these perceptions to overcome my fear, the physical state into which I placed myself faded. I know I am going to die, but I plan to be in control of my emotions when I do."

"Don't give up on yourself, Jim. No one else is," Glen said, impressed with Jim's words but not ready to accept his conclusion.

Jim smiled. "Sir, if you watch the video in the lab, you'll see that we are dealing with a toxin that results in one hundred percent mortality. All of our experience indicates that the response in humans is similar to the response in mice."

Glen shook his head. "Then explain a couple of things to me. You cut yourself at about 0800, correct?"

"Yes, sir."

"It's been over six hours since you were infected. Yesterday, weren't all of your specimens showing at least some symptoms six hours after infection?"

"That's true, but I said the response of humans and mice is similar, not identical. We're much larger animals; it's logical that the onset of symptoms would occur later."

"Maybe so, but explain this." Glen handed Jim the clipboard containing his chart, which documented all of the blood analyses performed to date. Jim scanned the columns on the chart until his eyes reached the column labeled Bacteria (mg/ml). The hourly results showed the concentration of bacteria increasing from the time he was admitted until the 11:00 a.m. sample. The three readings since showed no increase in bacteria level in the blood.

"This doesn't make sense," Jim said. "These data show the bacteria levels stabilizing. All of our tests indicated that the organism would continue to multiply at an exponential rate until death occurred. If the bacteria aren't reproducing, they're not secreting any more toxin."

Glen was still cautious. "That's one thing that might be happening. It's also possible that something in your body is killing off the bacteria as fast as they reproduce."

"I hadn't thought of that. The fact that humans can react differently to toxins than lab animals could discredit much of our ongoing work and the work of countless other labs around the world."

"I'm not convinced we can make that generalization, Jim. It could be that the contrasting responses only relate to this particular organism and not to other toxin producers. On the other hand, it's you who may be unusual."

"What!" Jim exclaimed, astonished at the suggestion of his unique invulnerability to deadly poisons.

"It could also be that the bacteria are in a dormant state before they become active again, or that the results of the analysis are inaccurate."

Jim's expression turned sullen again.

"It's too early to tell exactly what's going on here. I'm not trying to give you false hope, Jim. I just don't want you to give up on the hope that's still real. There's a lot to be said for a positive attitude in terms of combating disease. I've known a lot of cancer patients who have survived because of their will to survive. If you promise to stay positive, I'll promise to do everything in my power to sort out these results. Do we have an agreement?"

"It's a deal, Commander."

The two men shook hands, and Glen left the hospital room. On his way back to the doctor's office, he passed by an empty administrative office with a photocopier. Without anyone's knowledge or permission, he made a copy of Jim's chart and returned the original to the clipboard. On his way out of the building, he replaced the clipboard on the hook from which he took it.

* * * * * * *

After arriving back at the police station in Bothell, Harry Boland and Darrell Wolczyk felt somewhat less overwhelmed than they did when they first entered the building three hours ago. The basic plan designed at dinner the evening before was still a reasonable one—focus on who the terrorists are, where they're staying, and what they're driving.

Bernie Cushman had dropped the two agents off at the front door along with the canister, which they transferred to their Nissan. He told them to use his office as a base of operations, then headed downtown with Joey Caviletti. Hopefully, Joey's memory of the terrorists, together with a capable artist and a decent computer program, would generate an accurate representation of the faces they were attempting to find. This would help in the "who they are" part of the plan.

Where they're staying was undoubtedly the most critical part of the plan, but still the largest unknown. If the agents found out this piece of information, the element of surprise would shift to them. All of the terrorists' comings and goings could then be monitored, and any move to release the toxin in another reservoir could be intercepted. Hopefully, the third component, what they're driving, would help lead Boland and Wolczyk to where they were staying. Following up on this lead was the number one priority as the two men took over Cushman's cubicle and began thinking out loud.

"We know the make, model, color, and license plate number," Wolczyk said. "That doesn't buy us a whole lot in a town with almost as many cars as people."

"You're right, Darrell. The chances of a random encounter with this car are about a million to one. However, we also know it's a rental and the agency that rented it. I think our best bet is to find out who rented the car and follow up on that lead."

"Fine," Wolczyk agreed. "I'll start making phone calls to the various Avis agencies in the area."

Boland nodded, then commented, "I think we better give Bud Kershaw a call first. I'm sure he'll be interested in our progress." He unclipped his phone from its holster and dialed.

* * * * * * *

After the morning meeting with the president, Bud Kershaw had returned to his Ballston office, realizing that his primary role during the afternoon was going to be that of a communications conduit. He had already received calls from Lisa Kennelly and Rudy Moss. More calls were expected. One he hoped he would not receive was a call from Lisa informing him of a positive biosensor reading. Although technically he was in charge of the entire operation, at this moment, every aspect of it was in the hands of someone else. As he sat in his office waiting on phone calls and trying to keep himself otherwise occupied, Kershaw couldn't avoid feeling a bit helpless.

The ring of the phone disrupted this thought. "Kershaw," he said, answering after the first ring.

"Hey, Bud, it's Harry. I bet you're just dying for an update."

Kershaw confirmed Boland's presumption. "Am I ever. What's happening out there?"

"Well, you're not going to believe this—we're still having a hard time believing it ourselves—but we stumbled into one of the local police stations where a teenage boy had reported seeing two men plant a metal bottle in a reservoir. He just happened to be fishing there on Sunday when all of this happened."

"Did they see him?" Kershaw asked.

"Apparently not."

"Is anyone else aware of this?"

"Other than Darrell and me, only the kid and one police officer."

"What now?"

"We've already been out to the reservoir. I disarmed the detonator on the canister and removed it from the water. It's in the back of our rental car as we speak."

"That's great news, Harry. Of course, there are probably several of these canisters planted in several reservoirs," Kershaw cautioned.

"We're well aware of that fact, but we do have some leads we're working. The kid saw the car they were driving and got the plate number. We know it's an Avis rental, and we'll be trying to find out who rented it and when. Also, Joey—that's the kid's name—got a good look at the guys. We're definitely talking Middle Eastern ancestry. Joey is on his way downtown to work with a computer artist on facial composites. Between the car info and knowing what these guys look like, we're a lot closer than we were when we started out the day."

Kershaw was relieved that so much progress had been made, but still extremely anxious about the situation. "Harry, you've done great so far, but listen. You have to maintain the low profile. These people have no principles whatsoever. They'll kill without a second thought if they think someone is onto them. And believe me, if just one of those bottles of toxin is released into the water supply, it will be the worst environmental disaster in history."

"I hear you, Bud. We'll do our best."

"I know you will. Just one more thing, a favor."

"Name it."

"Glen Hargrove's wife and his wife's parents are in Seattle. We want to get them out of there without creating a stir. I want to have flight information delivered to them tonight. Could you or Darrell take half an hour off and make the delivery?"

"No problem. Where do they live?" Boland asked.

"7144 16th Avenue West in Kirkland."

"Kirkland, even less of a problem. It's only about ten minutes from where we are here in Bothell. Can you email me the info? We'll find a way to print it out here at the station."

"I'm hitting 'Send' right now," Kershaw replied, and then urged caution one more time before they said goodbye.

Wolczyk was already calling the various Avis rental agents in the region. His first and second calls were to the Bellevue and downtown Seattle branches of Avis. Neither had rented the blue Malibu. His third call was to the Sea-Tac airport branch, which did in fact rent the car in question for a two-week period starting on September 7. When Wolczyk asked who the renter was, the man on the phone said that he was not permitted to disclose that information without the approval of his manager and then only to someone who provided the appropriate credentials.

Wolczyk thanked the agent, told him he would be there in less than an hour, and asked him to obtain the necessary permission prior to his arrival. The agent said he would gladly comply with Wolczyk's request.

"I need the keys, Harry. I have to go back to the airport to find out who our mystery renter is."

"Good luck," Boland said as he tossed the keys. "I'll start calling around to the hotels and motels and see what I can find out."

"Good luck yourself. See you in about an hour and a half."

* * * * * * *

"What do you make of these results?" Glen asked Cheryl as he handed her the copy of Jim's chart.

"Impossible," she answered. "There has to be a mistake."

"What if there isn't?"

"It would mean that some unknown attribute of the human anatomy is capable of counteracting one of the most lethal organic substances ever encountered."

"Or some unknown attribute of Jim Thunderhill's anatomy," Glen countered.

"True, but we can't very well ask for another volunteer to subject himself or herself to infection in order to see which theory is correct."

"I agree with you there, Cheryl. So what do you suggest we do?"

"At the moment, nothing different. First, I'm not sure I believe these numbers. Having done blood work myself, I know that the methods are subject to error and the results themselves can be off by several percent. Even if the theory has merit, I have everyone focused on a particular goal now, and I'd hate to derail the effort to chase a hypothesis that is still pure speculation. Besides, if we disprove the theory and Jim starts getting very sick very quickly, we'll have lost valuable time."

Glen pondered Cheryl's position. "All right, I'll trust your judgment for now, but I think we need to prepare ourselves for a complete redirection if these numbers are correct and the trend continues."

"You're the boss," Cheryl said, her tone reflecting a rare attitude of defiance.

Glen bristled at the comment. "I've never pulled rank on you before, and I don't intend to start now. Please think about an alternative approach, should the next couple of readings show a continued stabilization of bacteria levels."

"I will . . . uh, sorry, Glen. I guess we're all a bit too tense right now."

Whenever Glen and Cheryl were at odds, it never lasted for long. "Apology accepted," he said. "I think I'm going to check out some reference material before I head back to the hospital."

They parted on a conciliatory note, and Glen headed out of the lab and down the hall to his office, where he intended to hunt for literature that could provide some insight into Jim's condition. First, however, he intended to place a call to Bud Kershaw.

* * * * * * *

The end of Lisa Kennelly's flight was even more trying than the beginning. At the baggage claim, one of her parcels was missing. Fortunately, no critical components of the biosensor equipment were in the missing bag. At the car rental counter, the van she had reserved was not yet ready because the previous renter, several hours late, had just returned it. The apologetic agent offered Lisa a spacious full-size car, but realized it was a bad suggestion when Lisa turned and pointed to the crates behind her.

In light of the delay in getting the car, Lisa decided to grab a cab and pick up the burner phones first, per Admiral Kershaw's direction. However, it took ten minutes to get through to Red Cable Wireless in Tukwila. When she finally got through, the service agent on the other end of the line sensed Lisa's frustration and offered to have the phones delivered to the rental car facility. With that act of kindness, things started to go smoother for the biosensor team.

The phones arrived twenty minutes after the call, and five minutes later, a Chrysler Grand Caravan, with the back seats removed as requested, was brought directly to their location, a small consolation for the inconvenient delay. A half hour later, with Kurt driving and Sanjay navigating, the van pulled into an open parking space directly in front of the Seattle Municipal Tower.

Before the van doors were locked behind them, they were greeted by a man, about forty-five and thinning on top, wearing a pair of khakis and a short sleeve denim shirt.

"You must be Lisa Kennelly," he said, as he thrust his hand in her direction. "Craig Evans, ma'am. Glad to be of service."

After Lisa returned the greeting and introduced the rest of her team, she commented on how fortunate they were to find an open parking spot right in front of the building.

Evans laughed and asked rhetorically, "Do you know how many people I've chased out of that spot waiting for you to show up? Nothing much happens by chance here in Seattle, ma'am."

"Thank you for holding it for us, Mr. Evans. And please, call me Lisa. I don't respond very well to ma'am."

"Only if you call me Craig."

"Agreed."

The group, now all on a first name basis, followed Evans into the building and onto the elevator, which carried them to the 49th floor. Evans showed them to his office, a multi-windowed corner office overlooking Elliot Bay, the Port of Seattle's entryway into Puget Sound. Coffee was offered and accepted by all but Sanjay, who sipped only herbal teas.

"Now, Lisa," Evans said, ready to get down to business, "I understand from the admiral I talked with, Admiral . . ."

"Kershaw," Lisa reminded Evans.

"Right, Admiral Kershaw. He said you needed to monitor a variety of sites where water enters the Seattle supply."

"That's right—a routine evaluation that we perform for a number of municipal water systems, and also the opportunity to field test some new equipment."

"And what exactly are you looking for in our water?" Evans was willing to cooperate but was also very protective of the outstanding reputation of the Seattle Water System.

Lisa had anticipated the interrogation and had embellished the admiral's basic cover story to address any questions. "Strictly trace elements," she replied. "We're compiling a data base of the chemical content of the major US water sources as a service to the Center for Disease Control. The Seattle water was selected as the standard for comparison because of its well-known and documented quality."

Evans beamed as Lisa completed her explanation. The mild praise was all that was required to secure his complete cooperation. "Well, Lisa, we certainly feel that we have the best water in the country. It's nice to see that our reputation has made it all the way to the nation's capital."

"How do you suggest we proceed, Craig?" Lisa asked.

"I think it would benefit your team if I spent ten minutes giving you a brief overview of our water system. Then we'll head out to the field and get your equipment set up."

"Sounds good."

Craig Evans actually spent twenty minutes giving his brief, but it was time well spent. Lisa and her team learned more about how water moves through the Seattle system in that short period than they could have learned in three days of library research. Evans truly was a wealth of information on his city's water supply.

He started with a brief history, discussing the vision for a city water system in the late nineteenth century and how that vision became a necessity when the Great Seattle Fire of 1889 destroyed the entire business district of the city. He discussed the look eastward to the Cascade Mountains as the source for a gravity-based water system, the acquisition of tens of thousands of acres of watershed land over the years, and the continuing efforts to expand the system to serve a greater number of residential, industrial, and wholesale customers.

After presenting the historical perspective, Evans placed a large geographical chart on the lip of his white board. The chart diagrammed the entire water supply infrastructure, including the most minute details. The well-conceived illustration made it perfectly clear how 200 million gallons of water a day makes its way from the sources to the spigots of Seattle area users.

Using the chart, Evans explained that the water system consisted of three principal components: supply sources, transmission system, and distribution network. The two major sources, the South Fork Tolt Reservoir on the Tolt River and the Chester Morse Lake on the Cedar River, provided 94 percent of Seattle's water, the other 6 percent coming from a well field near the Sea-Tac airport. The transmission system, with its 160 miles of pipeline and 800 valves and meters, transported water over the rural countryside to the distribution network. The distribution network contained the smaller reservoirs, elevated tanks, treatment facilities, pump stations, and countless pipes, valves, and meters necessary to deliver a plentiful supply of water to every Seattle area customer.

Finally, Evans addressed what he considered the most critical element of Seattle's municipal water system—water quality management, which involved a rigorous and continual effort to ensure that Seattle enjoyed the best water in the country. Evans claimed that this objective was met by tapping only the purest of water sources and then maintaining that level of purity as the water was transported through the delivery systems.

As he came to the end of his formal presentation, it was obvious to the four listeners that Evans was extremely proud of his city's water program, and justifiably so. "Any questions?" he concluded.

"Just a couple," Lisa replied. "Then it's important that we head out to the field. First, according to your chart, the sources you mentioned serve metropolitan Seattle. What about nearby areas like Tacoma?"

"Tacoma has its own supply fed by the Howard Hanson Reservoir and the Green River. Unlike Seattle, the Tacoma area users are predominantly industrial rather than residential. In fact, a single user, the Simpson Kraft mill uses over 30 million gallons of water a day, about 40 percent of the total Tacoma supply. A similar situation exists in Everett to the north of Seattle. The Scott Paper mill uses 45 percent of the Everett supply."

"That's amazing." Lisa was shocked that any consumer could use that much water. Having spent several of her formative years in southern California and experienced severe droughts, she had been conditioned to think twice before flushing the toilet. "One more question, Craig. You mentioned treatment facilities. What methods do you use to treat your water?"

"There are three basic processes. Chlorine is used as a disinfectant, fluoride is added for dental purposes, and calcium oxide is added to reduce corrosion in the system piping. The Tolt River water has a tendency to be more corrosive than the Cedar River water, so larger amounts of the chemical are added to the Tolt System."

Lisa looked around at her team members to see if they had any questions. They did not, so she thanked Craig and suggested they move on to the discussion of locations for establishing a base of operations and monitoring stations.

"How many stations do you want to set up?" Evans asked.

"I have twelve sensors," Lisa replied, "so I would say twelve stations, unless you think that's overkill."

"Not at all. With twelve stations, we can give you geographic coverage across the two major watersheds and the well field, and sample points at several locations along each distribution path."

Lisa remembered that during his briefing, the admiral mentioned the reservoirs specifically as the point where the toxin could be introduced, so she said, "I don't think we're really interested in the well field, Craig, just the two watersheds. That means we'll have six sensors for each of the main supply paths. Am I correct?"

"If you say so. The well field is out."

Lisa was pleased that the monitoring sites were falling into two distinct geographic groups, as she had hoped. This would make assigning responsibility for obtaining the water samples logical.

Evans turned back to his regional chart and pointed to specific geographic locations as he talked. "Let's look at the Cedar River System first. I would suggest three sites near the Chester Morse Lake, one in the lake itself and one downstream of each of the two dams. That leaves three for the rest of the system. I would have one site near the Landsburg Diversion—that's where the water is first screened, chlorinated, and fluoridated. Then we can have one in the Lake Youngs Reservoir. Lake Youngs is the regulating basin for the Cedar River System. By maintaining a constant level in Lake Youngs, we regulate the water pressure for most of the city. For the final site, we can take a tap off of the main Cedar System supply line downstream of Lake Youngs."

Evans then described a similar monitoring plan for the Tolt System, with monitoring sites in the Tolt Reservoir, Tolt River, Tolt

Regulating Basin, and main supply line. "The only real difference," he said, "is that the Tolt Reservoir has only one dam, so I suggest two taps on the supply line. It makes sense since the pipeline is four times as long as the Cedar pipeline."

Lisa's team all nodded in acceptance of Craig Evans's design for the water monitoring sites. As Evans put down his laser pointer, Lisa stood up, and everyone else followed her lead. "Where to now?" she asked.

"Let's hop in your van and head out to the Cedar River Watershed Education Center. This will be an ideal place to set up your base of operations. There's a reasonable indoor facility with reliable electricity, phones, running water, the essentials. Also, it's relatively near to your Cedar System monitoring sites. There's always an empty office or two, so you should have plenty of room to spread out."

As everyone left Evans's office and walked toward the elevator, Lisa was certain that within a couple of hours, she would be using her biosensor equipment to analyze the very first water sample of its very first field test. She couldn't help but feel gratified.

* * * * * * *

"Hello, Bud, it's Glen."

"Thanks for calling," Kershaw said. "I'm going crazy sitting in this office waiting for the phone to ring."

"I'd be happy just to sit down for five minutes," Glen retorted.

"I'm interested in hearing where your effort stands, but first let me brief you on what I know. Harry Boland called a while ago from Seattle. They've located one of the toxin sources. Apparently, a teenager was fishing at one of the reservoirs when two guys showed up and placed a canister in the water. Harry has already disarmed and removed it."

"Talk about a stroke of luck."

"We can't get too comfortable, Glen. Harry doesn't have a clue yet who these guys are, where they're hanging out, and how many more of these canisters they've placed. We both know what will happen if just one of them has its contents released."

"Don't worry. We won't be slowing down on our end."

"Good. I also talked to Harry about delivering the e-tickets to Jennifer's parents' home tonight. He said he would do it."

"Thanks." Glen was starting to feel more comfortable about Jennifer's safety. There were still two days left until the deadline for the ultimatum. By then, Jen will have been back in New Hampshire for almost a day.

"Next, I have the bad news and the good news. The PI that's investigating the names on your list called. He's come up with nothing. In fact, he's sure that two of the men, Levy and Halpin, are definitely not involved. He's still digging for more information on Corrigan and Broussard. Broussard looks to be the only likely candidate at this time."

"What's the good news?" Glen asked.

"Your problems with Halpin are over. He finally found the woman to replace Jennifer. He's been enjoying marital bliss for over a year, and baby number one just arrived."

"I'm sure Jen will be thrilled," Glen said, relieved that there was one less complication in his life.

"Finally, our water monitoring team should be in Seattle now setting up their equipment to monitor for the toxin. That's all I know, Glen. How about you?"

"It's been a bizarre day since we said goodbye at your office. I arrived back at the lab to find out that one of my research assistants had accidentally infected himself with the biotoxin and was in the hospital. Since then, I've visited him twice. It's almost inconceivable, considering what we know about this toxin, but the bacterial levels in his blood appear to have stabilized and he's showing no symptoms of toxic poisoning six hours after infection. It just doesn't correlate with our observations in lab specimens."

"Are you saying that humans might have a natural immunity to this toxin being used to hold Seattle hostage? That sounds to me like a stupid mistake on the part of whoever is behind this. It's sort of like holding up a bank with a water pistol."

"I agree, Bud. That's why I think this immunity, if it exists, may be limited to this one person. Or it could be that the poison is just slow in taking effect. We're really not sure yet."

"What does the rest of your team think?" Kershaw asked.

"Cheryl Forrester, the one whose opinion I trust the most, isn't convinced that it's anything more than inaccurate blood analysis."

"What's the next step, Glen?"

"I'm going to do a little literature research, then head back over to Walter Reed to check the latest blood results. I'll defer a decision until then."

"Please keep me informed. If this toxin is in fact less harmful than we think, it changes our whole bargaining strategy."

"Don't worry, I will. Anything else?"

"Not that I can think of. Keep in touch, Glen."

"Will do. See you tonight."

"That's right. I better call Eileen and make sure she remembered we're having a dinner guest. Take care."

After Glen hung up, he stood and scanned the rows of books on the shelves behind his desk.

He pulled out three publications that looked like they might provide some useful information, then sat back down and began reading.

* * * * * * *

Harry Boland sat at Bernie Cushman's desk and gazed at the computer renditions of the two faces Joey had described to the artist. Although both of the faces appeared sinister and undoubtedly Middle Eastern, one of the faces, the thinner one with the more pencil-like moustache, evoked a particularly strong feeling of hatred in Boland. "How do you feel about these pictures, Joey? Are they accurate?"

"They're good, Harry. The guy on the computer was a whiz."

"Good," Boland responded. "It's time to start searching."

In fact, Boland had been searching for the past hour with little success. He had called the majority of hotels in Bellevue, asking if two Middle Eastern men with dark hair and moustaches were staying at their establishment. The responses from the hotel employees ranged from "It's none of your business" to "Are there any other kinds of Middle Eastern men in the world?" No one had anything positive to contribute to Boland's search effort.

"Where's Darrell?" Cushman asked, sitting in the seat that Boland had occupied during their previous discussion.

"Hopefully on his way back from the Avis rental office at the airport," Boland answered. "They wouldn't give him the name of the person who rented the Malibu unless he personally presented his government ID."

"So what do we do now?" Joey asked.

Not knowing when Wolczyk would arrive back in Bothell, Boland suggested that he and Bernie take two copies of the computer images of the men and continue the search effort in the Bellevue area face-to-face. Meanwhile, Joey would stay at the station and wait for Darrell. When he returned, the two of them could either follow up on the information Darrell had obtained on the car or pick up the search in another town on the eastern side of Lake Washington.

No one objected to Boland's plan, so Cushman made the copies of the facial composites, and the twosome headed out to the cruiser for their trip south to Bellevue. Joey made his way to the other side of the desk and sat in Bernie's chair. He swiveled the chair back and forth for a few moments, then leaned back and propped his legs up on the corner of the desk. "Not bad," he said to himself, thinking that he just might like to do this on a full-time basis a few years from now.

* * * * * * *

The education of Lisa and her team continued on their way out to the Education Center. As they cruised eastward along Interstate 90 through Issaquah, with Tiger Mountain in the foreground and the Cascades looming beyond, Craig Evans was explaining the ownership of the land that comprised the watersheds.

"The City of Seattle owns about seventy thousand of the ninety thousand acres in the Cedar River Watershed. The US Forest Service owns the rest, but the city is continually negotiating with the Forest Service to buy more land. It's not a matter of greed, just control."

"What about the Tolt System?" Kurt Wagner asked from the driver's seat.

"That's a different story," Evans replied. "The Cedar River System dates back to the beginning of the twentieth century. We've had plenty of time to acquire the land. Development of the Tolt System didn't even start until the late 1950s. Of the thirteen thousand or so acres in the Tolt Watershed, the city owns only about four thousand of them. Some of the remaining acreage is owned by the Forest Service, but the big owner is Weyerhaeuser."

"The lumber company?" Wagner asked.

"Lumber and a lot more. They're a huge corporation out here, and they're not interested in selling their land. We've reached some cooperative agreements on land usage though, and they appear to be working out. Also, Weyerhaeuser has indicated a willingness to consider some land swap proposals."

Craig Evans continued to explain more about the Seattle Water System, from the politics to the practical, while simultaneously giving directions to Kurt. The van turned off Route 90 at 436th Avenue SE and, four miles later, pulled into the parking area of the Education Center.

In addition to being the facility where Water Management conducted day-to-day oversight of the Cedar River Watershed, the Center also served as an educational facility for tourists and school children. The grounds were replete with placards, mounted in rustic log frames, describing the history of the watershed and illustrating its current extent and layout. Also scattered around the grounds were relics of a past generation's effort at channeling water to Seattle residents. Most interesting of the artifacts was a five-foot-diameter wooden pipe section through which water flowed over half a century before.

Evans led the group to the inside of the main building, saluted the on-watch field supervisor, and found an empty office for Lisa to set up shop. Within five minutes, all of the crates marked "mother" had been brought into the office. He suggested that the Cedar System sites be set up first, followed by the Tolt sites later in the afternoon.

Lisa agreed, then assigned Kurt and Robin to accompany Evans to establish the remote monitoring stations. Meanwhile, she would set up the two mothers, one for each set of six sensors, and Sanjay would work on installing the dish antenna and central telecommunications equipment.

It was time for Craig Evans to be impressed. Over the next hour, he would witness an efficient and well-trained team construct a complete fiber optic chemical monitoring system, including a central data analysis station and remote data collection and transmission sites, as if they could do it in their sleep. In truth, all of them had done precisely that at one time or another.

* * * * * * *

Darrell Wolczyk didn't arrive back in Bothell until 2:00 p.m., nearly three hours after he had left. First, he had lost half an hour in the Seattle traffic, statistically the sixth worst in the country. Upon finally arriving at the airport Avis desk, the agent with whom he had talked earlier was gone for the day, having told his relief nothing about obtaining permission to turn private customer information over to an agent of the US Government. It had taken another half hour to track down the manager and confirm that the information transaction was in fact acceptable. When given the renter's name alone, Wolczyk had told the clerk that he also needed an address and credit card information. Obtaining additional permissions had consumed another twenty minutes. Lastly, the renter, a man named James Johnson, lived only a few miles from the airport in Burien, so Wolczyk had decided to pay him a visit since he was in the area. After finding a vacant apartment at the address given, Wolczyk had slowly made his way back to the station, fighting traffic in the opposite direction the entire way.

Now exhausted from his highway ordeal and frustrated at not being able to confront the terrorists' accomplice, he fell into one of the chairs in Bernie Cushman's cubicle. "Where is everybody, Joey?" he asked.

"Harry and Bernie took off to look for these guys at some of the nearby hotels," Joey said, as he passed Wolczyk copies of the computer-created facial images. "What do you think?"

"Pretty nasty-looking people. Looks like you did a good job with the pictures."

"Yeah, it was fun. Say, Darrell, are we going to start looking for them too?" Joey asked.

"In a different way. Now that we know who rented the car for these two," Wolczyk said, holding up the two computer images, "we can try to find that person and encourage him to tell us where his friends are staying."

Joey recognized the softening of the terminology. "Encourage, that means with hot prods and bamboo shoots under the fingernails, right?"

"You watch too many movies, kid. We're much more civilized than that. Nowadays, we rely on truth serum, electrical shock, and running fingernails across a blackboard."

They both got in a good laugh before Darrell suggested getting down to business. "Let's swap seats. I need to make a couple of calls."

Wolczyk moved to behind the desk and took the seat vacated by Joey. He then placed his first call, which was to the post office in Burien, Washington. He asked the postal clerk for the forwarding address of Mr. James Johnson and was immediately transferred to the office manager.

"Do you know something about James Johnson?" the irritated manager asked, without extending the courtesy of a hello.

"Only that he doesn't live where he used to live," Wolczyk replied.

"We know that much," the manager responded sarcastically. "He moved and didn't leave a forwarding address. His mail has been piling up for weeks. If I don't find out where to forward it soon, I'm going to throw it out."

"Well, it seems we're both trying to find out the same information. Thank you anyway."

"You call me back if you hear anything, you hear," the manager said brusquely.

"Right," Wolczyk said as he hung up, intimating that he was not inclined to take orders from employees of the US Postal Service.

With no help from the Postal Service, Wolczyk's next move was to attempt to locate Johnson by means of his credit card number. A five-minute Internet search revealed that the Issuer Identification Number or IIN—the first six numbers of the card—was associated with a Signature Visa issued by Bank of America. He was dismayed that he would be dealing with a mega bank and not a small local bank.

He immediately followed up with a call to the Bank of America 800 number. After being transferred three times, he was finally talking to someone with authority in the Credit Services Department. The apologetic representative informed him that he would have to personally appear at a Bank of America Financial Center—not a local branch—and show proper identification in order to obtain a client's credit card information. When asked about his location, Wolczyk informed her he was in the Seattle area. She suggested stopping by the Financial Center in the Safeco Plaza in downtown Seattle first thing in the morning, as it was near closing time this afternoon.

After saying thank you and exchanging goodbyes with the helpful representative, Wolczyk put away his phone, frustrated that he would be unable to pursue the best lead yet until the following morning. Resigned to the delay, he spent a moment in thought, then said to Joey, "Well, kid, let's hit the streets. If we can't do what we want, let's do what we can."

He grabbed the copies of the computerized faces and with Joey in tow, headed out to the Nissan, vowing to not go anywhere near the downtown Seattle area and its interminable sea of cars.

* * * * * * *

The literature search had been futile. Glen had been hoping to uncover some obscure facts concerning unique human responses to specific toxic agents or rare cases of universal toxic immunity. He had found none. Disappointed, he was now in his car on the way back to the Walter Reed Hospital.

When he arrived, he stopped by Jim's doctor's office, but both the doctor and the clipboard with Jim's chart were absent.

Glen then proceeded to Jim Thunderhill's room to find the same nurse by his bedside who had been keeping him company during Glen's previous visit. He hoped that, should Jim survive his current trauma, he would succeed at changing his bachelor status, a pursuit that was secondary only to his work over the course of the past year. When he approached Jim's bed, the nurse again excused herself; however, Glen urged her to stay while he tracked down Jim's doctor. She told Glen that the doctor had been in the room only moments before making his rounds and was probably either in one of the two adjacent rooms or across the hall. Glen thanked her and exited the room.

He looked right and left in the corridor and saw the doctor departing the room adjacent to the left.

"Excuse me, Doctor," Glen said. "Do you have a minute?"

"Certainly, Commander," the doctor replied. "You must be interested in how your associate is doing."

"Very much so."

"Quite well, actually," the doctor advised, "despite the gloomy prediction of Lieutenant Commander Forrester. Look at these results." He passed Jim's chart to Glen. "The bacteria count stabilized five hours ago. The last two samples show the level dropping substantially. The lieutenant's on the road to recovery. There's no doubt in my mind . . . not that he was ever sick in the first place."

Glen scrutinized Jim's chart, astounded that at 4:00 p.m., the bacteria count was one-fourth of what it was two hours before. Cheryl would in no way be able to attribute the observed trend to procedural error or measurement inaccuracy. Assuming Jim's estimate of his own health reflected the clinical evaluation, he was going to redirect Cheryl's efforts. He didn't want to pull rank, but if necessary, he would.

Glen handed the chart back to the doctor, expressed his thanks, excused himself, and stepped back into Jim's room. He told the nurse that there was no need to move because he would only be a minute, then asked Jim, "How are you feeling?"

"Great, never better," he answered. "I'm a little tired of being poked so many times; I'm going to look like a junkie before I leave here. I don't feel sick at all, though."

"Looking at your blood analysis, you shouldn't. I'm going to send Cheryl back soon. I want the two of you to figure out how and why your immune system is defeating this toxin. It's absolutely critical to know this within the next twelve hours. I'm glad you're going to be all right, Jim. Now let's use the experience to our advantage."

"I'm ready to help with all my energy," Jim replied, feeling like a prisoner who just had his death sentence suspended.

"You two can get back to your socializing now," Glen said, winking at Jim as he turned to leave the room.

* * * * * * *

The fountain of knowledge that was Craig Evans was still spewing forth information on the Seattle Water System as the Grand Caravan, now with Robin Stoddard at the wheel, was driven back into the Education Center parking area. As she pulled into the first empty space and got out, Robin was certain that her insight into the operation of the multi-stage water filtration and treatment process was second only to Evans.

The setup of the three Cedar River sites closest to the Morse Lake was now completed. The sites had been named Cedar One, Two, and Three, starting with the station that was the furthest upstream. Kurt Wagner had suggested that Robin and Craig rejoin Lisa and Sanjay while he remained at Cedar Three, which was just below the downstream dam of the Morse. They could perform a complete end-to-end system check before retrieving him and continuing with the remaining Cedar River site installations.

When Craig and Robin walked into the office-turned-laboratory, Lisa and Sanjay were sitting enjoying a Pepsi, having been finished with their part of the system assembly for twenty minutes. Kurt had already called Lisa to arrange for a system test at 2:30 p.m., exactly five minutes from now.

Lisa stood and told the two recent arrivals to not get too comfortable, as the data would start flowing within a matter of minutes. Sanjay headed over to his communications equipment by the window, where he had a view of the antenna dish and could make minor orientation adjustments based on the fidelity of the received data. Lisa took station next to the computerized analysis equipment that she had labeled Cedar System Mother.

At precisely the pre-arranged time, a visual and audible alert informed her that the first transmission from Cedar Three had been received and processed. Using the mouse, she moved the pointer on the computer screen to the List Messages menu selection. She clicked the mouse button and a listing containing a single item, the message just transmitted by Kurt Wagner, was displayed. Lisa double-clicked on the item and the content of the message was presented on the screen:

Lisa frox Krrt, Xmsssion checj. No datv cxntained in this messfge. Will cwll to verifl receipt in fcve minutes.

"The text is a bit garbled, Sanjay," Lisa complained. "Can you work on it?"

"I'm working on it already. The signal strength wasn't adequate. I think I've made the appropriate adjustments. The next transmission should tell."

No sooner were Sanjay's words spoken than a second message alert was received. Lisa repeated the steps to call the message to the screen:

Lisa from Kurt, Xmission check. No data contained in this message. Will call to verify receipt in five minutes.

"All right, Sanjay, you got it!" Lisa exclaimed excitedly. "No errors at all that time."

Two minutes later, Lisa's phone rang. "Hello, Kurt," she answered, realizing that no one else would likely be calling her.

"How did it look?" Kurt asked.

"Your first transmission was garbled. Sanjay made some antenna adjustments, and the backup message came through error free."

"Are you ready for some real data?"

"You bet. Let's get this show on the road," Lisa answered.

"I'll need about ten minutes to get the sample and run it through the sensor."

"We'll be waiting," Lisa said, getting more excited by the minute. "Call me back after you transmit."

"Will do. Bye for now," Kurt said as they both hung up.

* * * * * * *

"Impossible!" Cheryl argued, after Glen told her about the diminishing bacteria concentration in Jim's blood.

"Difficult to believe, I'll grant you, but true." Glen hoped that Cheryl would decide on her own to change her course of action. "We're not talking accuracy of the test anymore. There are 75 percent fewer toxin producers than there were two hours ago."

Cheryl was as strong willed as most in her field, but when she was wrong, she admitted it. This was one of those times. "Okay, it looks like Jim is beating this toxin. Let's figure out what we're going to do."

"Do you think the tolerance is unique to human beings or unique to Jim?" Glen asked.

"It's hard to tell at this point. If it's a human immunity, your problem with the toxin, whatever that problem is, appears to go away. If the tolerance is unique to Jim Thunderhill, the problem with human infection is still very real. I think the conservative approach would be to assume Jim is immune to the toxin and not the whole human race. We need to find out the reason for his immunity."

"Any thoughts?"

"Could be any one of a number of things: physical makeup, heritage, lifestyle, genes, diet, environment, habits, or something else. Whatever the key, he's going to have to lead us to it."

"I agree totally. Can you work with Jim tonight? I can help, but not until after 1900." Glen remembered both his nightly phone call from the terrorists and his dinner engagement. The latter could be postponed; the former could not.

"Absolutely. In fact, everybody on the team is ready to work until we find an antidote for this stuff or drop in our tracks trying. Let me take ten minutes to brief the team and give them some alternative tasks. Then I'll head back to the hospital."

"Thanks, Cheryl. I knew I could count on you."

"It's my job. So let's go kick some microorganic butt."

* * * * * * *

At the same time Cheryl Forrester was saying "impossible" to Glen Hargrove, Lisa Kennelly was mumbling the same word to herself, under her breath so that Craig Evans wouldn't sense her confusion and mild dismay.

When the first of the data was sent by Kurt Wagner from the Cedar Three monitoring site, Lisa had assumed that the message was garbled, similar to the first transmission check ten minutes before. When she had asked Sanjay to make the necessary antenna adjustments, he assured her that the signal strength was satisfactory. She had then called Kurt and asked him to repeat the transmission. The second message contained the same data values, which indicated the definite presence of a botulin-like toxin in the water. Her next call to Kurt had requested a fresh sample. That sample was also apparently contaminated with a measurable quantity of the toxin.

"Impossible," she repeated to herself, as she excused herself from the group, found an empty office, and again dialed Wagner's phone.

"It's Lisa, Kurt," she said as he answered the call. "I'm looking at identical readings for the second sample. Did you purge the sensor before sampling?"

"Yes, I did," Kurt answered.

"And the detector warm up time was sufficient?"

"Of course."

"How about the amplification setting?"

"Lisa, it's me, Kurt. We've been through this drill a thousand times. I assure you I didn't make any procedural errors. If your gear says the sensor is detecting, it's detecting."

"I don't doubt your competence, but we have to be absolutely certain," she said, her voice showing noticeable anxiety.

"Must be some pretty serious toxin," Kurt retorted. As Bud Kershaw had withheld certain facts that Lisa had no need to know, Lisa did likewise with Kurt and the rest of her team.

"Here's what we'll do. I'll send Robin in the van to pick you up and take you to Cedar Two. It's upstream of Cedar Three. If the Cedar Two sample is clean, then the Cedar Three site really is contaminated and the introduction point is somewhere between the two sites."

"All right," Kurt said, a bit defensively, despite Lisa's reassurance of her confidence in him. "I'll be waiting."

"And I'll be standing by for your data transfer. Talk to you later."

"Bye for now."

Lisa called Robin Stoddard into the office and asked her to pick up Kurt and transport him to Cedar Two.

"I'm on my way," Robin replied, and was gone.

When Lisa returned to the room serving as the central data analysis station, Craig Evans asked if anything was wrong.

Lisa lied, "We're just trying to iron out a few equipment problems. It should only take another twenty minutes or so."

"Anything I can do?" Evans asked.

"No, Craig, thank you. For now, all we can do is wait."

Lisa began to pace back and forth across the room, an activity she would pursue with vigor over the next fifteen minutes.

* * * * * * *

"How's your associate doing?" Kershaw asked after the customary phone greetings.

"His blood bacteria levels have dropped off substantially over the past several hours," Glen answered. "We have to assume that Jim Thunderhill is a human anomaly. Cheryl and I seriously doubt that a broad segment of the population is immune to this biotoxin."

"So in terms of how we deal with the terrorists, nothing changes," Kershaw concluded.

"Not yet, Bud. However, our analysis approach changes considerably. Cheryl and Jim are at the hospital now trying to determine why his resistance to this toxin is so high. Once we've gotten a handle on the reason, we can isolate the immunity trigger in his body and develop either a natural or synthetic treatment that makes every human body respond like Jim's does naturally."

"And how long might that take?"

"It's really hard to say—somewhere between several hours and several months." Glen regretted being so noncommittal, but his answer was an honest one. "Even after we've developed a candidate serum, we have to ensure that the drug is safe for administering to humans. And then there's the problem of producing it in quantity. I'm afraid to say it, but I don't think you can count on me for an alternative solution to negotiation."

"You're not painting a very bright picture," Kershaw lamented.

"For the short term, I agree. For the long term, we really may be onto something, but I realize that doesn't help us with the current crisis."

"Okay, Glen, keep doing the best you can."

"We will," Glen assured his friend. "By the way, anything else from the West Coast?"

"Nothing. I hope no news is good news."

"One more thing, Bud," Glen said with an apologetic tone. "I hate to do this to you and Eileen, but I'm going to have to take a rain check on dinner tonight. My whole staff is working straight through the evening. I couldn't very well justify a social evening of my own when they're all hard at work."

"I understand, and Eileen will also. Remember she's married to me, Mr. Unreliable. How about Thursday for that rain check? Eileen has bridge club tomorrow night."

"I'd love to, but I've already said yes to another invitation. My Academy roommate is getting a few of the guys in our company who live in the area together for dinner. Assuming this whole mess is history by Thursday night and I'm not yet free to join Jen in New Hampshire, I think I'll go. Maybe next week sometime if it's convenient."

"I think that'll be okay, but let me check with Eileen. Have a great time with your company mates. Sounds like great fun."

"Yeah, should be," Glen agreed. "I haven't seen some of these guys for years, and I don't think I've seen Chuck Renard—the guy who's throwing the party—since the day we graduated."

"Well, you need to get home for a phone call, and I need to let my wife know about the change in plans. Give me a ring after they call tonight."

"All right. Talk to you later."

"Bye."

* * * * * * *

Lisa Kennelly's pacing was interrupted by the audible message alert. She covered the twenty feet to the Cedar System Mother in less than two seconds, then went through the motions of calling up the message to the computer screen. The short text read:

I'm at Cedar Two. Purging, warming up, and checking settings. Data to follow in three minutes. Kurt.

The dart hit home. Lisa realized she had challenged Kurt's knowledge and ability a quarter hour earlier at Cedar Three, and he had remembered.

The next three minutes were among the longest three minutes Lisa Kennelly could ever remember. She spent the time contemplating her response to each of the two possible outcomes of the Cedar Two sample. A positive biosensor reading would be inconclusive. It could confirm that toxin was present in the sample and had entered the system upstream of Cedar Two. It could also indicate a system-wide problem with her equipment. She would have to experiment further, perhaps move Kurt to Cedar One and sample yet another location. On the other hand, a negative biosensor reading would prove that the equipment was operating properly and that there was definitely a toxin concentration at Cedar Three. In the case of the latter, she would have to call Admiral Kershaw immediately and let him know the results.

Finally, after what seemed like an eternity, the transmission alert was received. She made all of the selections necessary to display the message text except the last one, which she delayed for a moment while she closed her eyes and took a deep breath. She opened her eyes and, still holding her breath, double clicked on the newest message in the list. The text appeared on the screen. She let out her breath and went into the office to make a call to the East Coast.

* * * * * * *

When Cheryl Forrester walked into Jim's room, he was enjoying the fine hospital cuisine and yet another conversation with his nurse acquaintance. Upon Cheryl's arrival, he looked up and sighed, realizing that it was time to get down to serious work. He and the nurse shared some parting comments, whereupon she pecked him on the cheek and left the room.

"Do we have a romance in the making?" Cheryl asked, trying to elicit a blush from the normally straight-laced Thunderhill.

"It's nothing," Jim replied, hoping that he was in fact incorrect.

"Feeling well?" Cheryl asked.

"Better than ever," Jim replied.

"You should be. I checked with your doctor. The toxin levels are way down. Ready to go to work?"

"You bet."

Cheryl found the most comfortable chair in the room, pulled it over to Jim's bed, and sat down with pad and pencil in hand. "All right, do you have any idea why your reaction to the most lethal toxin in existence might be different from every other human being and rodent on the planet?"

"Not off the top of my head," Jim replied.

"Okay, let's start with what you did this morning from the moment you got up until you arrived at work."

During the next several hours, the two researchers would cover every aspect of Jim's life history, daily routine, and lifestyle. By the time midnight rolled around, Cheryl would know more about Jim Thunderhill than she ever cared to know. And he would remember more about himself than he ever thought possible.

* * * * * * *

The phone rang just as Bud Kershaw was putting on his cap to leave his office for the night. "Hello," he answered in an uncharacteristically informal manner.

"Hello, Admiral, it's Lisa. This is the call you didn't want to receive."

"Oh no."

"I'm afraid we've detected a concentration of the toxin at one of our monitoring sites on the Cedar River."

"No chance of an error?" Kershaw asked, hoping for even the slightest chance of a false alarm.

"The probability of an error is extremely small. All of the sensors are identical in their basic structure. We've performed several backups. Less than a mile upstream of the positive reading, the results are negative. I'm convinced that the toxin you're looking for has been introduced into the water supply between these two sites. I'm sorry to be the bearer of bad news, Admiral."

"There's nothing to be sorry about. This is not good news, but it's not your fault. You've done the job you were sent to do. Now I have to figure out what to do at my end."

"I don't envy your position," Lisa said.

"Frankly, I'm not too wild about my situation either. But it goes with the job. Keep me updated, and thanks for being prompt."

"Yes, sir, I will. Good luck."

"Thanks."

As Bud Kershaw hung up the phone, he removed his cap and turned his desk lamp back on. Not only would Glen Hargrove be missing dinner at his house, he would likely be missing it also. He gave Eileen a quick call to let her know he wouldn't be home soon. Then he flipped through the W section in the Rolodex until he reached the card for the White House. He dialed and prepared himself for one of the most difficult phone calls of his thirty-two-year naval career.

CHAPTER 9 -
TUESDAY, SEPTEMBER 16,
EVENING

For Bud Kershaw, when human lives were at stake, there was only one acceptable decision alternative—the conservative one. At college, his NROTC studies included lessons learned from the Navy's involvement in the controversial Vietnam War. One eye-opening event involved a destroyer providing gun support off the coast of Vietnam. Kershaw learned that during numerous bombings of the coastal regions, American soldiers had been killed by "friendly fire" during more than one of these bombings. He didn't blame the sailors, who loaded and fired the enormous guns, or even the junior officers, who gave the orders to fire. These young men were merely following the direction of their superiors. He blamed the senior officers on the ship who blindly followed orders without question, even though their own intelligence indicated that American troops could be near the targeting points. He also blamed the politics behind the bombings, the compelling need to demonstrate a show of force despite the potential consequence of losing the lives of American boys hardly old enough to shave.

Kershaw had experienced at an early age how easy it was to feel comfortable when the danger was distant. He likened the feeling to that of the pilots dropping the bombs on Hiroshima and Nagasaki during World War II. He had vowed at that early age to never allow distance from the danger or the lack of a threat to his own well-being to influence his decisions. He had thought briefly about asking Lisa Kennelly to perform additional verification checks, but in recalling his discussions with Glen Hargrove earlier, he knew that time was critical. Anyone who consumed contaminated water could be dead within hours. Another hour spent in testing could mean countless additional lives lost, and he was not willing to take that chance. It took only the moment between ending his conversation with Lisa and dialing the White House to determine his recommendation to the president.

"Admiral, let me patch you through to the president," said the White House operator, recognizing Kershaw's name immediately. "He's having dinner with his family, but said that certain interruptions were acceptable."

Within two minutes, the familiar voice of Jackson Tyler was speaking to Kershaw. "Bud, what is it?" Tyler said, still chewing on a morsel of food.

"Mr. President," Kershaw replied solemnly, "I hate to tell you this, but it looks like we have a positive detection of contamination at one of the Seattle area monitoring sites. I just got off the phone with Doctor Kennelly, and she is certain that her evaluation is accurate."

Kershaw heard the long and weighty sigh of a man with the weight of the world on his shoulders, followed by a one-word question, "Suggestions?"

"Mr. President, I realize that I am recommending the conservative approach, but I feel a public warning is warranted, and that it should be issued as soon as possible. The quicker the city is warned to not drink the municipal water, the more lives I believe will be saved."

"I hear you, Bud, but I want additional advice on this one. Are you in your office?" Tyler asked.

"Yes, I am."

"Fine. Please stay there. The Chief of Staff is still in the White House. I'll have him arrange a conference call with you and the others in about fifteen minutes."

"I'll be here."

"Good. Talk to you then," the president closed.

"Goodbye, sir."

As the call ended, Kershaw realized how little he envied the president's position. Although he wasn't exactly an admirer of the man, Kershaw nonetheless respected his courage in even wanting to assume the awesome responsibilities of the job. He sat back in his leather chair and, for the next fifteen minutes, pondered this latest turn of events and postulated where it might lead.

* * * * * * *

At the Cedar River Watershed Education Center, Lisa Kennelly had done a satisfactory job of shielding her concern from Craig Evans, but Robin Stoddard knew Lisa all too well and recognized the look on her face when she emerged from her private phone call with the admiral.

"Are you okay?" Robin asked, as Lisa approached.

"Fine," Lisa answered for Evans's benefit. "Robin, could you join me over at the equipment for a moment? Excuse us, Craig."

Evans nodded as the two scientists moved out of his hearing range.

"Robin, we have a positive indication of contamination at the Cedar Three site. Cedar Two is clean. We need to move the Cedar Three sensor upstream and Cedar Two downstream until we find the toxin introduction location. I want you to work together with Kurt to find the source ASAP."

"I'm right on it, Lisa," Robin said. "Don't worry, we'll find it."

"There's roughly a mile between the two sites," Lisa thought out loud. "I think moving the sensors in tenth-of-a-mile increments is appropriate. At fifteen minutes a sample, we should be within a couple of hundred yards of the toxin introduction point within an hour."

"Sounds like a plan," Robin agreed. "I'll call Kurt from the van and fill him in."

"Fine. Please keep me updated frequently, so I can keep Washington informed."

"Will do," Robin said as she turned to head for the front door.

* * * * * * *

The hastily arranged conference call began exactly fifteen minutes after Kershaw and the president hung up. Tyler and Clive

Donner were in the Oval Office. Lou Bernstein was home in his study. George Wilkes, who normally put in a seven-to-seven workday, was still in his office, as was Kershaw. The conversation lasted twenty minutes and was replete with disagreement, raised voices, and widely varying opinions on both the public reaction to an announcement concerning the contamination and the long-term political ramifications. Only Bud Kershaw seemed genuinely concerned with the Seattle area lives that were in jeopardy.

Jack Tyler weighed the opinions and alternatives carefully, then ended the argumentative conversation with the words, "Gentlemen, I've reached a decision."

The silence was immediate, as all of the advisors waited for the president's next words.

"At 7:15 this evening," Tyler started, "an announcement will be made from the White House press room, cautioning the residents of metropolitan Seattle to avoid any consumption, oral or otherwise, of municipal water until further notice. For now, we'll avoid details of the contamination problem." He turned to Donner while everyone else still listened over their respective speakerphones. "Get Marjorie Stone over here now and work on the precise wording of the statement," he said, referring to the on-duty White House spokesperson. "I want to approve the text within fifteen minutes."

"Yes, sir," Donner responded.

"That's all for now, gentlemen," Tyler said, again speaking directly into his speakerphone. "Bud, anything you find out, I want to know within minutes."

"Will do, Mr. President. Goodbye."

Everyone else on the line took their cue from Kershaw and hung up. When certain that there were no other listeners, Donner said to Tyler, "This won't make us any points in the polls you know."

"I know," Tyler said pensively, "but every now and then, you have to say screw the polls. This is just one of those times."

Donner nodded as he turned to walk away and work out the details of the press announcement. When Donner was gone, Tyler lowered his head into the palms of his hands and reflected. He had experienced this feeling before, many years ago on the ball field. He had come to the plate with the opportunity to win a critical playoff game with one swing of the bat. He had felt it was his destiny to win the game with a hit, but then the opposing pitcher intentionally walked him to face a less capable batter. The batter had struck out and the game was lost. Just like that moment so many years ago, control of the current situation had been taken out of his hands. His future as the country's leader was at risk, and there was little he could do about it. He mused briefly how externally controlled circumstances and events could do more to determine how history judged the success of a presidency than the competence of the president himself. He lamented a moment longer, then swiveled his chair and assumed his favorite Oval Office position, surveying the expanse of the White House lawn.

* * * * * * *

The call on this Tuesday evening from the terrorists to Glen Hargrove came later than the two previous calls. The phone rang at precisely 6:35 p.m.

After Glen's customary curt greeting, Ad-Faddil asked if all of the preparations were proceeding according to plan. Hargrove reassured the terrorist that the requested money had been assembled and that preparations to release the prisoners were likewise on schedule. Unaware of any of the recent developments in Seattle and Washington and the impending press announcement, Glen was being perfectly honest when he assured Ad-Faddil that knowledge of the toxin crisis was being closely held by a very small group of presidential advisors.

Ad-Faddil acknowledged, then said, "As for the delivery of the money, the transfer is to take place at the Seattle Aquarium, Pier 59 on the waterfront. There is a circular room surrounded by a fish tank. Ensure your courier is there at precisely nine o'clock. Have her wear a yellow dress and carry an umbrella, and of course make certain she has the money in her possession. Do you understand?"

Glen answered in the affirmative. He thought that the conversation was nearly over, as all of the details of the terrorists' demands had now been specified. Then Ad-Faddil dropped yet another bombshell. "By the way, Hargrove, we've added an additional criterion for release of the toxin. We know that your wife is in Seattle and that she is staying at the home of her parents. If for some reason she leaves the city, the reservoirs will be contaminated." Ad-Faddil paused and awaited a response, which was not immediately forthcoming.

On the other end of the line, Glen could not believe what he was hearing. The "how on earth" question he asked himself during the pause, which was only a moment but seemed like an hour, led only to some sort of White House connection. As the incredulity passed, Glen became paralyzed by the pronouncement. Within a few hours, e-tickets for a flight to Boston were to be delivered to Jennifer and her parents. He needed to end this call and get Kershaw to stop

Harry Boland from carrying out the plan. He finally responded to the terrorist. "I understand."

"Good. That's all for now," Ad-Faddil said and hung up.

Immediately, Glen called Bud Kershaw at home, to discover from Eileen that he was still at work. Glen thought it odd that Bud was still working, considering that two hours ago he was planning to host a supper, but the thought was fleeting. Glen thanked Eileen for the information, ended the call, and called Kershaw's office. The line was busy. Glen redialed the number at least twenty times during the next ten minutes, but the line remained busy. His frustration and concern grew with each attempt.

* * * * * * *

Lisa Kennelly was upset that she hadn't thought of the experiment earlier. The night before had been hectic. She had made all of her group's travel arrangements, calibrated the biosensors, treated the optical fibers, and packed all of the equipment, in addition to her personal effects. There was a remote possibility that in her haste, she had made an error in the calibration procedure for one of the sensors.

The idea for the test came to her after both sensors, Cedar Two and Cedar Three, had been moved once with no change in the results. She called Robin first, then Kurt, and told them to meet halfway between the original monitoring sites, sample the identical water, and transmit the results.

Ten minutes after the phone calls, Robin and Kurt were ready for the test. The two decided that in order to be absolutely certain of the results, the Cedar Three sensor should analyze the water at a site slightly upstream of the Cedar Two site. The two samples were taken and the results transmitted.

As the results were displayed on the computer terminal, Lisa didn't know whether to feel relief or apprehension. The upstream sensor was now indicating the presence of toxin while the downstream sensor showed none. The impossible combination of readings indicated that a sensor was in fact out of calibration. She pushed both emotions to the back of her mind and again retreated to a private office to call Admiral Kershaw, hoping that any action he had taken based on her first report could still be reversed.

* * * * * * *

All of the network and cable news anchors were informed of the press statement only moments before their 7:00 p.m. programs. Those for whom the seven o'clock program is a rebroadcast decided to run the news live a second time to accommodate what was obviously an important breaking story.

At 7:13, spokesperson Marjorie Stone entered the White House press room and greeted the assembly of fifteen television, newspaper, and wire service journalists. Far fewer were present than would normally be present for such an event because of the short notice. As Ms. Stone approached the podium with her notes in hand, a reporter from the *Baltimore Sun* asked her about the subject matter of the statement. She replied that the statement dealt with an environmental concern in the state of Washington and that nothing more would be said until the cameras were rolling.

At precisely 7:14 and 30 seconds, each of the news organizations cut to the press room in time to view an out-of-breath White House staffer approach Marjorie Stone and speak for thirty seconds into her ear. As the staffer departed, Ms. Stone cleared her throat and presented her new, extemporaneously revised statement.

"Ladies and gentlemen of the press," she began, "at this time, it was my intention to address a certain domestic situation of national concern. However, I have just been informed that the circumstances surrounding this situation have changed and that there is no longer the need for a statement to the public at this time. I apologize for bringing you all here for this false alarm and assure you that if the circumstances again warrant a statement, the press will be informed and hopefully given more notice than you were given this time. Please disregard any comments I made before this official statement. Again, thank you. That is all."

As Marjorie Stone left the podium, she received a barrage of questions from all directions, to which she replied, "I have nothing more to say." Of the journalists present, only Nathan Crowe was silent, his mind already focused on the content of the short article about a curious Washington State environmental situation and an aborted press conference, which within forty-five minutes would be electronically transmitted to the AP's subscribers around the country.

* * * * * * *

The follow-up call to the president from Bud Kershaw hadn't reached him in time to stop completely the forward motion of the press statement. He relayed to Tyler how an embarrassed Lisa Kennelly had called a second time to say that the positive biosensor reading was the result of an equipment calibration error and to express her deep regret at passing on the misinformation. Kershaw explained that he was partially to blame for having rushed Lisa's preparations. Both he and the president verbally shared the hope that no damage would result from the aborted statement to the press.

As soon as Kershaw hung up with the president, Glen Hargrove finally got his call through.

"You've been on the phone forever, Bud," Glen said with obvious frustration in his voice.

"I know," Kershaw said. "It's been a rather tense hour. You wouldn't believe what's been . . ."

"They know Jen's in Seattle," Glen interrupted, deciding that his news was the more important.

"What?!" Kershaw exclaimed, shifting the phone to the opposite ear.

"Somehow, the terrorists found out Jennifer is in Seattle. They've added a new rule to the list. Jen leaves Seattle, the toxin gets released."

"But how the . . ."

Glen again interrupted, "It has to be someone in the White House. No one knows except you, me, a few of my associates, and the people at these morning meetings in the Oval Office."

"I wouldn't be too quick to jump on the president's staff, Glen. People have ways of finding things out. Jen didn't head out there under cover, you know." Kershaw paused briefly to ponder Glen's assertion. "We will, however, bring the matter up at tomorrow's meeting and observe faces for a reaction."

"I take it you'll call Harry Boland and call off the delivery," Glen said, dejected.

"I guess I'll have to. I'm awfully sorry. I thought we had a solid plan."

"Me too."

"Any other surprises from these people?" Kershaw asked, purposefully changing the subject.

"Not much," Glen replied. "They gave me a few more specifics on the rendezvous. They want to have the money transferred at the Seattle Aquarium, and they want our courier dressed up like the Morton Salt girl."

"Anything else?"

"No. They wanted the same old assurance that everything was coming together according to their directions, and I gave it to them." Glen remembered that Bud had said something earlier about a tense hour. "Now what was this you've been up to lately?"

"It's a bit of a long story, and it looks like everything will turn out without incident, so there's no use bending your ear about it. You've got enough on your mind. Besides, you've got a busy evening ahead of you, and Eileen is probably beginning to wonder if I'm anchored to my desk for the night."

"No doubt," Glen said, realizing that, due to work requirements, the trend of sleeplessness could very well continue for a fourth straight night.

"Call me at home if there are any breakthroughs," Kershaw urged.

"I will," Glen said. "So long, Bud."

"Good night, Glen."

Bud Kershaw had a couple of loose ends to tie together before he headed home. When his call to Harry Boland's cell phone went to voicemail, he called the police station phone number given to him earlier by Boland. The officer who answered the phone indicated that both civilian visitors were out of the office for the time being and offered to take a message. Kershaw left the message for Boland to cancel the airline e-ticket delivery and to call him at home when he arrived back at the station for further details. Next, Kershaw called Rudy Moss to determine if he had found out any more on Jack Broussard. After listening to a new and equally amusing answering machine message, Kershaw started to leave a message when Moss picked up.

"I'm here, Bud. I screen my calls after working hours."

"Good, Rudy. It's been a busy day, and I've been on the phone a lot. I wasn't sure whether you called or not."

"I hadn't but I was about to call soon," Moss said. "We may have something on this Broussard character. It's not much, but it's worth mentioning. He does live in the D.C. area—the Maryland suburbs to be precise—but he has an unlisted phone number. I finally tracked him down through a travel agency. It seems that over the past five months, he's made three trips to Egypt. I couldn't find out anything about why he went or what he did while he was there, only that each of his visits lasted about a week."

"Anything else?" Kershaw asked.

"Not really, but I'm still working the problem."

"Okay, Rudy, thanks for the update."

"You bet, Bud."

After hanging up, Kershaw pondered the Broussard trips. Egypt was becoming more of a tourist destination, but it was doubtful that anyone would go on three sightseeing trips to the same destination within so short a time frame. The purpose of the visits could have been business. But what business could an immunotoxicologist have in Egypt? Kershaw didn't picture Egypt as a haven for the world's great scientific minds in this field. He remembered what Glen had said in his notes about Broussard's technology thievery. Perhaps Egypt was the country where technology-for-money exchanges were being made. The longer Kershaw thought about it, the more possible motives for Broussard's trips came to mind. As he grabbed his cap and headed out of the office, however, a single motivation for the visits dominated his thoughts. What better place than Egypt to secure the services of mercenary terrorists for the purpose of destroying a professional rival and embarrassing the US Government in the process. Maybe Broussard was behind this whole mess. However, finding him and coercing him to stop the ever-progressing series of events in Seattle would at this point be next to impossible.

* * * * * * *

Scoop Scanlon sat in his partitioned cubicle at the *Seattle Times* fuming at his misfortune of the morning. If it hadn't been for the train, he would have been able to tail Cushman, the kid, and the visitors to wherever it was they went. He was certain they were headed out toward the Cascades, but he had no idea why. In the past, his efforts to gather information for a story had been stymied more than once. However, this time he was particularly frustrated because at each turn, there was a new obstruction blocking his path. He had been so unnerved by the railroad crossing incident that afterward, he hastily drove his Focus straight back to the office, picking up a reckless driving citation and a crunched front right fender along the way. These mementos of his trip to Bothell only added to his outrage.

Now at 5:00 p.m. Pacific Time, his fury had diminished and he was reluctantly starting to accept a rare defeat. His lamentations were interrupted by the voice of the reporter in the next cubicle, Pete Winters, speaking over the partition.

"What's the matter with you, Scanlon? You've been moaning and cursing your luck for the past two hours. Just give it up."

"I'm about to, Winters. It's just that I can usually make my own breaks, and I failed miserably on this story."

Winters walked around the partition and said, "Some days you ride the elevator. Other days you just get the shaft."

Scanlon chuckled. "It's been a shaft sort of day," he said as he started paging through the latest AP articles on the computer, his last planned event before calling it a night.

At first, in his haste to end what had thus far been a miserable day, Scanlon paged right past the article. Then two articles later, the phrases "Washington State" and "environmental situation" had their delayed mind-jogging effect. He paged back two articles and read aloud the text slowly and carefully, absorbing its total significance. Somehow, he knew there was a connection with Cushman's secretive mission, but there were not enough details in the article to confirm his suspicion.

"I'll bet that's what that lady and her team are doing out here in Seattle." It took a moment for the focused Scanlon to register the words spoken by Winters from behind his back. When Winters's comment finally hit home, he turned and asked, "What on earth are you talking about?"

"On the plane back from D.C. today, the whole row behind me was full of scientists on their way out here to do some water sampling. Just a minute," Winters said as he reached into his shirt pocket for the three-by-five card with his notes from the flight. "I didn't understand much of what they were saying, but it sounded important so I jotted a few things down. The leader, a real looker in her thirties, did all of the talking. She said something about a network of sensors that uses telecommunications links to send data to, catch this, its mother."

"What else? What else did she say?" Scanlon asked, intent on pumping Winters for every shred of information he overheard.

"Well," Winters continued, "she said the team would be working six-hour shifts around the clock . . ."

"Doing what?" the weasel interrupted, his appetite for information apparently insatiable.

"Calm down," Winters chided Scanlon. "I'll get to everything. The people on duty were going to move about between the different sites where these sensors were located, sample the water, analyze it, and transmit the data. She didn't say anything about where these sites were located, why they were sampling the water, or what kind of data they were sending."

"How about names?" Scanlon asked. "Did she mention any names?"

"Only two, and one's just a title. At one point, she talked on her phone to somebody she called 'Admiral.' The other was the name of a point of contact at Seattle Water Management given to her by this admiral. His name is Craig Evans, and he works on the 49th floor of the Seattle Municipal Tower over on 5th Avenue."

"That's just a few blocks from here," Scanlon said excitedly. "Anything else, Winters?"

"Not really. Most of the time they just read or listened to music. You pretty much know what I know."

"Thanks a million, Winters. You've helped salvage what until now has been a very bad day." Scanlon glanced at his watch and realized he had to move quickly if he wanted to catch anyone still working. He pressed the PRINT key on the computer, rose from his chair, and patted Winters on the shoulder as he grabbed his jacket and left the cubicle. "Gotta run," he said as he headed toward the printer room to pick up his paper copy of the AP article.

* * * * * * *

Twelve miles to the northeast in Bothell, Harry Boland arrived back at the police station, dejected from his futile visits to over twenty Bellevue hotels and motels and tired from jet lag. When he and Bernie Cushman had arrived in Bellevue, they decided to split up to cover more ground. Cushman had visited another fifteen places of lodging with similar results. No one in their travels recognized the two faces in the composite computer drawings.

Cushman tried to console Boland. "Metropolitan Seattle's a big place, and there's no guarantee these guys are even staying in a hotel. We both knew today's hunt was a crap shoot."

"You're right, Bernie," Boland lamented. "But that doesn't make failure an easier pill to swallow."

"Maybe Darrell had some luck with the rental car agency," Cushman added.

"I hope so. It's time we had another break." Boland looked at his watch. "Say, weren't you supposed to go off shift two hours ago?"

"Yeah," Cushman said, "but this is too important to worry about punching a clock. I'm here while you're here."

Boland was impressed with Cushman's attitude. In his years at the DSS, he had run into many police officers who only cared about putting in their time and collecting their paychecks. Cushman was obviously a different brand of cop.

During this thought, Wolczyk and Joey walked through the front door of the station building. Boland could tell from the looks on their faces that their afternoon was about as successful as his was. "No luck?" he asked.

"Nothing with our hotel search over in Redmond and Kirkland," Wolczyk answered. "I think tracing the car's renter is still our best bet, but my efforts were stymied, at least for today."

"What do you mean?" Boland asked, making himself comfortable in one of the cubicle chairs.

"I got the information on the renter from Avis. His name is James Johnson. They gave me an address, which I visited, but he doesn't live there anymore. The most important piece of information I got was Johnson's credit card number. I determined it was a Bank of America Visa card. We need to stop at the BoA Financial Center downtown first thing in the morning and get copies of his statements for the past couple of months. Maybe he arranged a place to stay for these guys and paid for it with the same card." Wolczyk concluded, "I would have done it today, but they close early."

"Sounds good," Boland commented. "I just hope we're not losing too much precious time between now and then."

"It's out of our hands; you know bankers' hours," Wolczyk retorted cynically. "Besides, I don't know about you, but I'm not sure how much longer I can function intelligently today."

"Right," Boland agreed. "My clock's out of whack too. Okay, let's sit down and set up an agenda for tomorrow. Then we have a small errand to run in Kirkland before we call it . . ."

"Excuse me . . ." His statement was interrupted by an officer whom he had not previously met coming around the partition to Cushman's cubicle. "Is one of you two gentlemen Harry Boland?"

Boland waved a hand to identify himself, and the officer handed him a message, then departed. Boland read the message out loud. "Don't deliver e-tickets as previously discussed. Call me when you get back to the station. Kershaw."

"Speaking of our errand, sounds like something's come up," Wolczyk said.

The confused looks on the faces of Cushman and Caviletti would remain. They did not need to know anything about a plan to get Hargrove's wife out of Seattle.

Boland dialed Kershaw, while the others sat and listened.

"Bud, Harry," Boland said after Kershaw answered. "Got your message. What's going on?"

"Can we talk freely?"

"No problem. I'll be cryptic when I need to be."

"Harry, no one around here knows how it happened, but the terrorists have found out that Glen Hargrove's wife is in Seattle.

They've threatened to release the toxin if she leaves the city. Obviously, we have to call off the plan to get her out."

"Any idea of the source of the leak?" Boland questioned.

"No, only a few people were aware of her whereabouts. Glen thinks someone in the White House may be the problem."

"Sounds serious."

"I'm not so sure I agree with him," Kershaw said. "But I don't have any better ideas."

"All right, the delivery is off," Boland concluded. "Now I have a few things for you if you have some time."

"Absolutely. Shoot," Kershaw said.

"First, our young friend Joey came up with some decent composites of the terrorists. All of us have been out for the past two hours with the pictures checking the hotels and motels, but we haven't had much luck. No one seems to recognize these characters."

"Send me scans of the sketches," Kershaw suggested. "I can't do much to help you track the men down, but maybe we can get Langley to ID them."

"All right. They'll be on their way soon."

"Great. You mentioned the terrorists' rental car earlier today. Any progress?" Kershaw asked.

"Some, but we came to a standstill this afternoon. Darrell got the renter's name and address. Unfortunately, the address is an old one. He also got the credit card number used to rent the car. It's a Bank of America Visa, but the bank's financial offices are closed until morning and all client information has to be transferred in person. Our first priority tomorrow is to get a copy of the guy's recent credit transactions. We're keeping our fingers crossed that he's the same person who arranged for lodging and that he paid for it the same way. It's a long shot, but it's the best lead we have for now."

Kershaw got very serious as he moved on to his next subject. "I've debated whether to even tell you about this next incident because as far as I know, it's over and nothing will come of it. However, it does re-emphasize the importance of your mission. A couple hours ago, one of the sensors at our toxin monitoring stations got a positive detection. It was reported to me, and I called the president. The senior scientist informed me that the detection was a false alarm just in time to prevent what would have been a disastrous press announcement about a deadly pollutant in the Seattle water supply."

"Close call. If that announcement had been broadcast, the water would have been contaminated in short order, and we couldn't have prevented it because we don't know where the terrorists or the other toxin canisters are."

"Exactly," Kershaw reiterated. "That's why it's critical that you find these criminals . . . tomorrow. The time and place of the rendezvous to transfer the specified amount of money has been set. It will be Thursday, 9:00 a.m. your time, at the Seattle Aquarium."

"So someone gives them the money and they call off the action," Boland suggested, unaware of the full extent of the terrorists' demands.

"I wish it were that simple," Kershaw bemoaned. "They've also asked that their friends in prison for the Chicago and Baltimore bombing plots be released. This morning, Tyler showed signs of relenting on his stance against releasing terrorists in prison, but I still feel he'll play hardball. The more I think about it, the more I'm convinced that the only way out of this situation free and clear is if your team manages to find these men and stop them from carrying out their insane plan."

Harry Boland really didn't need any more pressure put on his shoulders right now, but that is what just happened. "Bud, I assure you we're doing all we can," he said defensively. "It's not easy finding two people in a metropolitan area with millions, but we're getting closer. Tomorrow will be an all-out effort to find them and stop them in their tracks."

"That's all I'm asking, Harry. I know you and Darrell will give it your best. Take care now and rest up for tomorrow."

"We will. Have a good night yourself."

Boland closed his eyes and shook his head as the call ended. "We don't get paid enough for this, Darrell."

"You got that right," Wolczyk concurred.

The foursome spent another ten minutes setting up the Wednesday agenda, decided on an early start at about 7:45, and broke for the evening.

* * * * * * *

The receptionist at the Seattle Public Utilities offices had never dealt with anyone as obnoxious as the newspaper reporter who was now asking for the third time, "Where is Craig Evans? I want to see Evans."

"Mr. Evans is not here," the receptionist answered for the third time, only slightly agitated by Scanlon's rude persistence. "He's currently in the field. I am not aware of his precise location, and I don't expect him to report in until morning."

Finally, Scanlon asked to see Evans's immediate superior.

"One moment, sir," she said, immediately regretting having extended the courtesy of calling the irritating man "sir." She dialed a three-digit number at her terminal and when the ring was answered, said, "Mr. Halverson, there's a newspaper reporter here to see Mr. Evans. I told him that Mr. Evans was out, so he insists upon seeing you."

The receptionist stopped talking for a moment, obviously receiving a response from Halverson, then said, "Sir, I don't believe he will leave until he talks with someone other than me."

A moment later, she tapped the end call button and directed Scanlon to a seat.

Marv Halverson was used to dealing with reporters. As Director of the Seattle Public Utilities Water Management Branch, he was the media representative whenever the local water supply made the news, which due to the water's excellent reputation for quality was infrequent. He didn't know why the press was in the Department's offices today, but he decided to make this reporter sweat for ten minutes for being so impudent and stubborn. He remembered receiving a note from Craig Evans earlier in the day and rifled through his cluttered desk until he found it. The note stated that Evans would be helping some scientists from Washington, D.C. perform some random water samplings and routine analyses around the region, and that he would be spending considerable time in the field over the next few days.

Halverson trusted Evans completely, and the project sounded innocent enough. He decided to be civil with the reporter but to withhold comment on any accusations he might present.

Precisely ten minutes after his conversation with the receptionist ended, Halverson arrived in the lobby to find a restless and slightly seething reporter with whom he had never had a prior encounter.

He extended his hand and introduced himself. "Marvin Halverson, how may I help you, Mr. . . ."

"Scanlon. Listen here, Haverman," Scanlon started, without returning the handshake, "you've got a water crisis on your hands, and the public has a right to know. Now, are you going to tell me what's going on or am I going to have to find out what you're hiding some other way?"

As Halverson lowered his hand, he counted two strikes against Scanlon in the first five seconds of their conversation. He had a hard time respecting someone who didn't have the common courtesy to shake an offered hand or get a person's name right immediately after being introduced. Then this presumptuous and arrogant little twit had the audacity to threaten him. Strike three. He felt like throwing Scanlon out of the office without a response but bit his tongue and tried to remain calm. "I'm sure I have no idea what you're talking about, Mr. Scanlon. We have no problems with our water whatsoever."

"Wrong answer." Scanlon was now ranting, gesticulating wildly with one hand and pointing a crooked index finger at Halverson with the other. "I have evidence that several scientists flew out from Washington, D.C. today to find out what's polluting or going to pollute the water supply and that the Federal Government, the Bothell Police Department, and your Mr. Craig Evans are trying to cover up the fact that there's a problem. Now, one way or another, the people of this city are going to find out about this."

Halverson had just about dismissed Scanlon as a raving lunatic. Then he remembered that this lunatic had direct access to the minds of the citizens of Seattle, and that fact scared him to death. He mustered one more ounce of self-control for his final statement. "Mr. Scanlon, for the last time, I assure you that if there were a problem with this city's water, I would be the first to be informed. Now, this conversation has continued much too long already. I have business to take care of before I go home, so if you will excuse me, I think you can find your own way to the door."

Scanlon got in the last word as Halverson turned to head back to his office. "The people will find out what's going on here, and I'll be the one to tell them." He then left the Seattle Municipal Tower and headed back to the *Times* Building.

When Halverson arrived back in his office, he immediately called the number of the Cedar River Watershed Education Center. He had no idea where Craig Evans was, but he figured there was a reasonable chance that he was there. His hunch was correct.

"Hello, Mr. Halverson," Evans said when handed the phone by one of the on-shift supervisors.

"Craig, is everything okay out there?" Halverson asked.

"Yes, sir, I believe so. What exactly do you mean?"

"A newspaper reporter was just here making accusations about pollutants in our water supply. Are you sure these people from D.C. are leveling with you?"

"Absolutely, Mr. Halverson. Their tests are strictly routine, and so far, everything is turning up normal. You and I both know our own quality checks would find any contamination in the water."

"Of course you're right. I just wanted to make sure this guy's allegations were unfounded," Halverson said.

"I'm sure he's been misinformed, sir. Anything else?" Evans asked.

"No. Thanks, Craig. That's all. Have a good evening."

"You too, sir. Good night."

As he hung up, Halverson reflected on the events of the past half hour. He believed that there were few things more dangerous than a self-righteous reporter who passed on to the public misinformation that he perceived was truth. He hoped Scanlon would come to his senses. His hope would be in vain.

* * * * * * *

Glen Hargrove arrived back at the NMRC laboratory at around 8:30 p.m. and briefed his team of researchers on recent events that were critical to their efforts to develop a treatment for the biotoxin. He told them of Jim Thunderhill's amazing immunity to the toxin and how Cheryl Forrester was at the hospital with Jim, trying to pinpoint a reason for his unusual response. Meanwhile, it was their job at the lab to proceed along the path Cheryl had prescribed earlier, that path being to isolate a substance, possibly a treated derivative of the toxin itself, that would cause the human immune system to destroy the parent organism quickly and efficiently.

Glen started a fresh pot of coffee brewing and settled in for a long evening of intensive research and experimentation.

* * * * * * *

Shortly after Glen Hargrove briefed his researchers at NMRC, Scanlon arrived back at his desk in the *Times* Building. His first order of business was to call the Bothell Police Department and confront Cushman with his recently obtained evidence. He was dismayed to find out that Cushman had left only a few minutes prior to his call but pleased to discover that he was speaking with Cushman's immediate superior.

On the other end of the line, Lieutenant Bill Brewster was picking the caked mud out of his golf cleats with a tee while he held the phone between his cheek and shoulder. He had played a mediocre round during the afternoon, so he was neither gleeful nor glum. As Scanlon began his tirade criticizing the department's cover-up of a major environmental crisis, however, Brewster's mood turned serious. He put his golf shoes down and listened carefully. When the reporter finished his speech with the question, "Do you confirm or deny that the department is aware of this situation?" Brewster was more than a bit flustered. He cleared his throat for at least fifteen seconds during which time he fashioned a response indicative of the true bureaucrat that he was.

"Mr. Scanlon," Brewster began, "my position within this department requires that I be informed of all incidents of the nature you describe. I am certain that if Officer Cushman were pursuing such a case, his first action would be to brief me on the events to date and his proposed plan. I can assure you that it is not the practice of this department to withhold information concerning a situation that could jeopardize the public safety. Therefore, I state with full confidence that the situation to which you are referring does not exist. Confirmation or denial of our awareness of the situation is therefore a moot point."

Scanlon didn't buy Brewster's line for a minute. He didn't know whether Brewster was being kept in the dark by Cushman or was part of the cover-up. It didn't really matter though. Despite the denials of a crisis by Water Management and the Bothell Police, Scanlon already had most of the pieces of the jigsaw puzzle. He needed to merely put the pieces he had together and write his story. As soon as tomorrow's *Times* hit the streets, the rest of the pieces would fall into place quickly. He would be a hero for exposing the cover-up of a serious environmental situation at both the national and local levels. There would undoubtedly be serious accolades, a promotion, and maybe even a book deal. Scanlon ended the conversation with Brewster by saying, "We'll see about that." He hung up without a goodbye and turned to his computer terminal to begin writing.

As Brewster hung up his phone, he mentally labeled Scanlon an idiot and returned to the important process of preparing his golf shoes for tomorrow's round. Unlike his more competent counterpart at Seattle Public Utilities, Brewster did not place a call to his subordinate in order to validate or disprove the reporter's claims.

As Scanlon's fingers started tapping out the words of his story, he recalled the AP article from the previous evening about the president's canceled trip to Savannah, Georgia, and decided that the change of plans was also related to the Seattle crisis. The words flowed nicely as all of the puzzle pieces fell neatly into place. It took about an hour for the article to come together to Scanlon's satisfaction. He spell-checked, then printed a paper copy and reviewed the text a final time, making a couple of last-minute grammatical changes. The normal submission deadline for the morning edition was 8:00 p.m. He had a half hour to spare.

The only hitch was his section editor's endorsement, which in this day and age of computers, was a confidential code that indicated approval and forwarded the article to the layout department. Two months before, as Scanlon was rifling through his vacationing editor's desk for a lost memo, he stumbled upon the four-digit code underneath the desk blotter. Figuring that the information would come in handy at some point, he copied down the code.

The time had come to use the pilfered information. The section editor usually gave Scanlon a fair amount of leeway with his stories. However, this one might be perceived to contain too much conjecture for his liking. Therefore, Scanlon decided to apply the adage "it's easier to get forgiveness than permission." He felt only slightly uncomfortable in bypassing his section editor, because tomorrow the entire staff, including the publisher himself, would be offering congratulations on an exceptional piece of investigative reporting.

Scanlon saved the final version of the story, then transferred the file to the section editor's directory for articles awaiting approval. He scurried into the editor's office, now vacant for more than an hour, and powered up the computer terminal, which was the only terminal that would recognize the approval code. He accessed the file for his own article, then clicked the mouse on the *Approve/Forward* menu item. When prompted by the "Enter Approval Code" message on the screen, he typed in the four-digit alphanumeric code and hit the *Enter* key. His correct entry was rewarded with the screen message "Article Forwarded." After turning off the section editor's terminal and office lights, Scanlon returned to his own cubicle, where he placed a call to the layout department.

"Is Russo there?" he asked when his ring was answered.

"Just a minute," the impassive voice on the other end of the line answered.

Russo was on the phone ten seconds later. "Hello."

"Hey, my friend, it's Scanlon here."

"What do you want, Scanlon?" Russo asked, his tone indicating that the friendship was not exactly mutual.

"An article of mine was just sent over to you," Scanlon said, being careful to use the passive voice to conceal his deception. "Can you get me on page 1?"

"No way, Scanlon. Even if I had room left, you know everything on page 1 gets the boss's okay," Russo replied, referring to a privilege reserved for the editor-in-chief. "How long is the story?"

"About ten inches, single column."

"All right. I've got two five-inch columns available for you near the bottom of page 2."

"Thanks, Russo."

"Yeah, so long."

His work completed, Scanlon propped his feet up on his desk and imagined the expressions of Cushman, Evans, and everyone else who was party to the cover-up when they read his article the next morning. He guessed that before noon, there would be a full disclosure of the pending crisis by both water and police departments. He just knew that heads were going to roll. He was right about that, but wrong about which ones.

* * * * * * *

"All right, Jim, let's go through your day one more time," Cheryl Forrester said, tired and frustrated at the lack of significant progress toward finding why Jim Thunderhill's body successfully resisted the virulent toxic organism.

Over the past several hours, Cheryl had become familiar with every aspect of this Navajo-turned-naval officer's life, past and present, and had undoubtedly surpassed his mother in terms of knowledge of her son. Cheryl had learned about his ancestry going back several generations and how his parents had been the first in the family to attempt to integrate a child into the broader society. She had been fascinated by his upbringing on the Ramah Reservation, his experiences at public school, and the amazing story behind his appointment to the Naval Academy. She had learned about his Annapolis years and his career path to NMRC. Of more recent note, she had learned all about his daily routine, from the moment he opened his eyes in the morning to the moment they closed again sixteen hours later. She had analyzed what he ate, drank, and otherwise consumed; where he spent his time outside of working hours; whom he saw; and what he did for relaxation. She had been over his medical record several times looking for hints. Now at 11:30 p.m. Eastern Time, fatigue and the tedium of the question-and-answer process were causing her to lose her focus.

"All right," Jim started, also showing signs of frustration. "I get up at 6:15, throw on a robe and slippers, go downstairs, and feed the cat. I start a pot of coffee—Maxwell House—never another brand. Then I go upstairs and take a shower, being sure to take the robe and slippers off before I get in."

As Jim continued to recount his morning routine, he instinctively reached into the pocket of his hospital robe and pulled out a small wad of a brownish, pasty substance wrapped in cellophane. He opened the wrapper, pulled off a piece the size of a dime, and put it under his tongue.

Cheryl looked up from her notes in time to catch the last part of the routine. "Jim! I didn't know you chewed. That stuff will kill you."

Jim laughed off her disapproval. "It's not tobacco, Cheryl. Actually, the stuff is quite sweet. I suck on it four or five times a day, and it curbs my appetite for sugar."

"What is it?" Cheryl asked.

"I don't really know. My mother sends me a supply once a month. I think she makes it from some root she gets out of the New Mexican desert."

Cheryl's curiosity was now piqued. "Jim," she said, "didn't it occur to you once during the past five hours that this little ritual of yours with the nasty-looking sweet stuff could have something to do with your immunity to the toxin?"

"Not at all," Jim said frankly. "If our roles were reversed and you ate four or five breath mints a day, would you have thought to mention it to me?"

"No, but . . ."

"That's all I've ever considered this stuff—a cheap alternative to store-bought candy. I've been sucking on it for as long as I can remember. Of course, now that you've made the connection, I agree that maybe we should investigate it further."

"I'm glad you agree," Cheryl said, a little miffed at being interrupted while making a point. "Okay, tell me everything you can remember about this alternative to Tic Tacs."

"There's really not much to tell. When I was a kid, my little sister and I each had a sweet tooth like most other kids on the reservation. Now and then, some of the kids were allowed to eat a real candy bar, like a Snickers or a Milky Way, but Mom had strict rules about what sis and I ate. We had three square meals a day, and the only treats we were allowed to eat were these hard doughy sticks that she made—they tasted like sweet pretzels—and this stuff." Jim pointed to the still open cellophane wrapper with the pasty substance.

Cheryl took another look at the tobacco-like matter and made an expression like she was gagging. "You're sure that stuff is really sweet?"

"Absolutely. Want to try some?" Jim asked.

Cheryl declined without saying a word. Her face said it all. "Tell me, did your mother ever mention whether or not this root had any medicinal value?"

"Not to me. Kids don't care much about what's good for you. We just wanted something that tasted good. I guess by the time I was old enough for that argument to make sense, I was already hooked on the stuff. It's been a habit ever since."

During the previous few minutes of the conversation, Cheryl had been reviewing Jim's medical record once again. "You know, Jim, you have a remarkable health history. This has to be the thinnest medical record for a lieutenant I've ever seen. How many doctor visits have you had since you graduated?"

Jim thought for a moment. "Other than physicals and shots, I don't think I've ever been to the doctor . . . until this trip."

"I believe it. What about your sister; do you know anything about her medical history?"

"I don't think she's ever been seriously ill, but I don't see her enough to know the details of her health," Jim admitted.

"How about your parents? They're probably in their late forties or fifties, right? Are they in good health?"

"As far as I know. Do you really think this root paste is responsible for my family's good health and my immunity to the toxin?" Jim asked.

"I really don't know," Cheryl answered. "But I do know that it's almost midnight and we have nothing better to go on."

"What do you suggest?" Jim asked.

"If you can live without the remainder of your wad," Cheryl said, pointing to the substance, "I'd like to take it back to the lab and run some tests on it."

"It's yours," Jim said, wrapping the root paste back up and handing it to her. "There's a lot more where it came from."

"You're here for the night?" Cheryl asked.

"Hospital policy. Hopefully, I can be back to work early tomorrow, assuming I don't have a relapse."

"Somehow I don't think you will. Enjoy your sleep, Jim. You'll be the only one getting any tonight."

"Good night, Cheryl, and good luck."

Cheryl got up from her chair and immediately realized from the stiffness in her body that it had been hours since she'd moved. After stretching her tightened muscles, she closed her note pad and returned it and the pencil to her pocketbook. She dragged the chair back to the corner from where it came, turned and smiled at Jim, then left the room.

* * * * * * *

Harry Boland had suggested to Darrell Wolczyk that they each enjoy a two-inch-thick steak and a beer before turning in for the night. Wolczyk merely licked his chops in reply. They hunted down the Seattle Ruth's Chris Steak House on Pine Street and, like the night before, requested a secluded table so they could talk freely.

They shared small talk until the beers came, then Boland asked, "Well, Darrell, what do you think our chances are of finding these guys tomorrow and stopping them?"

"I'd be a liar if I told you I thought they were good," Wolczyk answered.

"I'd like to disagree with you," Boland retorted, "but I can't. Too many things have to fall into place, and they're not just a bunch of random happenings. Each event depends on the outcome of the previous event."

"Exactly," Darrell agreed.

"First, we have to have the bank's complete cooperation in giving us the documents we need," Boland continued. "Next, we're counting on Johnson having used the same card he used for the car to make payment on a hotel or house for his friends to use as a base of operations while they do their dirty work."

"A professional wouldn't do that," Wolczyk argued.

"Probably not, but a true professional would have covered his tracks better than Johnson has done so far. You never know, he may have slipped up more than once, figuring no one would ever get this close."

"Okay, so we'll assume this Visa statement lists an advanced payment for some form of lodging," Wolczyk continued the train of thought. "We're still a long way from pulling all of the toxin bottles out of all the reservoirs."

"Right," Boland commented. "Next, we visit this place of lodging. If it's a hotel or motel, we have to be fortunate enough to find a cooperative desk clerk. We find out all we can about the comings and goings of these guys, if of course they haven't checked out and gone somewhere else."

"And if it's a house," Wolczyk continued, "we stake out the place and find the information ourselves."

Boland's tone got sarcastic. "So now we're lucky enough to find who we're looking for. All that remains is the trivial little task of preventing them from releasing their toxic sludge into the reservoirs, which according to Bud Kershaw, could very well be in automatic. They just sit around and do nothing. Then when all of their demands aren't met on time, the stuff gets released with no further action on their part."

"We'd make a move before then," Wolczyk protested.

"We have to be careful about that, Darrell. Even if there is only a small probability of successful negotiation remaining, we need to keep a low profile. Otherwise, this water supply is history. Remember the timing device on the canister we found? With today's technology, it may only require a signal from a cell phone to dump the contents. It's too dangerous to let them know we're onto them unless it's the absolute last resort."

"I suppose you're right," Wolczyk agreed. "I hate being helpless."

"Me too, but I don't see that we have a choice. We can't make a move until they make a definitive move first. And that will be a tough one to call."

The server delivered two delightful-looking filets, medium rare, with baked potatoes smothered in butter and sour cream on the side. With their strategy about as solid as wet concrete, the two agents concluded that tomorrow would likely turn out totally different from the way they had just envisioned it. They decided to take the day a step at a time and, for now, to enjoy their dinners. For some strange reason, both felt like prisoners being served their last meals before execution. They banished the thought and dug into their food.

* * * * * * *

By the time Cheryl arrived back at the NMRC lab, Glen had collapsed on his desk from exhaustion. Although the rest of the research crew was going through the motions of productive work, none was at full mental capacity. While she hated to disturb Glen, realizing certain events that he would not disclose had deprived him of sleep for the past several nights, Cheryl felt she had to give him an update on her progress at the hospital. She shook his shoulder gently while calling his name.

After hearing his name the third time—the first two times, he was called by some dream character—Glen responded with a groggy "Huh."

"It's me, Glen . . . Cheryl. I may be onto something."

Glen started to show signs of coherence. "What . . . oh, Cheryl, how's Jim doing?"

"Jim's fine. He's going to make a full recovery. I found out he's been taking daily doses of a substance derived from a root found in the New Mexican desert. His mother has been sending him supplies of the substance in a paste-like form for years. There may just be some immunity-enhancing ingredient in the stuff. I brought some back for evaluation."

Glen looked at his watch. "It took you six hours to discover Jim's been taking some Navajo health tonic for most of his life?"

"Glen," Cheryl protested, "he eats the stuff like candy. I know it sounds absurd, but he didn't make the connection between candy and medicine until I saw him put a piece into his mouth an hour ago. I felt he should have thought of the connection earlier, but apparently, his mother never presented the stuff as anything other than an alternative to store-bought sweets. He's been conditioned to think of it as nothing more than that."

"So where do we go from here?" Glen asked.

For a change, Cheryl Forrester was taking on the job of director and, considering his current state of fatigue, Glen was more than willing to accept the role shift. "I'll do some composition tests on it," she started, "and try to find out what it's made of and why it produces this immunity, if in fact it does. If there's anyone else in the lab who's still coherent, I'd like that person to liquefy some of the paste, administer doses to a few specimens, then infect them with the toxin an hour later to see if a one-time dose provides any immunity-enhancing benefit. By morning, I want to know what kind of substance I'm dealing with and have a plan for producing a toxin antidote if at all possible."

"Rather ambitious," Glen said. "How can I help?"

In a rare display of mild insubordination, Cheryl said, "In your state, you'd be better off staying out of the way and getting some sleep so you can take over in the morning. By that time, the rest of us will be wiped out. Don't worry, we can handle the night shift."

"Whatever you say, Lieutenant Commander," Glen said, while moving a limp hand to his brow in a mock salute. Even in his current weary condition, he perceived that Cheryl's suggestion was both prudent and practical.

"Go home, Glen. Have a good night," she commanded, taking advantage of her transitory role as the boss. She then sought out the most alert of her lab technicians—it turned out to be the Richmond intern who had not been party to the Thunderhill stabbing incident—and assigned him the task of working with the specimens. She watched the other technicians' heads bobbing and weaving and decided to let them do what they were doing until, like Glen Hargrove, they dropped to their desks from exhaustion. She headed to her own work surface, gathered the necessary equipment for her analysis, and focused her entire attention on the tedious job ahead. It was going to be a long night for Cheryl Forrester.

* * * * * * *

As the witching hour visited Washington, D.C. and the surrounding Maryland and Virginia suburbs, sleep came easily for some and with greater difficulty for others. In a town where many practiced the arts of deception, backstabbing, and malicious slander to achieve personal gain, promotion, vengeance, or reelection, the more experienced at their craft slept soundly. Others, whose consciences had not yet been completely desensitized to the corruptive influence of the city, would need a little help falling asleep in the form of pills, alcohol, or both.

Lou Bernstein was one person who was having difficulty finding rest. He didn't know exactly how, but he knew his little conversation with Nathan Crowe the previous evening would have some far-reaching impact on the Seattle crisis. He prayed that he was wrong, then lay awake for an hour before the sleeping pills took effect.

Across town in the master bedroom of the White House, Jackson Tyler finished the last of his toddy, placed his tablet with the digital *Newsweek* magazine on the nightstand, and turned off the light. Despite the pressures of the office, he would fall asleep quickly and sleep soundly through the night. The alcohol in the hot drink always helped. He'd gotten into the habit of taking a toddy before bedtime when he played baseball. No matter how big a game was scheduled for the next day, he was always well rested. He never gave up the habit.

Glen Hargrove slept, but like the previous three nights, his sleep was troubled. Dreams that bordered on nightmares periodically disturbed his rest. In one dream, great goblets of toxin-laced water sat on the dining room table of Jennifer's parents' home. Each time Jennifer or one of her parents would reach for a glass, Glen, who observed the scene from a dimension beyond their collective consciousness, would attempt to stop the person from drinking, but he was powerless to make his presence felt. Then someone would say something, the conversation would be stimulated, and they would replace their glasses on the table, postponing the danger for the moment. Peril was certain, however, when Jen's father proposed a toast to family closeness. Hysterical at the prospect of the three relatives consuming their death potion, Glen hurled himself through the transparent yet soundproof barrier that separated dimensions, only to wake up in a cold sweat. After an hour, he would fall asleep again to repeat the cycle with a different dream. Such was the Tuesday night of Glen Hargrove.

About a third of the way around the Washington Beltway, Bud Kershaw kissed his wife good night, then retreated to his side of their king-size bed. His mind drifted to Lisa Kennelly and the near-crisis situation six hours earlier. She had placed him in a very difficult position. He knew that the incident would henceforth influence the way he viewed Lisa, and he felt relieved. For months, he had known his attraction to her was unfair to Eileen. She was an exceptional woman, and now he knew she was the only woman he would ever need. He thought for a moment about suggesting a little romance; however, making love while such a crisis loomed over the country somehow seemed improper. Bud reflected one last time on the near-disastrous news conference. He mumbled "close call" to himself, then shook off the notion and closed his eyes. He'd faced many a crisis over the course of his career, and he'd never once lost a minute of sleep over one of them. He wasn't about to start.

At the NMRC laboratory in Silver Spring, Maryland, Cheryl Forrester would indeed make it through the night, although it would require the assistance of three Rockstar Energy drinks and a couple of Vivarin tablets.

In the Maryland suburbs to the northwest of D.C., one man would not sleep until nearly 2:00 a.m. By all external indications, his objectives were being carried out according to plan. However, an uneasiness about the day to come precluded an easy transition to sleep. When he finally decided that his concern was unfounded and that even if there were problems, his backup plan would be a suitable means to the same end, he slept comfortably through the night. He was not one whose conscience presented a problem.

On the other side of the country, Harry Boland and Darrell Wolczyk, who still suffered jet lag, would experience a rerun of the previous night's sleep pattern. They would fall asleep effortlessly at 9:30, but wake up well before sunrise. Boland would occupy the time before breakfast with a workout consisting of a jog and some calisthenics. Wolczyk preferred a long hot bath and a good book. Both, however, had a difficult time keeping their minds off the day ahead. They knew that one way or another, it would be a climactic one.

Twenty miles to the east in the foothills of the Cascade Range, Lisa and her team were also feeling the effects of jet lag. After her mid-afternoon scare, the faulty sensor was recalibrated and the remainder of the sensor installation was accomplished without incident. Shift work had begun at 4:00 p.m. with Kurt and Sanjay covering the Cedar and Tolt sites, respectively, while Robin took a nap. Lisa had spent the past several hours monitoring normal indications from all sites and occasionally chatting with Craig Evans until he departed at about 8:30. Now at 10:00 p.m., Lisa rousted Robin from one of the several cots that Evans had provided so that she could relieve Kurt. With all of the sensors operating normally and all of the toxin readings below the minimum detectable level, she decided to reward herself with some much-needed rest. After Robin left, she stretched out on a cot, completely dressed. She was asleep almost before her head hit the pillow and slept so soundly that she didn't even dream.

One other person involved in the Seattle water crisis slept like a baby this Tuesday night. Scoop Scanlon usually slept uneasily because he always had thoughts of tomorrow's potential news events rattling through his brain. Tonight, however, he decided to savor the success of the afternoon. His story in the morning *Times* would at long last bring him the credit he had sought and deserved. Tomorrow would be a once-in-a-career day, and he planned to enjoy it. He allowed his mind to go blank so he could be fully rested for the experience.

CHAPTER 10 - WEDNESDAY, SEPTEMBER 17, MORNING

By six in the morning, Cheryl Forrester was weary beyond words but elated at the progress she had made during the night. Jim's sweet root paste indeed had some components that could be the key to his immune system's ability to fight the toxin-secreting bacteria. She was glad she had kept some of the books from her time at medical school. The one on pharmaceutical effects came in handy as she analyzed the offensive-looking food. The similarity between the chemical composition of the substance and some common prescription medicines had helped lead to her conclusions. Now, as the first shafts of morning sunlight streamed through the lab windows, she realized that she had very little energy left and started summarizing her findings in a turnover log.

Unable to make his intermittent sleep last until sunrise, Glen Hargrove decided at 4:45 to end the struggle. He rose, showered, shaved, and finished his bowl of cold cereal and toast within an hour of opening his eyes. He hopped in his Camry and made it to work by 6:20.

"Still at it?" he asked Cheryl as he entered the lab.

"I made it through the night, but I'm running on empty," she answered. "Pretty good progress too. I think I'm onto something here. Take a look."

Glen scanned her notes for a moment and nodded in agreement.

He knew his next request was not going to be well received, but he also knew more than Cheryl about the crisis that was driving the schedule.

"Cheryl," he said apologetically, "I know how exhausted you must be right now, but I have to ask you to keep working through the morning on a treatment. I need my best to stay focused on this problem, and you are the best there is. Unfortunately, my morning is going to be tied up in a meeting. I promise that when this is over, I'll put in a special request for extended leave for you. If there's anything else I can do, just let me know."

Cheryl liked being called the best, and she liked it when Glen said he needed her. She also saw a window of opportunity open. "Actually, with just an hour of shut-eye and a couple cups of coffee, I think I can handle the day." She paused for effect and Glen knew he should have stopped talking before the "anything else I can do" line. "By the way," she said, "are you ready to fill me in on what's really happening here?"

"Cheryl, you know I can't . . ."

"You did say anything," she interrupted, then immediately realized she was taking advantage of him. "Never mind. It's just that I think I could focus even better if I knew who or what was at risk."

Glen pondered silently for a moment. He trusted Cheryl explicitly, and within a day and a half, no matter what the outcome, the crisis would be front-page headlines anyway. He decided to fill Cheryl in on the details, trusting that she would hold the information in confidence.

For the next five minutes, Glen shared his knowledge of the events that began, from his perspective, four days earlier. He told her of the terrorist threat to release countless billions of toxin spores into the reservoirs serving the city of Seattle and of his role as the middleman between the terrorists and the White House. He related the details of the Tuesday Oval Office meeting and the story of Jennifer's poorly timed trip to Seattle. He discussed the ill-fated plan to rescue her because, by some unknown means, the terrorists had discovered she was in Seattle. Finally, he shared some of his personal trauma over the past several days, at one point almost breaking into tears.

At that moment, Cheryl Forrester was just what Glen needed—a shoulder and a caring ear. There was healing in just talking, and Glen felt that he had done the right thing.

"How many are at risk?" she asked, after emotions returned to normal.

"It's hard to say," Glen answered. "A million, maybe two million. It depends on how many people tap into the municipal water supply and how fast the word gets out if the toxin does get released."

"I understand now what you've been going through," Cheryl said sympathetically. "And I want you to know I'm here for you, both professionally and personally."

"Thanks, it's a help. So you'll grab an hour or so of sleep . . ."

". . . take a pot of strong coffee intravenously, and be back to work shortly," she finished his sentence. "See you later."

Cheryl patted Glen on the shoulder and left the lab. She headed down the hallway to her office, where her high-backed leather chair, which she had purchased out of her own pocket, looked more comfortable than it ever had before. After shutting the door and setting the alarm on her wristwatch for 8:15, she closed the vertical blinds on the window to keep out the light. She sat down, leaned back, and propped her feet up on her desk. Within two minutes, the luxurious leather carried her into a deep and dreamless sleep.

* * * * * * *

Glen spent the next hour reviewing the specifics of Cheryl's findings. Once again, she had proven her thoroughness and attention to detail. Her conclusions were logical and well founded. She had hypothesized that Jim's long-term consumption of the New Mexican root had resulted in two significant and sustained positive effects on his immune system. She had subsequently confirmed her theory with data from Jim's medical record, graciously provided by the hospital in the middle of the night.

The first effect related to the number and location of lymphocytes—the white blood cells that attack foreign pathogens—in Jim's body. In humans, the lymphocyte count is generally low at birth, increases dramatically during the first four years of life, and then gradually diminishes to a fixed level in adulthood. Remarkably, the latter transition never occurred in Jim. The proportion of total white blood cells that were lymphocytes was several percent higher in him than in the general population. Moreover, in most humans, the majority of lymphocytes sit around dormant in various tissues, waiting to be rallied into action. However, in Jim, a greater percentage of the cells resided permanently in the bloodstream, ready to be instantaneously transported to the site of infection to begin the battle.

The second effect of the root was to strengthen Jim's nonspecific immune system, the protective elements that fight the day-to-day invasion by the millions of microbes and parasites with which the body comes into contact. He had a higher than normal concentration of the blood protein transferrin, which removes from the gut the iron needed by bacteria to grow. He had greater numbers of interferons, the proteins that inhibit the duplication of viruses. Finally, the scavenger cells known as macrophages or big eaters, normally lethargic and late in arriving at the site of disease, seemed to be supercharged in Jim's body, as if on amphetamines. It was no wonder he had enjoyed such extraordinary health throughout his life.

Glen felt that the weakest part of Cheryl's theory was her assertion that the immunity realized by Jim Thunderhill after a lifetime of consuming the root paste could be achieved in a short time period with a few highly concentrated doses of the root's active ingredient. Last night's experiment, in which lab specimens were infected with toxin after consuming a liquefied form of the root paste, was designed to confirm this speculation.

As Glen was getting up from his chair to check on the health of the specimens, he was astonished to see Jim walking into the lab. Glen rose to greet him. "They let you out!" he said excitedly.

"No reason to keep me, Commander," Jim responded. "Everything in this body is the same as it was before I came to work yesterday. Remind me to never get sick again. It's not much fun."

"You look terrific," Glen commented. "How do you feel?"

"Totally healthy, except my arms will probably look like a junkie's for the next two weeks. Anyway, I'm ready to go to work."

"You're just in time," Glen said. "Cheryl was up all night trying to make the connection between this terrible-looking stuff you eat and your immunity. I believe she's onto something, but the proof is in the specimens. I was on my way in to check on them now. Care to join me?"

No answer was necessary. The two men walked into the specimen room with Cheryl's log and the lab specimen diary that the Richmond intern who performed the tests had completed the night before.

The scene was in part reminiscent of the scene from the morning before, and Jim reacted with expected revulsion. The first cages coming into view all contained dead specimens that had obviously experienced severe trauma at the end. A closer inspection of the remaining cages, however, revealed that some of the specimens were still living, although they showed early symptoms of toxic poisoning. Glen quickly flipped through the diary pages until he came to the September 17th entries. He compared the cage numbers with the notes in the diary for the corresponding numbers, then let out a triumphant "Yes!"

Jim asked, "What did you find?"

"None of these mice over here," Glen said, pointing to the dead specimens, "were given any treatment before infection with the bacteria. Half of them were given treatment after they were infected. They all died. On the other hand, the mice that are still living were all given a dose of your miracle drug before being infected."

"They still look like they're going to die," Jim commented.

"Maybe," Glen replied, "but the fact that they've lasted longer than the others confirms Cheryl's theory about rallying the immune system to prepare for imminent danger. Obviously, the root paste delays the onset of symptoms if administered prior to infection. Now the trick is to turn the raw material into both a vaccine, which will promote an immunity as it did in you, and an antidote, which will bolster the immune system to kill the bacteria retroactively."

"Sounds like Cheryl's territory," Jim commented.

"Definitely, and she'll be back to work the problem in . . ." Glen paused to look at his wristwatch. ". . . about half an hour. Jim, I have to leave for a meeting. Will you brief her for me when she wakes up?"

"No problem, sir."

"Thanks. Gotta run."

As Glen Hargrove left the NMRC lab, he knew already that he was cutting the time close for his nine o'clock Oval Office meeting. Not knowing who would be where at what time, he and Bud Kershaw had decided in advance to proceed to the White House independently. Glen hustled to his car and sped out of Silver Spring toward the nation's capital.

* * * * * * *

At 5:15 a.m. Pacific Time, Harry Boland and Darrell Wolczyk sat frustrated in the lobby of the Red Lion, waiting for the six o'clock opening of the hotel restaurant. They had run into each other outside their rooms an hour earlier. Boland was returning from his morning run at the same time Wolczyk was exiting his room to search for a *USA Today*, a futile effort for at least another hour. They briefly compared sleep schedules, then decided on an early breakfast.

At 5:30, both hungry and irritable, they decided to forego the complimentary hotel breakfast and eat at the Denny's across the street. During breakfast, they kept the chatter to a minimum, content to consume large portions of eggs, bacon, and pancakes while listening to the early morning planes take off for points east. They purposely steered clear of the "what if" game they had played at dinner the previous night, realizing it would only intensify their sense of helplessness to control the upcoming day's events.

After breakfast, they walked back to the Red Lion, picked up a couple of *USA Todays*, and headed for their rooms. Safeco Plaza, their first stop of the day, would not be open for another forty-five minutes. They agreed to meet in twenty minutes in the parking lot. For the next fifteen minutes, both agents sat on their beds, their eyes scanning the words of the newspapers but their minds preparing for what was destined to be one of the more eventful days of their lives.

* * * * * * *

Out of breath from his mad dash to make the meeting on time, Glen was escorted into the Oval Office with less than a minute to spare. The last of the meeting's attendees to arrive, he unobtrusively found the one remaining seat and sat down silently.

The president, however, didn't let his near-tardiness go unnoticed. "Now that the last of our group has arrived, we can get started."

Bud Kershaw shot a quick glance at Glen. His eyes said the words, *Don't cut it so close next time.*

Glen responded with a *Don't worry, if there's a next time, I won't* expression.

"First, the money situation," Tyler started. "What have you heard, Clive?"

Donner cleared his throat as he pulled a note card and pen out of his shirt pocket. "The money is ready to go. Treasury has put the package together, and our friend Ms. Birnbauer has enthusiastically accepted the job of making the delivery. Now, what I need to know is where to send her for the drop."

Everyone in the room looked in Glen's direction for the details.

He hesitated briefly, not expecting to be called on to speak so early in the meeting. "Uh, well . . . the delivery is supposed to be made tomorrow morning at the Seattle Aquarium. There's a circular room where the tank surrounds the observers. That's where Ms. Birnbauer needs to be at nine o'clock sharp; and she's supposed to wear a yellow dress and carry an umbrella."

The sniggers around the room were clearly audible, as those who knew Birnbauer imagined a large human canary delivering ten million dollars under the watchful eyes of several hundred fish.

When the levity died down, Tyler asked Glen if there were any other details of the previous night's conversation with the terrorists that should be mentioned at this time.

Glen shot another look at Kershaw, wondering if now was the time to bring up the terrorists' knowledge that Jennifer was in Seattle. Kershaw shook his head slightly, realizing that the productivity of the meeting would diminish rapidly if the subject were broached this early. There were too many other important issues to be addressed before instigating what was certain to become a shouting match. Glen took the hint and simply said, "No sir, not really."

"All right, next issue," Tyler said, continuing to look at Glen, then glancing also at Kershaw. "Are we getting any closer to a cure?"

With a nod, Kershaw deferred to Glen for the answer.

"We've had a very interesting twenty-four hours at NMRC, Mr. President," Glen started. "One of my researchers working on the toxin analysis, a young lieutenant of Navajo Native American ancestry, accidentally infected himself yesterday morning. Initially as expected, the bacteria levels in his body increased dramatically as the organisms multiplied. Then, several hours after infection, the concentration started to diminish for some unknown reason. This was totally contrary to our observations in laboratory specimens. My senior assistant spent half the night with him trying to figure out how he came to have this remarkable immunity. At about midnight, the two of them stumbled onto the fact that he's been consuming quantities of a sweet chewy substance made from a New Mexican desert root every day since he was a kid. His mother sends him a new supply every month. He eats the stuff like candy, so the possibility of the root having some therapeutic value never occurred to him. My assistant spent all night doing compositional analysis on the root and concluded that if administered prior to infection, the root could help fortify the immune system to neutralize the bacteria. It seems her theory was correct. Several specimens were infected with the organism last night. The ones treated with a liquid abstract from the root held up better than those that were not."

The group was intrigued by the extraordinary tale. "Does this mean the complexion of our problem has changed?" Tyler asked. "I mean, do we now have a bargaining chip to use with these madmen?"

"Not in the short term," Glen replied. "Although the treated specimens are putting up a better fight than the untreated ones, they're still very sick critters and will probably die. They don't have the benefit of a lifetime of building up the immune system to resist the organism like our Navajo friend. We've got a lot of work to do before we create either a successful vaccine or post-infection antidote. It would be a miracle if we came up with either within a week or even a month, let alone a day. Then there's the time associated with testing, production in quantity, and distribution. And of course, the FDA is going to want to get in their two cents. Even though I'm working my people around the clock, there's no way on God's earth that the wheels will turn fast enough to protect those in Seattle before these people strike tomorrow."

The mood grew sullen as Glen's words hit home. An unbelievable stroke of luck had produced an accident involving the one person in ten million whose reaction to the toxin could have helped reverse the odds. Yet there wasn't enough time to capitalize on the good fortune.

Tyler let out a mild expletive before moving to the next subject. "Not much more we can do, I guess. I trust you'll give it your best effort, Glen."

Glen nodded. "Certainly, sir."

Tyler continued, "As you are all aware, we had a bit of a scare last evening. If Bud's call confirming a false alarm had been two minutes later, the whole country would have known about this situation, and we would probably have had a real contamination crisis on our hands."

Glen looked puzzled, and Kershaw mentioned to the group that Glen was hearing about the incident for the first time. He turned to Glen and said, "The topic we didn't cover last night," to which Glen responded with a nod.

"But we did stop the announcement in time," Lou Bernstein commented, adding little but words to the conversation.

"Let's hope so," Tyler said. "I guess you didn't get beyond the comics in the morning paper again, eh Lou?"

The president allowed the quizzical looks to persist for a full ten seconds before he nodded at Donner, who produced a copy of the morning *Post*, already opened to the page containing the small AP article on the aborted press conference. "It seems that Marjorie Stone committed the cardinal sin of introducing her subject matter before beginning her official remarks, and Mr. Nathan Crowe of the Associated Press decided the world should know what she said. Please listen carefully, gentlemen. I want your views on this." Tyler read the short article. The same key words that caught Scanlon's eye the previous day in Seattle—environmental situation and Washington State—now stuck with all of those present in the Oval Office. Tyler allowed another twenty seconds to pass before saying, "Any thoughts?"

Bud Kershaw spoke first, asking, "Do we know whether any of the Seattle newspapers are AP subscribers?"

Donner replied, "Both the *Times* and the online-only *Post-Intelligencer* use the AP as a source. So, to answer your implied question, it is likely that what the president has just read us will be read by Seattle's citizens and visitors as they sit down to breakfast this morning."

George Wilkes spoke for the first time. "My office will be inundated with calls all day long. Should I tell them it's all a big mistake?" he asked, the question posed to no one in particular.

Donner was peeved that Wilkes had missed the point of his comments. "Mr. Wilkes, just tell your people to reiterate that the press conference was called off for a reason and that any supposition derived from Ms. Stone's preliminary remarks has no basis of truth. Now, can we address the real issue?" he asked rhetorically.

George Wilkes was perplexed. He decided to keep his mouth shut for the rest of the meeting.

Donner continued, "The question the president and I would like to have answered is this: How much would a couple of terrorists have to read between the lines in order to relate this article to their little escapade? Therein lies our true concern."

Lou Bernstein had been frozen in his chair, feeling sick to his stomach for the past few minutes. Tyler's verbal spanking for not reading the newspaper had annoyed him and almost provoked him to retaliate on the spot. However, the mention of Nathan Crowe's name in connection with the crisis sent a paralyzing wave of nausea through his body. He felt the need to respond now, if only to ease his sense of guilt. "I would say that the term environmental situation is sufficiently ambiguous that one would have to take extreme liberty with the definition to make the connection."

"Oh, would you now, Lou," Tyler said sarcastically, then directed his comments to the group. "Well, I don't think it's that far a stretch. If I were behind this stunt and read this article in the paper, I think I'd make the connection right away. What do you think, Bud?"

Kershaw was not pleased that the question was directed at him specifically. He had been observing the personal conflict between Tyler and Bernstein for three days and felt that Tyler's comments to Bernstein were far from objective and often motivated by matters beyond the context of the Seattle affair. In this instance, Kershaw agreed more with Bernstein than Tyler and was now faced with the undesirable task of expressing a difference of opinion with his Commander-in-Chief. He decided to tread carefully.

"Mr. President, there is a whole sequence of events that would have to fall into place for this article to deserve our concern. First, the story had to have been considered worth printing by the editor-in-chief of the Seattle newspapers or whoever makes those decisions. Remember that Ms. Stone gave plenty of reasons for respectable journalists to avoid the subject matter. Next, a decision would have to have been made to rush the article into the morning edition, despite the potential consequences. The article would need to appear in a prominent place in the specific newspaper that the terrorists have chosen to read while in Seattle, they would have to see the rather small article, and they would have to equate the cited 'environmental situation' as the situation they themselves have created. Frankly, sir, I believe it would be an incredible fluke if all of these pieces fell into place as I just described them."

Tyler and the others considered Kershaw's response for a few moments and decided that there was some merit to his logic. What no one could begin to imagine was that all of the pieces had already been helped into place by an insufferable reporter named Scanlon. He had extrapolated the vagueness of the AP article into an amazingly accurate description of events, expanded the brief article into ten column-inches of highly visible story on page two of the *Seattle Times*, and bypassed all of the normal checks and balances on article approval.

Finally, Tyler decided to propel the meeting forward. "Bud, before we leave the subject of the near-disastrous press conference, can you confirm that all of the toxin detection devices are operating properly?"

"Absolutely . . . I mean I'm assuming that no news is good news. I've heard nothing from Dr. Kennelly for the past fifteen hours."

"Good," Tyler retorted. "That's one problem for which we don't need an instant replay. Now, how about Glen's list of potential enemies. Anything from your friend, the PI?"

"Three out of four names have virtually been eliminated. The fourth, Jack Broussard, is still under investigation. So far, we know that he lives in Maryland, and he's made several trips to Egypt this year, an unusual place for an immunotoxicologist to visit on a routine basis. Hopefully, we'll know more later today."

"And how about the DSS agents in Seattle?" Tyler asked.

"I think our best hope for a solution other than concession lies with Harry Boland and Darrell Wolczyk," Kershaw began. "Yesterday, they ran into a police officer and a teenage boy who had by chance stumbled upon one of the toxin canisters. It was located at the edge of a reservoir called the South Fork Tolt, where the kid fishes, twenty-five miles northeast of the city. They've recovered the canister and disabled it. Apparently, the kid got a good look at the terrorists' faces and he's helped them construct some computer composites."

Kershaw opened the large envelope he'd been holding, pulled out copies of the facial images sent by Boland the day before, and placed them side-by-side on the president's desk. "Sir, I'd like permission to turn over copies of these composites to Langley for identification. Of course, no one there needs to know any details of the situation."

Tyler looked around the room to see if anyone had a good reason to withhold the pictures from the CIA. None forthcoming, he said, "Sure, go ahead."

"Fine, I'll make it happen," Kershaw said, then continued his report. "In addition to seeing the terrorists' faces, the kid got a look at the car they were driving—an Avis rental that was traced to the Sea-Tac Airport rental office. They know the name of the person who rented the car and are hoping he arranged for lodging as well. This morning, they'll be tracing his other credit purchases in an attempt to find out where the terrorists are."

Clive Donner stated what everyone else was thinking. "I think it's great that your friends have found one of the toxin canisters and know what kind of car these guys are driving around Seattle. On the other hand, who knows how many of these disasters-in-a-bottle are planted in reservoirs around the city. And this front man would have to be truly inept to leave a trail of stupid credit card purchases that leads to his friends. Somehow it strikes me that we're not crediting these people with the degree of intelligence and professionalism they deserve."

"You're absolutely right," Kershaw agreed. "I know Boland and Wolczyk are doing their absolute best, but I believe it will take a minor miracle for them to track these guys down before tomorrow's deadline."

Kershaw's conclusion was followed by a collective sigh of frustration.

"So let's figure out where we stand," Tyler finally said. "The probability of coming up with a wonder drug in the next several hours that can be used to protect humans from the toxin is near zero. We still have no idea who is behind the conspiracy, and we won't know any more about this Broussard character until it's almost too late to do anything about it. We've found only one of an unknown quantity of toxin canisters and have no idea how to find any of the others or the men who've put the canisters in the reservoirs. Meanwhile, we have ten million dollars waiting for delivery, a newspaper article that may provoke the terrorists to release the toxin despite our efforts to meet their demands, and less than twenty-four hours to resolve the whole mess. Would you call that an accurate summary?" he asked the group.

Ten seconds of silence passed before Bud Kershaw said, "Accurate, sir, but not quite complete." As all of the eyes in the room shifted toward him, Kershaw knew it was time to drop the bomb about Jennifer Hargrove. "At our meeting two days ago, if you recall, I mentioned that Glen's wife and parents were in Seattle. For obvious reasons, the knowledge of her current whereabouts has been kept to a small group, the present company comprising the majority of that group. When Glen was relating last night's call with the terrorists, he left out one major detail. Somehow, these men have obtained the knowledge that his wife is in Seattle and, based on that knowledge, have established one more criterion for releasing the toxin—her leaving town. This turn of events is particularly disturbing, as we had planned to fly Jennifer and her parents back to Boston today."

The men in the room reacted with a mixture of incredulity and defensiveness. Lou Bernstein went white for the second time in the meeting, although he couldn't figure out how he could have had anything to do with this particular information leak. He wondered whether someone else in the room also had it in for Tyler.

Finally, Clive Donner spoke for the group. "Admiral," he said in a formal tone, "are you insinuating that someone in this room has been passing on the confidential proceedings of these meetings to the people responsible for this crisis?"

"Mr. Donner," Kershaw replied, maintaining the formality, "I'm not insinuating anything. I'm merely informing this group that someone, either knowingly or unknowingly, has divulged private information, and that information is now being used against us. That person may or may not be in this room. However, I am obliged to remind everyone of yesterday's AP article concerning the president's canceled trip to Georgia. We're not exactly talking about an isolated incident."

"All right," Tyler interrupted, "let's not blow this out of proportion." He turned to Kershaw. "C'mon, Bud, put yourself in the shoes of the person behind all this. Remember we're talking about a personal vendetta against Glen, at least in part. Don't you think the guy's going to go out of his way to find any means possible to hurt him?" Tyler looked at Glen, his eyes apologizing for the painful truth he had just spoken.

"That's right," Bernstein added, doing his best to deflect suspicions away from himself. "He could have accomplices locally checking on Glen's every move."

Glen shuddered. He had plenty of reasons to feel uncomfortable right now, and he didn't want to add being stalked to the list.

Tyler concluded the Jennifer Hargrove issue. "Bud and Glen, I just think there are many ways that this information could have fallen into the terrorists' hands, and you've thought of only one." He turned to address the group. "Nevertheless, I'll repeat what I said yesterday. If anything we say is leaving this room and I find out who is responsible, there will be hell to pay. Do I make myself clear?"

All of the heads in the room nodded, save one. Lou Bernstein swallowed hard and tugged a starched white collar away from his perspiring neck.

"That leaves one remaining topic," Tyler said. "I can think of nothing more offensive to me than letting convicted felons out of prison, especially those whose crimes have been motivated by a hatred toward the United States. It is unfair to the country and to the unfortunate victims who suffered because of their crimes. However, from what I've heard this morning, it sounds like there's only a slight chance of resolving this crisis on our terms."

The president looked around the room to see if there were any differences of opinion before continuing. There were none. "We must put the safety of the people of Seattle first. Therefore, today we'll make the initial arrangements for the release of these prisoners. Clive, I want you to talk to the wardens personally. Let them know we will be working on an alternative solution until the very last minute and that the order to release these men will come directly from me."

"Yes, sir," Donner replied.

"Anything else, gentlemen?" Tyler asked.

When no one responded, the president dismissed the group. "Then I thank you for your time."

* * * * * * *

After leaving the Red Lion Hotel, Boland and Wolczyk headed toward Interstate 5 for the short trip to downtown Seattle. With a little time to spare, however, Boland decided at the last minute to take the Marginal Way past the enormous complex of buildings, hangars, and runways that embodied the Boeing Aircraft Company, where much of the history of aviation had unfolded.

As the skyline of the Emerald City loomed ahead, it was easy for the two agents to sight their destination. One of the most prominent and unadorned of the Seattle skyscrapers, Safeco Plaza was jokingly referred to by some as the box that the Space Needle came in. Boland merely pointed the car toward the building and made the necessary turns to stay headed in the right direction. As they arrived in front of the building, they were fortunate to find an open parking space just across the street. Boland parallel parked, and he and Wolczyk headed toward the lobby, arriving at seven o'clock sharp. They scanned the building directory until they determined the location of the Bank of America Credit Services Department, then found the elevator.

They presented their credentials to the receptionist and asked who might help them with obtaining credit card records linked to a US Government investigation. The receptionist escorted them to the office of Ellie Barton, made introductions, and departed.

"Good morning, Ms. Barton, thanks for your time," Wolczyk said.

"Oh, it's Miss Barton." She was quick to correct his use of the ambiguous female title. "You never know when Mr. Right will walk through those doors into your office. Please call me Ellie, though. What can I do for you?"

Both agents again produced their credentials. "Ellie, we are interested in obtaining the recent credit records of a Mr. James Johnson. This information is related to an ongoing investigation critical to national security."

Ellie's eyes widened. She had never before been in any way involved in a national security investigation and was eager to help. Wolczyk handed Ellie the scrap of paper from his wallet containing Johnson's Visa number and expiration date.

Ellie excused herself to call up the appropriate records on her computer terminal. Two minutes later, she walked across the common office area to a network printer and picked up three sheets of paper, then returned to her office. She handed the sheets to Wolczyk and said, "I can retrieve the past three months fairly easily. That's what I've given you. After three months, the data is archived in another location that can't be accessed without a special password that I don't have. Will this be sufficient?" she asked, almost apologetically.

"Perfect, Ellie. Thank you very much," Wolczyk said.

"If there's anything else I can do for you, just let me know."

"We will, but I believe this is all we'll need."

Boland and Wolczyk said their goodbyes to Ellie Barton and departed. Ellie returned to her desk, began her day's work in earnest, and remained on the lookout for Mr. Right.

* * * * * * *

Wolczyk was behind the wheel on the drive to the Bothell Police Station so that Boland could review the credit card statement. First, he scanned the purchases for a listing with the word hotel, motel, inn, or realty, or for any of the familiar lodging chain names. He found none, although the liberal use of abbreviations made it impossible to eliminate many of the items on the list. Next, he analyzed dollar amounts of purchases, conjecturing that a one-to-two-week stay would cost over five hundred dollars.

It took Boland a mere five minutes to determine that there was no obvious record of a purchase for extended lodging. However, several of the entries on Johnson's account record were sufficiently cryptic and costly that they were worthy of further investigation. Boland placed a check mark next to these items and tucked the sheets into his jacket pocket. As soon as they arrived at the station, he would make a few calls.

"Anything interesting?" Wolczyk asked, when he saw the list go into Boland's pocket.

"Nothing that reaches out and grabs me, but I haven't given up. We need to make some calls when we get to Bernie's office."

They arrived at the station twenty minutes later and were greeted by Bernie Cushman and Joey Caviletti as they approached Cushman's cubicle.

"Good morning, guys," Cushman said. "Any good news to report?"

"Good news and bad news," Wolczyk answered. "We got ahold of Johnson's Visa statement for the past three months, but there's no obvious record of a long-term lodging rental or lease. There are several ambiguous purchases over five hundred bucks; Harry's going to check them out."

"Maybe you guys can save me some phone calls," Boland interjected. "Are any of these businesses that I've checkmarked familiar?" He placed the three-sheet Visa statement on the desk. Cushman picked it up and read, with Joey looking over his shoulder.

"You'd think they could come up with better abbreviations or use two lines for some of these items," Cushman commented as he attempted to discern the listing of vendors and service providers on the sheets. "Okay, here's one I know," he said as he found an abbreviation he could decipher. "Gardiners is an upscale hardware store to the southeast of the city. Anything for the home can be bought there. Looks like James is a bit of a do-it-yourselfer."

"Hey, Bernie," Joey chimed in, "that FeinApplWorld item on the list, could that be the crazy dude that does the ads on TV? You know, the ones where he claims that if you can find a stereo or washer or whatever for a better price than his, he'll blow his brains out in his next TV ad."

"I think you're right, Joey," Cushman replied. "Merv Feingold of Feingold's Appliance World." He looked at the two disbelieving agents and said, "Seattle merchandisers are not known for their conventional marketing techniques."

"I guess not," Boland chuckled.

Cushman continued to scan the list of purchases Boland had marked. "I don't believe WysdeofRent has anything to do with renting a place of lodging. If I'm not mistaken, there's a furniture store in Renton named Wayside."

All of sudden, a light went on in Cushman's head. "Wait a minute. I think I'm beginning to see a couple of trends here. Darrell, didn't you say you tried to visit Johnson's apartment yesterday?"

"Yeah. The address Avis gave me was in Burien, but the place was vacant."

"Right," Cushman responded, the wheels turning. "So he's moved, and by the looks of these purchases, he's furnishing his new place. Home furnishings, appliances, and furniture—all big-ticket items. I bet if we check the list further, we'll find that he also spent money at places like carpet and lighting stores."

"Good thought," Boland commented. "Perhaps he's getting a big payoff for his contribution to this job, and he's using it to set himself up with a nice place to live."

"But he hasn't told anybody his new address yet," Wolczyk added.

"I know I wouldn't tell anyone until I knew for a fact there wouldn't be any repercussions from what I was doing," Cushman said. "Would you?"

"No way," Boland answered. "Bernie, you said a couple of trends. What's the other?"

"Right. Joey, you know the area as well as I do. Correct me if I'm wrong, but aren't the majority of these purchases falling within a couple of relatively small geographic areas?"

Joey quickly scanned the entire three-page list, recognizing immediately that Bernie was correct. "You're right. The first two months, he did everything down around the airport—shopping, going out to eat, and getting his car tuned. This past month, he's spent his money in places like Renton, South Bellevue, Issaquah, and Maple Valley."

"So how does that help us, Bernie?" Wolczyk asked.

"It may be a long shot, but I'm suggesting that even though Johnson didn't use his Visa card to get his friends a place to stay, he may have set them up not too far from his own residence. What I'm saying is that we may have spent yesterday afternoon scouting the wrong neck of the woods. We concentrated on downtown Bellevue, Redmond, and Kirkland—all in the northern section of the east side. Lately, Johnson seems to be operating out of the southern section."

Wolczyk was the perpetual devil's advocate. "Of course, it may be that Johnson didn't have anything to do with renting these guys rooms or a house. Maybe they just breezed into town, found a place, and laid down a stolen credit card."

"That doesn't fit the general terrorist mode of operation," Boland retorted. "From the little I know about these kinds of jobs, all of the logistics are normally set up by a third party. The nasty guys come into town, get the job done, and leave—no traces left behind, all of their own purchases made in cash. I think Bernie may be onto something."

"So where do we go from here?" Wolczyk asked, looking at his watch and realizing that time was running out.

"I suggest we proceed in several directions," Boland said. "Bernie, you and Joey know the area better than Darrell and me.

How about picking up where we left off yesterday. Take the facial composites and hit all the hotels and motels you can in the region you've just localized."

"You got it," Cushman responded.

"Darrell and I will start calling the rest of these cryptic entries on the Visa record. Then we'll call real estate companies in the area and see if our Mr. Johnson has made a purchase with something other than his Visa card."

"Sounds like a plan," Wolczyk added.

"Bernie, let's keep in touch in case one of us gets lucky," Boland said.

"Absolutely, it might be easier to use police radio. The chief has one in his office that's on line with all of our vehicles."

"Great," Boland replied. "I guess it's time to get this show on the road."

With that comment, the effort representing the last genuine hope of ending the crisis on terms favorable to the US Government began. Wolczyk remained at Bernie Cushman's desk, Boland headed toward the office of the department chief, and the now inseparable team of Cushman and Caviletti headed in a police cruiser toward the suburban and rural regions to the southeast of Seattle.

* * * * * * *

By the time Glen arrived back at NMRC after the morning Oval Office meeting, Cheryl and Jim had been working together for nearly two hours. Their further analysis of the organic structure of the root had identified certain components with a remarkable similarity to the generic immunogen the team had been developing for the past year. Only the number and location of a few of the carbon atoms distinguished the two compounds. Of course, in the world of organic chemistry, such a variance could mean the difference between something good to eat and something with which you can make explosives. Nonetheless, the two researchers were encouraged and expressed their optimism to Glen as he returned to the NMRC lab.

"So tell me, what did you do after you discovered this similarity?" Glen asked, sharing the enthusiasm of his associates.

Cheryl grabbed Glen by the hand and led him to her work area, with Jim following behind, then began recounting their recent efforts. "First, we used a separation process involving a combination of chemicals and centrifuging to extract the therapeutic component of the root paste. At least it's the part we believed was therapeutic because of its likeness to our own compound. After that, we chemically combined the root component with our immunogen base using a distillation process, then mixed in a common antibiotic. Finally, we put a drop or two on bacteria samples to test the reaction."

"And?" Glen asked.

"The results were very interesting. Do you remember the other day when I mentioned how thick and impenetrable the cell wall of this organism was?"

"Yes," Glen answered.

"Well, that membrane appears to be the full extent of the critter's defenses. Once you break through, it takes very little potency to make the organism roll over and die. Our mixture seems to do a better job of eating away at the membrane than anything we tested the first day."

"It sounds like there were some flaws in the resiliency part of the engineering process," Glen noted.

"Maybe," Cheryl said, "or more likely, the creator put all of the bacteria's defensive eggs in one basket. He probably didn't figure anyone would stumble upon the key that unlocks the organism's front door."

"So how close to a treatment are you?"

"We're not there yet," Cheryl explained. "Based on our discussion earlier this morning, I figured that the vaccine was more critical than the antidote, so that's what we've been pursuing. For a vaccine to work, you have to get the body's lymphocytes producing the right kind of antibodies. To do this, the vaccine has to include a little bit of the bacteria you're trying to kill. As you know, incorporating even a few cells of this organism into the drug could be extremely hazardous to one's health. We want to protect the people, not kill them. Jim's been working on developing a harmless culture of the bacteria that will contain the identity of the organism but none of the damaging effects. Meanwhile, I've been experimenting with different concentrations of the new immunogen to maximize its potency. I figure we have at least another hour or so of pure research, then who knows how much production time after that."

Glen was clearly pleased with the team's progress. "I'm proud of both of you. Now that I'm available, what can I do to help?"

"Right this way," Cheryl said, as she led Glen to her workstation and the unorganized pile of scribbled notes. "As busy as it's been around here, we've fallen a tad behind in our documentation. We sure could use your assistance."

"Not a problem," Glen said, happy to help. He collected the papers and headed to one of the lab's office workstations. For the first time in days, the enormous burden on his shoulders felt a little lighter.

* * * * * * *

None of the last few ambiguous purchases on James Johnson's Visa statement were even remotely related to temporary lodging. However, during the past half hour, Boland and Wolczyk had confirmed Johnson's penchant for expensive cars, alcohol, and first-class entertainment. The remaining purchases over five hundred dollars included an automobile servicing at a Jaguar dealership in Bellevue, a considerable expenditure at a package store in Renton, possibly to stock the bar in his new home, and season tickets to the Seattle Symphony. Somewhere in Johnson's recent past, there had been some newfound money, and he was wasting no time in spending it.

Satisfied that they had extracted every possible clue from the report, the two agents tackled the job of contacting real estate agents in the geographic area southeast of the city. They were overwhelmed with the number of firms in the business of selling and leasing property but proceeded with the cold calls, Boland taking A to M and Wolczyk N to Z.

Meanwhile, Bernie and Joey had reached Bellevue and begun visiting the scores of hotels and motels on the city's south side. After the first two visits, their routine was well rehearsed. They would introduce themselves, show the reception clerk the two Middle Eastern-looking faces created by Joey and the computer, ask if any guests resembling the men were staying at their establishment, receive a negative reply, and leave a phone number to call, should the men show up. They had completed the third visit when the call came in from Harry Boland.

"Cushman, this is Boland. Come in," the police radio was squawking as Bernie opened the driver's side door and slid into the cruiser. As he settled in his seat, the radio squawked again. "Cushman, this is . . ."

"I read you, Harry," Cushman replied, grabbing the microphone. "Not bad radio chatter for a fed," he quipped. "What's up?"

"I think we may have hit pay dirt," Boland replied, his tone cautiously optimistic. "Darrell and I were working our way through the alphabet of realtors. I got to Eastside Realty in Issaquah. The agent I talked with checked the company's records and determined that a Mr. J. Johnson had recently arranged for the short-term lease of a mobile home. I started to dig for more information, and she hit me with the privacy act. I told her I was an agent of the US Government, but it didn't fly."

"Uh huh," Cushman grunted, understandingly. "It's getting harder and harder to get information over the phone. I guess that's where Joey and I can help out."

"You're reading my mind. How far are you from Issaquah?"

"Ten minutes. Just tell me where we're headed."

"The address is 160 Northwest Gilman. The agent's name is Donna Whitcomb. I'll call her back and tell her you'll be coming over to get the address of the place."

"What then, Harry?"

"I don't want to waste a second. Darrell and I will start driving south now. When you get the address, call us. We should already be halfway there."

"What do you plan to do when you get it?" Cushman asked.

"Watch and wait," Boland replied. "We can't very well just walk in and arrest them. They would keep their mouths shut and smile those defiant terrorist grins while the timers on the rest of the canisters ran down to zero. We wouldn't have accomplished anything except maybe save the country ten million bucks. We need to do a low-profile surveillance until they lead us to the rest of the toxin bombs. That may be before or after the deadline tomorrow. Honestly, from now on, we'll have to play everything by ear."

"What about us?" Cushman asked.

"I think you'll be the most help back at the station. If we need reinforcements of one type or another, you can muster the help best from your office. Also, you can be our information conduit to back east if we run into communication problems."

"All right, Harry, we're on our way to Issaquah. We'll call as soon as we have anything."

"Good," Boland said. "You've both been a great help. We won't forget it. See you later."

Cushman grunted into the microphone.

Boland realized he was being mildly chided for his informal sign-off. "Oh yeah," he said. "Roger your last. Boland out."

"Not bad, not bad. Ciao, Harry."

They both laughed out loud. It would be the last laugh either would have for several hours.

* * * * * * *

In the NMRC lab, Glen Hargrove's team of researchers was focused entirely on their sole objective—finding the precise recipe for the prototype vaccine that would stimulate the immune system to destroy the lethal organism before it got a foothold in the body of an infected human. By noon, Cheryl, now working on sheer adrenalin, felt she had finally determined the correct combination of ingredients. She hastily produced several samples of the vaccine and gave them to Jim for the experiment. Jim administered the vaccine to a half dozen specimens in various dosages, then waited an hour for the drug to be absorbed by the bloodstream before giving the mice oral doses of the bacteria.

While most of the research team members waited—some hoping, some praying, some with fingers crossed, depending upon their perceived source of good fortune—Cheryl moved forward with the work toward an antidote, pushing through the limits of fatigue to find her third wind. She knew that developing an antidote serum would be even more difficult than producing the vaccine. However, she was on a roll now and she knew Glen and her country were counting on her.

* * * * * * *

Boland made one more call before leaving the Bothell Police Station. He dialed Bud Kershaw's number, thinking that it might be his last update until the crisis was over, no matter what the outcome.

"Bud, it's Harry," he said when Kershaw answered at his office.

"How are things? Anything positive?" Kershaw asked.

"We think we're about to get an address for their base of operations. If it turns out to be the right place, we'll be on their tails continuously until they make a move."

"Don't be too conspicuous," Kershaw cautioned.

"We're well aware of how much depends on what happens out here. I promise we won't get careless."

"I know you won't. By the way, I just got off the phone with Rudy Moss, the PI trying to find the mastermind behind the crisis. A half hour ago, his investigation of the last feasible candidate led to a dead end."

"Not good. How's Hargrove coming with the toxin research?" Boland asked.

"His team is making good progress, but there's no way they can develop and produce a drug in time to treat a whole city before tomorrow."

"So it's still up to us," Boland said, resigned to continue carrying the weight of the crisis personally.

"I'm afraid so. We're all pulling for you, Harry. If there's anything else I can do, let me know."

"Thanks. Anything else?"

"Not right now. Keep me posted. So long."

"Yeah, so long, Bud."

After the call to Kershaw, Boland and Wolczyk left Bothell in their rented Nissan and headed for the southbound lanes of Interstate 405 toward Issaquah.

* * * * * * *

Bernie Cushman asked Joey to wait in the car while he went into the Issaquah office of Eastside Realty, promising he'd only be a few minutes.

Having anticipated the arrival of a police officer, Donna Whitcomb was quick to rise from her desk and walk over to welcome Cushman as he walked through the door. “Officer Cushman, I presume. A pleasure to make your acquaintance. Please have a seat. May I offer you some coffee?”

“No thank you on the coffee,” Cushman said. He mused at Ms. Whitcomb’s well-rehearsed greeting, obviously designed to make potential property buyers feel comfortable in her presence. Maybe she figured him for a future sale. He took one of the two seats facing her desk.

“Let me get my records here,” she said as she sat down in her chair and opened her bottom desk drawer. She pulled the file labeled August to October Rentals and opened it on her desk blotter. “Mr. Boland was interested in a lease by a Mr. James Johnson . . . here we are.” She extracted the paperwork and closed the folder. “Mr. J. Johnson leased some property on August 27 and paid for it in advance with cash. Now I’m not sure this man’s name is James, Officer Cushman.”

“He’s probably our man,” Cushman said, the cash payment reinforcing his conclusion. “Now where is this property, Ms. Whitcomb?”

“Lot Number 24 at the Shady Retreat Trailer Park. It’s a beautiful village, for which Eastside is the sole representative. This particular mobile home is one of the few two-bedroom homes in the park. The couple that owns it . . .”

Cushman interrupted the sales pitch. He already knew that it was a wonderful home and that the owners kept it in immaculate condition and only drove it to church on Sundays. “Ms. Whitcomb . . .

excuse me, but I have to be going. If you could just tell me where the park is."

"Yes, of course, Officer. Issaquah-Hobart Road, two miles south of I-90."

"Thank you very much, Ms. Whitcomb. You've been a tremendous help," Cushman said while rising.

"So happy to be of service. If you are ever interested in property in the Issaquah area . . ."

"I will certainly contact you," he said, finishing her thought as he left the building.

As soon as he got into the cruiser, Cushman called Boland who, with pencil in hand, answered on the first ring.

"I'm ready to copy," Boland said, realizing that there was only one reason for the call.

"The address is Lot 24 of the Shady Retreat Trailer Park," Cushman stated. "Where are you now?"

"We're still on 405, about two miles from the junction with Interstate 90."

"Good. Get onto 90 East. Go six miles to exit 17. Head south on the Issaquah-Hobart Road for two miles to the trailer park."

"Thanks, Bernie. You guys can head back to Bothell now. We'll stay in touch as the situation evolves."

"Will do, Harry. Good luck."

"Thanks. We'll need it."

CHAPTER 11 - WEDNESDAY, SEPTEMBER 17, AFTERNOON AND EVENING

After a mere fifteen minutes of surveillance, the blue Malibu pulled out of the carport at Lot Number 24 of the Shady Retreat Trailer Park. Both occupants of the mobile home were in the car. Boland and Wolczyk didn't associate the excessive acceleration and accompanying tire screech with any sense of urgency in the terrorists' departure. The two DSS agents concluded that the Middle Eastern driver had a heavy foot, because where he came from, there was plenty of gas to waste. The agents considered following the car but, with a day until the deadline, decided rather to take a calculated risk and use the opportunity of the men's absence to check out the contents of the home.

As they approached the front door, Boland reached into his pocket to remove a special tool he carried for such occasions. Wolczyk tried the door and found it unlocked. "You can put it away,

Harry. It's unlocked," he said, puzzled as to why the home was left open to inspection or burglary, as the case may be.

"Darn it, Darrell, I was hoping to test out my skill with this little device; maybe next time."

The agents entered through the front door and began their search. The trailer had been kept in decent order. The beds were made. The bathroom was clean. Belongings were stored neatly in the drawers and closets. The only out-of-place items in the entire place were a few empty beer cans and a copy of the daily newspaper lying on the floor by the door in the shape of a tent. They spent a few more minutes checking out the drawers and closets, being careful to leave all items just as they had found them. Convinced that no evidence was to be found in the mobile home, they headed back to the front door.

Boland had reached the door and was opening it, when Wolczyk's eye caught an abnormal marking on one side of the newspaper tent. It was a combined rip and ink mark. He stooped down for a closer look and the mark's identity was confirmed; it was five inches long, located along the right side of a two-column article of equal length. Then his eyes glanced at the headline of the article, and his heart skipped a beat. It read: "President's Canceled Trip to Georgia Linked to Water Crisis in Seattle."

"Harry, we've got a problem," he said, stopping Boland in his tracks halfway out the door.

"Huh?" responded a confused Boland, certain that everything in the trailer had been thoroughly inspected.

"Read this."

Boland came back inside while Wolczyk picked up the paper. They both carefully read the article on page two of the *Seattle Times* by Scoop Scanlon, their concern and anger increasing with every sentence. The article was full of vagueness and conjecture. It spoke of a White House press conference that related the canceled Savannah trip to an environmental situation in Washington State. It correlated increased local covert police activity and trips to the Western foothills of the Cascade Range with the presence of US Government representatives conducting an analysis of the municipal water supply. The article concluded that a crisis of unknown magnitude was about to threaten the entire water supply of metropolitan Seattle and called for the Government to perform its duty to keep the public informed. Of course, the article neglected to mention that the White House terminated the press conference before it began and retracted all statements made up to that point. It also ignored statements by the Bothell Police Department and Seattle Public Utilities that all ongoing operations were strictly routine.

By the time they finished the article, Boland and Wolczyk despised Scoop Scanlon. Cushman was right; he was a pain . . . no, he was far worse. He was a hazard to humanity, a type they knew well. This so-called defender of the public's right to know couldn't care less about the welfare of the public. The story and the personal glory that it could bring were all that mattered to reporters like him. Unfortunately, Scanlon had guessed right. Because he was right and because he felt it necessary to put his speculation into print, two terrorists who read his words were on their way to bring about the very event he prophesied. Little did this smug, meddling reporter know that his own public warning was the event trigger.

The agents ran to their car, the thought processes in motion. The hurried exit by the blue Malibu, the unlocked door to the mobile home, and the cast aside newspaper all made sense now. There was no time to lose. Boland threw Wolczyk the keys and said, "You drive, Darrell," while he retrieved the carefully wrapped Tolt Reservoir canister from the trunk. He was relieved to see the countdown continuing, implying that the toxin could not be released from a significant distance. As they got into their respective sides of the car, Wolczyk started the engine and pulled out, leaving a cloud of smoky gravel in his wake, while Boland called Bernie Cushman.

"Bothell Police Department, may I help you?" the voice on the other end of the line answered.

"Officer Cushman, please," Boland replied.

"One minute."

Much to Boland's frustration, it took much longer than the promised minute to get Bernie Cushman on the line. Finally, he answered. "Cushman here."

"Bernie, Harry Boland. Listen carefully. The situation's taken a turn for the worse. We think the terrorists are on their way to the reservoirs to release the toxin. We . . ."

"What the . . . why? How do you know?" Cushman responded, clearly distraught by the turn of events.

"One of their conditions was met. They said no leaks to the media. Check out page two of today's *Times*."

"Not Scanlon, I hope," Cushman said.

"That's the guy. Your buddy has blown this thing wide open. We know they saw the article. We can only assume they're taking the action they promised. Now, please listen because time is critical. We can't be sure where they're headed first. If it's not the Tolt Reservoir, we may have a lost cause on our hands. If it is the Tolt, we've still got a chance, and I believe it's a good one. I'll explain when we meet up. Is our friend Joey still with you?"

"Right by my side," Cushman answered.

"Good. Both of you jump in a car and head to the town of Carnation. If I remember from yesterday, it's the last vestige of civilization on the way to the Tolt."

"Right."

"How soon can you be there?"

"About half an hour." Cushman knew that driving at the speed limit would put him in Carnation in forty-five minutes. The benefits of being a policeman would gain him fifteen.

"Great. Remember that Shell Station on 203, the main road through town? We can meet there."

"No problem."

"Meanwhile, have Joey figure out the quickest route to the Tolt from Carnation. I'll explain the plan when we get together. One last thing, bring some binoculars."

"Okay, Harry. We're on our way. See you soon."

Cushman took a pair of binoculars from his lower desk drawer. He grabbed Joey by the sleeve and hustled him toward the building exit, briefing him on what he hadn't overheard of the phone conversation along the way.

"Wait a minute," Joey exclaimed, suddenly stopping and causing Cushman to do the same. "Does the cruiser have all-wheel drive?"

"No."

"Then we'll need my Blazer on the roads we're going to take."

"All right," Cushman replied, "the Blazer it is, but I'm driving."

"And we'll need one of those gumballs for the roof and a siren."

Joey was right. Cushman had counted on the lights and siren to get him through any traffic on the way to Carnation. He told Joey to wait by the door and was back within forty-five seconds with a portable flashing light and siren.

In another minute, they were out of the parking lot and headed toward their rendezvous with Boland and Wolczyk.

* * * * * * *

The Chevy Blazer arrived at the planned meeting point exactly thirty-one minutes after Cushman and Boland ended their call. The agents' rental car was in the parking lot of the Shell station. Wolczyk was standing by the driver's door, while Boland was inside the mini-mart getting a six-pack of Cokes. Cushman pulled the Blazer up next to the Nissan, and he and Joey got out.

"You guys made good time," Wolczyk said.

Joey decided that he would answer since it was his car. "We lost a minute or so in traffic. Not bad, though."

Boland emerged from the mart at a slow jog. "Are you guys ready to roll?"

"You bet," Cushman answered. "Joey has the route planned, but he says there are some rough roads. That's why we brought his Blazer."

"Sounds good to me. Can you drive fast, Joey?" Boland asked.

At first, Joey didn't know quite how to answer. "Yes" would be a risky reply with a policeman present. But saying "no" might disqualify him from the assignment he was being offered. Finally, he said, "As fast as I need to."

The answer seemed to please everyone. Cushman handed him the keys, and Joey jumped into the driver's seat. Boland claimed the front passenger seat, while Cushman got in behind Joey. Wolczyk grabbed the canister from the Nissan and took the remaining back seat.

Boland handed out Cokes and they were off. Joey proved himself the best choice for driver. He knew every turn and bump in the often-tortuous route to the Tolt Reservoir and negotiated each with ease and confidence.

Boland did most of the talking along the way, checking the security of his seat belt every few minutes. "Since we already have the canister from the Tolt, they can't do any damage there, but they can help us out if things go our way. Assuming that's where they're heading first, here's how I see the situation developing. The device we recovered from the Tolt is still in countdown mode. If they had a cell-phone-based or other high-tech signaling device, they would have already initiated the toxin release, or at least thought they had. There isn't a switch on the device itself, so they must have a remote trigger that requires proximity to the device. That's why they're on the road."

Boland continued, "The best case scenario is this. They are in fact going to the Tolt as we speak. Their Malibu is not the best car for these roads, and they certainly don't know Joey's short cuts. So we beat them there and find a secure hiding place. They show up and initiate what they believe to be the toxin release. Hopefully, they're in enough of a hurry that they don't visit the cove to make sure the stuff is flowing. They get back on the road and head for the next site. We follow close enough to not lose them but far enough behind to avoid suspicion. We make our move at the second site. Otherwise, they release the toxin there and we fail. We capture both of them alive, they tell us where all of the remaining bottles, if any, are located, and Seattle and the world are safe for democracy."

"Why don't we nab them at the Tolt?" Joey asked, then answered his own question. "Oh yeah, they keep their mouths shut and some other bottle spews poison when its countdown reaches zero."

"What's the worst-case scenario?" Joey continued with the obvious next question.

"The worst-case scenario is that right now, they're headed somewhere other than the Tolt. If they are going to the Tolt first and any of the events turn out different from the way I just described them, some in-between case happens."

"What do we do then?" Cushman asked.

"We wing it," Boland answered matter-of-factly.

* * * * * * *

Without the benefit of Joey Caviletti's intimacy with the back roads to the Tolt, Ad-Faddil and Hassan managed to zigzag their way to the reservoir using the mostly paved roads they found on their first trip. It had been a toss-up as to which reservoir to go to first. Hassan had suggested that security around the Tolt was more lax and they could realize a more certain success if they went there first. Lacking any good reason to do otherwise, they headed east on the Issaquah-Fall City Road toward the Tolt.

There was little conversation during the trip to the reservoir. Each man was deep in thought about the unexpected turn of events. Both men surmised that information had been either intentionally or accidentally leaked to the press. Whether the reporter's article was an accurate representation of fact or pure conjecture was unimportant. One of their criteria for release of the toxin had been met, and they would live up to their threat.

Hassan was somewhat disappointed in the outcome. He would have preferred the extra money and the release of some of his friends in prison, both of which would add to his notoriety and place a much steeper price on his head. Ad-Faddil, on the other hand, was pleased that the Americans failed to live up to their part of the bargain. They would be punished severely for their insolence and the carelessness that resulted from it. To him, that was as important as the money.

As Ad-Faddil rounded the last bend on the cove access road, he asked Hassan to open the glove box and hand him the device labeled TOLT. After the small actuator, which resembled the remote control for a garage door opener, was given to him, he moved the power switch to the on position, rolled down his window, held the device out the window, and depressed the button marked SYNC. As expected, nothing happened. Fox had told them that the actuator's range was 100 yards, and he knew they were at least 150 yards from the canister. Ad-Faddil turned off the car ignition. He and Hassan got out of the car and started walking through the trees toward the cove.

* * * * * * *

For the second time in as many days, good fortune had descended upon Harry Boland, but he was going to need a lot more before the day was over. The Blazer had been in its hiding place and everyone in position for less than five minutes when the blue Malibu pulled up. Joey had correctly guessed the terrorists' arrival route, so he parked well down the access road in the opposite direction. Boland had surmised that the timer on the canister, even though disconnected from the detonator, would provide critical feedback to the remote device. So he sent Wolczyk and the canister, along with Cushman as a backup, in the direction of the cove. He, Joey, and the binoculars remained concealed behind two large trees thirty yards deep in the woods and on a fifty-yard diagonal to the blue Chevy that had just arrived.

Boland raised the binoculars to his eyes and observed the car's driver roll down his window, hold his arm out the window, and press a button on an electronic device in his hand. Then he watched both men get out of the car and start walking into the woods. He hoped that the device had been out of range from the car and that the men were moving closer for a second attempt rather than on their way to verify the successful release of the toxin from a bottle that was no longer where they expected it to be. The first presumption proved true when the two men stopped about fifty yards into the woods and the one with the device repeated his previous action. Boland observed that this time, the terrorist was apparently successful, because he held the device in the air for at least fifty seconds. Their next move would be critical, and Boland still wasn't sure how he would handle all of the contingencies.

* * * * * * *

When they arrived at a point in the woods where they thought the actuator might be within range, Ad-Faddil stopped, with Hassan following the lead of his self-appointed superior. He pointed the device toward the cove and again pressed the SYNC button. This time, he was rewarded with three short successive beeps. The timer readout on the device, which since it was energized had indicated all dashes, now read 29:11:14 and was counting down. He then pressed the button labeled MANUAL, and the countdown sped up to a rate of about five hours every ten seconds. Ad-Faddil silently cursed Fox for his amateur electronics skills. For all his apparent brilliance in other sciences, one would think he could have come up with a more elegant way of signaling the device to deploy its contents. Nevertheless, Ad-Faddil patiently held the MANUAL button until the countdown reached 00:00:00.

* * * * * * *

Wolczyk and Cushman were only mildly startled when the timer on the canister beeped three times. Wolczyk once again inspected the timer's two wires, as he had done several times since their arrival at the cove, to make certain they were not attached to the detonator. As the numbers on the timer started counting down at a much faster rate, Wolczyk quietly commented, "It's show time." Cushman could feel his heart pounding a bit faster and a lot harder. He reached down to make sure his weapon was exactly where he expected it to be.

* * * * * * *

Through the binoculars, it appeared to Boland that the two terrorists were arguing about something. The one who had operated the actuator was pointing toward the cove. The other was shaking his head and motioning toward the car. He could hear only their loudest words, but it didn't matter anyway, since the words weren't in English. He hoped the one who apparently wanted to return to the car would win the argument, but his hopes were dashed when both men started walking in the direction of the cove.

His mind was frantically searching for a course of action when he realized that Joey was no longer by his side. Boland spun his head in all directions until his eyes caught the figure of the slim teen, who had circled to the left and forward so that he was now positioned on the opposite side of where the terrorists had been relative to Boland and only twenty yards from their current location.

Boland wanted to shout and tell him to take cover or run to him and drag him out of the way, but both actions would only exacerbate an already unacceptable situation. Boland started moving into position to create a diversion when Joey pulled an unbelievably bold and reckless stunt. He watched helplessly as Joey picked up several branches from the ground and broke them across his knee. The loud crack was audible for fifty yards in all directions. As expected, the terrorists interrupted their stroll to the cove, turned with pistols drawn, and began pursuing the rapidly retreating figure through the woods.

* * * * * * *

Having heard the sound of breaking branches, Wolczyk and Cushman carefully made their way back to Boland's location.

"What's going on?" Wolczyk asked.

Boland was still shaking his head. "You guys were about to have visitors down at the cove when Joey decided to play hero. He intentionally diverted their attention away from you toward himself."

"Brave kid," Cushman commented.

"Some might call him crazy," Boland responded. "Whatever he is, I haven't seen him or the toxin twins for several minutes. I hung around here for a couple of reasons. First, I don't know these woods like Joey and would probably get hopelessly lost. Second, if by some miracle, he pulls off his little exploit and the bad guys decide to call off their walk to the cove and move on, plan A might still be in effect. For all they know, Joey's just a curious kid who unintentionally stumbled onto the scene. If they saw me or either of you, they'd be sure something's fishy in Seattle. I guess the good news is there haven't been any shots fired, so our little buddy may have lost them."

The three of them decided there wasn't much they could do at that point, so they sat and waited.

* * * * * * *

After ten minutes of pursuit, the last five of which had been spent chasing shadows, Ad-Faddil and Hassan gave up looking for the mysterious person who had interrupted their mission. They concluded that the intruder's presence was a coincidence and that even if it wasn't, the person was helpless to stop their forward progress.

"Shall we still check the canister?" Hassan asked as they returned to the car.

"No," Ad-Faddil replied, "we have wasted enough time already. We must continue to the next site."

* * * * * * *

"Look," Cushman said excitedly, as the two men emerged from the woods on the other side of the road, "they're going to their car. Joey's plan worked."

Then reality hit all three of them simultaneously. Wolczyk verbalized what they were all thinking. "They're leaving. And guess who's got the keys to the car? Joey! Great! What do we do now?"

As they watched the blue Malibu disappear around the bend, the joint state of depression was severe. Then, a minute later, an angel of mercy visited in the form of a brave and possibly crazy nineteen-year-old driving a tan Chevy Blazer. "C'mon, guys," Joey shouted out the window while lightly honking the horn, "time's a'wastin'."

* * * * * * *

"That was a stupid trick you pulled, Joey," Boland commented, as the three men took their previous seats in the Blazer.

"It worked, didn't it?" Joey responded, his ego slightly bruised by Boland's mild reprimand.

"Yes, it worked, but you could have gotten yourself killed."

"Listen, Harry, I knew what I was doing. I know these woods like the back of my hand. There was no way those guys were going to keep up with me."

Boland let it rest for a minute, then said, "Now you listen to me. What you did back there took a lot of guts, and it may have saved a lot of lives. I think I speak for all of us when I tell you that we're proud of you and we're glad you're on our team. But I don't want to have to walk up to your mother's front door and tell her she's lost another family member so soon after losing her husband. From here on out, you'll do what I tell you to do when I tell you to do it and nothing more, got it?"

The praise in Boland's comments helped offset his previous reproach. "Got it," Joey said, happy to comply, knowing he had already helped save the day.

The attention turned back to the task at hand. They had to catch up to the blue Malibu before it left the Tolt Reservoir access road, yet remain undetected in the process. Fortunately, there were plenty of bends in the road to stay behind. Once they were on the open highway amidst other vehicles, it would be easier to follow the car, assuming mid-day traffic didn't present too much interference. At some point, the problem would get tougher again as they got closer to another reservoir.

Joey applied the brakes just in time. The Blazer was rounding a bend within visual range of the Malibu's rearview mirror, when Bernie Cushman spotted, through the trees, a shade of blue uncommon to the woods. "Slow down," he said abruptly and anxiously. "There they are."

"Good call," Wolczyk said, "I sure couldn't see it."

"I hunt a little in my free time, so I recognize odd shapes and colors in these woods."

For the rest of the drive on the Tolt access road, Joey had three back seat drivers. Each felt he knew exactly the right distance to remain behind the Malibu to avoid being spotted. Joey breathed a sigh of relief when the terrorists finally turned south on Route 203. He gave them a half-minute head start. When he was certain they would not see his own car pulling out of the same road, he turned left onto 203 and quickly caught up.

Following the Malibu on Highway 203 and Interstate 90 was a piece of cake. The half hour or so on the open road gave the four occupants of the Blazer their first chance to relax in more than two hours. For the first time, they noticed the beauty of the day that surrounded them and the rare clarity of the Washington air. These became all the more apparent as they crested a hill and the majestic panorama of Mount Rainier was revealed from behind a nearer pine-shrouded ridge. The snow-covered peak of the dormant volcano appeared to be suspended above the southern horizon, and both Easterners took out their phone cameras.

"We do have a beautiful state," Cushman remarked, bringing the other riders out of their temporary trances.

"Yes, you do," Boland said, now more confident than ever of the natural tendency for good to triumph over evil, "and we're going to keep it that way."

* * * * * * *

When the Malibu turned off Interstate 90 onto 436th Avenue SE in Riverbend, Cushman, who had been periodically checking the local road map, said, "It looks like they're heading for Chester Morse Lake." Joey slowed and postponed his turn to follow until he was sure that they would not be seen. The trip to the Morse was a mirror image of the trip from the Tolt, each rider again advising the driver when to slow down, speed up, get closer, or back off as he saw fit. Joey did a fine job of driving despite the coaching. Over the course of the ten-mile drive to the water, the road transitioned from pavement to gravel to packed dirt, and finally to a combination of rocky dirt and grass.

The terrorists' car finally pulled off the road into a small clearing of pine needles about twenty yards from a fifteen-foot-high chain link fence topped with three parallel barbed wire cables six inches apart. Joey slowly brought the Blazer to a stop one bend short of the parked Malibu, making sure the best view through the trees was achieved. The territory was new to Joey and Bernie Cushman as well as the agents. However, it was obvious from the curvature of the fence and the orientation of the barbed wire section that the reservoir was on the opposite side from where they were located. The big unknown was how far. If the electronic actuator was effective from this side of the fence, their action would have to be immediate and decisive.

All of these thoughts raced through Harry Boland's mind. He decided to assume the worst-case scenario, and then quietly and quickly presented his plan to the rest. "Joey, remember what I said. Stay here in the car for now; no more heroics. Bernie, stay close to the car but keep your weapon ready. If things go awry, you need to protect yourself and Joey, then get out of here, get to a phone, and give Admiral Kershaw a status report. You can reach him at one of these numbers." He handed Cushman a small slip of paper with Kershaw's work, home, and cell numbers.

"Darrell, you and I get to play one-on-one. I'll take the driver. He's probably the device operator again. You have the passenger. I think we need to assume that they're within effective range of the canister from where they are now. Weapons off safety, gentlemen. Let's go."

Boland's hunch was right. As he, Wolczyk, and Cushman were getting out of the car, the driver of the Malibu was doing likewise. He immediately lifted his left arm, which remained up, indicating to Boland that the actuator was in fact within range. Judging by the time the accelerated countdown took at the Tolt, Harry figured he had less than forty-five seconds to act. He covered forty of the fifty yards between the Blazer and the terrorist at a crouching jog in about thirty seconds.

Boland lifted his pistol, held it straight-armed with two hands, aimed, and shouted, "Drop it if you enjoy life."

The man initially appeared startled by the unexpected company, but recovered, refocused his attention, and continued his action.

"Did you hear me?" Harry screamed again. "Drop it now!"

The second threat apparently had no effect at all. The man was obviously on a mission, and the threat of death was not going to jeopardize it. With time running out, Boland was left with a single alternative. He took careful aim and fired.

The bullet ripped a hole through Ad-Faddil's upper left arm, damaging muscle but missing the bone. The actuator dropped to the ground. Annoyed more than hurt, he stooped to pick up the device with his right hand. Boland moved a few steps closer, fired, and again hit his mark.

Meanwhile, Wolczyk had silently moved to the passenger side of the Malibu. He opened the front door rapidly and, before Hassan could react, a metal barrel was positioned at his temple.

The second bullet passed through Ad-Faddil's right wrist, shattering several bones, and the actuator again dropped to the ground. He looked up and his eyes met those of Boland, who continued to move closer, his gun poised for another shot. Each man's gaze revealed mutual contempt for the other man and what he represented. Ad-Faddil broke off the stare first and again reached for the actuator with his left hand.

Boland spoke to him conversationally. "You just don't get it. How many holes do I have to put in you before you see that I really don't want you holding that thing?" He was now facing the terrorist directly, less than eight feet away.

"You'll have to kill me, American," Ad-Faddil responded defiantly as his hand grasped the device.

Boland didn't need any more of an invitation. He'd given this slime more chances than he deserved. "Suit yourself," he said matter-of-factly, as he squeezed off a round that planted itself squarely in Ad-Faddil's abdomen. He avoided the heart because he wasn't finished with the conversation.

The terrorist grimaced as he took the slug and hunched over, shifting from a stoop to a kneel and then forward onto his face, dropping the actuator for the last time.

Boland walked the remaining distance to Ad-Faddil, kicked the actuator beyond his grasp, then grabbed him by his bloody upper left arm and rolled him face up.

"You really think you won, don't you?" Boland said, incredulous of Ad-Faddil's insolence to the end.

Ad-Faddil tried to speak, coughed up and spit some blood, then managed a few words. "My mission is complete. The first reservoir is contaminated and soon the entire water supply to the city. Allah is pleased." The last words were spoken for effect only, as he had no belief whatsoever in any superior being.

Boland turned toward Wolczyk, who was heading back to the Blazer with Hassan in tow, and said, "Hey, Darrell, how about bringing me that souvenir from the Tolt."

He turned his attention back to the dying Ad-Faddil and started his lecture. "Okay, I'm sure the last thing you want to do before you die is listen to a speech, but you're going to get one anyway. As for Allah being pleased, I don't think you'd recognize God if he came down and paid a personal visit. You don't treat the real God with any reverence. You use the name whenever you don't want to accept responsibility for your own actions, when you want a little divine justification for your miserable treachery. Just call on the Creator and bingo, you're exonerated. Well, let me tell you, it doesn't work like that. I believe in God, but I don't believe in a god who condones, let alone endorses, your kind of crime. So let's cut the crap. You and I both know that Allah is not pleased."

Boland paused a moment to let his comments sink in. Ad-Faddil started to have trouble breathing as the blood from his gut made its way to his lungs through his mouth. He lay silent except for an occasional gurgling cough, disdainful eyes fixed on Boland. "Hand me that thing, Darrell." Wolczyk handed him the canister, and Boland held it six inches from Ad-Faddil's face.

Boland continued in his most patronizing tone, "Now that we agree on where God stands, let's talk about the Tolt Reservoir. How do you suppose that reservoir got poisoned when I distinctly remember pulling this bottle out of the water and disconnecting these two little wires. I would say your visit there was a wasted effort, wouldn't you? So, let me summarize. Your mission was a failure, your life's been a failure in my book, and now it looks like your health is failing. Strike three. End of lecture. I can't stand to look at you for another second."

Boland went to the actuator and picked it up. He noticed the time and said a silent thank you. The display read 00:02:17. He found an on-off switch and turned it to the off position, then put the device in the pocket of his trousers. He decided it would be beneficial to foster a cooperative spirit in the other terrorist, so he asked Wolczyk to take Hassan over to where his friend was dying.

Ad-Faddil's gaze was now more distant as life ebbed from his body. He knew his wound was fatal. He had always believed death would come in a violent manner, but he had thought it would be in triumph as he completed a mission of great importance. Now, the words of his adversary had stripped him of even his opportunity to die with dignity.

Strangely, the agonizing pain was disappearing, but it was being replaced by a much more horrifying sensation. As darkness rapidly encroached upon his peripheral vision, his first feeling was that of profound loneliness. This was quickly replaced by a sense of utter and complete isolation. He realized two things in these desperate moments: first, that everything the American had said about his selfish irreverence was true, and second, that the end of this life was not the total nothingness he had come to believe, but a very real existence in one of two very real and different places. Finally, as his last few tortured breaths came and went, absolute fear took over his consciousness as he realized his own destination. This fear was imprinted as the final expression on his lifeless face. With one quiet and shallow last breath, Ahmad Ad-Faddil slipped into an eternity totally separated from the God whose name he had so often invoked, yet whom he never really knew.

Under the careful supervision of Wolczyk, Hassan watched his compatriot die. After this experience, he was more than willing to cooperate. He immediately led the two DSS agents to the canister in the Chester Morse Lake, which was promptly removed and disabled. On the way back to the police station, he gave a complete account of the past several weeks' events. He started with the initial offer of an opportunity, passed from a go-between to himself and Ad-Faddil. If successful, the scheme would inflict serious damage upon the United States while providing a handsome contribution to their bank accounts. He spoke of their American contact for the operation, whom they had learned was also the source of their funding. This man, known only as Mr. Fox, provided all of the instructions and materials required for the job, including the canisters, the phony IDs, the points of contact, the timetable of events, and funding for the car and temporary residence. He told the agents of their conversations with Mr. Fox and the number they called to talk with him. He described in detail their every action from the pickup of the car in Canada on the previous Friday morning to the arrival at the Morse a half hour ago. The only detail that Hassan intentionally omitted was the existence and location of the third canister of toxin. When pressured for information on the location of any more toxin canisters, he swore that he knew of only two bottles, the two that were in the agents' possession. Satisfied that they could squeeze no more out of Hassan in the car, they let him relax the last ten miles of the trip back to the police station.

* * * * * * *

"Admiral Kershaw, a phone call, sir. It's Harry Boland." The Flag Lieutenant was standing in the doorway to Kershaw's inner office. "Line 2, sir."

"Thank you, I'll take the call," Kershaw replied as the aide retreated to his own office. He picked up the receiver and punched the flashing button for line 2. "Kershaw here. What's up?"

"It's over, Bud . . . for the most part." Boland sounded more at ease than he had sounded since arriving in Seattle. "There were two terrorists involved, Middle Eastern background, though you couldn't tell from their speech pattern. One's dead, the other is safe behind the bars of a jail cell for now. We recovered two bottles of toxin from reservoirs, one from the Tolt and one from the Chester Morse. Some day over a beer, I'll tell you how close we came to having one big pollution problem out here. The second guy spilled his guts big time after he saw his partner go to meet his maker. As you figured, they weren't acting on their own. They were getting orders from a guy they knew as Mr. Fox. I doubt if that's his real name. He has a number that they used to contact him at various times during the mission. It's 888-456-8902. You can check it out, but I doubt if it'll lead you to him. This guy says that we've got all the toxin bottles now, but I think he's holding back information. They're not set up to interrogate out here, so we may not be able to extract the truth for a while. I suggest you work the Fox connection with Hargrove; maybe the name will ring a bell."

Boland's report was music to Kershaw's ears. "Excellent job, Harry. I'll be putting you and Darrell in for citations."

"Skip it, Bud. There are a police officer and a young boy, though, who do deserve some serious recognition. As for Darrell and me, we'd be happy with a prime rib dinner when we get back."

"I'll do both. Wrap things up out there within a couple of days and head back for a debrief. The FBI will take care of the surviving terrorist from this point. By the way, the CIA did identify both of them from your computer-generated pictures. Are you interested in any details?"

"Not in the least," Boland answered, ready to start putting the events of the past few days behind him. "Oh, one more thing. The guy that's been doing Fox's logistics legwork out here for the past couple of months goes by the name James Johnson. His Visa card number helped lead us to his friends, but we still don't know his current address. I'll text you the credit card information. Maybe one of your mega computers in D.C. can track him down."

"I'll see what I can do. See you guys in a few days."

"Right, Bud. See you then."

* * * * * * *

Within a minute of ending his phone call with Harry Boland, Kershaw was talking to Glen Hargrove. "Glen, Bud here. You can rest easy. Jen and her family are safe. Boland and Wolczyk have neutralized the threat and recovered the toxin."

"That's great news, Bud." Glen felt a huge burden removed from his shoulders as Kershaw's words sunk in. "We're making some pretty significant progress ourselves. Thanks to Lieutenant Thunderhill's little accident, we should have an effective vaccine developed by later today and a post-infection antidote by mid-day tomorrow, although now it looks like we might not need it."

"I'm sure it wasn't a wasted effort. Your long-term research will certainly benefit from the progress. Listen, Glen, we're not totally out of the woods yet. There's still the matter of this acquaintance of yours who conceived the whole operation. One of the terrorists identified him as a Mr. Fox. At least that's the name he's been calling himself. Any thoughts?"

Glen thought for a moment. "I really don't think I know anybody with the name Fox."

"It may not be an actual name. It could be a pseudonym. Someone who's sly and cunning could call himself Fox. It could also be an acronym; F-O-X could stand for something. I used to know a submarine skipper in the 1980s we called the Silver Fox because of his totally gray head of hair." Kershaw was grasping at straws, but he was doing everything he could to stimulate Glen's mind to think of a possible connection between his past associates and the name Fox.

"Right now, I can't think of anyone who fits, but I'll try to come up with something."

"That's all I ask."

"I'll call you if I think of anything."

"Do that. Get some sleep tonight too."

"I don't think sleeping will be a problem tonight." Glen felt a debt of gratitude to his longtime friend and decided that now was the time to express it. "Bud, I can't tell you how much I appreciate everything you've done this week. If not for you, Jen and . . ."

"It was a team effort, and you know it," Kershaw interrupted, having always felt uncomfortable with excessive praise.

"Whatever you say," Glen replied, one humble person to another. "I'll talk to you soon."

"Bye, Glen."

One more call to the White House completed Bud Kershaw's action items.

CHAPTER 12 – WEDNESDAY, SEPTEMBER 17, NIGHT, AND THURSDAY, SEPTEMBER 18

Until the night of September 17, Glen Hargrove felt that nothing constructive ever came out of a dream. Several years ago, when working particularly hard on a project, he often took work home with him and even carried it into his sleep world. During his dreams, he would come up with solutions to complex problems, but without pen and paper at his bedside, the thoughts were lost by morning. He decided at one point to keep the necessary writing tools by his bed so he could capture the ideas. Then one night, a spark of brilliance came to him in the middle of a dream. He immediately sat up, turned on the light, and wrote it down. Satisfied that he had captured the essence of the idea and could work out the details in the morning, he slept peacefully for the rest of the night. When he awoke, he excitedly checked out his 3:00 a.m. revelation. Not only was half of what he wrote illegible, but what he could read made no scientific sense at all. He concluded that no matter how wonderful an idea seemed during a dream, the light of day would reveal its true worth, which was likely next to nothing.

For some unknown reason on this particular Wednesday night, in the midst of the soundest sleep he'd had in five nights, Glen found himself dreaming through a high school French class. The endless repetition of phrases was the key to learning French, his teacher used to say.

"Now, repeat after me, first the English and then the French," Mrs. Pourier would encourage her students.

"Hello, how are you? *Bonjour, comment allez-vous?*"

"Fine, thank you. And you? *Très bien, merci. Et vous?*"

"May we come into your house, please? *Pouvons-nous entrer votre maison, s'il vous plaît?*"

"Come in. The door is open. *Entrez. La porte est ouverte.*"

"Your house is very clean. *Votre maison est très propre.*"

"Thank you, we have a maid. *Merci, nous avons une servante.*"

"Do you have any animals? *Avez vous des animaux?*"

"Yes, three dogs. *Oui, trois chiens.*"

"May we see your dogs? *Pouvon-nous voir votre chiens?*"

"Perhaps later. The dogs are fox hunting. *Plus tard, peut-être. Les chiens sont chasse au renard.*"

Within an instant, Glen was fully awake and making a phone call to Bud Kershaw.

The groggy voice of Kershaw answered the call. "Hello."

"Bud. Glen. I know who our man is."

"I'm glad, but I'm also very tired. How about 0700 at my office? Whoever he is, he's probably sleeping too. We can talk when I'm more coherent."

"Okay. See you then. Good night."

* * * * * * *

Glen arrived at the CNR's Ballston office at 7:00 a.m., appearing well rested and alert. Kershaw greeted him at the door, anxious to hear who Glen believed was the man behind the terrorist activity.

"All right, Glen, let's have it. Who's our man?" Noticing that Glen appeared to have gotten plenty of sleep, Kershaw concluded that the name he was about to hear was the product of Z-time and not hours of brain racking. He was naturally suspicious.

"It's Chuck Renard, the guy who's having the dinner party tonight."

"And what led you to this remarkable conclusion?" Kershaw asked, no less skeptical than before he heard the name.

Glen started his explanation with a little science. "You know, dreams aren't just collections of random sensations and images like a lot of people think. Studies have shown that most of the time, there's a connection between your dreams and the past day's events. Although it's sometimes hard to understand the relationship after you wake up, it still exists."

"What are you getting at?" Kershaw was growing impatient for Glen's point.

"It's simple. Yesterday, I spent a lot of time trying to associate someone from my past with this Mr. Fox. I fell asleep thinking about who it could be. After I dozed off, my subconscious finished the job. I dreamed I was in French class in high school, reciting phrases. The last phrase I recited before I woke up had the word fox in it. The French word for fox is renard."

Kershaw wasn't totally buying Glen's conclusion. "And so this Academy roommate you haven't seen in years is the one behind this near-disaster on the West Coast?"

"There's no doubt in my mind that he's the one. First, although we were roommates, we were never that close. He was an introvert and not very forthright. You could never know what he was thinking, and he wasn't about to tell you. Also, nothing ever seemed to get to Renard. Then on service selection night, he returns to our room and throws this world-class tantrum because he doesn't get picked up for medical school. He blames his bad luck on me because I do get a medical research billet. Here's a guy I've roomed with for four years, Mr. Unflappable, and now he goes berserk right in front of me. So you see, I know he's got enough madman in him to pull a stunt like this Seattle business.

"Second, Renard loved biology to the point of being fanatic. He used to spend plenty of off-duty hours in the lab performing oddball experiments. He would come back to the room talking about how close he was to creating a new life form. The guys in the company called him Frankenstein Junior because of his weird biology experiments. When you think of it, though, what he was doing then probably wasn't that different from the gene splicing he did to create the new biotoxin. I did some digging after I got up this morning, and he's been working in the biolab out at Fort Detrick, so he had access to the source materials.

"The clincher is that I haven't heard a word from this guy since the day we graduated. Now, after fifteen years and out of the blue, he calls and wants me to come over for dinner. It's just too much of a coincidence. I think what happened is that his terrorist buddies either didn't make a scheduled call, or else they phoned and told him that things weren't going quite according to plan. This dinner invitation may be part of plan B."

"All right, Glen . . ."

"Oh, and one more thing just hit me," Glen interrupted. "When Chuck asked me to dinner, he also invited Jen. I told him she was visiting her parents. Jen and I dated during my Academy days, so Chuck would have known her maiden name and that she was from Seattle. All he had to do was find out her parents' Seattle address, then persuade the terrorists to add her departure to the criteria list. The source of that particular leak wasn't the White House after all."

A couple things still puzzled Kershaw. "Why do you think he would choose the pseudonym Fox, realizing that you might make the connection with his real name?"

"Good question and maybe I'll find out more when I meet up with him. It could be that subconsciously, he recognized his guilt, and he wanted to be caught and pay for his treachery. Why do so many criminals choose suicide by cop?"

"Makes sense. One last question. Why wasn't Renard on your short list of those who might be behind this scheme?"

Glen paused for a pensive moment. “In retrospect, I guess he should have been. But honestly, Bud, I’ve never known anyone to hold a grudge for fifteen years. Have you?”

“Hmm. Can’t say that I have.”

Kershaw was starting to put some credence into Glen’s hypothesis, but wasn’t yet 100 percent convinced. “Okay, let’s say there’s a fifty-fifty chance that Renard’s our man; how do you suggest we proceed?”

“It came to me in the shower.”

Kershaw laughed out loud. “Okay, you identified the culprit in your sleep, and you figured out what to do with him in the shower. Did you solve the federal deficit problem while shaving?”

“No, no, seriously,” Glen said, chuckling along with Kershaw, “here’s what we do.” For the next five minutes, Glen explained his plan for dealing with Renard at tonight’s dinner. When he was done, Kershaw sat back in his chair, interlocked his fingers, and began to philosophize. “I like it in theory, but it’s dangerous. If he’s not the one, you and I will spend the rest of our natural lives in court as defendants in libel cases or worse.”

“It’s him, I’m sure of it,” Glen protested.

“I hear you,” Kershaw responded, “but I still give your dream a 20 percent margin of error. Also, your new product isn’t exactly FDA approved yet. Finally, it’s dangerous for you. This guy is borderline insane and maybe completely gone. There’s no telling what he’ll try to do to you when you show up.”

Glen got very serious. “I’m prepared to take the risk and accept the total blame if I’m wrong. You and I both know that we won't feel completely comfortable until we're sure that no more of that toxin exists."

They both sat in silence for a good thirty seconds, then Kershaw spoke. "Okay, it's your call. Just one thing, and it's an order, not a request. You will wear a bulletproof vest. I have a good friend who's a cop. He'll have it delivered to your house this afternoon."

"It's a deal . . . I mean aye, aye, sir."

"Go with God, my friend."

"Thanks, Bud. It'll work out; I'm sure of it."

They both rose, shook hands, and then Glen Hargrove was gone. Bud Kershaw hoped he would have the privilege of shaking Glen's hand tomorrow.

* * * * * * *

Glen showed up at Chuck Renard's house promptly at 6:00 p.m. It was going to require the best acting job of his life to facilitate his plan's execution.

"Where are the rest of the guys?" Glen asked, not expecting that anyone else had actually been invited.

"Oh, they should be along soon," Renard replied.

The two former roommates spent ten minutes encapsulating the fifteen years of their respective careers since graduation from the Naval Academy. As expected, Renard described his own career as replete with opportunities, both missed and failed. As the conversation proceeded, Glen found it hard to believe that Renard was so nonchalant after having plotted and nearly carried out such an unthinkable act of environmental and human destruction. After the initial small talk, Renard suggested a drink.

"You enjoy California Chardonnay if I remember correctly. Am I right, Glen?"

"You have a good memory, Chuck."

"Yes, I've been blessed with the ability to remember many details of my past."

Glen only nodded. To recall events that caused anger and resentment fifteen years ago seemed more like a curse than a blessing.

Renard poured two glasses of Chardonnay and lamented a while longer about the unfair hand that life had dealt him. When he excused himself to use the bathroom, Glen seized the opportunity to carry out step one of the plan. He removed a small syringe from the pocket of his sport coat and injected its contents into the remainder of Renard's glass of wine.

When Renard returned to the conversation and his wine, Glen carefully observed the level in his ex-roommate's glass. When he decided that Renard had consumed a sufficient amount of the liquid, he decided it was time to end the small talk.

"Chuck, or is it Mr. Fox," he said, both forcefully and with a touch of pity, "the game is over."

The sudden change in the content and tone of the conversation didn't seem to faze Renard in the least. It was almost as if he expected the comment. "Excuse me, Glen . . . the game?"

"You know what I'm talking about. Seattle, the biotoxin, the guys you hired. One's dead and one's in custody, you know."

"Yes . . . of course. More wine?"

What was with this guy, Glen thought. *He's in his own little world. Doesn't he hear what I'm saying?*

"Listen to me. Don't you realize what you've done? You've jeopardized a million lives, including the woman I love, just to get back at me for a reason that God only knows. Have you no conscience?"

Renard stared blankly at Glen.

Perhaps it was time. Glen delivered the punch line. "Chuck, you just drank enough of your own poison to kill you within six hours. We developed an antidote, but you're going to have to cooperate to get a dose. I don't have any of it with me, so it won't do you any good to hurt me to get the stuff. What I need to know is whether there were more than the two canisters of toxin, the ones we found in the Morse Lake and Tolt Reservoir."

Renard totally ignored Glen's demand for information and launched into a passionate justification of his actions. He attacked Glen for ruining his future fifteen years ago by taking the last of the three medical officer billets available to graduating midshipmen. He cursed the Navy for relieving him as chief engineer of a destroyer for an incident that he believed was not his fault. He slandered the US Government for relegating him to menial tasks at his civil service job and refusing him promotion above GS-11.

Then Renard suddenly became silent and introspective, as if he had made his argument and was now analyzing its logic. Glen knew he was dealing with a very disturbed man when his former roommate took another couple of sips from his wine glass. When Renard walked to the dining room hutch, opened the top drawer, and took out a pistol, Glen was scared for the first time during the visit. *He's going to shoot me anyway,* he thought. *He doesn't care if the toxin kills him, as long as he gets his revenge.* He was pleased that Bud had talked him into the vest; then another frightening thought flashed through his brain. Renard had qualified as pistol expert at the Academy. At ten feet, it would be hard to miss a head shot, and no vest was going to protect his head. Glen glanced around the room for anything that could offer protection.

Renard, still in a pensive mood, then spoke with unusual serenity in his voice, considering the tense circumstances. "I'll tell you what you want to know, Glen. There were three canisters. The third one is still inside the rear-passenger side door of their car, unless they moved it. The three canisters plus the vial they sent you—that's all the biotoxin I made." He then tilted his head sideways, smiled slightly, and said, "Telling you that was the most decent thing I've done in fifteen years."

"We'll get you help, Chuck, and I'll get you the antidote, just put down the . . ."

"Thanks, anyway. Goodbye, Glen," Renard said, as he lifted the pistol to head level. Then with the same calm indifference with which he must have conceived his entire traitorous plan, he shoved the barrel of the gun four inches into his mouth, closed his eyes, and pulled the trigger.

The sound seemed deafening to Glen Hargrove within the confines of the small room. It may or may not have been the last thing Chuck Renard ever heard.

EPILOGUE - FRIDAY, SEPTEMBER 19

During the search of Chuck Renard's home, more than enough evidence was uncovered to implicate him in the commissioning and subsequent direction of the Seattle terrorist activity. Receipts from hardware, electronics, and explosives vendors for the materials used to build the toxin canisters were found in his den in a desk drawer. A veritable library of reference material on recombinant DNA, gene transfer, and other forms of genetic engineering was discovered scattered throughout the den and in an oversized closet that he had converted into a makeshift laboratory for his experiments.

Digging into Renard's phone records indicated more than a few calls to Middle Eastern and European locations. A variety of bills and other correspondence were addressed to a post office box in a town ten miles away from Renard's house. Boland's hunch that the instigator's locating information would be difficult to trace was correct. The investigative team had been directed to inform the Seattle FBI immediately if any evidence implicating a Washington State accomplice was found. More than twenty calls to the same area code 206 number during August and early September was deemed sufficient evidence. The call history was transmitted to the FBI, which began the process of checking out all suspicious phone numbers.

No one understood how Renard managed to finance his elaborate research and the services of the terrorists until his previous year's tax return was found. Apparently, he came from a very wealthy family, a fact that he concealed from Hargrove during his Academy years. His already widowed mother had died early last year, leaving her only child, Charles, the entire multi-million dollar inheritance. She probably would have rolled over in her grave had she known what her son was doing with the money.

The most unique of the recovered documents was a chronology of two careers, Glen Hargrove's and his own, organized side-by-side in scrapbook fashion. Hargrove's side of the book revealed a career of notable achievements, early promotions, and special awards. Renard's side, on the other hand, depicted an entirely opposite career. It contained, among other things, a variety of critical newspaper and magazine articles, the findings of a Navy board of inquiry, a half dozen underwhelming Navy fitness reports, and a transcript from Yale University showing the attainment of a master's degree in genetics with a 2.9 grade point average. Next to each document was Renard's own personal commentary.

At first glance, Renard appeared to have a career filled with hardship and failure. It didn't take too much reading between the lines, though, to see that his world of misfortune was created more by his own perception of and reaction to events than by the events themselves. The types of setbacks he suffered were not uncommon to others involved in similar career pursuits. However, instead of picking up the pieces and moving forward or turning adversity into advantage, Renard allowed his self-inflicted misery to swell like an uncontrolled cancer until it reached unbearable proportions.

It was a safe assumption that at one point, something inside Renard snapped. From that point on, his all-consuming passion was to seek revenge on those whom he most closely associated with his downfall. Glen Hargrove became a target because of a lingering fifteen-year grudge. The US Government became a target of convenience because of his chosen method to get back at Hargrove. Renard ultimately became a target of himself because, in truth, he was his own worst enemy.

As the body of evidence was gathered, placed in folders, bottles, or bags, and labeled, one was left with the impression that regardless of the outcome of the events in Seattle, Renard's own personal scenario had played out to its inevitable conclusion. From all indications, he was a perpetual malcontent. Success in his vengeful plans could bring only short-lived satisfaction if it brought any satisfaction at all. Sooner or later, he would have devised another plot against another innocent past associate and another unsuspecting city, and the entire roller coaster ride of the past week would start all over again.

As the door of the suburban brick colonial was locked and the police barrier tape stretched across the entrance, everyone on the investigative team was arriving at the same conclusion: the world would be a much better place without Chuck Renard.

* * * * * * *

James Johnson's first mistake had been making too many purchases in the same geographic region on the same credit card. His second mistake was not changing his phone number when he vacated his apartment on August 27. With a little help from AT&T, it took the Seattle FBI less than fifteen minutes to track down his new address.

Two agents paid a visit to his newly purchased townhouse in South Bellevue just after 8:00 a.m. A surprised yet cooperative Johnson sat silently as he was informed of his arrest for conspiring to commit a grave act of environmental destruction. The arresting officers would later determine that James Johnson was one of several American aliases used by Mr. Anwar Haleel, a former active participant in terrorist activities who had semi-retired to the Pacific Northwest.

* * * * * * *

At noon, Glen Hargrove and Bud Kershaw met for lunch at the Food Court of the Ballston Quarter Shopping Mall in Arlington. They had already talked briefly about the previous evening's events on the phone after Glen finally finished briefing the police at 10:30 p.m. The first thing Kershaw did as they approached each other in the mall was to grab Glen's hand and shake it long and hard. "It is good to see you, my friend," he said, refusing to let go of the hand. "Yesterday when we said goodbye, I wasn't sure I'd have the opportunity to see you today, or ever again for that matter. Let's get a bite and you can fill me in on the details of last night."

They split up to sample different offerings from the Food Court, then rejoined at a table for two. Glen spent about ten minutes describing the events at Renard's home, often shaking his head in lingering disbelief at the outcome. "The whole evening seems so surreal now. One minute we're having a conversation, and the next . . ." Glen's voice trailed off as he tried to avoid invoking the image of Renard's last moment on earth.

Kershaw recognized Glen's uneasiness and changed the subject. "I passed on the location of the third canister to Harry Boland, and he'll be trying to retrieve it this morning. Unfortunately, they already took the car back to the rental agency. Hopefully, he doesn't have a problem chasing it down."

After a short pause, Kershaw turned to yet another subject. "So tell me, Glen, how will your findings this week impact your long-term research objectives?"

"I'm pretty excited, Bud. I guess I've always been conservative when it comes to our group's research agenda. I've discouraged unconventional approaches to unlocking the secret of the generic immunogen. I think from now on, though, I'll have to base my evaluation of ideas more on merit and less on my preconceived notions about their value. As for the miracle Navajo drug, it's a very interesting concept that we'll be pursuing. Obviously, Jim Thunderhill's long-term consumption of the substance prepared his body to fight off one of the most virulent biotoxins in the world. There's definitely something we can learn from this experience, but I won't get too excited until we have a lot more analysis behind us."

"Sounds like the benefit to your work is the real silver lining in the rain clouds of the past week. By the way, when does Jen come home?"

"She flies from Seattle to Boston today. I talked with her last night after I talked with you. We decided to get together for a long weekend in Newport. This afternoon, I'll fly to Providence, and she'll pick me up on the way south."

"Excellent. You deserve the break after this week. Does she suspect anything?"

"No. Her family doesn't take a daily newspaper or watch TV news. I told her that the crisis was resolved, and she didn't ask any questions."

Both naval officers spent about thirty seconds pondering the amazing series of events over the past week. Finally, Kershaw spoke. "You know, there are about a hundred different ways this crisis could have played out. Only a couple of them had happy endings."

Glen thought for a moment before responding. "Bud, I think you and I both know who's really in charge. I would say things happened exactly as the Lord planned them. Sometimes the odds against you don't mean a thing. You just have to be on the right team."

"Perhaps you're right, Glen, perhaps you're right."

* * * * * * *

Harry Boland was a little less into the concept of divine intervention than Glen Hargrove and Bud Kershaw. He figured he needed his string of luck to last a few more hours. Regardless of its source, his good fortune did continue.

His first stop on this cool and hazy Seattle morning was at the Sea-Tac Airport Avis Car Rental desk. The clerk was a bit bewildered by the request to determine if a particular blue Chevy Malibu was available, not for rental but for a fifteen-minute inspection. The Government agent's credentials appeared to be in order, so she honored the request. Her computer screen showed that the car was available and still in the lot, so she gave Boland the parking space number. It took him and Wolczyk less than ten minutes, after finding the car, to remove the right-rear door panel, extract the canister, disable the detonator, and reassemble the door. They took the bottle back to police headquarters where, with the two similar bottles, it was carefully packaged for transport back to Washington, D.C. for further analysis and final disposition.

After the trip to headquarters, Boland made a solo trip downtown to the offices of the *Seattle Times*. There, in the presence of the publisher and editor-in-chief, he explained how a certain employee of the paper had been the catalyst of a near-disaster in the metropolitan Seattle environment. He accused the reporter of demonstrating irresponsible reporting methods, having been remiss in researching the facts, knowingly misrepresenting those facts he had obtained, and writing an article with the sole motivation of causing sensationalism at the expense of the public's welfare. The visitor recommended that the reporter be strongly admonished for his careless action.

The two heads of the newspaper took great pride in their product and therefore acknowledged with concern the comments of this representative of the US Government. In fact, the visitor had validated the accusations of reckless journalism that had been pouring in since Wednesday.

* * * * * * *

Thirty feet away as the crow flies, but much further through the maze of newsroom cubicles, Scoop Scanlon sat despondent and confused. Since his story had appeared two days ago, the events had not transpired as envisioned. His so-called facts proved to be speculation, as the water crisis he had forecast never happened.

Many formal denials of a problem had been issued to the media by various local authorities, and apparently several complaints had been lodged with the newspaper. Instead of the expected accolades, Scanlon was receiving only stares of anger and mistrust from his fellow *Times* employees as the official and public reaction to his article became evident. Throughout the ordeal, however, his bosses had remained strangely silent. Rather than enduring the uncertainty any longer, Scanlon decided to pay a visit to the office of the editor-in-chief.

When the editor's office came into view around the last cubicle partition, Scanlon noticed both his bosses in conference with a stranger who looked vaguely familiar. He lingered in the vicinity of the office for the remainder of the outsider's visit, straining to catch an earful of the conversation, but to no avail.

* * * * * * *

As the visitor prepared to leave, the two chiefs of the paper assured him that the matter would be addressed promptly and that appropriate action would be taken. In truth, the action to follow was a foregone conclusion. It had not been the first time Mr. Scanlon's questionable reporting standards had been brought to their attention, but it would be the last.

Scanlon scarcely allowed the visitor to get around the corner before he knocked on the door to the publisher's office and invited himself in. "Got a scoop for old Scoop, boss?" he asked in a vain attempt at levity with the ever-present grin on his face.

With a nod and a smile, the publisher gave the editor-in-chief the privilege of confronting Scanlon. "Well, Mr. Scanlon, what a fortuitous visit. Now I'm not sure the firing of an unscrupulous reporter is newsworthy, but you're welcome to write about it."

For the next five minutes, Scanlon was in the receive mode. He was lectured on both the inadequacies of his performance in general and the specifics of his reporting of recent events. He was given no opportunity to defend himself but would have had no credible justification if he had been. Finally, the editor-in-chief made it clear to Scanlon that he would be ill-advised to request either of them to draft a letter of recommendation for his next job.

Shell-shocked beyond words after the heavy barrage from the editor, Scanlon simply turned and left the office. His sole consolation was that the *National Enquirer* did not require letters of recommendation.

* * * * * * *

Joey Caviletti sat on his favorite rock at the edge of the Tolt Reservoir, fishing pole in hand, two trout already in his basket. With him sat his new fishing partner, Officer Bernie Cushman, zero fish in his basket.

"It takes more than a good fishing spot," Joey said. "You also need the right technique."

"Did your father teach you that, Joey?"

"Sort of," Joey answered pensively. "Bernie, do you think he knows what we did this week . . . I mean, capturing honest-to-goodness terrorists and all?"

"I don't know for a fact, but if he does, I'm sure he's real proud of his boy right now." Cushman realized that acceptance by a male adult was critical to this young man's growth at this point in his life. He decided at that moment to be Joey's pseudo-father, if he would let him. "I'll tell you one thing though, I'm very proud of you . . . son."

Joey seemed to light up as Cushman said the word "son." Cushman noticed the reaction and knew that the two of them would be spending considerable time together. "So," he said, "are you going to teach me this technique of yours? Maybe I can give you a few hunting lessons in return."

"Excellent," Joey said excitedly, "let's get started."

The two of them fished and talked for the rest of the daylight hours, knowing that the future of both their fishing spot and their relationship was secure.

* * * * * * *

Jackson Tyler returned to the Oval Office at 1:50 p.m. after a thousand-dollar-a-plate luncheon at the Waldorf Astoria Hotel, designed to help fund the upcoming media blitz of his reelection campaign. Kershaw had called him early in the morning with news of Renard's suicide, closing the books on a tumultuous week of events and allowing the president to get back to his normal schedule.

As Tyler sank into his leather swivel chair, the unmarked envelope positioned squarely in the middle of his desk caught his attention. He opened the envelope and read the brief correspondence:

Dear Jack,

We've known each other too long for me to be other than completely honest. My personal life, as you so frequently and publicly remind everyone, is in disarray. Stresses at work, together with the existing anxiety at home, have created a burden almost too great to bear. Living this way for much longer would force me to do something even more painful than the action addressed herein. Therefore, please consider this letter notice of my resignation, effective immediately. I sincerely regret any difficulties or embarrassment caused by my actions over the past several months. I assure you they were strictly reactionary and were not intended to reflect on you personally or on the office of the Presidency.

Lou Bernstein

Tyler refolded the note and tucked it back in the envelope. On the outside of the envelope, he wrote the letters C-O-S and a large A with a circle around it, his standard symbol to indicate required action by the chief of staff, then threw the letter in a box that was emptied by one of the staff admins every hour. Before the afternoon was over, Clive Donner would have started the search for a suitable replacement. Tyler's thoughts on his relationship with Bernstein were fleeting as the top-of-the-hour news broadcast approached.

Tyler opened the doors of a beautiful Victorian-era cherry cabinet, his own contribution to the Oval Office furniture, and turned on the TV. The top story included a rebroadcast of the noon statement made by Marjorie Stone, which fully disclosed the chronology of events associated with the threatened terrorist action in Washington State. The carefully worded statement, to which Tyler had provided significant input, cited the rapid and decisive action of the president's Crisis Management Committee as the reason for the mission's failure. On behalf of the president, Ms. Stone apologized for withholding information during the situation and explained that such secrecy was critical to the successful outcome of the committee's efforts. Little did the media or viewing public realize that no such committee existed until the statement was written four short hours ago. Nor were they told the names of those who in truth were responsible for frustrating the terrorist plans. The purely political statement was not much more than free advertising for the president.

As the reporter provided her commentary, Tyler justified in his own mind taking full credit. He thought to himself, *Why not? I would have taken the heat if Kershaw and Hargrove had failed. Besides, no matter how things turned out, they would both have jobs after Election Day. I'm the one who needs the political boost right now.* His rationalization was reinforced as the anchor concluded the segment with a follow-up poll showing the president gaining four crucial percentage points on the Republican front-runner.

As Tyler switched off the television, his thoughts returned to Lou Bernstein. It was true that Lou's brilliant strategy contributed to his successful election campaign. But so did his baseball career. All of Lou's salesmanship would have been meaningless if he didn't have the right merchandise to sell. Tyler concluded that Bernstein's departure would be a personal and professional loss but certainly a surmountable one. People and events responsible for putting him in office would soon be forgotten. In the long run, history would remember not the means, only the results. As Tyler sat in his swivel chair staring across the White House lawn, he silently thanked Lou for the contribution to his cause, then bid his memory farewell.

If Lou Bernstein had known his life's work had just been equated in importance to the game of baseball and both had been reduced to rungs on Jackson Tyler's ladder to destiny, he might have put less sugarcoating in his resignation letter.

* * * * * * *

After a leisurely dinner at one of Newport's finer seafood restaurants, Glen and Jennifer Hargrove headed to the Cliff Walk, one of the town's more popular spots for an evening stroll. With the Atlantic Ocean to the south and east and the summer mansions of a bygone era to the west, it was the perfect way to digest their meal. The sun had an hour or so before it departed for the night and cast a beautiful orange reflection on the rippling surface of the ocean.

"I do love you, Jennifer Hargrove," Glen said, as they stopped and gazed over the expanse of one of the mansion front lawns.

"I love you too," came the response from Jennifer, a little too matter-of-factly for Glen's liking.

"I mean it, Jen."

"I know you do . . . Wait a minute. Are you trying to get me in a romantic mood or something?"

"No, just stating a fact."

"I get it. This is one of those 'absence makes the heart grow fonder' conversations."

"Well, you have to admit that being absent from the one you love is far better than losing that person forever."

"What are you getting at, Glen? Is there something you're not telling me about what went on this week?"

"We'll talk about it sometime but not right now. Let's just enjoy the scenery and each other's company. Promise me one thing, though. Whenever we start to disagree or have an argument about something, let's both imagine what life would be like without each other. That should help us put our small differences into perspective. Is it a deal?"

"Sure, Glen, whatever you say. But I don't understand . . ."

"Shhhh, I'll explain sometime. For now, enjoy the moment."

They walked a while longer, absorbing the peacefulness of the Newport evening, then turned around and headed back to the beginning of the Cliff Walk. As they got back into the car and started driving toward their hotel room, Glen finally broke the twenty-minute silence. "So tell me, Jen, how was Seattle?"

There was a slight grimace in her expression as she answered. "It was good to see my family, but to be honest, after a couple of days, I was pretty bored. There was nothing at all going on out there."

Glen simply smiled and kept on driving.

ABOUT THE AUTHOR

Robert Dorsey (Bob) Smith is thankful his parents gave him the middle name Dorsey so that he might be distinguished from nearly all of the other Robert Smiths in the United States.

Following his graduation from the U.S. Naval Academy, Bob served as an officer in the submarine force as part of a 28-year combined active duty and reserve career, retiring at the rank of Captain. During one of his two-week active duty periods as a reservist, he was immersed in the missions and work of the many government research and development organizations in the Washington, D.C. area. This experience, together with a parallel civilian career in the defense industry, provided the impetus for writing *Countdown* and the breadth of knowledge to make it an interesting and technically stimulating story.

Concurrent with the reserve portion of his naval career, Bob helped grow a small defense enterprise between 1978 and 2000. He spent the latter part of his career focused on business growth at a large defense firm. Since retiring from that company, he has continued to pursue defense-related consulting.

In the midst of a successful career in defense, Bob has pursued many extracurricular activities with passion and dedication. He has written over 200 songs, the majority of them in the contemporary Christian genre, he swims competitively in senior Olympic competitions, and annually, he leads a team on a mission trip to build a house for a family in Mexico. He is a deacon in his church and is an active member of the Gideons International ministry. Bob was on the Academy Award-winning sound effects team for *The Hunt for Red October*, and his *Out of My World* CD was on the ballot for the Contemporary Christian Album of the Year Grammy in 2013.

Bob has previously published the book *Ten Things I Wish I'd Known When I Was Younger*, which is a perspective on the Christian life. The following website has information on this book:

https://www.christianfaithpublishing.com/books/?book=Ten-Things-I-Wish-Id-Known-When-I-Was-Younger

For information about his songwriting and recording activities, visit:

https://message-songs.com/

To stream songs at no cost, visit:

https://bobsmith.hearnow.com/ or

https://www.jango.com/stations/270602471/tunein

Bob was born and raised in the Philadelphia, Pennsylvania area, has lived in nine states since leaving for Annapolis, and currently resides in the greater Tucson, Arizona area.